ELEVATOR
PITCH

ELEVATOR PITCH

A NOVEL

LINWOOD BARCLAY

WM

WILLIAM MORROW

An Imprint of HarperCollins*Publishers*

HarperCollins books may be purchased for educational, business, or sales promotional use. For information, please email the Special Markets Department at SPsales@harpercollins.com.

FIRST EDITION

DESIGNED BY WILLIAM RUOTO

Library of Congress Cataloging-in-Publication Data

Names: Barclay, Linwood, author.
Title: Elevator pitch : a novel / Linwood Barclay.
Description: First edition. | New York, NY : William Morrow, 2019. |
Identifiers: LCCN 2019014755 (print) | LCCN 2019017134 (ebook) | ISBN 9780062678300 (E-book) | ISBN 9780062678287 (hardcover) | ISBN 9780062678294 (paperback) | ISBN 9780062946683 (mass market) | ISBN 9780062912107 (large print)
Subjects: LCSH: Psychological fiction. | BISAC: FICTION / Suspense. | GSAFD: Suspense fiction.
Classification: LCC PR9199.3.B37135 (ebook) | LCC PR9199.3.B37135 E44 2019 (print) | DDC 813/.54—dc23
LC record available at https://lccn.loc.gov/2019014755

ISBN 978-0-06-267828-7

19 20 21 22 23 LSC 10 9 8 7 6 5 4 3 2 1

For Neetha

ELEVATOR
PITCH

Monday

Prologue

S tuart Bland figured if he posted himself close to the elevators, there was no way he could miss Sherry D'Agostino.

He knew she arrived at the offices of Cromwell Entertainment, which were on the thirty-third floor of the Lansing Tower, on Third between Fifty-Ninth and Sixtieth, every morning between 8:30 and 8:45. A car was sent to her Brooklyn Heights address each day to bring her here. No taxi or subway for Sherry D'Agostino, Cromwell's vice president of creative.

Stuart glanced about nervously. A FedEx ID tag he'd swiped a couple of years ago when he worked at a dry cleaner got him past security. That, and the FedEx cardboard envelope he was clutching, and the FedEx shirt and ball cap he had bought online. He kept the visor low on his forehead. There was every reason to believe the security desk had been handed his mug shot and been advised to keep an eye out for him. D'Agostino—no relation to the New York grocery chain—knew his name, and it'd be easy enough to grab a picture of him off his Facebook page.

But in all truth, he was on a delivery. Tucked into the envelope was his script, *Clock Man*.

He wouldn't have had to take these extra steps if he hadn't overplayed his hand, going to Sherry D'Agostino's home, knocking on the door, ringing the bell repeatedly until some little girl, no more than five years old, answered and he stepped right past her into the house. Then Sherry showed up and screamed at him to get away from her daughter and out of the house or she'd call the police.

A *stalker,* she called him. That stung.

Okay, maybe he could have handled that better. Stepping into the house, okay, that was a mistake. But she had no one to blame but herself. If she'd accepted even *one* of his phone calls, just one, so that he could pitch his idea to her, tell her about his script, he wouldn't have had to go to her house, would he? She had no idea how hard he'd been working on this. No idea that ten months earlier he'd quit his job making pizzas—unlike the dry-cleaning gig, leaving the pizza place was his own decision—to work full-time on getting his script just perfect. The way he figured it, time was running out. He was thirty-eight years old. If he was to make it as a screenwriter, he had to commit now.

But the whole system was so terribly unfair. Why shouldn't someone like him be able to get a five-minute audience with her, make his pitch? Why should it only be established writers, those assholes in Hollywood with their fancy cars and big swimming pools and agents with Beverly Hills zip codes. Who said their ideas were any better than his?

So he watched her for a couple of days to learn her routine. That was how he knew she'd be getting into one of these four elevators in the next few minutes. In fact, it would be one of two elevators. The two on the left stopped at floors one through twenty, the two on the right served floors twenty-one through forty.

He leaned up against the marble wall opposite the elevators, head down, trying to look inconspicuous, but always watching. There was a steady flow of people, and it'd be easy for Sherry to get lost in the crowd. But the good thing was, she liked bright colors. Yellows, pinks, turquoise. Never black or dark blue. She stood out. And she was blond, her hair puffed up the way some women do it, like she went at it with a bicycle pump in the morning. She could be standing in a hurricane, have every stitch of clothing blown off her, but there wouldn't be one hair out of place. As long as Stuart kept a sharp lookout, he was pretty sure he wouldn't miss her. Soon as she got on the elevator, he'd step on with her.

Shit, there she was.

Striding across the lobby, those heels adding about three inches to her height. Stuart figured she was no more than five-two in her stocking feet, but even as small as she was, she had a presence. Chin up, eyes forward. Stuart had checked her out on IMDb, so he knew she was nearly forty. Looked good. Just a year or two older than he was. Imagine walking into Gramercy Tavern with her on his arm.

Yeah, like that was gonna happen.

According to what he'd read online, she'd started in television as a script supervisor in her early twenties and quickly worked her way up. Did a stint at HBO, then Showtime, then got lured away by Cromwell to develop new projects. The way Stuart saw it, she was his ticket to industry-wide acclaim as a hot new screenwriter.

Sherry D'Agostino stood between the two right-hand elevators. There were two other people waiting. A man, sixtyish, in a dark gray suit, your typical Business Guy, and a woman, early twenties, wearing sneakers she'd no doubt change out of once she got to her desk. Secretary, Stuart figured. There was something anonymous and worker bee about Sneaker Girl. He came up behind the three of them, waiting to step into whichever elevator came first. He glanced up at the numbers. A tiny digital readout above each elevator indicated its position. The one on the right was at forty-eight, the one on the left at thirty-one, then thirty.

Going down.

Sherry and the other two shifted slightly to the left set of doors, leaving room for those who would be getting off.

The doors parted and five people disembarked. Once they were out of the way, Sherry, Business Guy, Sneaker Girl, and Stuart got on. Stuart managed to spin around behind Sherry as everyone turned to face front.

The elevator doors closed.

Sherry pressed "33," Sneaker Girl "34," and the Business Guy "37."

When Stuart did not reach over to press one of the many buttons, the man, who was standing closest to the panel, glanced his way, silently offering to press a button for him.

"I'm good," he said.

The elevator silently began its ascent. Sherry and the other woman looked up to catch the latest news. The elevator was fitted with a small video screen that ran a kind of chyron, a line of head-lines moving from right to left.

New York forecast high 64 low 51 mostly sunny.

Stuart moved forward half a step so he was almost rubbing shoulders with Sherry. "How are you today, Ms. D'Agostino?"

She turned her head from reading the screen and said, "Fine, thank—"

And then she saw who he was. Her eyes flickered with fear. Her body leaned away from him, but her feet were rooted to the same spot in the elevator floor.

Stuart held out the FedEx package. "I wanted to give you this. That's all. I just want you to have it."

"I told you to stay away from me," she said, not accepting it.

The man and woman turned their heads.

"It's cool," Stuart said, smiling at them. "Everything's fine." He kept holding out the package to Sherry. "Take it. You'll love it."

"I'm sorry, you have to—"

"Okay, okay, wait. Let me just *tell* you about it, then. Once you hear what it's about, I guarantee you'll want to read it."

The elevator made a soft whirring noise as it sped past the first twenty floors.

Sherry glanced at the numbers flashing by on the display above the door, then up to the news line. *Latest unemployment figures show rate fell 0.2 percent last month.* She sighed, her resistance fading.

"You've got fifteen seconds," she said. "If you follow me off, I'll call security."

Stuart beamed. "Okay! Right. So you've got this guy, he's like, thirty, and he works—"

"Ten seconds," she said. "Sum it up in one sentence."

Stuart suddenly looked panicked. He blinked a couple of times, his mind racing to encapsulate his brilliant script into a phrase, to distill it to its essence.

"Um," he said.

"Five seconds," Sherry said, the elevator almost to the thirty-third floor.

"Guy works at a factory that makes clocks but one of them is actually a time machine!" he blurted. He let out a long breath, then took one in.

"That's it?" she said.

"No!" he said. "There's more! But to try to explain it in—"

"What the hell?" Sherry said, but not to him.

The elevator had not stopped at her floor. It shot right past thirty-three, and then glided right on by thirty-four.

"Crap," said Sneaker Girl. "That's me."

The two women both reached out to the panel at the same time to press the button for their floors again, their fingers engaged in a brief bit of fencing.

"Sorry," said Sherry, who'd managed to hit the button for her floor first. She edged out of the way.

US militant group Flyovers prime suspect in Seattle coffee shop bombing that killed two.

As the elevator continued its ascent, Business Guy grimaced and said, "Guess I'll join the club." He put his index finger to the "37" button.

"Someone at the top must have pushed for it," Sneaker Girl said. "It's going all the way up first."

She turned out to be right. The elevator did not stop until it reached the fortieth floor.

But the doors did not open.

"God, I fucking hate elevators," she said.

Stuart did not share her distress. He grinned. The elevator malfunction had bought him a few extra seconds to make his pitch to Sherry. "I know time travel has been done a lot, but this scenario is different. My hero, he doesn't go way into the past or way into the future. He can only go five minutes one way or the other, so—"

Business Guy said, "I'll walk back down." He pressed the button to open the doors, but there was no response.

"Jesus," he muttered.

Sherry said, "We should call someone." She pointed to the button marked with the symbol of a phone.

"It's only been a few seconds," Stuart said. "It'll probably sort itself out after a minute or so and—"

With a slight jolt, the elevator started moving again.

"Finally," Sneaker Girl said.

Storm hitting UK approaching hurricane status.

"The interesting angle is," Stuart said, persisting, "if he can only go five minutes into the past or five minutes into the future, how does he use that? Is it a kind of superpower? What kind of advantages could that give someone?"

Sherry glanced at him dismissively. "I'd have gotten on this elevator five minutes before you showed up."

Stuart bristled at that. "You don't have to insult me."

"Son of a bitch," the man said.

The descending elevator had gone past his floor. He jabbed at "37" again, more angrily this time.

The elevator sailed past the floors for the two women as well, but stopped at twenty-nine.

"Aw, come on," Business Guy said. "This is ridiculous." He pressed the phone button. He waited a moment, expecting a response. "Hello?" he said. "Anyone there? Hello?"

"This is freaking me out," Sneaker Girl said, taking a cell phone from her purse. She tapped the screen, put the phone to her ear. "Yeah, hey, Steve? It's Paula. I'm gonna be late. I'm stuck in the fucking eleva—"

There was a loud noise from above, as though the world's largest rubber band had snapped. The elevator trembled for a second. Everyone looked up, stunned. Even Stuart, who had stopped trying to sell his idea to Sherry D'Agostino.

"Fuck!" said Sneaker Girl.

"What the hell was that?" Sherry asked.

Almost instinctively, everyone started backing up toward the walls of the elevator, leaving the center floor area open. They gripped the waist-high brass handrails.

"It's probably nothing," Stuart said. "A glitch, that's all."

"Hello?" Business Guy said again. "Is anybody there, for Christ's sake? This elevator's gone nuts!"

Sherry spotted the alarm button and pressed it. There was only silence.

"Shouldn't we be hearing that?" she asked.

The man said, "Maybe it rings someplace else, you know, so someone will come. Down at the security desk, probably."

For several seconds, no one said anything. It was dead silent in the elevator. Everyone took a few calming breaths.

Average US life expectancy now nearly 80.

Stuart spoke first. "Someone'll be along." He nodded with false confidence and gave Sherry a nervous smile. "Maybe *this* is what I should be writing a—"

The elevator began to plunge.

Within seconds it was going much faster than it was designed to go.

Stuart and Sherry and the two others felt their feet lifting off the floor.

The elevator was in free fall.

Until it hit bottom.

One

Barbara Matheson was impressed by the size of the crowd. The usual suspects, more or less, but the fact that they'd turned out meant her story had made an impression.

This was a TV event, really. Get the mayor walking out of City Hall, lob a few questions his way, get video of him denying everything. The *Times*, the *Daily News*, the *Post* could all write their stories without being here. But NY1 and the local ABC, CBS, and NBC affiliates had crews waiting for Richard Wilson Headley to show. He might try sneaking out a back way, or leaving in a limo with windows so deeply tinted you wouldn't know whether he was inside or not. But then the evening newscasts would say he made a point of avoiding the media, imply that he was a coward, and Headley never wanted to come across as a coward.

Even if he could be one at times.

Barbara was here on the off chance that something might actually happen. And yes, she was enjoying the shit she'd stirred up. This show of media force was her doing. She'd broken the story. Maybe Headley would take a swing at somebody who put a camera in his face, although that seemed unlikely. He was too smart for that. The TV stations were here for a comment, but she'd already gotten one and put it in her column.

"That's a load of fucking horseshit," Headley had said when Barbara ran the allegations past him. Her editors at *Manhattan Today* printed the response without asterisks to disguise the profanity, but that was hardly daring these days. The *Times* still avoided curse words except in the most extreme cases, but even *The New Yorker*, that staid institution, didn't blink an eye about f-bombs and hadn't for years.

"You really put his dick into the blender this time."

She turned. It was Matt Timmins, instantly recognizable by his multidirectional black hair and glasses thick enough to see life on Mars. He worked for an online site that covered city issues, but she knew him back when he worked for NBC, before he got laid off. He had a phone in hand, waiting to take video, which would be good enough for the political blog he wrote.

"Hey, Matt," Barbara said.

"Wearin' Kevlar?"

Barbara shrugged. She liked Matt, vaguely remembered sleeping with him nearly ten years ago when they were both in their early thirties. The local press had been camped out in front of the house of a congressman in the midst of a bribery scandal. Barbara and Matt had shared a car to keep warm while waiting for the feds to arrive and walk the politician out the front door. After, they went to a bar, had too much to drink, and went back to his place. It was all a bit foggy. Barbara was pretty sure Matt was married now, with a kid, maybe two.

"Headley won't shoot me," she said. "He might *hire* someone to shoot me, but he wouldn't do it himself."

A woman with a mike in one hand looked up from the phone in her other. She'd been reading a text. "Dickhead's on the move," she said to the cameraman standing beside her, loud enough that it created a low-level buzz among the collected media. The mayor was on his way.

Of course, Mayor Richard Wilson Headley always went by

"Richard," sometimes "Rich," but never "Dick." But that didn't stop his detractors from referring to him that way. One of the tabs, which had it in for him nearly as much as *Manhattan Today* did, liked to stack DICK over HEADLEY on the front as often as it could, usually with as unflattering picture as they could find of the man. They also took delight in headlines that coupled GOOD with HEADLEY.

Headley knew it was a losing battle, so sometimes he'd embrace the word so often used against him, particularly when it came to the city's various unions. "Am I going to be a total dick with them on this new contract?" he asked the other day. "You bet your ass I am."

"Here we go," someone said.

The mayor, accompanied by Glover Headley, his twenty-five-year-old son and adviser, communications strategist Valerie Langdon, and a tall, bald man Barbara did not think she'd seen before, was coming out the front door of City Hall and heading down the broad steps toward a waiting limo. The media throng moved toward him, and everyone stopped halfway, allowing Headley a makeshift pulpit, standing two steps above everyone else.

But it was Glover who spoke. "Hey, guys, we're on our way to the mansion, no time for questions at this—"

Headley shot his son a disapproving look and raised a hand. "No, no. I'm more than happy to take a few."

Barbara, hanging at the back of the pack, smiled inwardly. Standard operating procedure for Headley. Overrule your aides; don't hide behind them. Act like you want to talk to the press. The whole thing would have been rehearsed earlier. Valerie touched the mayor's arm, as though asking him to think twice about this. He shook it off.

Nice touch, Barbara thought.

Even though the bald guy was standing back of the mayor and trying to be invisible, Barbara was sizing him up. Trim, over six feet, skin the color of caramel. Of the three men standing before the assembled media, this guy had the most style. Long dress coat over his suit, leather gloves even though it wasn't that cold out. Looked like he'd stepped off the cover of *GQ*.

A looker.

She thought of the people she knew in City Hall, the ones who regularly fed her information. Maybe one of them could tell her who this guy was, what the mayor had hired him to do.

Then again, she could just go up and introduce herself, ask him who he was. But that would have to wait. NY1's correspondent, a man Barbara knew to be in his fifties but could pass for midthirties, led things off.

"How do you respond to allegations that you strong-armed the works department to hire an independent construction firm owned by one of your largest political donors for major subway upgrades?"

Headley shook his head sadly and smirked, like he'd heard this a hundred times before.

"There is absolutely nothing to that allegation," he said. "It's pure fiction. Contracts are awarded based on a long list of factors. Track record—no pun intended—and ability to get the work done, cost considerations, and—"

The NY1 guy wasn't done. "But yesterday *Manhattan Today* printed an email in which you told the department to hire Steelways, which is owned by Arnett Steel, who organized large fund-raisers for your—"

Headley raised a shushing hand. "Now hold on, right there. First of all, the veracity of that email has not been determined."

Barbara closed her eyes briefly so no one would have to see them roll.

"I would not put it past *Manhattan Today* to manufacture something like that. But even if it turns out to be legitimate, the content of that message hardly qualifies as a directive. It's more along the lines of a suggestion."

In her head, Barbara composed her next piece.

"Headley alleges the email uncovered by Manhattan Today *could be phony, but just to cover all his bases, says that if it turns out to be the real deal, it's not that much of one."*

In other words, suck and blow at the same time.

"Everyone knows that *Manhattan Today* has an obsession with me," Headley said, waving an accusing finger in Barbara's general direction.

He's spotted me, she thought. Or one of his aides alerted him that she was there.

Headley's voice ramped up. "It's been involved in a relentless smear campaign from day one. And that campaign has been led by one person, but I won't give her the satisfaction of repeating her name before the cameras."

"You mean Barbara Matheson?" shouted the reporter from the CBS affiliate.

Headley grimaced. He'd walked into that one, Barbara thought.

"You know who I'm talking about," he said evenly. "But even though this vendetta is being led by a single individual, I have to assume this kind of character assassination is approved from the top. Maybe the opinions of this journalist, and I use the term loosely, are slanted the way they are because of direction from upstairs."

Barbara yawned.

"That's why I'm announcing today that I will be filing a defamation suit against *Manhattan Today.*"

Oh, goodie.

Textbook Headley. Threaten a lawsuit but never actually file. Act outraged, grab a headline. Headley had threatened to sue every news outlet in the city at some point. He'd used the same tactics back when he was in business, before he embarked on a political career.

"Furthermore," he said, "I—"

Headley noticed Valerie waving her phone in front of Glover, who winced when he read what was on her screen. The mayor leaned her way as she turned the phone so he could see it. While he was reading the message, there was a stirring in the crowd as some received messages of their own. The NY1 guy and his cameraman were already on the move.

"Sorry," Headley said. "We're going to have to cut this short. You're probably getting the same news I am."

With that he continued on down the steps, Valerie, Glover, and the bald man trailing him. They all got into the back of the waiting limo, which was only steps away from Barbara. But she had her eyes on her phone, attempting to learn what it was everyone else already seemed to know. She was vaguely aware of the whirring sound of a car window powering down.

"Barbara."

She looked up from her phone, saw Glover at the limo window.

"The mayor would like to give you a ride uptown," he said.

Her mouth suddenly went very dry. She glanced quickly to both sides, wondering if anyone else was witnessing the offer. Matt, to her left, was smiling.

"I'll always remember you," he said.

Barbara, having made her decision, sighed. "How kind," she said to Glover.

She made as though she was turning off her phone, but set it to record before dropping it into her purse.

Glover pushed open the door, stepped out, let Barbara in, then got back in beside her. The limo was already pulling away as he pulled the door shut.

Two

The stairwell on West Twenty-Ninth Street that led up to the High Line, just west of Tenth Avenue, was blocked off with police tape, a uniformed NYPD patrolman standing guard.

Detective Jerry Bourque parked his unmarked cruiser directly under the elevated, linear park that at one time had been a spur of the New York Central Railroad. He got out of his car and looked up. The viaduct was only about one and a half miles long, but it attracted millions of people—locals and tourists—annually. Lined with gardens and benches and interesting architectural features, it had quickly become one of Bourque's favorite spots in the city. It cut through the heart of lower Manhattan's West Side, yet was a ribbonlike oasis away from the noise and chaos. When it first opened, Bourque jogged it.

Not so much these days.

There were half a dozen marked NYPD cars, some with lights flashing, cluttering the street. As Bourque approached the stairwell entrance he recognized the patrolman standing there.

"Hey," Bourque said.

"They're expecting you," the officer said, and lifted the tape.

Bourque still had to duck, and the tape brushed across his short, bristly, prematurely gray hair. He was a round-shouldered six foot three. When circumstances demanded he stand up straight, he pushed six-five. He started up the stairs. Halfway, he paused for several seconds, a slight wave of anxiety washing over him. It was still hanging in there, this sense of unease before he reached the scene of a homicide. It hadn't always been this way. He reached into his pocket, feeling for something familiar, something reassuring, and upon finding it, he carried on the rest of the way to the top.

When he reached the High Line walkway, he looked left, to the north. The path veered slightly to the west, where the High Line crossed West Twenty-Ninth Street. A gently curved bench hugged the walkway on the left side, with a narrow band of greenery between the back and the edge.

This was where everyone—police, the coroner, High Line officials—were clustered.

Bourque walked on with a steady pace, his head extending slightly ahead of his body, as though tracking a scent. There was no need to run. The subject would still be dead when he got there. Bourque had turned forty only three months earlier, but his creased and weathered face would have allowed him to pass as someone five or ten years older. A woman had once told him he reminded her of those trees that grow out of the rocks up in Newfoundland. The relentless winds from the ocean caused them to lean permanently to one side, the branches all going in one direction. Bourque, the woman said, looked like someone who'd been worn down by the wind.

As he got closer, another detective, Lois Delgado, saw him and approached. Seeing her, his anxiety receded some. They were more than partners. They were friends, and if there was anyone Bourque trusted more than Delgado, he couldn't think who it might be.

And yet, he didn't tell her everything.

She had an oval face, the way she let a curl of her short dark hair fall across her upper left cheek where she had a port-wine stain about the size of a quarter. Bourque understood why she tried to disguise it, but he found it one of her most beautiful features. She pulled her hair back on the right side, usually tucking it behind her ear, giving her face a kind of lopsided quality. She was a year older than Bourque, but unlike him she could have passed for someone younger.

"Well?" he said.

"Dead male," she said. "No ID on the body. If I had to guess, late forties, early fifties. Early-morning jogger noticed something behind the corner of the bench that turned out to be a foot."

Bourque looked around. The High Line wound among countless apartment buildings. "Somebody must have seen something," he said.

"Yeah, well, that part of the bench is up against a nearly windowless wall on the left, and an open area on the right, and then there's the rink just up there, so . . ."

Delgado shrugged, then continued. "Had to have happened in the middle of the night when there was no one going by. Tons of pedestrian traffic up here through the day. Thousands of people walk along here."

"High Line closes at what, ten or eleven?"

"Yeah," Delgado said. "They roll down the gates at all the access points then. Opens up again at seven in the morning. Wasn't long after that that the body was discovered. You couldn't do this to someone during the open hours."

Bourque gave her a look. "Do what?"

"Easier if you just come and see for yourself," she said.

Bourque took a breath.

I'm fine.

As they approached the bench, he saw the dirty white rubber sole of the shoe the jogger had spotted.

"We think he got dragged into the tall grasses and that was where it happened," Delgado said, pointing to all the vegetation at the edges of the walkway that made it such a popular place for people to stroll. "I guess, just before they close the High Line and security does its walkthrough, someone could hide in the grass and not be seen."

A couple of other officers made some room for the two detectives, who stepped off the main part of the path and into the greenery at the left edge. Bourque knelt down close to the body.

"Jesus," he said.

"Yeah," said Delgado.

"Did a real number on the face."

"Hamburger," Delgado said.

"Yeah," Bourque said, feeling a tightening in his chest.

"Check the fingers. At least, what's left of them."

Bourque looked. "Fuck me."

The fingertips on both hands were missing.

"All cut off," Bourque said. "What would you need for that? Small pruning shears? The kind you use in the garden? Who walks around with one of those, unless it's one of the people who maintains this area."

"Don't think he used pruners," Delgado said. She parted some grass to reveal a rusted ribbon of steel, one of the original tracks when the High Line was used to bring rail cars into the heart of the city. "See the blood?"

Bourque slowly nodded. "He holds the guy's fingers over the rail, using it like a cutting board. Could have done it with a regular pocket knife, although he'd have had to press hard to get through bone."

"Our guy would have to have been dead by then, Jer," Delgado said.

"Would make it a tad easier," Bourque said. He paused to take a breath. "You cut the ends off ten fingers, you're going to get some objections if your guy is alive."

They looked back from the bloody rail to the body.

"Why?" Delgado asked.

"Hmm?"

"I've seen a finger get cut off as a way of getting someone's attention, of making them talk, of punishing them, but why cut 'em all off after he's dead?"

"Identi—"

"Of course," Delgado said. "So we can't take fingerprints. And the smashed-in face keeps us from knowing who he is."

"Maybe the killer's never heard of DNA," Bourque said, pausing to take another breath.

"You okay?" Lois asked. "You comin' down with something?"

He shook his head.

Delgado said, "DNA takes time. Maybe whoever did this wants to slow us down. Or maybe our guy here isn't in the database."

"Could be."

"Why not just cut off the hands? Why *all* the fingers? Why ten cuts instead of two?"

Bourque thought about that. "If he just had a simple knife, cutting through fingers was easier than sawing through wrists."

Delgado nodded. "Yeah."

Bourque raised his head over the top of the bench and looked down the walkway. "You walk off with ten fingertips, maybe you leave a blood trail."

"It rained around five this morning," Delgado said.

He sighed, looked at the body again. He took out his phone and started taking pictures. His gaze wandered farther down the body. The man's tan khakis had inched up one leg far enough to reveal his socks.

"Check it out," Bourque said, his voice barely above a whisper.

They were novelty socks, imprinted with several images of the shark from Jaws.

"*Daaa-duh, daaa-duh,*" Delgado said.

Bourque took some close-up shots.

"I've seen those for sale somewhere," he said.

"Lotta places sell novelty socks these days," Delgado said.

They both stood. Bourque gazed along the High Line, first to the north, then the south. "So if this happened after hours, and this is all locked up, how'd our killer get away?"

Delgado said, "Before you got here, I walked a block in each direction. One or two places, if you were really brave, you could jump onto a nearby roof. There's some rooftop parking up that way. Get onto a roof, or a fire escape, work your way down."

"Like Bruce Willis in *Die Hard*," Bourque said. The words came out in a whisper.

"What?"

Bourque repeated himself, louder this time.

"Yeah, could be done," Delgado said. "If you're in good shape."

Bourque coughed, cleared his throat. "I don't ever remember a murder on the High Line. Nothing bad happens up here."

Delgado said, "It's lost its cherry."

Bourque put a hand to his chest, indicating he had a call or a text coming in. "Give me a sec," he said.

He took the phone from his pocket, glanced at it, put it to his ear as he came out from behind the bench and walked a few yards up the High Line, still within the area that was taped off, but free of police or any other city officials.

Bourque nodded a couple of times as he walked, as though responding to whatever his caller was saying. But there'd been no call, and no text.

And Bourque was not talking. He was wheezing. His windpipe had started constricting at the sight of those fingers with the missing tips.

When he felt confident he was far enough away from the murder scene to not be seen, he reached back into his pocket for that familiar object.

He brought out the inhaler, inserted it into his mouth, and inhaled deeply as he depressed the top of the tiny canister. A barely detectible puff of medicine entered his lungs. He held his breath nearly fifteen seconds, exhaled, and repeated the process.

Bourque tucked the inhaler back into his pocket. He took a few breaths through his nose, waiting for his air passages to open up again.

He turned around and walked back to have another look at the man with no fingertips.

Three

Barbara sank into a leather seat opposite the mayor and Valerie. Glover and the good-looking bald guy made space for her in the middle, so her feet had to straddle the driveshaft hump. Even though the car was roomier than most, she found her shoulders squeezed by the two men. She was picking up a cheap aftershave scent from Glover. But the bald guy was giving off something subtler, an almost coffee-like scent. Barbara wondered whether it was an actual cologne, or if he'd been in the Starbucks line for too long. Either way, she kind of liked it.

She turned her head to face the bald man. "You're new."

He smiled.

"I'm Barbara Matheson, but I'm guessing you know that." When he didn't say anything, she looked at Headley. "Does he talk? Stomp his foot once for yes, two for no?"

"That's Chris Vallins," Valerie said. "Say hello, Chris."

"Hello," said Chris. Deep voice. If brown velvet could make a sound, Barbara thought, this would be it. "Nice to meet you." He snaked a gloved hand around in the tight quarters and offered it.

"A pleasure," Barbara said, shaking it. "And what do you do for His Holiness?"

"Part of the team," he said. "Whatever the mayor needs."

Barbara didn't see her new friend Chris as much of a chatterer, so she turned her attention back to those sitting across from her. She wondered whether to make anything of the fact that Valerie was sitting next to the mayor. There was a foot of space between them, but Barbara tried to read the body language. If Valerie found her boss as unappealing as Barbara believed she should, she'd be pressing herself up against the door. But there was a slight shoulder lean toward Headley.

Maybe she was reading too much into it. And what did it matter, anyway? If Headley wanted to screw the help, and the help was okay with it, then what business was it of Barbara's? Valerie was a grown woman capable of making an informed choice. Surely she had to know the mayor's background, what a shit he reportedly had been to his late wife, Felicia. Everyone knew that, ten years earlier, the night Felicia died in their uptown brownstone after a long fight with cancer, Headley was fucking the brains out of one of her caretakers in a room at the Plaza. It was a young Glover who called 911 to report that his mother had stopped breathing.

Headley was already one of the most famous, if not most notorious, businessmen in the city, so when the media picked up an emergency call at his address, a couple of TV vans were dispatched to the scene. What ended up on the news was a shot of a weeping Glover, his father nowhere to be seen and not reachable by phone. Headley claimed later he had muted his cell because he'd been meeting with a possible investor whose name he was not at liberty to reveal. No one believed it for a second.

Barbara had wondered if that was when Headley's relationship with his son had soured. The boy had humiliated him. Unwittingly, of course, but that was what he'd done. Headley had been on the cusp of a mayoral bid way back then but delayed it, hoping that as time passed his reputation would be rehabilitated. When he finally did announce his candidacy, he had created a myth about himself as the sad widower who had raised his teenage son on his own.

Felicia had been a looker in her day, a onetime model who worked her way up to a senior editor position at Condé Nast. Valerie had some of Felicia's attributes, at least those the mayor valued. In her late thirties, she was younger than him by more than a decade. Long legs, busty enough without being too obvious about it, dark, shoulder-length hair. Probably bought all her clothes at Saks, went to some trendy salon like Fringe or Pickthorn to get her hair done. Unlike Barbara, whose salon was the bathroom sink, did quite well pulling together a wardrobe at Target, and whose makeup budget was a pittance compared to what she spent on pinot grigio.

More than once, at political events, when Valerie was looking the other way, Barbara had observed the mayor checking out his communication director's ass as if it harbored some mystical secret. Not that hers was the only one.

But now, in the back of this limo, Headley had a very different expression on his face as he sized up Barbara. He was scowling at her, like she was a teenage daughter who'd ignored curfew for the fifth night in a row.

"So what's happened uptown?" Barbara asked, looking out the window. The driver had found his way from City Hall to the FDR and was making good time heading north.

Beside her, Glover said, "Some kind of elevator accident."

Barbara was underwhelmed. Elevator accident, crane collapse, subway fire. Whatever. It was always something in a city this big. It'd be news if something *didn't* happen. If Headley felt a need to attend, it had to be more serious than usual, but still. Headley liked being seen at catastrophes. Say a few things for the evening news, give the impression he knew what he was talking about, show his concern.

Barbara was willing to cut him some slack on this. It was something all mayors did, if they were smart. A mayor who couldn't be bothered to show up when New Yorkers endured something particularly tragic would be pilloried. Rudy Giuliani had set the standard, way back on September 11, 2001, as he walked through the rubble, holding a handkerchief to his mouth. Say what you wanted about the guy's shenanigans since, you had to give him credit for his service back in the day.

Barbara doubted Headley had it in him to be that kind of mayor. She just hoped he—and the city—would never be tested like that again.

"They're saying four dead," Valerie said.

Barbara nodded again. It wasn't that she didn't care. But industrial accidents, car crashes, drive-by shootings, apartment fires, these just weren't her thing. She covered city politics. Let the youngsters chase ambulances. She'd cut her teeth on that kind of stuff, and it was valuable experience, but she'd moved on.

"Nice of you to give me a ride, but this isn't the way to my place," Barbara said to Headley, who was still looking at her through narrowed eyes. "So, what? Am I grounded? Being sent to bed without my dinner?"

"Barbara, Barbara, Barbara," Headley said, looking weary and disappointed at the same time. "When's it going to stop?"

"What?" Barbara asked. "Your love of quid pro quos or my love of writing about them?"

"You think you can keep poking the bear and never get a scratch," he said. "You're not untouchable."

Untouchable. Interesting choice of word.

"Well, you told everyone you're suing me and *Manhattan Today*. So I guess I'm not untouchable. But while we're on that issue, how's the suit against the *Times* for saying you were registered to vote federally in three different districts? And how long's it been since you threatened to sue that actress who said you had performance anxiety?"

Valerie shot a glance at Barbara but said nothing.

Headley forced a smile. "Well, I think we know which of those accusations was the more ridiculous." The smile faded. "Anyway, these things take a while to work their way through the courts."

Barbara settled into the leather seat, taking advantage of the head-rest. *Don't let them rattle you,* she thought. Sure, there were four of them, not counting the driver, who was getting off at Forty-Second Street and heading crosstown. The one Barbara really wanted to know more about was this Chris dude beside her, who looked like he could get a job playing a Bond villain's bodyguard if he lost his City Hall gig. Not that that was necessarily a knock against him. He was a handsome piece of work. Was being surrounded supposed to put her on edge? Did they know how much she was actually *loving* this? If Headley and his gang ignored her, gave no hint of how annoyed they were with her, well, that would be unbearable.

"I honestly don't know why you seem to have it in for me," Headley asked. "Why so angry?"

"I'm not angry," Barbara said. "I just have this thing about hypocrisy."

"Oh, please," the mayor said. "Hypocrisy is the fuel that keeps the world running. Let me ask you this. Be honest. Have you ever had a source who did something bad, something worth writing about, worth exposing, but you looked the other way because they had good intel that gave you an even better story? Something that would give you an exclusive? Are you going to sit there and tell me you've never done that?"

Barbara said, "There are a lot of considerations when you're working on a story."

Headley grinned. "That sounds as evasive as something I would say. We're really not that different, you and I. It's all a game, isn't it? Politics and the media? And it can be great fun, I'm not denying it.

But sometimes"—and at this point his face grew stern—"it all starts to get a little annoying."

"Am I annoying you?" Barbara asked, almost hopefully.

He held his thumb and forefinger apart a fraction of an inch. "Just a titch. But," he said slowly, "we'd like to give you an opportunity to redeem yourself."

Barbara eyed him suspiciously. "What's that supposed to mean?"

Headley glanced at Glover and gave him a subtle nod.

Glover said, "The mayor certainly has his differences with you, but he also recognizes your skills as a journalist, that you are an accomplished writer. And he respects you for that."

Headley looked out the window, watched the city go by as they traveled north on Third.

"Needless to say," Glover continued, "the mayor, and the rest of the team here, wish you'd at least occasionally focus on the things that are getting done. This subway story you've latched on to, that's a really positive story. But instead, you're portraying it in a negative light. The current signal system is based on technology from the 1930s and desperately needs to be overhauled. And then there's the switchover to electric cars. The mayor wants every city vehicle to be converted to electric power within his first term. Soon you'll be seeing those little green stickers on the back of every car and truck that's—"

"Glover, move it along," Headley said to his son, still looking out the window, an edge of irritation creeping into his voice.

"We're not announcing anything at the moment," Glover said, "but in due time it may be in the mayor's interest to tell his story to a broader audience, so voters have a better sense of who he is. That there's more to him than two-bit scandals and salacious headlines. That he's a man who wants to make a difference, but on a broader canvas."

"Ah," said Barbara, looking at Headley. "You want to move up the political food chain. After mayor of New York, there's only governor, or president. Or going on TV endlessly to defend a *corrupt* president. How do you know someone wants to be the leader of the free world? They suddenly come out with a book, like the world's been dying to hear their life story. Comes out, sells a few copies, then the primaries come, someone else gets the nomination, and the book ends up on the seventy-five-percent-off table at Barnes & Noble, and even then they can't unload the copies. In the end, their life story gets pulped."

Glover waited to see if she was done. When Barbara said nothing more, he continued. "As I was saying, we're looking for someone who can assist the mayor in telling his story."

Barbara nodded. "A ghost writer."

Glover smiled. "My sources tell me you're no stranger to that kind of work."

It was true. Over the years, Barbara had ghostwritten three memoirs. One for a Broadway actress, one for a sports hero who'd lost both legs in a car accident, and one for a pop star who was once at the top of the charts but now would be lucky to get a gig singing in a SoHo night club. None of those assignments would have given her a shot at a Pulitzer, but they'd certainly helped pay the bills.

When Barbara failed to confirm or deny what Glover had said, he carried on. "We've started speaking to publishers. We're meeting later with Simon & Schuster. They're looking for possible writers to work with Da—with the mayor, but we have final approval on that and can make suggestions of our own. We think you'd be a leading candidate."

"Seriously."

Headley cleared his throat, turned away from the passing scenery, and looked directly at her. "There's a feeling that choosing someone who's had an antagonistic history with me would lend the project considerable credibility. That it wouldn't be a whitewash."

"It would be particularly credible if I were working for you at the same time you were suing me."

Headley grimaced. "I suppose we could let that slide. There's still enough of a history of animosity, I should think."

Barbara nodded slowly. "Of course, you'd still have final approval on the manuscript."

"Well," said Valerie, weighing in for the first time, "of course, but we're looking for a fair and balanced portrait. Warts and all. The mayor wants to lay everything out on the table. America's becoming accustomed to candidates who are less than perfect. If you're running for office these days, it helps if you're relatable."

"Warts and all," Barbara said slowly. "Are you sure you want to go there?"

"And I haven't mentioned perhaps the most important thing of all," Glover said. "You'd be looking at a mid-six-figure fee. With the potential for bonuses should the book stay on the bestseller list for an extended period of time." He grinned. "Or if anyone ever wanted to turn it into a movie. You know. A biopic. Despite your little speech, it could happen."

Headley had the decency to blush. Barbara figured even he had to know that was over the top. She poked the inside of her cheek with her tongue. "Golly. That's something."

Headley leaned forward, lowered his voice, as if they were the only two in the car. He locked eyes with her and said, "I believe, despite our differences, we could work together."

Barbara appeared to consider the offer as the mayor leaned back in his seat. "I could probably carve out some time from my *Manhattan*

Today duties." An eyebrow went up as she looked at the mayor. "Maybe weekends?"

"Oh," said Glover, who had glanced down for two seconds to read a text on his phone. "Working on this book would be a full-time proposition. At least for the duration of the project, which I think would take the better part of a year. Wouldn't you agree, Valerie?"

"I would," she said.

"Jesus." It was the driver. They all looked forward up Third, through the windshield—Barbara and Glover and Chris had to turn around in their seats—to see the traffic stopped dead at Fifty-Eighth. Police cars blocked any further passage northward. The limo driver snaked the car between some taxis, heading straight for the makeshift barricade of emergency vehicles. He powered down the window as a police officer approached.

"You can't—"

The driver said, "I got the mayor here."

The cop leaned forward to peer into the back to be sure, then nodded and waved them through. But it wasn't possible to go much farther. Emergency vehicles clogged the street.

Glover, waving his phone, said, "Latest is three dead, not four. Elevator dropped at least twenty floors. No word yet on the survivor's condition."

Headley nodded solemnly.

"We'll walk from here, David," Valerie told the man behind the wheel.

The limo came to a dead stop. The driver jumped out and opened the door on the mayor's side.

Chris Vallins opened his door and, once out, extended a hand to Barbara to help her out. Her first inclination would have been to refuse. *I can get out myself, thank you very much.* But some other, perhaps more primal, instinct overruled that inclination, and she accepted the offer. His grip was strong, his arm rigid enough.

"Thank you," she said.

Vallins nodded.

Glover had gotten out the other side and ran around to Barbara. Quietly, he said, "It was my idea."

"I'm sorry?"

"About the book. To see if you'd be interested. My father took some convincing. I think you'd be perfect."

"Keep your friends close and your enemies closer," Barbara said.

"No, it's not like that. You'd do a good job." His voice went even softer. "I'd never admit this to Dad, but I've admired your work for a long time."

She hardly knew what to make of that.

They caught up to the rest of the group as they walked toward the office tower where, it appeared, the accident had occurred.

"Son of a bitch," Headley said, more to himself than anyone else.

"What?" Valerie asked.

"Morris Lansing's building," he said. Valerie looked at her boss blankly, clearly not immediately recognizing the name. "Seriously?" he said.

A CBS camera crew spotted the mayor and zeroed in on him.

"Mr. Mayor!" someone shouted. "Do you know when this elevator was last inspected?"

A camera was in his face. Headley looked appropriately grim.

"Look, I've only just arrived, and haven't been briefed, but I can assure you I'll be speaking to all the involved parties and bringing all the powers of my office to bear on . . ."

Barbara slipped through the media throng and headed for the main doors in time to see the paramedics wheel out a gurney with a bloodied woman strapped to it.

"Make way!" one of them shouted, and the crowd scattered so that they could reach the open doors of the waiting ambulance.

The gurney passed within a few feet of Barbara, who got a look first at the woman's sneakers, and then, as she was hustled past, her face.

Barbara only caught a glimpse of her. Two seconds, tops.

But it was long enough.

"Paula," Barbara whispered.

Four

Detectives Jerry Bourque and Lois Delgado decided to split up duties.

Delgado was going to look for overnight surveillance video. There were cameras on the High Line and undoubtedly on nearby buildings. She was also going to be tracking down the city workers responsible for locking up access to the High Line at the end of the day to ask whether they had seen anything that, in retrospect, might seem important.

Bourque would check reports of any missing person whose description might match their victim. He also had an idea where to get a lead on those shark socks.

After the chief medical examiner had arrived, the body would be moved to the Manhattan forensic pathology center, where a DNA sample would be retrieved. If the deceased's genetic ID was on file, they'd know with certainty who he was. The only problem, of course, was that it could take weeks or months to get those results. Fingerprints would have been a faster route, but that was obviously not an option this time.

An autopsy would tell them more about how those fingertips were removed, and how, exactly, the man had died. Those blows to the head, most likely, Bourque figured. When the lab was done scouring the man's body for clues, his clothes would be searched and analyzed.

A four-block-long stretch of the High Line was to remain closed for the day as forensic experts examined every inch of it. Maybe they'd be able to pull up a shoe print with a hint of blood on it. The rain might not have washed away everything. Maybe the killer had dropped something. Handrails on the stairs at access points north and south of the scene were to be searched for blood traces, and dusted for fingerprints, although that was not expected to produce much in the way of results, considering thousands of people touched those handrails every single day.

Officers were dispatched to knock on the doors of every single apartment along the High Line with a view of that curved bench. Any apartment where no one was home through the day was to be revisited that evening. Bourque also wanted someone there after midnight to make note of apartments that remained lit right through till morning. One of those night owls might have been looking out the window at just the right time.

I'm doing okay, he thought. *I got through all that just fine. As long as I don't think about it, I'll—*

Which, of course, made him think about it.

About those drops. Blood drops. Falling like red rain onto the lips of that—

"Jerry?" Delgado said.

"Yeah," he said.

"You off?"

"Yeah, I'll catch up with you later," Bourque said, feeling his throat start to constrict.

Bourque headed for his car. Once he was behind the wheel, he took another hit off the inhaler. He held his breath for ten seconds as he slipped the device back into his pocket, then glanced at his watch.

He had a midmorning appointment he'd failed to mention to his partner, but there was still enough time to check out one lead ahead of that. He started the engine, turned the car around, and headed east. He'd seen those socks at the Strand Bookstore. That didn't mean their homicide victim had bought them there, but he might find out who distributed them, and how widely.

The truth was, he just wanted an excuse to go to the bookstore.

He headed for Broadway and Twelfth and left the unmarked cruiser half on the sidewalk, half on the street. One of the few benefits of being a cop. You never had to hunt for a parking spot. He entered the store, went past the front counter and tables stacked with new releases, then took a left into the clothing section. It wasn't as though one could pull an entire wardrobe together here, but the store carried novelty T-shirts and hats and plenty of pairs of offbeat socks.

He'd dragged a date in here one night a couple of months ago. Wendy was her name. A waitress from a diner up on Lex in the Seventies. She'd bought a pair of socks imprinted with a library card design, nicely ruled with a "Date Due" stamp and everything. They'd been displayed right next to the ones with the shark images. Bourque hadn't paid a lot of attention to the socks, having wandered off to the section with books on architecture. At the cash register, Bourque offered to pay for the socks, which came to ten bucks, and she let him. "Just for that," she whispered to him as they headed back out onto Broadway, "I'll model them for you." A sly smile. "*Just* the socks."

And so she had.

Bourque had not spent the night. He had to be up early, and so did she. The following morning, he went to a different diner. He hadn't seen her since.

On this morning's visit to the bookstore, he checked out the sock display and quickly found the *Jaws*-inspired design. He took one pair off the rack and compared it to the picture he'd taken of the dead man's foot. The socks were a match. He took them to the counter, where a young man with frizzy hair smiled and said, "Yeah?"

Bourque said, "I got an email that a book I ordered was in."

"What's the name?"

"Bourque."

"And the book?"

"*Changing New York*, by Berenice Abbott."

"Give me a sec. And you want those socks?"

"Can you check on the book first?"

The clerk slipped away. Bourque leaned against the counter, killed some time looking at his phone.

The man returned, set the book on the counter for Bourque's inspection. It was art book sized, nine by twelve inches and an inch thick, with a crisp, black-and-white cover photo of downtown New York. "It's used but in nice shape. Couple of pages are slightly creased."

"That's okay," Bourque said, thumbing quickly through the book, scanning the hundreds of photos of New York from the 1930s. "It's great. I'll take it."

"Have you seen the book on Top of the Park? Came out last week. Thought you might be interested." He pointed to one of the new release tables. "Over there."

Bourque walked over to the table, found what the man had been pointing to. Another large book, an artist's rendering on the cover of a gleaming skyscraper soaring upward above a park. "I didn't know they were doing a book on this," he said, flipping through the pages, looking at more architectural drawings, floor plans, comparisons to other buildings, around the world, of similar height. There weren't many.

He brought it over to the counter. "Nice book. They've documented everything. Early concepts, final plans, bio on the architect." Bourque slowly nodded his head. "Gorgeous book." He flipped the book over, looking for a price. "Jesus," he said.

"Yeah," said the clerk. "But you're getting the other one for only fifteen bucks. And we can take five off the forty for the other one."

While Bourque considered that, the clerk tapped the cover of the more expensive book and said, "I think it officially opens this week. Supposed to be the tallest residential tower in the world, or just the U.S. I'm not sure. Only thing I know is I won't be going up it. I got a heights thing. I've never even been to the top of the Empire State."

Bourque had reached a decision. "I'll take both of them."

"And the socks?"

"Just a question about them. How many places in the city other than you sell these?"

The man shrugged. "I'd guess all kinds. Why? You want us to match a price?"

Bourque shook his head. At this point, he displayed his badge and put it away. "Do you remember a guy coming in here buying a pair like this?"

The clerk blinked. "You kidding? We sell lots of those. And there's lots of others work the checkout."

Bourque was not deterred. "Every item in this store has a different UPC number, right?"

The young man shrugged. "Yeah, sure."

"So then if you enter that UPC number, up will come all the purchases of this particular sock. And if they were paid for with a credit card, you'd know who made the purchase."

"Maybe, yeah."

Bourque smiled. "That's what I'd like you to do for me."

The clerk grinned. "So let me see if I understand this. You want to find a guy who bought a pair of these socks."

"Right."

"If I did sell a pair to your guy, maybe I'd recognize him. You got a picture?"

"No," the detective said.

"Okay, so, I'd need one of the managers to okay looking through our records, but I've already got your email."

Bourque handed him a card. "That's got my phone number on it, too."

———

"I don't have a lot of time," the detective said, dropping into the plastic chair in the small examining room. "I need a new scrip."

The doctor, a short, round man in his midsixties with a pair of glasses perched atop his forehead, sat at a small desk with a computer in front of him. He lowered the glasses briefly so he could read something on the screen. He tapped at the keyboard, slowly, with two fingers.

"I hate these goddamn computers," the doctor said. "Whole clinic has changed over to them."

"So just write me one the old-fashioned way," Jerry Bourque said. "On a piece of paper, Bert. With your illegible handwriting."

"That's not how it works anymore," Bert said, squinting at the screen. He paused. "Hmm."

"What, hmm?"

"You're going through these inhalers pretty fast," he said.

"Come on, Bert."

Bert perched the glasses on his forehead again and turned on his stool to face his patient. "Inhalers aren't the answer."

"They work," the detective said.

The doctor nodded wearily. "In the short term. But what you need is to talk—"

"I know what you think I need."

"There's no physiological reason for your bouts of shortness of breath. You don't have, thank God, lung cancer or emphysema. I don't see any evidence that it's an allergic reaction to anything. It's not bronchitis. You've identified plainly what brings on the attacks."

"If there's nothing physiological, then why do the inhalers work?"

"They open up your air passages regardless of what brings on the symptoms," Bert said. "Has it been happening more often, or less?"

Bourque paused. "About the same." Another pause. "I had one this morning. I got called to a scene, and I was okay, but then I had this . . . flash . . . I guess you'd call it. And then I started to tighten up."

"Is it almost always that one memory that brings it on? The drops—"

Bourque raised a hand, signaling he didn't need his memory refreshed. "That does, for sure. But other moments of stress sometimes trigger it. Or a tense situation brings back the memory, and it happens." He paused. "There doesn't always have to be a reason."

Bert nodded sympathetically. "The department doesn't have anyone you can talk to?"

"I don't need to talk to anyone in the department. I have you."

"I'm not a shrink."

"I don't need a shrink."

"Maybe you do. You either need to talk to someone, or—"

"Or what?"

"I don't know." The doctor waved his hands in frustration. "Maybe you're like Jimmy Stewart in that Hitchcock movie. He gets vertigo after suffering a trauma. It takes another trauma to cure him of it."

Bourque scanned the walls, looking at the various framed medical degrees.

"What are you looking for?" Bert asked.

"Something from the New York Film Academy. I'm guessing that's where you got your medical degree."

Bert ignored the shot. "It's been eight months. You need to see someone who can bring more to the table than I can."

"I'm not baring my soul to anyone in the department."

Bert sighed again. "Maybe the department is the problem."

Bourque looked at him, waiting for an explanation.

The doctor said, "Maybe you're in the wrong line of work. Do you actually like what you do?"

Bourque took several seconds to answer. "Sure."

"That was convincing."

Bourque looked away. "I'm okay at what I do. It's not a bad job."

"I've been seeing you since you were in short pants," Bert said. "I know this was never your first choice."

"Okay, I couldn't get accepted into architectural school. I got over it. Dad was a cop. His two brothers were cops. So I went into the family business. It was what they wanted for me, anyway."

Bert turned back to the computer, fingers poised over the keyboard. But he had a change of thought and swiveled his chair back to face Bourque.

"Have you tried that exercise I gave you, for when things start tightening up, you have trouble bringing in air?"

"Tell me again."

"When it starts happening, try not to focus on it. Focus on something else. You think, what are five things I see in front of me? What are five sounds I'm hearing? What are the birthdays for people in my family? List the Mets in alphabetical order. The ten most-wanted list. Or here's a good one for you: New York's ten most historic buildings. Or most popular with tourists. Tallest, I don't know. That would seem to be right up your alley."

Bourque looked at him dubiously. "Seriously?"

"Just try it."

It was Bourque's turn to sigh. "If it's all in my head, it's not like it can kill me. Right? If I lost my inhaler, it's not going to get so bad that I can't breathe at all. It's not like I'm going to die."

Bert slowly shook his head, then went back to the keyboard. "I'll do you one more scrip," he said.

Five

So far as Barbara knew, Paula Chatsworth had no family in the city. She hailed from Montpelier, had come to NYU to study journalism, and never went back. Barbara got to know Paula three years earlier when she did a summer internship at *Manhattan Today*. Barbara had seen a lot of herself in the young woman. An eagerness to learn matched by a healthy contempt for authority. And she swore a lot. For some reason, Barbara didn't expect that from a Vermont girl, but she was pleased. Paula had assured Barbara that Vermont girls could cuss with the best of them.

Manhattan Today didn't take Paula on permanently, and Barbara lost touch with her. She'd run into her once in the Grand Central Market, getting a taco at Ana Maria. Three minutes of small talk, enough time to learn that Paula had not found a job in her field of study, but was working as a copywriter for a firm that managed a number of websites. "I'm right up by Bloomingdale's," she said. "So I don't have to go far to get rid of my paycheck."

Paula hadn't mentioned anything about being in a relationship, but it was only a quick meeting, and there was no reason why she would have. She hadn't looked conscious as she was wheeled to the ambulance, but the police would probably be looking through her phone for a contact, if it wasn't password protected, or talking to her coworkers to find next of kin.

Barbara thought she might be able to help.

Once she'd learned which hospital Paula had been taken to, Barbara headed there. While she waited in the ER to find out how she was doing, Barbara tracked down her parents in Montpelier. She hoped someone, maybe from Paula's work—she had, after all, been injured at her place of employment—had already been in touch, but it turned out Barbara was the first to call.

"I don't understand," Paula's mother, Sandy, said, her voice breaking. "How does an elevator just fall?"

"They'll be looking into that," Barbara said. "Some kind of fluke accident, I'm guessing."

"We were always so worried about her going to New York," Sandy said. "All the things that could happen. Muggings, shootings . . . I told her, don't you dare get a bicycle, don't be trying to ride around the city on a bike because everyone there drives crazy and you'll get hit for sure. But an *elevator*?"

"I know." Barbara hardly knew what else to say. And offering comfort had never been one of her strengths. *Shit happens* was her basic philosophy. But still, her heart ached for the woman. Barbara asked if there was anyone in the city she should call. Sandy said if Paula had been seeing anyone, she and her husband didn't know anything about it.

"We haven't heard from her for weeks," Sandy said, and Barbara could hear her crying. "She might . . . we said some things . . ."

Barbara waited.

"Paula's been sorting out who she is," Sandy said quietly. "If you know what I mean. It's been hard for me and Ken to . . . to accept."

Barbara remembered Paula mentioning once, during her internship, about going to the Cubbyhole, a well-known lesbian bar, one weekend. She'd made no effort to hide her sexual identity, so Barbara had an idea what Sandy might be hinting at. Maybe it was Paula's parents who'd been sorting out who she was, more than Paula herself.

"Sure," Barbara said. "I understand."

Paula's father, Ken, got on the line.

"I've never driven into Manhattan," he said. "What's the best route?"

His voice was all seriousness, as if focusing in on travel arrangements could push the image of his injured daughter out of his head.

"I'm really not the best one to ask. I don't have a car. I don't even have a driver's license."

"Are there tolls?" he asked. "Will I need lots of change? Is there parking at the hospital?" He said they were going to leave within the hour.

Barbara suggested they consider a train. Or better yet, there was probably a flight they could take from Burlington.

Ken said catching a plane made sense, and that he'd look into that as soon as he got off the phone. Barbara promised to call back if she learned anything, and gave Paula's parents numbers for the hospital, as well as for her own cell. In turn, Ken gave Barbara their cell number so she could update them, if there was news, as they were en route.

Once the call was over, Barbara felt emotionally wrung out. Paula's mother was on to something when she'd said the last thing you worried about when your child went to the big city was an elevator accident. A million other perils came to mind before something like that. Hit-and-run, botulism, alien abduction would all be higher up on the list. How many elevator mishaps did New York have in a year? One? Two, maybe?

Barbara went looking for a coffee, although what she needed was something much stronger. She came back to the ER, asked the woman at admitting how Paula was doing and whether she'd been moved to a room.

The woman, eyes focused on a computer screen, said she would check when she had a chance.

"I've got a number for her parents," Barbara offered.

The woman kept staring at the screen and tapping away at the keyboard.

Fuck it, Barbara thought.

She wandered into the curtained warren of the emergency ward, peeking into the various examining areas to see whether she could find Paula.

It didn't take long.

Paula lay in a bed, connected to various wires and tubes and machines, including a beeping heart monitor. The woman's face was mottled with blue and purple bruises, and her body had been immobilized. Barbara assumed she'd have suffered multiple fractures. If she'd been standing when that elevator hit bottom, the shock wave would have run straight up her entire body, shattering bones, particularly those in her legs, compressing her insides. It would be like jumping off a building.

God, what must it be like to be in a plunging elevator? Barbara wondered. *Knowing what's coming? Knowing there's nothing you can do about it?*

Barbara hoped a doctor or nurse would appear so she could get an update on her condition. If they asked if she was family, she'd tell them she was Paula's aunt or a much older sister.

As she took another step closer to the bed, it occurred to Barbara that Paula was pretty close in age to her own daughter, Arla. Paula was in her early twenties, Arla would be twenty-five on her next birthday, Barbara thought.

I should call her.

Paula stirred slightly, her head shifting slightly on the pillow.

"Hey," Barbara said softly.

Paula's eyes did not open.

"Don't know if you can hear me or not, but it's Barbara. Barbara Matheson, from *Manhattan Today*. From your internship?"

Nothing.

Paula's right eye opened a fraction of an inch, then closed.

"I've called your folks," she said. "In Montpelier. Hope that was okay. Figured you'd want them to know. They're coming."

Paula's lips parted, closed, parted again.

"You want to say something?" Barbara asked.

Her lips opened again. Paula's tongue moved slightly.

"Don't push yourself. It's okay. Save your strength."

But then a word, light and as soft as a feather, drifted from Paula's mouth.

"What was that?" Barbara said, turning her head sideways, placing her ear an inch from Paula's lips.

She whispered the word again, just loud enough for Barbara to hear.

"Floating."

"Floating?" Barbara said.

"Like floating."

Barbara pulled away, nodding. "I'll bet," she said. "You were basically in freefall. You'd have felt weightless, and—"

The heart monitor went from a beep to a sustained, alarming tone.

"What the—"

Barbara looked at the machine, saw the flat line travel across the screen.

"Oh, shit," she said.

She threw back the curtain and called out: "Hey! *Hey!* I need help here!"

From the far end of the ward, a nurse came running.

Later, when it was over, and Barbara had made the call to Paula's parents to tell them that there was no longer a sense of urgency, she found her way to a bar over on Third north of Fiftieth and ordered a scotch, neat.

She was on her fourth when it occurred to her that maybe "floating" was not a reference to plummeting in the elevator. Now Barbara wondered whether Paula was being slightly more metaphorical as she slipped away. In the short time she'd worked at *Manhattan Today*, Paula had shown a flair for words.

Six

By late afternoon, just about everything anyone could want to know about the elevator accident at the Lansing Tower was available. Everything, that is, except for why it had happened.

Various news sources had posted brief profiles on the dead. They were:

Paula Chatsworth, twenty-two, single. Tribeca resident, originally from Vermont, worked for Webwrite, a firm that produced copy for firms working on their online presence. Paula had initially survived the elevator plunge, but later died at the hospital.

Stuart Bland, thirty-eight. Lived with his mother in Bushwick. He'd held a variety of odd jobs, none for very long, including a stint at a dry-cleaning operation. That, police speculated, might have been where he acquired a FedEx ID. The courier company reported that he was not, and never had been, an employee, which got the police wondering what he was up to. Found on the floor of the elevator was a script with his name attached. Initial speculation was that Bland hoped to meet with someone in the building to discuss the project, although there was no record of him having made an appointment.

Sherry D'Agostino, thirty-nine. Vice president of creative at Cromwell Entertainment. Married to Wall Street stockbroker Elliott Milne. Mother of two children: a daughter, five, and a son, eight. She lived in Brooklyn Heights. "An immense loss," said Cromwell president Jason Cromwell, "both personally and professionally. Sherry had an unerring eye for talent in all fields and was not only a vital member of our team, but a close, personal friend. We are beyond devastated."

Barton Fieldgate, sixty-four. Estate lawyer at Templeton Flynn and Fieldgate. Married forty years, father of five. Lived in an $8 million brownstone on West Ninety-Fifth. Said Michael Templeton: "That something like this could happen, in our own building, is unimaginable. Barton was a friend and colleague of the highest order. He will be missed." There was also a report that the firm was already in the process of suing the owners of the Lansing Tower for failure to maintain the elevators properly.

The cause of the accident was under investigation by multiple agencies, including the fire department and the city body that oversaw the licensing and operation of elevators and escalators. New York, it was pointed out, had thirty-nine inspectors to check on some seventy thousand of them.

Richard Headley was flopped on the office couch in Gracie Mansion, the official New York mayoral residence, jacket off, feet on the coffee table with his shoes still on, tie loosened, and remote in hand. He was looking at the large screen bolted to the wall, flipping back and forth between the various six o'clock news reports. He'd decided to stay awhile on NY1.

They had a few seconds of his arrival at the Lansing Tower, then a clip of him conferring briefly with Morris Lansing, the major New York developer—and long-time friend of the mayor's—who owned the skyscraper.

The door opened and Valerie Langdon walked in, moving quickly so as not to obstruct the mayor's view of the news.

"Get me Morris," Headley said, muting the TV and handing her his cell phone. "I want to see how he's doing." He glanced at his aide. "You know who he is *now*?"

"I know he gave half a million to your campaign," Valerie said. "It slipped my mind before." She added, "You have a lot of donors."

Valerie tapped the screen and put the phone to her ear. She spoke to someone, said she had the mayor on the line for Lansing, then looked at Headley. "They're getting him."

While he waited, Headley continued to watch the news. They were on to another story, out of Boston. A reporter stood out front of a building Headley recognized as Faneuil Hall. When he saw the word "bomb" in the crawl he turned the volume back on.

"—four injured when what police are calling an explosive device of some kind went off inside the market. Of the injured, one is reported in serious condition. Police believe the device was left in a backpack inside a trash container in one of the food court areas. The incident brought back memories of the horrific Boston Marathon bombing in 2013, in which three people were killed and hundreds injured. If this most recent event had been during the busier lunch hour period, it's very likely more people would have been injured and possibly killed. The Marathon bombers, two brothers, were motivated by Islamist extremism, but this event may find its roots far closer to home. It's similar to other acts linked to the domestic extremist group known as the Flyovers, although authorities have not yet confirmed that the group is involved, despite some vague claims of responsibility on Twitter that—"

"Richard," Valerie said.

He muted the set again as she handed his phone back to him.

"Morris?" he said.

"Hello, Richard," Lansing said.

"We didn't have long to talk today. I wanted to check in, see how you were, see what else they've learned."

"It's horrible," Lansing said. "Beyond horrible. Sherry was a friend. We were out to her place on Long Island three weeks ago. And Barton was a good man. The other two, I have no idea who they were. This one guy, posing as a courier, that sounds fishy to me. Someone at security is going to be fired, I can promise you."

"If anybody can get into the building that easily, yeah, you're going to want to look into it. But is there anything that connects that guy to the elevator malfunction?"

"Well, no, not at this time," Morris Lansing said. "They don't know what the fuck happened there. There's so many safeguards built into the damn things, but once in a while, they still let you down. Jesus, no pun intended."

"I just wanted you to know that if there's anything you need, all you have to do is call," Headley said. "The office of the mayor is here to help you in any way it can."

There was a pause from Lansing's end.

"Morris?"

"Yeah, well, about that," Lansing said. "There's gonna be lawsuits comin' outta my ass on this one. Fieldgate's firm is already making noises. But we've got our own ax to grind. We're going to be turning our sights on the city."

"Christ, Morris."

"It's nothing personal, but damn it. I don't intend to take the fall—shit, there I go again—the blame for this. We're seeing a major liability issue for the city here. Whatever was wrong with that elevator the city inspectors should have caught."

Now it was Lansing's turn to go quiet.

"You must believe these things can't work both ways," Headley said through gritted teeth. "You don't think elevator inspectors did due diligence in your building? Maybe what I should do is send every fucking inspector—food, air quality, rodent infestation—your way and do a complete inspection from roof to basement. And not just in that building, but every other one you've got across the city. That seems to be what you're asking for here."

"Richard, for God's—"

"That's Mr. Mayor to you, you fuckin' ass pimple."

"No wonder so many people call you *Dick*," Morris said.

Headley ended the call and tossed the phone onto the coffee table. Valerie looked at him expectantly, but he did not fill her in.

There was a light rap on the door and Valerie went to answer it. Chris Vallins strode in with a touch screen tablet in his left hand, his right tucked casually into his pocket.

Headley looked up but said nothing.

"Mr. Mayor, something you might want to see," Chris said, handing him the tablet. "Matheson's latest column just dropped."

Headley grabbed a pair of reading glasses that were sitting on the coffee table and slipped them on. The headline on the page, "Headley Takes Me for a Ride," was enough to make him wince.

"Christ almighty," he said. He tossed the tablet in the direction of the table, but missed. Chris didn't wait for the mayor to pick it up. He bent over and got it himself.

"Give me the gist," Headley said.

Chris said, "She tells about the offer. To write your bio. That she'd get mid–six figures to do it. That she'd have to take a break from *Manhattan Today*. Implying this was your way of getting her to stop writing critical stories of your administration. That you were buying her off. Bribing her, essentially."

Headley said, "We deny the whole thing. It's a total fabrication."

Chris slowly shook his head. "She quotes everything that was said in the car so perfectly I'm betting she recorded it."

"Shit," Valerie said. "I remember her doing something with her phone just before she got into the car. I thought she was just turning it off."

Headley slumped further into the couch. "Glover," he said under his breath.

Neither Chris nor Valerie said a word.

Headley, feigning a cheerful tone, said, "Bring her into the loop, Glover says. Get her on our side. Throw enough money at her that she'll jump at the chance." Headley shook his head, then managed a wry smile. "I guess this means she's not taking the job."

"Nothing against Glover," Valerie said, "but you know I advised against this from the beginning."

"I know," Headley said, grimacing.

"Matheson's piece also raises the question of *why* you want to do a book. It encourages speculation that you're giving serious consideration to running for something besides reelection for mayor, before you're ready to tip your hand. That was the other reason why I didn't want to pursue this matter with Matheson."

"I shouldn't have listened to him," Headley said. "I should have known better."

"At the risk of stepping over the line, sir," Valerie said tentatively, "I'm not sure Glover has enough experience to be advising you on these sorts of matters. He understands you better than any of us, of course, but where he's most valuable is in the data mining end of things. Analyzing trends, surveying." She shrugged. "There's nobody in the whole building who can help me with a computer problem the way he can. But when it comes to advising you on matters like—"

Headley raised a silencing hand and Valerie went quiet.

Chris said, "There's a bit at the end of the column."

Headley gave him a pained look, expecting even more bad news.

"No, it's not about you," he said. "Someone Matheson knew was killed in that elevator accident."

The mayor was about to look relieved, but quickly adopted a look of moderate concern. "Sherry D'Agostino, I bet. Everybody knew Sherry." He managed a wry grin. "I even went out with her a few times, back in the day."

Valerie looked slightly pained, as though only Headley could boast about dating someone who'd recently died.

"No," Chris said. "Paula somebody. She'd interned at *Manhattan Today*."

"Oh," Headley said. There didn't seem to be much else to say. He looked at Valerie, then Chris, then back to Valerie. "Can you give us the room?" he asked her.

She looked momentarily taken aback, but said nothing as she headed for the door and closed it behind her.

"Chris," he said, "have a seat."

The man sat.

"Chris, in the time you've been with us, you've shown yourself to be very valuable. One part bodyguard, one part detective, one part political strategist." He chuckled. "And whenever Glover isn't here to fix my printer, you know just what to do."

Chris smiled. "Thank you, sir."

"You're good at finding things out. Turns out not all the great hackers are teenagers living in their parents' basements. You've been very helpful for someone in my position."

"Of course," he said.

"I might not be in this office today if it weren't for you."

"I'm not so sure about that, Mr. Mayor."

"Don't be modest. *You* found that woman, talked her into coming forward, telling her story to the *Daily News*. Wouldn't be sitting here now if she hadn't told the world how my opponent forced himself on her when she was fourteen and he was forty. Even dug up the emails he wrote to his lawyer where he as much as admitted it."

Chris only smiled.

Headley grinned. "Thank Christ you weren't digging into my *own* history."

Chris shook his head dismissively. "I guess if someone's looking hard enough, they'll find a few skeletons in anyone's closet."

"Yeah, well, I might need a *walk-in* closet for all of mine. But I believe you understand where I'm coming from, that I want to make a difference. I've been an asshole for much of my life, Chris, but I hope I'm doing what I can to make up for that now."

Chris nodded, waiting.

Headley's face went dark. "I'm worried about a couple of things."

"Yes, sir?"

"The first is . . . Glover."

"He's eager to please you. He means well. He wants your approval, sir."

"Yeah, well, that may be. But his instincts . . . just let me know if you see him doing something particularly stupid, would you?"

"Of course. And the other thing?"

"Barbara."

Chris nodded slowly.

"Let's face it. She's good at what she does. People feed her stuff. She has good sources. Some working right here at City Hall, people who've not been loyal to me. She's a pit bull. If she bites down on your leg you've as good as lost it."

"I understand your frustration," Chris said.

"If there were some way to get her off my back, some way to neutralize her . . ."

Chris was silent for a moment. Finally, he said, "I'm not quite sure what you're talking about here, sir."

Headley looked at him, puzzled at first, then horrified. "Christ, you didn't think I meant . . ."

Chris gave him a blank stare. "Of course not."

"Jesus, no." He shook his head. "No, I'm thinking more . . . about those skeletons in the closet. If there were a way to discredit her somehow." The mayor put a hand to the back of his neck and tried to squeeze out the tension, like he was wringing a sponge dry.

"Let me nose around," Chris said.

"Good, that's good," the mayor said. "You had me worried there for a minute."

Chris Vallins tilted his head to one side, as if to say, *Yes?*

"That you might have thought, even for a second, that I was suggesting we push the woman out a window or something."

"Forgive me," Chris said. "I know you'd never hurt a soul."

Seven

Jerry Bourque's first stop on the way home had been an art supplies place down on Canal Street. Then he'd gone into a grocery store with hot table service and filled a container with a few steamed vegetables, lasagna, a dollop of mashed potatoes, two chicken fingers, and some shrimp chow mein. The fact that some of these items did not typically go together did not bother Bourque. They charged by the weight of the container, so you could throw in a bit of whatever you liked.

As he came through the door of his fifth-floor, two-bedroom apartment in the Lower East Side, he tossed his keys in a bowl on a table in the hall, then went into the kitchen. He took his phone from his jacket pocket and set it, and his food, on the counter. He placed the bag from the art store on the already cluttered kitchen table. He slid out ten sheets of white illustration board, each twenty by thirty inches. He stacked them neatly at one end of the table by several small, screw-top bottles of art paint, a selection of box cutter–type knives, a metal ruler, some brushes and pencils, several three-foot-long strips of balsa wood, a glue gun, and a large, eighteen-inch-square paper cutter with an arm strong enough to slice through the art board. Or his fingers, if he wasn't careful.

Fingers.

He tossed his sport jacket and the book filled with photos of old New York onto his bed in the bedroom. The other book, about the nearly completed Manhattan skyscraper, he set on the kitchen counter. He took his dinner out of a bag, opened the lid of the rigid cardboard container, and took a fork out of the cutlery drawer. He picked up a remote to turn on a small television that hung from the underside of the cabinetry.

He went through the stations until he landed on a local news-cast, took a bottle of beer from the fridge, then leaned up against the counter and ate his dinner while standing. There'd been a truck rollover on the Van Wyck, spilling a load of bananas across two lanes. Four were dead in an elevator accident. The mayor was fighting alle-gations of giving a big city contract to a friend.

"So what else is new," Bourque said, his mouth full of chow mein.

Some nut set off a bomb in Boston. England was still being battered by high winds.

Bourque finished his meal, put the food-stained container into a garbage bin under the sink and his fork into the dishwasher, next to three other forks, the only other items in the appliance. He took five minutes and looked at the pictures in the skyscraper book.

"Wow," he said to himself several times.

Then he went into his bedroom to take off his tie and dress shirt and suit pants. He tossed the shirt into a bag that would be dropped off at the dry cleaner at week's end. The pants he lay carefully on the bed, then took a gripper hanger from the closet, clamped it to the cuffs, and hung them up. He stripped off his socks and tossed them in a laundry basket. Come Sunday morning, he'd fill his pocket with quarters, head to the basement laundry room, and do a wash.

Now, dressed only in boxers and a T-shirt, he went back into the kitchen and sat at the table. Next to the paints was a twelve-inch metal ruler, which Bourque used to draw several long, straight lines on the cardboard sheets, then several small boxes in a grid formation.

Standing, he sliced off some of the cardboard sheets with the oversized paper cutter, then with the box cutter lightly scored the art board along some of the pencil lines, allowing him to bend the cardboard to a right angle without separating the pieces. Sitting back down, he cut some strips of the balsa wood to match the length of the scored lines, applied some hot, drippy adhesive from the glue gun, and used them to brace the corners. The tip of his index finger touched some of the hot glue.

"Shit!" he said. He peeled the set glue off and sucked briefly on the finger.

He spent the next hour making three rectangular boxes of different sizes, painting them various shades of gray, then detailing the perfectly arranged boxes on the sides, making them look like windows. At the bottom edge, he drew detailed entrances and oversized windows. He did all of this without drawings or plans or blueprints of any kind. What he saw in his head he turned into three dimensions.

One of the purposes of this exercise, beyond the fact that he just liked doing it, was to push out of his head the events of the day. Some evenings it worked, some evenings it did not.

This was one of those nights when it did not.

Bourque's mind kept coming back to the body with the smashed-in face on the High Line. After his appointment with Bert, he and Delgado had paid a visit to the coroner's office. The naked body, minus fingertips, yielded at least one clue that might lead to an identification. On the dead man's right shoulder was a two-inch-long tattoo of a coiled cobra.

A DNA sample had been taken. A search of his clothes yielded nothing helpful. No credit card or time-stamped gas bar receipts had been found in the dead man's pockets. His jeans and top were cheap off-the-rack items from Old Navy.

Bourque had taken another look at the socks. They looked

relatively new; the area around the big toes did not show signs of an imminent hole. And the corpse's toenails had been due for a trim. Bourque had heard back from the bookstore and been told the shark socks were made somewhere overseas, sold online and in countless stores across the city, but if he still cared, they had sold twelve pairs in the last month. Six were put on credit, six were paid for with cash. Bourque took down the credit card information.

His one pleasant memory of the visit to the coroner's office had been standing close enough to Delgado to smell her hair. Whatever shampoo she used had a scent—mango?—that was strong enough to overrule the lab's stench of bleach and antiseptic.

Bourque forced the investigation from the front of his mind as he held out at arm's length the first completed building of the evening. He turned it around and admired it. If he noticed a spot where the paint was thin, he gave it a touch-up.

"Okay," he said to himself. "Installation time."

He got up from the kitchen table and opened the door to the second bedroom. But there was no bed, or dresser, or even a chair. There were four metal card tables, arranged into a large square roughly six by six feet, and almost entirely covered in boxes similar to the ones Bourque had just made. They were arranged in a grid, with space between to replicate streets.

Bourque placed that evening's effort onto one of the tables. He moved some of the existing ones to make way for the new one. He viewed his work from various angles. Some of the boxes soared as tall as four feet, others only a foot or so. Many were recognizable. There were crude interpretations of the Chrysler Building, the Empire State Building, the Flatiron Building, 30 Rockefeller Plaza, the Waldorf Astoria Hotel.

The model city was in no way exact. The landmark structures he was re-creating were, in his version, within steps of each other, rather than scattered across the city. This was more an appreciation of the city, not a replica.

Bourque leaned up against one wall and crossed his arms, admiring his handiwork. At first, his gaze took in the project as a whole, but then his focus narrowed on one spot near the edge.

He stepped away from the wall, knelt down so that his eye was at the model's street level. He studied the street in front of his re-creation of the Waldorf Astoria.

His airway began to constrict.

If only I hadn't moved. If only I hadn't dived out of the way.

The drops.

He breathed in, then out, heard the wheeze.

He wasn't expecting it to happen now. Here, at home, working on his project. Away from people with bashed-in faces and missing fingertips. But then he had to look at the sidewalk in front of the Waldorf Astoria.

Bourque immediately thought of grabbing the inhaler from his sport jacket in the other room, but then remembered what his doctor had suggested.

"Okay, Bert, we'll give it a try." He closed his eyes and concentrated.

Find a category.

Got it. The city's tallest structures, starting with the highest.

Aloud, he said, "One World Trade Center. Top of the Park. 432 Park Avenue. 30 Hudson Yards. Empire State Building." He stopped himself.

Could he include Top of the Park? The luxury apartment building on Central Park North, the subject of his new book, didn't officially open until later this week. Erected between Malcolm X Boulevard, otherwise known as Lenox Avenue, and Adam Clayton Powell Jr. Boulevard, or Seventh Avenue, the building came in at ninety-eight stories, making it two floors taller than the astonishing, and relatively recent, 432 Park Avenue, which towered over Central Park looking like some monolithic, vertical heat grate.

Did it really matter for the purposes of this exercise? He was still wheezing. He continued with his list.

"Uh, Bank of America Tower. 3 World Trade Center, uh, 53 West Fifty-Third. New York Times. No, wait. Chrysler Building, then the New York Times Building."

The tightening in his chest was not easing off.

"Fuck it," he said.

He went into the other bedroom, picked up his jacket, and reached into the left inside pocket.

The inhaler was not there.

"What the . . ."

He always tucked it into the left pocket. But maybe, just once . . .

The inhaler was not in the right pocket, either. Nor was it in either of the outside pockets.

Bourque felt his lungs struggling harder for air. The wheezing became more pronounced.

"Shit, shit, shit," he whispered.

Had he taken the inhaler out of his jacket when he first got home? He went back to the kitchen to check. It wasn't on the kitchen table or on the counter by the sink. Bourque returned to the bedroom, wondering if the inhaler had slipped out of his coat when he had thrown it onto the bed.

He got down on his hands and knees, patting beneath the bed where he could not see.

"Come on," he wheezed.

He found nothing.

In his head, he had an image of a snake coiling itself around his windpipe. Like that cobra tattoo on the deceased.

It was becoming increasingly difficult to breathe. If he didn't find his inhaler soon, he was going to have to use his last breaths talking to a 911 operator.

And that would be *if* he could find his phone. Where the hell had he left his phone? He hadn't noticed it in his jacket pockets as he searched for the inhaler. Had he left it in the kitchen?

He started to stand, and as his eyes were level with the top of the bed, he spotted something. Something small and dark, just under the edge of the pillow.

He grabbed the inhaler, uncapped it. He exhaled, weakly, then put the device into his mouth and, at the moment he squeezed it, drew in a breath. Held it for ten seconds. He breathed out, then prepared for a second hit.

He wrapped his mouth around the inhaler again. Squeezed. Started counting.

His cell phone rang. Out in the kitchen. He got to his feet, had the phone in his hand by the time he'd counted to four.

The name DELGADO came up on the screen. Lois Delgado.

Five, six, seven . . .

Delgado had not given up on him yet. Bourque had his finger ready to take the call.

Eight, nine, ten.

Bourque exhaled, tapped the screen. "Yeah, hey," he said, holding the phone with one hand and gripping the inhaler with the other.

"It's me," Delgado said. "You okay? Can barely hear you."

He got some more air into his lungs. "I'm fine."

"Okay. Anyway, sorry to call so late."

"It's okay. What's up?"

"I've got a tip for you."

He sighed mentally. "Go ahead. I'm all about self-improvement."

"Not that kind. A fingertip. Our guy dropped one."

Eight

Bucky had heard about the Boston bombing even before he saw the item on TV that night from his cheap hotel room. Mr. Clement had filled him in, and he sounded less than impressed when they had spoken late that afternoon about how that event had gone down.

Four injured, one seriously.

"It's a wonder it even made the news," Mr. Clement said when they had their brief meeting, standing almost shoulder to shoulder, feigning interest at the Central Park Zoo's penguin exhibit. They spoke softly, careful not to turn and face each other during their chat, as the penguins swam and splashed and waddled.

Mr. Clement made it clear he was not blaming Bucky for how unspectacular the Boston event turned out to be. Bucky had not been assigned to that one. Bucky didn't know who Clement had trusted to do Boston, but he was betting whoever it was, he wouldn't be doing any Flyovers missions in the future.

Bucky, however, was in the old man's good books. Bucky'd engineered the Seattle coffee shop bombing the week before, which left two dead. *That* made headlines, to be sure.

"New York's special," Mr. Clement had said. "That's why we have to be more ambitious here, Bucky. Not some simple coffee shop bombing."

"I hear ya," Bucky said.

His real name was Garnet—last name Wooler—but he'd gotten the nickname Bucky when he was a kid, before his parents managed to scrape up enough money to have him fitted with braces. But the name stuck, and just as well, because as names went, Garnet was no great shakes, either. These days, if anybody asked, he told them he was named after Captain America's sidekick, Bucky Barnes. There were those who thought the name made him sound stupid, like some country hick. But if he were some dumb rube, Mr. Clement wouldn't have been putting so much faith in him. That was for sure.

Bucky liked the man, and even though Bucky was now in his late thirties, he looked up to Mr. Clement, who was pushing seventy, as a father figure. Bucky had lost his own dad when he was seventeen, and he missed having someone older and wiser—and male—to mentor him, guide him. Mr. Clement, to a degree, had filled that role.

"We'll talk again tomorrow," Mr. Clement said. "A progress report."

"Sure thing," Bucky said. "Are you having a nice time?"

Without nodding, Mr. Clement said, "We are. Estelle has never been to New York before. Long way to come, all the way from Denver. So we're taking in the sights. Might see a show."

Bucky chuckled. "Oh, there'll be a show, all right."

Mr. Clement managed a smile. "Nice to have a front row seat. I didn't go to Seattle, or Portland, or Boston, and just as well. Would have been hard to explain how I just happened to be in those places at those times. But New York? This trip's been in the works for months. We're here celebrating our anniversary."

"I didn't know. Congratulations."

"Thank you, Bucky. You have a restful evening."

"You, too, Mr. Clement."

"I'd suggest you hang in here another five minutes after I leave."

"Sure."

With that, the older man departed.

Bucky didn't stay an extra five minutes. He stayed an extra twenty. The truth was, Bucky found watching the penguins very entertaining. Darned if they weren't the cutest damn things he'd ever seen.

Nine

Barbara had poured herself another finger of scotch, brought it into the bedroom with her, and decided, before turning off the light, to look one last time at online responses to her column. An argument could be made that the comments section on all websites should be disabled. It was just possible that giving an outlet to every anonymous wingnut on the planet to spew hate and spread lunatic conspiracy theories was not in society's best interests. Barbara sometimes thought wistfully back to the old days when if you wrote a letter to the editor of your local newspaper, you had to include an address and a phone number. Before they printed your letter, they had to confirm that you were really you.

Fucking quaint was what it was. The days before the trolls and the bots and the people with tinfoil hats.

Not every online comment was written by a crazy person, but enough were that it made sense to think twice before dipping in. After you'd read a few, you might feel the need for a shower.

And yet, Barbara could not help herself.

Sitting up in bed, she opened the laptop resting atop her thighs and went to the *Manhattan Today* website.

Readers who despised Mayor Richard Headley might give passing praise to the column, but mostly they wanted to hurl insults at the man himself. "Rat fucker," wrote **BoroughBob**. Well, Barbara thought, that certainly seemed, for New York, more appropriate than "goat fucker," and was, by current standards, relatively tame. **SuzieQ** saw the mayor as "a cum stain on the city's reputashun." Barbara wondered where **SuzieQ** had gone to school.

Then there were the Headley supporters who took out their anger against Barbara. "When's the last time you actually did anything for the city, you cunt Jew?" asked **PatriotPaul**. Was it worth replying to tell **PatriotPaul** that, while raised Presbyterian, she no longer belonged to any organized religion whatsoever? Perhaps not. The numerically named **C67363** asked, "How's anything ever going to get done in this city when people like you are always complaining?" It was downright charming when someone could express an opinion without being vulgar.

Barbara scrolled through a few more. On very rare occasions, someone might actually have something useful to say, maybe even point Barbara in the direction of a future article, although she wasn't seeing anything like that tonight.

But then there was this:

"Sorry about your friend. It's often the case that innocents are lost in the pursuit of a greater good."

Barbara blinked, read it again. It was a reference, of course, to the column's postscript about Paula Chatsworth. How she'd worked briefly at *Manhattan Today*, how she'd shown so much promise, how her life had been cut short by tragedy when she clearly had so much still to offer.

It was, for Barbara, an emotionally honest bit of writing, and her sadness at the young woman's death was genuine. People came to the big city to pursue a dream, not get killed in some freakish accident.

Barbara read the comment again.

"Sorry about your friend. It's often the case that innocents are lost in the pursuit of a greater good."

What the hell was that supposed to mean?

What "greater good" could the author possibly be referring to?

The author went by the handle **GoingDown**.

"Very fucking funny," Barbara said aloud, shaking her head. But then she thought, maybe it wasn't intended as an elevator joke. The writer could be an oral sex aficionado.

She was about to close the laptop when it dinged. An incoming email.

From Arla.

Barbara could not remember the last time she'd heard from her daughter. A few weeks, at least. Could it have been as long as a month?

Barbara clicked on the email.

"Hey," Arla wrote. No "Dear Mom." That would be too much to expect, Barbara knew.

It went on: "I have news. Want to meet for a coffee or something tomorrow?"

News? What kind of news could Arla have? So far as Barbara knew, she wasn't seeing anyone. Then again, Arla had never been big on sharing the details of her private life with her mother. It would have to be something big for Arla to actually propose getting together.

Maybe Arla had been seeing someone. Maybe Arla was engaged.

Would she be expecting her mother to foot the bill for a wedding? Christ, how much was Headley offering to ghost-write his bio again? Mid–six figures?

No. No way. Arla would have to need life-saving surgery before Barbara would sink that low.

Maybe Arla was pregnant.

Wouldn't that just be history repeating itself.

Anything was possible.

Barbara clicked on Reply and began tapping away.

"Sure," she wrote. "When and where?"

Ten

*T*he boy gently pats the woman's arm as she sits in the chair. He believed she was simply asleep, but he has to be sure. She does not look
well. Her forehead is glistening with sweat.

"Mom? Mom, are you okay?"

She opens her eyes slowly, focuses on the boy. "I guess . . . I nodded
off there."

"You're sweating like crazy. For a second it looked like you weren't
even breathing."

Her gaze moves beyond the boy. "Oh, Lord, I didn't even put the
groceries away. The ice cream'll be melted."

The boy gives her arm a squeeze. "I already put it away. You should
have sent me to the store instead."

"Don't be silly. I'm perfectly capable. A little extra exercise never hurt
anybody." She finds enough energy to smile. "Why don't you get us both a
little ice cream? It's chocolate. I'll sit right here. My legs are killing me."

The boy gets out a couple of bowls, takes the ice cream from the
freezer, and spoons out two small servings. He hands one bowl to his
mother, then perches himself on the arm of her chair while he eats his.
She eats hers very slowly, as if this simple task takes effort.

Chocolate is his favorite. But he finds himself too worried to enjoy it.
He doesn't know how much longer things can go on this way.

Tuesday

Eleven

The four elevators at the Sycamores Residences, a thirty-story York Avenue apartment tower just below Sixty-Third, were in constant use. Kids heading off to school. Men and women leaving for work. Nannies arriving to look after toddlers. Building maintenance staff heading to the top floor to vacuum hallways, working their way back down to ground level.

New Yorkers headed out from this residence to every corner of the city. Some worked at nearby Rockefeller University. Several units in the building were set aside for visiting professors and scientists who came to Rockefeller from all around the globe.

Although an exact count was not known because residents came and went, some people had guests, and others had sublet their apartments without informing building management, it was generally believed that any given time about nine hundred people lived in the Sycamores Residences. The building, like so many others in the city, was a small town unto itself.

Only three of those roughly nine hundred people were in Elevator Number Two when it happened.

Fanya Petrov, forty-nine, a visiting scientist from Russia, was staying on the twenty-eighth floor; she had been waiting the better part of five minutes and the elevator still had not arrived. She followed, with increasing frustration, the digital display above the doors, telling her where the elevators were. She'd hear them traveling through the shaft, whizzing past her floor on the way to the top of the building. Often, inexplicably, the elevator car would sail right past on its descent, not stopping to let her on. Was someone from building maintenance overriding the functions?

Since coming to New York three weeks earlier, she had learned that the magnificent view of the East River and the Queensboro Bridge that had at first so impressed her was not worth the aggravation of the slow elevators in the building. She'd have been happy with a room on the first or second floor. Who needed a view? She had learned that if she was to be on time for her appointments at Rockefeller, she had to allow herself an extra ten minutes because of the elevators. She'd take the stairs, but really, was she going to go down twenty-seven floors? It wasn't particularly exhausting—she had done it a few times—but it was time-consuming. And she just knew that the moment she entered that stairwell, the elevator doors would be parting.

She blamed the children. *And* their parents.

There were so many youngsters in the building, and they always forgot something. Only yesterday, after thinking she'd caught a break when the elevator showed up almost immediately, the doors opened at the twentieth floor to allow a young man and his ten-year-old son to board. As the doors were closing, the boy shouted, "I forgot my lunch!"

"For Christ's sake," his father said, sticking out his arm to stop the doors. "Go!"

The boy bolted from the elevator, ran down the hall to their apartment, fumbled about in his pocket, looked back, and said, "I don't have my key!"

Fanya had closed her eyes and said to herself, *You have got to be kidding me.* Well, not exactly that, but the Russian equivalent. Fanya spoke English fluently, but she was not up to speed on American phrases of frustration.

The father dug into his pocket and said, "Here!" He tossed the keys so the son could retrieve them halfway down the hall and, of course, he failed to catch them.

Future scientist, Fanya thought.

"Sorry," the father mumbled in the woman's direction.

The polite thing to do, she felt, would have been for him to step off the elevator and let her continue on her way. But no.

The kid got the apartment door open, ran inside, took a good two minutes to find his lunch, then came charging back down the hall to get onto the elevator.

Today, as she stood waiting, Fanya Petrov tried to think about the prepared remarks she would be delivering within the hour. Her area of expertise was "missing heritability," traits that are passed down through the generations that cannot be found in the genome. The world had come to believe that a person's DNA revealed everything, but it could not predict certain diseases or behaviors or countless other things, even when evidence existed that these characteristics could be passed on.

And while that was the subject of her talk for today, Fanya was an expert in other things, as well. Like bacterial pathogens, and how they could be spread among a population. Used, in effect, as weapons. Fanya knew a thing or two about what many in the world most feared: bioterrorism.

It was something she had studied a great deal back in Russia.

It was her expertise in missing heritability that had earned her an invitation to continue her studies in New York, but it was her vast knowledge about pathogens that might end up keeping her here.

Fanya Petrov did not want to return to Russia.

Fanya Petrov wanted to stay in America.

This was not something she had mentioned to her superiors back home. But she had mentioned it, discreetly, to another professor at

Rockefeller who had connections with the State Department. A few days later, a message was relayed to her that her situation was being looked at favorably. If she were to seek asylum in the United States, she would be accepted—provided, of course, she shared everything she knew about Russian research into pathogens.

That was fine with her.

But Fanya Petrov was now very, very anxious. What if her superiors were to learn of her treachery? Would they summon her home before her application for asylum had been approved? Would she be thrown into a car and put on a plane before anyone knew she was missing? And what would happen to her when she got back?

Very, very bad things.

She had become so consumed with worry that when the elevator's arrival was announced with a resounding ding, it startled her. Fanya sighed with relief and stepped into the empty cab as the doors opened.

She pressed G and watched as the doors closed.

The descent began.

"Please, no stops," she said under her breath, in Russian. "No stops, no stops, no stops."

There was a stop.

At the twentieth floor.

No.

Every time the elevator stopped, or there was a knock at the door, or someone dropped by to see her at her office at Rockefeller, Fanya feared it would be someone from the FSB, Putin's modern version of the KGB.

So when the door parted and there was no one standing there who looked like a Russian thug, Fanya felt momentarily relieved. But relief was soon supplanted by irritation when she saw that it was the same father and son who had delayed her on her last trip down this elevator. Her heart sank. Please let them have remembered everything, she thought.

The father glanced to see that G had already been pressed. As the doors started to close, he looked down at his son and asked, "You got your homework?"

The kid, suddenly panicked, said, "Shit."

American children, Fanya thought. So foul-mouthed.

The doors only had four more inches to go to close. But the father's arm went up with the speed of a lightning bolt, his hand angled vertically, sliding into the rapidly narrowing space. The rubber extenders bounced off both sides of his wrist and the door retracted.

"Please," Fanya said. "I am in a hurry."

He caught her eye and nodded. Fanya took that to mean that both father and son would get off, retrieve the forgotten homework, and catch another elevator.

But that was not the father's plan.

He said to the boy, "*You* hold the elevator. I'll go. It's on the kitchen table, right?"

The boy nodded and put his finger on the Hold button.

Fanya sighed audibly, but the father didn't hear it because he was already running down the hall, keys in hand.

The boy looked sheepishly at the scientist. "Sorry."

Fanya said nothing. She crossed her arms and leaned up against the back wall of the car. Down the hall, she saw the man slip into the apartment.

Five seconds, ten seconds, fifteen seconds.

Fanya felt her anxiety growing. She did not like to be in any one place for a long period of time. She felt exposed, vulnerable.

The apartments in this building were not huge. How long could it take for the man to run in, grab something off the kitchen table, and come back out?

"Remembering homework is your responsibility," Fanya said sternly. "If you forget, you forget. The teacher gives you a zero. Next time, you remember."

The boy just looked at her. But suddenly his eyes went wide. He said to Fanya, "Can you hold the button?"

"What?"

"Just hold it!"

She stepped forward and replaced his finger with hers on the button. The boy slipped off his backpack, dropped it to the floor, and knelt down to undo the zipper. He rifled through some papers inside and said, "Here it is."

Yet another sigh from Fanya.

The boy got up and stood in the open doorway. "Dad!" he shouted down the hall. "I found it!"

No response.

This time, he screamed, "*Daaad!*"

The father's head poked out the doorway. "What?"

"I found it!"

The dad stepped out into the hall.

Fanya, somehow thinking they were finally all on their way, let her finger slide off the button.

The doors began to close.

"Hey!" the kid said.

But he was less courageous than his father and did not insert his arm into the opening to stop the doors' progress. And Fanya wasn't about to do it.

She'd had enough.

The father shouted, "Hey! Hang on! Hold the—"

The doors closed. The elevator began to move. The boy looked accusingly at Fanya and said, "You were supposed to hold it."

She shrugged. "My finger slipped. It is okay. You wait for your dad in the lobby."

The kid slipped his backpack onto his shoulder and retreated to the corner, which was as far away as he could get from the woman in the tight space.

They traveled three or four floors when the elevator stopped.

This was just not Fanya's day.

But the doors did not open. The elevator sat there. The readout said they were at the seventeenth floor.

"What is happening?" Fanya asked. She looked accusingly at the boy. "Did your dad stop the elevator?"

The kid shrugged. "How would he do that?"

After fifteen seconds of not moving, Fanya began to pace in the confined area.

It's them. They know. I'm trapped.

"I have to get to work," she said. "I have to get out of here. I am giving a lecture. I cannot be late."

The boy dropped his backpack to the floor again, reached in and pulled out a cell phone and began to tap away.

"What are you doing?" Fanya asked, stopping her pacing.

"Texting my dad."

"Ask him if he stopped the ele—"

"I'm telling him we're *stuck*." He looked at the phone for several more seconds, then said, "He's going for help."

"Oh," Fanya said. She wanted to ask the boy to ask his father if there were any strange men around. Men who looked out of place. Men with Russian accents. But she decided against it. "Why do you think we are stuck?" she asked the boy.

The kid shrugged.

"Why won't the doors open?"

"We're probably between floors," the boy said.

Fanya looked at him and, for the first time, felt some kinship. They were, after all, in this together. "What is your name?"

"Colin," he said.

"Hello, Colin. My name is Fanya."

"Hi."

Keep talking to the boy, she told herself. It would help control her paranoia.

"What was your homework on?"

"Fractions," he said.

"Ah," she said. "I liked taking fractions when I was a little girl."

"I hate them."

Fanya managed an anxious smile. "I think we need to do something to get out of here. We cannot stay in here. It is not good."

"My dad'll get somebody."

"That could take a long time. We need to do something now. Don't you have to get to school so you can see how well you did on your fractions homework?"

Colin nodded.

"And I have to get to work. So let's figure this out." Fanya studied where the doors met, worked a finger into the rubber lining. "I bet we could get these apart."

"Uh, I don't think you're supposed to do that."

"Maybe we are not between floors," she said. "Maybe the hallway is right there and all we have to do is step off."

"Maybe," Colin said uncertainly.

She dug her fingers in and started to pull the door on the right side into the open position. The doors did not move.

Fanya said, "You look like a strong boy, even though you are little. You pull from the other side."

Colin said nothing, but did as he was asked. He got his fingers into the now-larger gap and pulled hard on the left door. Even with both of them pulling, the doors parted only about half an inch.

"Okay, okay, stop," Fanya said. They both released their grips on the doors and took a step back. "I do not think this is going to work."

And then, as if by magic, the doors parted. Fanya and the boy stepped back, startled.

"Well," Fanya said.

The woman and the boy were faced with a concrete block wall, and an opening.

From the floor of the car, and going nearly three feet up, was the gray cement wall of the elevator shaft. Above that, open space. Fanya and Colin were able to stare straight down the seventeenth-floor corridor.

"Success!" she shouted.

Fanya felt relieved not only that the doors had opened, but that there were not any men in black suits standing there in the hallway, waiting for her.

"I'm not going through there," Colin said nervously, backing away farther.

Fanya smiled. "We just have to be quick."

"No way," he said.

She smiled sympathetically. "Think of it as a fraction. The doors are how far open?"

The boy looked at her. "Half?"

"Very good. So it is half-open, and half-closed. Half-open is good enough for us to get out. But I will try it first." She grinned. "I just have to be fast."

She set her purse on the elevator floor. "I used to be a gymnast in Russia," she said. "When I was a girl." She grimaced. "It was a long time ago. But some things you don't forget. Climbing up three feet should not be so hard."

Fanya put both hands on the grooved metal strip on the hallway level, hoisted herself up enough to get her knee onto it, then moved her entire body through the opening. She was on her knees in the hallway, her feet hanging over the edge inside the car before she stood triumphantly.

"What are you going to do now?" Colin asked, looking up at her. "Are you going to leave me here?"

Shit. She really couldn't do that. She'd freed herself, could head to the university, but how would it look? "Visiting Professor Abandons Child in Stuck Elevator." Would a callous act like that prompt the State Department to reject her request for asylum?

"No," she said. "I will not do that. I will not leave you here." She glanced down at the elevator floor. How stupid of her. She'd dropped her purse there. It would have made more sense to have tossed it out onto the hallway floor before making her escape.

"Colin," she said, pointing. "Toss me my purse. Then we'll see about getting you out, too."

As Colin reached down to get it, Fanya dropped back down to her hands and knees to reach in to take it from him.

She leaned forward into the car. Colin picked up the purse and held it out for her. Fanya shifted slightly forward on her knees.

The elevator suddenly moved.

Down.

The roof of the car dropped toward Fanya's neck. She didn't have to glance upward to see what was coming. She saw the elevator floor dropping away from her. While physics had never been her area of expertise, she could figure this much out. If the car's floor was heading down, the car's ceiling would surely follow.

Without having to think about it, she began to withdraw her head from the elevator. She needed to get her entire body back into the hallway.

She was not quick enough.

The elevator continued on its way to ground level at a normal rate of speed. When the doors opened several seconds later, those who had been waiting—and not very patiently, at that—were greeted by the sight of a near catatonic, wide-eyed Colin, huddling in the corner as far away as possible from Fanya Petrov's arm and hand, still gripping her purse, and the scientist's decapitated head.

Twelve

Barbara got to the Morning Star Café on Second Avenue, just above Fiftieth, before her daughter, Arla, got there. She took a booth near the window, facing the street, and said yes to a cup of coffee when the waiter stopped by. Barbara scanned the menu to pass the time, but knew she'd be getting a Virginia ham and cheddar omelette. Arla, she was betting, would have only coffee.

Barbara glanced at the photos on the wall. A lot of famous people had dropped by the Morning Star over the years. There were a couple of Kurt Vonnegut Jr., who Barbara was pretty sure had lived in the neighborhood before his death in 2007. She'd seen him once, a couple of blocks north of here, but didn't say anything, even though she was a fan. You were always seeing somebody famous in New York and were expected to be cool about it.

She'd checked the menu, scanned the walls. Fidgety. Getting out her phone seemed the next logical step. Barbara had mixed feelings about meeting with her daughter this morning. She had reason to believe Arla'd been seeing a therapist lately, although Arla had not come right out and admitted it when Barbara asked. But Barbara knew Arla had a multitude of issues she was struggling to come to terms with. There'd been an eating disorder for a while there, but that seemed to be under control. When Arla was in her midteens, she'd gone through a cutting period, marking her arms with a razor. That one really had Barbara worried, but that, too, had passed.

Barbara was aware that whatever the issue, Arla was inclined to trace it back to her mother. She was, after all, the root of all of Arla's problems.

Well, fuck, Barbara thought. *I was never exactly June Cleaver.*

When Barbara found herself pregnant at eighteen, she was already working on a career in journalism. As a kid, inspired by watching reruns of *The Mary Tyler Moore Show* (she wasn't old enough to have seen it when it first came on), Barbara wanted to be Mary Richards. She wanted to work in news. And Mary showed how an independent woman could make it, after all.

When she was barely seventeen, she had landed a reporting gig at the *Staten Island Advance*, winning over the editors by showing up day after day with unsolicited stories about interesting people in the borough. They were good. They saw that the kid could produce. They took her on despite her young age and lack of a journalism degree.

Who needed a piece of paper to frame and hang on the wall? You went out, you asked people questions, you observed, you wrote it down. When someone wouldn't tell you what you wanted to know, you found someone else who would. You kept asking until you got an answer. How tricky was that? You needed to go to school for four years to figure that out?

Barbara threw herself into her work from the very beginning. The proverbial printer's ink ran through her veins. She was covering murders and gang wars and plane crashes and political scandals when she was no older than first-year journalism students.

She was having the time of her life.

Until she found out she was pregnant.

Getting knocked up was definitely not part of the plan. At first, she was in denial. She couldn't believe that it had happened. The home pregnancy test had to be wrong. So she did nothing, told no one.

But there comes a point when what you refuse to believe becomes painfully obvious.

So when her tummy began to ever so slightly bulge, she found the courage to find the man who'd gotten her pregnant. He deserved to know, right? Barbara figured there was a chance he'd even *want* to know. Okay, maybe that was being too hopeful. The guy was going to be shocked, no doubt about it. Especially considering that they hadn't even known each other until they'd had sex, and hadn't exactly been a couple since.

They hadn't even *seen* each other since.

It had been, Barbara was willing to concede, a night of very bad decisions.

Starting with going to a party at NYU given by a former high school friend who, unlike Barbara, had pursued higher education. More bad decisions followed. She smoked a little too much weed, drank a little too much gin. And then, going over to chat up that older guy in the corner. That was the big one.

He was no longer a student, having gotten his MBA a few years earlier. He'd tagged along with some girl who knew the host of the party.

So why was he all alone in the corner?

A shrug. Some guy was going on about having to leave because he played in a band and they had a late-night gig in SoHo. She left with him.

"The bitch," Barbara said.

Later, she wasn't entirely clear how events had progressed. They'd had more to drink. It was possible there'd been a walk. And then they'd ended up in someone's dorm. On a bed. Barbara remembered some fumbling with a condom, but hadn't paid all that much attention when the guy said, "Uh-oh."

In a few weeks, she'd have an idea what had alarmed him.

While some of the events from that night were foggy, Barbara knew there was no one else up for the role of father of her child. Sure, she'd gone to bed with other guys. But the last time she'd had sex before that evening had been a good (or bad, depending on how you looked at it) six months.

Other things she was sure of? What he looked like, and a first name. She asked the friend who'd thrown the party if she knew the guy's surname. No special reason, she said. Just, you know, wondering.

She found him.

Broke the news.

He said, "I have no idea who you are."

The way he said it, it almost sounded like he was telling the truth. Barbara refreshed his memory with every detail she could remember.

"Sorry," the guy said. "Honest to God, I don't ever remember meeting you. How long ago was this? I don't even remember being at that party."

"Yeah, well, we were both kind of flying."

"Maybe you were," he said. "Not me."

Barbara couldn't decide what to do. Go after him? Demand a blood test?

And of course, there was one other option.

But again, Barbara was paralyzed with indecision, and did nothing. By the time she found the strength to tell her parents, it was too late to end the pregnancy. Barbara's mother and father—fucking saints, that's what they were—didn't judge. Oh sure, they wanted to know about this man, and Barbara told them she'd talked to him, that he refused to accept responsibility, and had moved to Colorado or Wyoming and gone into real estate. It wasn't worth the time to pursue him, she said.

Okay, they said. These things happen, they said. No sense ranting and raving. What's done is done. Let's figure out what to do.

Give the baby up for adoption, Barbara decided. I'm not cut out to be a parent.

Well, okay, sure, that's a possibility, her mother said. But that *is* my future grandchild you're talking about. If you're absolutely determined that you do not want to raise this child, well, your father and I have still got a few good years left, and we've been talking about this, and we've agreed that if you're okay with it, we'll do it.

At first Barbara thought, no way. But as that child grew inside her, she started to come around to her mother's way of thinking. This could work. The world was changing. Alternative parenting options were in vogue. Sure, some people might look down their collective noses at Barbara, but when had she ever cared what anybody else thought?

She knew her mother was betting that when the baby arrived, Barbara would have a change of heart. She'd see that infant and decide to raise the child herself, even if there was no father's name to put on the birth certificate.

That whole mother-child bond would kick in.

Arla arrived.

The bond did not kick in.

Barbara was tormented that it did not. She was consumed with guilt that she did not want to raise this little girl. Did she love her? Of course, without question. But if there was a mothering gene, Barbara feared she did not have it.

So Barbara's parents honored their pledge and took Arla into their home. Barbara remained conflicted about how things had turned out. She felt less guilty that she had not given Arla up to strangers, that she was with family. But every time Barbara went home and saw her mother and father so fully engaged with Arla, the guilt bubbled back to the surface. It was an ache that never went away.

Every time she saw Arla, she was reminded of her abdication of responsibility. In those moments, she wondered whether adoption would have been the better choice. Out of sight, out of mind.

She hated herself for even thinking it.

Every week, Barbara sent a good chunk of her paycheck to her parents. She visited most weeks. She did love Arla. She loved her more than anyone or anything else in the world. No one pretended Barbara was not her mother. Arla was not raised to believe Barbara was the aunt who dropped by. No, Barbara was Mom. Barbara's parents were Grampa and Gramma.

No lies. No attempts to deceive. At least not on that score.

It all seemed to work out.

And when Arla was twelve, Grampa died. Liver cancer. Barbara's mother carried on alone. Barbara still came by, but as Arla moved into her teens and became the kind of hellion so many teenage girls turned into for a period of time, Barbara had to admit, deep down, that she was relieved to be spared the daily turmoil.

Thirteen months ago, Barbara's mother passed on. Heart attack.

"This is how I see it," Arla had told Barbara the last time they'd sat down together. "You leaving me with them is what drove them to an early grave. I was a bitch and a half, no doubt about it, but I should have been *your* bitch and a half, not theirs."

"I can't rewrite history," Barbara had said.

"Yeah, but you don't have a problem writing about others who've made a mess of theirs," she'd countered. "Bad things people have done, mistakes they've made, that's your whole shtick. But looking in the mirror, that's not so easy."

Barbara hadn't known what to say. The truth was always difficult to argue.

They'd had a serious argument six months earlier. Arla wanted to go out west, try to find her father. Barbara did everything to discourage her, and offered no clues that would help her track him down. "The man's not worth finding," she said. Arla was furious.

Barbara said something she wished she hadn't. "Maybe you'd have been happier if I'd given you up for adoption and you'd been raised by strangers."

"You're the stranger," Arla shot back. "Always have been."

And then Arla had gone in for the kill. "I have this friend who's getting married, and she says her mother's driving her crazy, wanting to be involved in every single detail about the wedding, and my friend's like, God, I can't take it anymore, and I said to her, hey, at least she's *interested*."

So there was every reason to feel unsettled about meeting with Arla this morning. What was Barbara to blame for now? What repressed maternal memory—or lack thereof—had Arla gone over with her therapist this week?

She'd said she had news.

Jesus, maybe it's about her father.

So far as Barbara knew, Arla had abandoned her idea of heading out west to look for him. Maybe she'd changed her mind.

Arla still was not here—being habitually late to meetings with her was, Barbara figured, a minor act of vengeance—so Barbara scrolled through her Twitter feed. Barbara was almost never without the phone in her hand. The advent of technology had made it nearly impossible for Barbara to be alone with her own thoughts. If she wasn't writing, or reading, or having a conversation with someone, she was on the phone.

She followed political leaders and countless pundits and various media outlets and even bulletins from the NYPD. And no one had to know that she also followed someone who tweeted, every single day, cute puppy pics.

So shoot me.

She continued to scroll, caught a glimpse of something, then thumbed her way back up the feed. It was a post from the NYPD.

There'd been an elevator accident in an apartment building up on York Avenue. The story was just breaking and details were few.

"Fuck," she whispered.

"I take it you're not talking to me."

Barbara looked up to find Arla standing there.

"Oh, hey, hi," she said, slipping out of the booth to give her daughter a hug. No matter how angry Arla might be with her, she'd still allow her mother to do that. And Arla would slip her arms around Barbara in return, even if she didn't pull her in for the big squeeze.

"You look good," Barbara said as they slipped into the booth, sitting across from each other.

And it was true. The thing was, Arla always looked good. She was tall and slender, with straight black hair that hung below her shoulders. She wore a black, clingy dress with a broad, black, patent leather belt. A lank of hair hung over one eye and she brushed it back, tucking it behind her ear.

"Thanks," Arla said. "Have you ordered?"

"Only coffee. I was going to get an omelette. What do you want?"

"Coffee's good."

"Go on, have something. I'm buying."

Arla shook her head. "That's okay."

The waiter came. Just because Arla didn't want to eat wasn't going to stop Barbara. She ordered two coffees and an omelette for herself.

"So how's it going?" Arla asked.

"Fine," Barbara said, then frowned. She told her daughter, briefly, about the incident the day before involving the young woman who'd interned at *Manhattan Today*. Even as she told Arla the story, she wondered why. Was she hoping to garner some advance sympathy, maybe ward off the latest grievance Arla wanted to air?

"That's awful," Arla said with what seemed genuine concern. "Are her parents down here yet?"

"Probably," Barbara said. "And now," she said, raising her phone, "there's another one."

"Another elevator thing?"

Barbara nodded.

"I get totally creeped out in them," Arla said. "It's not that I think they're going to crash or anything. It's just, when that door closes, there's no place you can go, and if you're trapped in there with someone weird, you can't wait to get to your floor." She shook her head. "Two in two days. They say things come in threes."

Barbara smiled. "I think that's celebrity deaths. So," she said slowly, "what's your news?"

Arla inhaled deeply through her nose. The arrival of her coffee gave her a moment to exhale and prepare for what looked to Barbara like a major announcement. She took a packet of Splenda, ripped it open, and sprinkled half of it into the cup.

Pregnant, Barbara was thinking. *History repeating itself.*

"So . . ." Arla said. "I got a job."

Barbara blinked. "You have a job. So this is a *new* job?"

"That's right."

"Well, that's good. Congrats. You didn't like what you were doing?"

"No, it was okay. And I learned a lot of stuff there that I can do at the new place."

"So where are you moving to?"

"Okay, so, you know at the job I had, I was doing all this survey stuff. Analytics, interpreting data, all that kind of thing."

"Right. What marketing is all about."

"No one makes a decision these days without looking at all the data. No one in business goes with just their gut."

"Gut feelings are all I've ever had," Barbara said. "I don't understand any of this stuff you're talking about."

"It's the way the world's going," Arla said. "I mean, even if you're sure your own instincts are right, no one wants to make a move without data to support it."

"And let me guess," Barbara said. "Sometimes the data tells you *what* the people want, so that's what you give them, even if, in your heart, that's not what you want to do."

Arla shrugged. "Pretty much. You find out what the people are hankering for and deliver it." She shook her head. "God, who uses a word like 'hankering' anymore?"

Barbara chuckled.

Arla continued. "Anyway, you want to know if your message is getting out there, and if it is, if it's reaching the target audience. All that stuff. It's pretty fascinating. The company I just left, we were doing a lot of work for the entertainment industry. What movies people like and why, data from advance screenings. Funny thing is, even when you have a movie you think will be a hit, it can go out there and sink like a stone."

"Sure," Barbara said.

"But I was thinking, what if I could take those kinds of skills and apply them in a way that would have some more meaning? You know, instead of finding a way to make some airhead pop star even more popular, what if you could expose people to issues that matter, and make them care?"

"That actually sounds like a good thing," Barbara said. "So who are you going to work for? Planned Parenthood? The ACLU? Save the Whales?"

"Not one of them," Arla said. "But still, a place where I can do some good."

"So, tell me," her mother said.

"You promise you won't get mad."

Barbara sat back on the bench. *Oh, no,* she thought. *She's gone to the dark side. She's working for Facebook.*

The waiter delivered the ham and cheddar omelette, but Barbara didn't even look at it. "Just tell me."

"I got a job with the mayor's office," Arla said.

Barbara was too stunned to speak.

"Pretty cool, huh?"

Barbara found her voice and said, "*This* mayor? The mayor of New York?"

Arla nodded and smiled. "I haven't actually met him yet. I mean, maybe I never will. You can work for someone like that and never come face-to-face. You're just one of the minions, right? But you never know." She leaned across the table and whispered conspiratorially, "I hear rumors he's thinking of going for a Senate seat, or maybe even something bigger than that. Imagine being on the ground floor if that happens."

Clearly, Arla had not read Barbara's latest column that put out that rumor. Barbara pushed her plate to one side and leaned in, their foreheads almost touching.

"I get it," she said.

"Get what?" Arla said.

"It's creative, I'll grant you that."

"I don't know what you're talking about," Arla said, leaning back into her seat.

"Don't be cute, Arla."

"Honestly, I don't know what you mean, *Mother.*"

"Did you actually plan it? Did you think, wouldn't it be great if I could work for the man my mother's been trying to get the goods on since he took office? The man is totally corrupt, you know. Always doing favors for his friends. Or did the mayor's office seek you out?" Barbara suddenly smiled. "I could see it happening that way."

"Not everything is about you."

"Headley figures out who you are and offers you a job just to stick it to me. Were you headhunted? Maybe he figures if I know you're working for him, I'll back off. Or I'll take him up on his offer."

"What offer?"

"Never mind."

"I saw the position advertised online," Arla said. "And I applied. I went for an interview, and I got it. If you're suggesting I was hired just to even some score with you, then thanks for the insult. I'm good at what I do. I got hired because I bring something to the table."

"You went after it to spite me."

"You're not even hearing me anymore."

"You wanted to rub my nose in it," Barbara said.

Arla eyed her mother pitiably. "I'd have thought, being a writer and all, you could do better than a cliché like that."

"Once they find out you're my daughter, they'll probably fire you."

"Well, unless you're planning to tell them, I should be fine."

Arla's last name was Silbert, as was Barbara's. Matheson was actually Barbara's middle name, which honored her mother's side of the family. She'd chosen to write under it years earlier, so Arla wasn't likely to be found out on name recognition alone.

"You know, it'd be nice, if just once, you could acknowledge that I can accomplish something on my own. Maybe even congratulate me."

Barbara said nothing.

Arla sighed resignedly and looked at her watch. "Shit, I have to run. Don't want to be late on my first day." She flashed a smile as she slid out of the booth. "Thanks for the coffee. Always nice to catch up."

She turned and walked out. Barbara watched as she reached the sidewalk, turned right, and walked past the window, heading south.

Barbara looked at the omelette. She was sorry she'd quit smoking years ago. She wished she had a butt to grind into it.

Thirteen

Jerry Bourque was at his desk. Lois Delgado sat across from him, drinking coffee from a paper cup.

"How's it going?" he asked.

"Kid's sick," she said. "Barfed her guts up first thing."

Delgado had been married ten years to a firefighter named Albert. They had a seven-year-old daughter, Abigail. Abby for short.

"Al's shift starts late, so with any luck I'll be home before he leaves, and if not, we'll get his mother to come over."

"That'll be nice," he said.

She shot him a look across the two desks. "Don't get me started."

"I didn't say anything."

"Bullshit." Delgado rolled her eyes. "She's a snoop. She went into the medicine cabinet last time, looking around."

"How do you know?" he asked.

"All the prescriptions, I had them all turned exactly halfway, so only the right side of the labels were exposed. Like, all you'd see of my name on the prescription is 'gado.' You know what I mean?"

"I get it."

"So after she's been there, I check, they're all facing every which way. Pretty much in the same spot—she covered her tracks that much—but not sitting the way I left them. I got one of those mini-safes, like they have in the hotels? Put it in our bedroom closet. One day she says, she just happened to see it when she found Abby in there, wanting to try on my shoes. Oh, she says, I see you have a safe? What's that for? It's driving her crazy. Thing is, it's the only place I can keep something where I know she won't see it. Financial papers, stuff like that. I tell her it's where I keep my gun."

"She buying that?"

"She knows I already have a lockbox for it. Maybe I can get her thinking I'm building an arsenal. But she probably suspects."

"Albert ever decides to have an affair, he hasn't got a chance of getting away with it."

"No kidding," Delgado said. "I've told him, you mess around, I'll kill you and I know how to cover my tracks."

Bourque believed she had the skills, if not the actual inclination. "And if *you* decide to have an affair," he said, "you'll know how to get away with it."

Delgado smiled. "No way Albert's finding out about Ryan."

Bourque grinned. Delgado had a thing for actor Ryan Gosling. She'd seen all his movies multiple times. Once, on a trip to Canada, she even drove by the Burlington high school he'd attended. A photo of him from a magazine was taped to the edge of her computer monitor.

"I think, maybe having his picture there would be a clue," Bourque said.

Delgado shook her head. "It's the opposite. If he and I were seeing each other, putting that picture there would be the last thing I'd do. It actually keeps anyone from being suspicious."

"Brilliant," Bourque said.

"Anything back on the DNA?"

"Don't make me laugh. How about the tip of the finger? Were they able to pull a print off it?"

Delgado said, "Waiting. Looks like a pinkie. They found it about twenty yards north of the bench the body'd been dumped behind, just to the edge of the path, in the flower bed. Once we get a print, and they do the DNA, we'll find out if our guy's in the system. The hands were callused, suggesting the vic did physical work."

"And the socks are a dead end. So far."

Delgado said the review of surveillance video along the High Line was also going nowhere, at the moment. "But at least there's this." Delgado pointed to her computer monitor. "I'm sending it to you."

Bourque signed in and called up the file his partner had shared. It was a picture from the coroner's report of the dead man's cobra tattoo.

"That tat might be the best thing we've got at the moment," he said.

Delgado nodded. "It's something. We can start hitting tattoo parlors. Wondering if it's time to put out a release. White male, best guess is between forty and fifty years old, photo of the tattoo, those socks."

"I'm gonna make another call to Missing Persons," Bourque said. "Maybe somebody's worried Daddy didn't come home."

"Knock yourself out," Delgado said.

Bourque first went onto the NYPD's Missing Persons Twitter feed, then its website. Most of the missing were categorized as "silver alerts," which applied primarily to senior citizens with Alzheimer's disease or some other form of dementia. These were folks who'd wandered away from home or a facility, and in most cases turned up okay. Many of the others were kids who'd failed to come home. But the likelihood that any of these were child abductions was low. These were youngsters who'd had a fight with their parents, or stayed over at a friend's house without thinking that a call home might be a good idea. If a child had been taken, odds were it was a parental abduction, a custody fight that spiraled out of control. That didn't mean it was any less serious an event. Some parental abductions ended up very badly. Murder-suicide, for example. Teach the other spouse a lesson.

What didn't come up on the Missing Persons list very often were middle-aged men or women without any history of mental disabilities.

Bourque didn't see any recent postings that sounded like the High Line victim. There were a couple of men who had been missing for several months who were, as the saying went, "known to police," and could very likely be residing at the bottom of the East River, but the man Bourque was hoping to identify was very recently deceased.

He put in a call to the Missing Persons bureau to ask if they'd had any reports about a middle-aged white male they'd not yet put on the website.

"Funny you should ask," they said.

———

The house was on Thirty-Second Street, between Broadway, to the south, and Thirty-First Avenue to the north, in the Astoria part of Queens. It was a two-story semidetached, gates across the driveway that were intended to keep anyone from ripping off the ten-year-old Ford Explorer parked there. It sat on a slab of concrete that sloped downward toward a single garage door.

Lois Delgado parked their unmarked Ford Crown Vic out front, although anybody who knew anything would immediately be able to spot it as a police car with its plain minihubcaps, lights inside the front grille and atop the rear window shelf, and antenna on the trunk lid.

Bourque got out the passenger side and waited until Delgado had rounded the car so they could approach the front door together. She rang the bell and stood ahead of him.

Seconds later, the curtain was pulled back an inch. A woman peeked out. They heard a deadbolt turn and a chain come off before the door opened.

"Mrs. Petrenko?" Delgado said. "Eileen Petrenko?"

The woman was in her forties, about five-four, plump, her brown hair pulled back tightly into a bun. She eyed the two of them with apprehension.

"Mrs. Petrenko, I'm Detective Delgado and this is Detective Bourque."

"Oh my," she said. "Have you found him? Please tell me you've found him."

"Could we come in?" Delgado asked.

"Yes, yes, of course," she said, holding open the door.

They entered a cramped living room that was a mess of newspapers, magazines, and small office boxes up against one wall.

"I've been going out of my mind," Eileen said, wringing her hands nervously. "Have you found him? Where is he? Has he gone back to Cleveland? He hates it here, I know that, but I can't believe he'd just go back there without saying a word. I called his sister, and she hasn't seen him, and if he was going back he'd have got in touch with her, I know he would."

"Can we sit down?" Bourque asked.

Eileen cleared the couch of newspapers so the two detectives could sit. She took a seat across from them. There was a framed photo of her and a round-faced man with grayish, brush-cut hair on the small table next to her.

"This is Mr. Petrenko?" Delgado asked.

The woman picked up the picture and looked despairingly at it. "I've barely slept for two days," she said.

Bourque had his notebook out. "I know you've been over this with the officers who spoke with you yesterday morning, but I wonder if you'd mind going over it with us."

The woman kept the framed photo in her lap and nodded.

"Your husband's full name?"

"Otto Mikhail Petrenko."

"Can you spell that?"

She did.

"Date of birth?"

"Um, February third, 1975."

"Where was Mr. Petrenko born?" Delgado asked. "What kind of name is that?"

"Russian," his wife said. "Except for Otto. That is German. He was named after an uncle in Germany. Mikhail was his father's name. He was born in Voronezh, but his parents slipped out of the country and into Finland shortly after he was born, and then, eventually, to America, when Otto was around four years old. They settled in Ohio, which is where Otto grew up, and where we met in Cleveland."

"And how long have you been married, Mrs. Petrenko?" Delgado asked, her voice soft and full of concern.

"Seventeen years," she said.

"The two of you have children? Or do you live here alone?"

"It's just us," she said, looking uncomfortable. "Otto had siblings, but . . ." Her voice trailed off.

"And you own this house?"

She shook her head. "We're renting. Otto didn't want to buy. He didn't know whether he wanted to stay here."

"In Queens?" Bourque asked.

"In New York. Anywhere here."

"You moved here from Cleveland?"

"Three years ago," she said. She glanced at the boxes along one wall. "We've still got things in boxes, if you can believe it. It's not important stuff. We'd move it to the basement, but it's awfully musty down there."

"What about the garage?"

"We've got furniture in there," she said. "Our place in Cleveland was bigger, so we had stuff we couldn't place, so we just leave it in there. We haven't been able to get the car in the garage since we got here. Is this important?"

"I'm sorry," Delgado said, offering an apologetic smile. "Sometimes we tend to wander. Tell us about when you last saw Otto."

"Two nights ago," she said. "Sunday night."

"What time would this have been?"

She thought a moment. "Around eight? I know it was after *60 Minutes*. The show had just ended when Otto said he was going out. He didn't show up for work yesterday, and he didn't show up today."

"Did he say where he was going on Sunday night?"

Eileen Petrenko shook her head. "I just thought, maybe out for a drink."

"I noticed the Icon when we were driving around," Bourque said.

Another head shake, but this one was more violent. "He wouldn't go to that kind of bar."

Bourque glanced at Delgado. She said, "I think it's a gay bar."

"Oh," he said. "Anywhere else he might have gone?"

"There's the Break, the billiards place," she said. "Sometimes he goes there. Mostly he watches the others play because he's not very good. But when he hadn't come home by eleven, I went down there looking for him, and he wasn't there. They hadn't seen him. Then I wondered if maybe he'd gone to a movie. I don't like movies, so sometimes he goes alone."

"He likes movies?" Bourque asked.

Eileen nodded her head toward the boxes along the wall. "Half of them are filled with DVDs. He likes to collect. There's even some of them on VHS. On cassette, you know? And we don't even have a VCR anymore. Threw it out years ago."

"What's his favorite movie?" Bourque asked.

She had to think. "He likes adventure ones. Like with Indiana

Jones or that John Wick person, that kind of movie. Action ones. He likes the fighting ones, where they're doing the kung fu or whatever it's called. I don't watch those."

"One of my favorites," Bourque mused, "is that one, with the shark? Where they had to close the beaches?"

She brightened. "Oh, right, *Jaws*. That's one of Otto's favorites." She looked curious. "I bought him some socks online with a shark on them. For his birthday."

Bourque exchanged a brief glance with Delgado. "Yeah, great movie."

Eileen said, "If he *had* gone to a movie, he'd have been home before midnight." She took a tissue from a box on the table next to her and dabbed the corner of her right eye.

"Do you think he was meeting with someone?" Delgado asked.

"He didn't say."

Delgado leaned forward, elbows on her knees. "This is a difficult question to ask, Mrs. Petrenko, but is it possible your husband is seeing someone?"

"You mean, a woman?" She looked aghast. "An affair?"

Delgado nodded.

"Oh, no, that's . . . I don't think so." She seemed to close in on herself, squeezing her arms closer to her body. "That wouldn't be like him, I don't think."

The room went quiet for a moment while the detectives let Eileen think about that one a little longer. Finally, Delgado asked, "Why did you say you thought he might have gone to Cleveland?"

She shrugged. "He doesn't like it here. He doesn't like New York. He doesn't like the big cities very much. At least, not the ones on the ocean." She sniffed, touched the tissue to her nose.

"The ocean?" Bourque said. "He doesn't like to swim? He hates boats?"

"No, no, it's not like that. There's the cities on the coast and then there's the rest of the country."

"I don't follow," Delgado said.

"Otto says one day there's going to be another civil war, but it won't be between the north and the south. It'll be between all the snooty people, you know, the elites, and all the other people, the real Americans."

"So people who live in, like, New York and Los Angeles and places like that aren't real Americans?" Delgado asked.

"They don't hold true American values," Eileen Petrenko said. "Otto would say they all want everyone to have abortions, to turn children into homosexuals, that kind of thing. But mostly, they look down their noses at everyone else." She shrugged, then tried to smile through the tears she was holding back. "But that's not me. I like people. I try to get along. I like people here. I like my neighbors. They're nice."

"Your husband's views," Bourque said slowly, "sound similar to those espoused by the Flyovers."

Eileen nodded. "That sounds like something Otto might have mentioned, but when he started in on this, I didn't listen to much. What are Flyovers?"

Bourque said, "It's an alt-right group that says the real Americans are the ones the elites fly over when they go from coast to coast."

Eileen looked confused. "It can't be the same group. I was watching the news yesterday, wondering if there might have been a car accident or something that might have involved Otto, and there was something about a bombing in Boston, and they mentioned that group. But Otto wouldn't want anything to do with people like that."

"Does Otto spend a lot of time on the net?"

Eileen's face darkened. "Maybe. But he's not some pervert if that's what you're asking. He's not on any of those porno sites. And he's not in some chat room talking to women, either. Not Otto."

Bourque glanced at Delgado, who was no doubt thinking what he was thinking. If Otto was their guy, and it was looking as though he might be, when they left this house they'd be taking his computer with them.

"Mrs. Petrenko," Bourque said, "do you know whether your husband was having any disagreements with anyone? Personally or professionally? Maybe there was someone who had a grudge against him?"

"No. Otto is a good man."

"Has he ever been in any kind of trouble?"

"Trouble?"

"With the police? Has he ever been arrested?"

She bit her lip. "It was a long time ago."

Delgado asked, "When was this?"

"Ten, eleven years, I think? It was a misunderstanding. Otto and a friend, they were on an out-of-town job, had too much to drink, and broke some furniture in a motel. The police were called. But Otto and the other man, they agreed to pay for the damages, and the charges were dropped."

Bourque slowly nodded his head. "So if he was arrested, they probably took his fingerprints."

Eileen shook her head. "It was long ago. He did the right thing. He paid them."

Delgado smiled. "I'm sure he did. Let's move on. Can you describe his behavior the last few weeks? Did he seem any different to you? Did he seem worried about something?"

Eileen thought about that. "Maybe a little." They waited. She put a hand to her forehead, then took it away, as if taking her own temperature. "He's been in touch with his family."

"Is that odd?" Bourque asked.

She shrugged. "Usually, at Christmas maybe, he calls his brother, asks how his kids are, or he'll check in with his sister if it's her birthday. But these last few weeks, he'd just call to say hi, or he'd send them an email. I mean, he likes them, they're family, but he's never shown all that much interest before."

"Did he say why he was doing that?" he asked.

She shook her head slowly. "It was like . . . it was like he was worried about them. I heard him say to his sister that they should have an alarm system. And I heard him ask his brother if he'd noticed anyone watching the house. I asked Otto about that, when he got off the phone, and he said we live in an age when we need to be careful, that was all."

"Where do his brother and sister live?" Delgado asked.

"His brother's back in Cleveland. His house is around the block from where ours used to be. And his sister lives in Vegas. She's a blackjack dealer."

"Have you talked to them since your husband went missing?"

Eileen Petrenko shook her head. "I didn't want to alarm anyone. And . . . and if Otto's just done something stupid, I don't want to have to explain it later."

"Stupid how?" Bourque asked.

"I don't know. Sometimes men do stupid things. They have too much to drink, they . . . have some midlife crisis or something." She tried to laugh. "Maybe he bought a motorcycle and decided to drive across the country." But her laughter turned immediately to tears. "He would never do that. It's not . . . it's not like him."

Bourque took out his pad. "Could you give me your brother- and sister-in-laws' names and numbers?"

"Anatoly Petrenko, and Misha Jackson. That's her married name."

She left the room briefly and returned with a cell phone. She sat back down, opened up the contacts on the phone, and recited two phone numbers for Bourque.

The two detectives gave each other a subtle glance. It was time.

"Mrs. Petrenko," Delgado said, "you provided a picture and a general description of your husband when you first called the police."

"That's right."

"I wonder if you could provide a few more specifics. Perhaps, identifying marks."

"Identifying marks? Like . . ."

Bourque said, "You know, birthmarks, perhaps a scar, a tattoo maybe."

"Oh," she said. "Otto does have a tattoo."

"There you go," Delgado said. "Can you describe it?"

"I can do better than that," she said, picking up the phone again. She tapped on photos.

"Last summer, we went up to Cape Cod for a couple of days to see my cousin and her husband." She swiped through the pictures until she found the ones she was looking for. "Here we go."

She handed the phone to Delgado, who leaned in closer to Bourque so they could look at the picture together.

The photo showed Otto standing on the beach, ocean behind him, hands on his hips. He was shirtless, wearing only a pair of black swimming trunks, his belly hanging over the waist.

The photo offered a clear shot of his shoulder, and the coiled cobra tattooed on it.

"Ah," said Delgado. "That is distinctive. What's the story behind that?"

"He got it when he was in his early twenties and didn't know better," she said. "He and some of his stupid friends, they were at some bar where they had a cobra in a big cage, and if you could stay in the cage with it for five minutes, you got free drinks."

"Jesus," Bourque said.

"Otto was the only one who lasted that long, so he got the tattoo as a reminder." Her voice dropped, as though someone were listening. "I bet it was defanged, or whatever they call it. The bar couldn't risk having their customers poisoned."

"You're probably right," Bourque said.

He looked into the woman's face. He hated this part, always had. Telling someone a loved one was dead. It was the worst part of the job. He felt a slight constriction in his windpipe.

He had a couple more questions before he'd break the news.

"So why did you move here from Cleveland if your husband hates New York so much?" he asked.

"The company he worked for went out of business," she said. "He sent out résumés all over the place, and the only firm that responded was here in New York. So even though he didn't want to move, there really wasn't much choice." She smiled sadly. "Have to put food on the table, you know. I've been working, too. I got a job waiting tables, but I haven't gone in since Otto's been gone."

"Right," Delgado said. "You said earlier he didn't show up for work yesterday or today?"

She nodded worriedly.

"We'd like the name of that boss," Bourque said.

"Sure, of course," Eileen said.

"What sort of work does your husband do, anyway?" Delgado asked.

"Elevator repair," she said. "Otto services elevators."

Fourteen

Mayor Richard Headley had arrived at his City Hall desk early and had made it clear to Valerie and the rest of his staff that unless the Statue of Liberty hiked up her skirt and waded over to Jersey City, he did not want to be disturbed. He muted his phone and brought up onto his screen a speech he was to deliver to the New York Conservation Authority the following week. Headley had speechwriters, but he hadn't been happy with their attempts at this one, and he wanted to take a run at it himself. The speech was one of a series the mayor had been giving to various groups about the need to reduce greenhouse gas emissions in the city. That included everything from establishing more charging stations for electric cars throughout the five boroughs to making all the cars in the city's fleet 100 percent electric. It was easier said than done, but Headley had made a greener city one of his campaign planks and he wasn't going to back down on it.

Converting larger vehicles, such as garbage trucks and fire engines, to electric power was a more formidable task, but scrapping conventional gas-powered cars, those that ran on fossil fuels, to battery power was an achievable goal. The city had already converted nearly 25 percent of its cars—basic four-door sedans—to electric power. They could be spotted by the small, green "NYG" logo on the back bumper. Glover had tried to talk his father into a big sticker that would cover most of the driver's door, really give people the message, but Headley had thought that too over the top.

While he had the speech on his computer screen, the mayor made a few changes. Just a line here and there so it didn't sound like he was giving the same speech he'd given the week before to a different group. He liked to work something fresh into each one so that the media would have something new to lead with. That assumed, of course, that the media was paying any attention at all. You tried to do what you thought was right, to make the city a better place, but did the media give you any credit for it? Not often. Certainly not when people like Barbara Matheson were making a big deal out of nothing. Sure, he gave a contract to Steelways, and yes, Arnett Steel had been a major contributor to his campaign, but Steelways had the best proposal for upgrading the subway's switching system. What was he supposed to do? Recommend a less competent company that came in with a lower bid?

Journalists didn't understand how the real world worked. They never had and never would.

Barbara Matheson was a perfect example of that. Never worked in business. Never hired or fired people. Never had to make distasteful, backroom payoffs with union leaders to make sure a job site wasn't sabotaged.

Headley didn't always like the way the world worked, but he wasn't naïve enough to think he could change it. Journalists were. They expected more of those in charge than they did of themselves.

Hypocrites, the lot of them.

And yet, when you were in a job like Headley's, you had to find a way to work with them. The media was one more obstacle to getting things done, like those unions, and government regulation.

Which was why Headley had been open to considering his son's idea to bring Matheson into the tent with that lucrative offer to write his bio.

An idea that had blown up in their faces. For the time being, the project was on hold. Meetings with prospective publishers had been canceled.

The mayor had brought Glover into his office earlier that morning to tell him how badly he'd screwed up.

"She made us all look like fools," Headley had said angrily while his son sat on the couch, knees together, head slightly bowed. "You should have known she'd say no, and that she'd go off and write about our proposal. What the fuck were you thinking?"

His son had raised his head long enough to say, "But you said to give it a—"

"So it's my fault," Headley had said. "You come up with a strategy that doesn't work, and it's my fault." He paused. "Maybe it is. Who I pick to advise me, that's on me."

Before Glover could say anything else, his father had pointed to the door and said, "That's all."

There'd been no point trying to completely refute Matheson's piece about what had transpired in the limo. As Chris had said, she'd probably recorded it. Valerie had issued a short statement to say that Matheson's experience made her a leading candidate for a possible project, and had nothing to do with undermining her work at *Manhattan Today*. Valerie also had to clarify what the mayor's political ambitions were. And that, she said, was to be the best mayor of New York that he could be.

As he reworked the speech, Headley found it difficult to concentrate. He hated personnel matters, especially when they involved Glover. He was still staring at the screen, struggling to find a way to give the speech some new life, when Valerie Langdon strode into the room. She pointed to the flashing light on his phone.

Valerie said, "It's Alexander Vesolov."

"Should I know who that is?" Headley said, slowly turning his head to look at her.

"The Russian ambassador."

"What does he want? A reception or something? Just take down the details."

"He wants to speak with you. Personally. He's quite insistent. He sounds pretty agitated."

Headley took his fingers off the keyboard and sighed. "Christ, somebody not notice his diplomatic plates and give him a parking ticket?"

Valerie said nothing. Headley sighed and reached for the phone. A smile came to his lips as instantly as if a switch had been thrown.

"Mr. Ambassador, always a pleasure."

"Mr. Mayor," said the heavily accented Vesolov on the other end.

"What can I do for you today?"

"We are very concerned, of course, about what has happened to Fanya Petrov."

The mayor didn't speak for several seconds, trying to place the name, wondering whether it was one he should know.

"I'm sorry, could you repeat that, Mr. Ambassador?"

As the ambassador did so, Headley scribbled the name on a scratch pad and held it up for Valerie to see. She made a *Huh?* face, but immediately got out her phone to do a search.

"This is a terrible, terrible thing," Vesolov said. "This is a terrible blow to my country. It's a terrible blow to the scientific community. Not just for Russia, but for the entire world."

Valerie set her phone on the desk, screen up, under Headley's nose. She'd found a Wikipedia page about the woman. Headley scanned it while he carried on the conversation.

"I can understand that," the mayor said, speaking slowly and deliberately while he struggled to get up to speed. "Dr. Petrov's work is certainly . . . groundbreaking. One of the leaders in her field."

"Not anymore," the ambassador said.

Headley decided he could not bluff any longer.

"I'm going to have to be frank here, Mr. Ambassador. You have me at a disadvantage. I've been in something of a bubble this morning. I do not know what has happened to Dr. Petrov. Has she been asked to leave the country? Is this a diplomatic issue? Because if it is, I'm not sure that I am the best one to talk to. I'd be more than happy to connect you with the State Department or any other appropriate agency."

"Fanya Petrov is dead, Mr. Mayor."

"I'm sorry. I did not know. My condolences. Perhaps you could bring me up to speed about what happened."

"You know about the elevator accident?"

Ah, Headley thought. Something he did know a little about.

"Yes, of course. Very tragic. A horrible thing. I did not know Dr. Petrov was among the casualties. I somehow missed her name in the accounts of the incident. I knew one of the victims. Sherry D'Agostino. I visited the scene personally yesterday, and have directed my staff to—"

"Yesterday?" said Vesolov. "No, not *that* elevator accident. This happened this morning."

Headley sat up in his chair, tossed the TV remote toward Valerie and pointed to the screen mounted on the wall. "This morning?" Headley said as Valerie started pushing buttons to bring the screen to life.

"You do not know this?"

One of the news channels popped up, but instead of local news there was a weather update. The mayor mouthed, *Fuck!*

Valerie came around the desk, forcing the mayor out of her way so she could start typing on his keyboard. She opened a browser and within seconds found an online news video, hit play with the volume off, and stepped back so Headley could watch it.

"I'm just getting more details now . . ." Headley said.

A woman was doing a remote outside the York Avenue apartment building, but the report was little more than her talking head. The chyron at the bottom of the screen read *One Dead in Grisly Elevator Mishap.*

"Of course," Headley said, "the incident on York. Horrible, just horrible."

"Fanya Petrov," the ambassador said, "could very well have been on the cusp of some startling scientific discoveries. We have been in touch with her family in Moscow, and they are devastated."

"I've no doubt. Please pass on our deepest sympathies."

"How could something like this happen?" Vesolov asked. "Her head cut right off! A decapitation."

Jesus, Headley thought. "It's a terrible tragedy. These types of accidents are very, very rare."

"Doesn't seem that way," the ambassador said. "One yesterday and one today?"

Headley struggled for an explanation. "I guess it's like airplane crashes," he said weakly. "We don't have any for months, then two or three in quick succession. Mr. Ambassador, I'm going to personally check on the progress of this investigation and will report back to you myself."

"Thank you, Mr. Mayor," Vesolov said. "I look forward to hearing from you." He ended the call.

Headley glared at Valerie. "Why didn't I know about this?"

"I'd only just found out about it seconds before the ambassador called."

"What's the actual address where this happened?"

Valerie looked to her phone for details, and told him.

"I've been in that building," he said. Headley put a finger to his chin, trying to remember. "A fund-raiser, I think. Last year."

"How would you like to proceed?"

Headley sighed. "Get the car," he said.

———

Alexander Vesolov took his hand from the receiver and leaned back in an oversized leather chair. He clasped his hands together over his considerable stomach and glanced at the large portrait of Vladimir Putin hanging on the wall to his right.

The door opened and a young, dark-haired woman with the most perfect posture in the world walked in.

"You were able to speak to the mayor directly?" she asked.

"I was," Vesolov said.

"And how did it go?"

Vesolov wore a satisfied smile. "I was suitably outraged."

The woman returned the smile and glanced, for half a second, at the portrait. "Would you like me to inform him?"

Vesolov shook his head. "No, I would like to do that myself."

"Of course," the woman said. "I will set up the call."

Vesolov took his hands from their resting place atop his belly and leaned forward over the desk.

"How do the Americans say it?" he asked.

The woman was not sure what the ambassador was referring to, and waited.

He smiled, remembering. "We caught a break."

Fifteen

W hat we're trying to do," Glover Headley explained to Arla Silbert as they entered a windowless City Hall office stocked with a dozen cubicles, "is not tell the public what it wants to hear, but gauge whether they're getting the message we're hoping to send. Are our policy proposals resonating? Is the message being heard?"

"Sure," said Arla. "And is it?"

Glover offered half a shrug as they walked into the room, which was eerily quiet. There was no one working at any of the desks. "It's mixed. That's why we're investing so much in the analytics. And we're also studying New Yorkers' feelings about Mayor Headley himself. This is one of my primary roles here in the mayor's administration, this assessing of public opinion."

"I looked you up," Arla said, smiling. "I went to some of the same marketing courses as you did, I think."

He nodded. "Yeah, I noticed that on your résumé, which was one of the reasons you were a leading candidate from the start. There are a lot of very good people in this department. You'll learn a lot. Although," and he grimaced, "you're not going to learn much today. I'm really sorry there's no one here right now. I forgot everyone's off to a seminar this morning."

"That's okay."

"Anyway, the mayor thinks very highly of the team down here. The work you'll be doing for him is critical for future strategizing."

Arla smiled. "You ever just call him Dad?"

Glover tucked his index finger between his neck and collar, as though his tie was too tight. "When it's business, I try to be as professional as possible. But yeah, some days, he's Dad."

"He's not Dad every day?"

Glover gave his dry lips a lick. "Well, of course he is."

Arla sensed she was making Glover uncomfortable, so she shifted gears. "I read that before you got into all this marketing analysis, you were in high-tech."

"I actually spent some time in Seattle, at Microsoft," he said. "I even worked for Netflix for a while. When I was twelve, I could take apart just about any device and put it back together with my eyes closed." He grinned. "If you're having trouble with your modem, I'm the man to call."

"Noted," Arla said. "So, all the work you've done so far, what does it say about how New Yorkers feel about the mayor?"

"Depends what side of the fence you're on, I guess. My father didn't run on a Republican or Democratic ticket, but historically he has more ties to the Democrats. His father served back in the sixties in Congress as one. But Mayor Headley is not an ideological guy. He's a pragmatist. He goes into a situation looking at both sides. He hasn't got his mind made up beforehand. And there's a lot he wants to do for the city. Improve transit. Keep taxes low. Boost tourism. And he has an ambitious environmental agenda. Electric cars, that kind of thing."

"It seems that he has—can I really speak my mind here?"

"Yeah, sure. That's what we're going to be paying you for."

"He has a lot of positives, like you say. The pragmatism, speaking his mind. But he's seen as brusque and dismissive at times."

Glover couldn't stop himself from slightly rolling his eyes.

"That's . . . certainly true."

"And he's been taking heat for favoring friends when it comes to awarding contracts."

"You can't believe everything you hear," Glover Headley said. "There's a lot that goes on behind the scenes that people never know about. So many things factor into the decision making. It may not make sense to the general public, but there are reasons things are done the way they're done."

"I'm sure that's true," Arla said.

"That's why what we're doing here is so important. One of our jobs is to counter the negativity, the false impressions that are created in the media. It doesn't matter what the mayor says or does, there are some media outlets that will always find the negative angle."

He stopped and waved his arm theatrically. "Anyway, this is your home away from home, right here."

It was little more than a cubicle with cloth-covered dividers on three sides that offered a token amount of privacy from coworkers.

"Awesome," Arla said.

Glover scanned the workerless room again. "I really wanted to introduce you to some people, but there's not much sense interrupting their seminar. They should all be here after lunch and then—"

The sound of a text came from inside his suit jacket. "Excuse me," he said, taking out the phone and reading the message. His forehead creased.

"What is it?" Arla asked.

"I'm going to have to cut your orientation session short," he said apologetically. "There's been an incident and the mayor wants to attend. I have to go."

"What kind of incident?"

"I can't believe it. Another elevator accident." He looked at his phone again as another text came in. "And this one may have diplomatic overtones. Look, I really have to go. Let me grab a few reports you can sift through before everyone comes back later."

Arla glanced about the empty room. "Let me toss out an idea."

Glover waited.

"What if I came along? Watch the mayor do his thing?"

Glover's expression bordered on fearful. "I'm not exactly in his good books today. I couldn't, I mean, no offense, but I couldn't, you know, take you in the mayor's limo, someone who's just been—"

Arla lightly touched his arm. "Relax. Tell me where you're headed and I'll get there on my own. I'll just observe. I won't get in the way. What better way to get a sense of the boss than to see him in action?"

Glover thought about it for two more seconds, then nodded. "It's up near Rockefeller University. I'll text you the exact address when I know it."

Arla nodded. "See you there."

Glover gave her a smile before spinning on his heels and running out the door.

Wow, Arla thought. *Talk about being in the right place at the right time.*

Sixteen

Bourque put Otto Petrenko's laptop, sealed in an evidence bag, on the floor in front of him as he got into the passenger seat. Delgado got behind the wheel. Both were subdued. Eileen Petrenko stood at her front door, watching them through eyes filled with tears.

Moments earlier, they had told her about the body found on the High Line. While a positive identification had yet to be made, evidence suggested it could be her husband. The dead man was the approximate age and weight of Otto Petrenko. There was the cobra tattoo. The shark socks.

They'd attempted to ask her a few more questions. Did her husband often walk the High Line? Could he have gone there to meet someone? But the woman was too distraught to handle any more of their inquiries.

Delgado turned the key and headed south.

"So Otto's killer," Bourque said, "somehow knows Otto's prints are on file somewhere."

"So he makes sure we can't take any," Delgado said. "But we should be able to get those prints, see if we can get a match on the tip our guy left behind."

"Confirmation'll be nice," Bourque said. "But it's him."

They were on their way to Petrenko's employer, Simpson Elevator Maintenance. Bourque looked on his phone to see how many firms in New York did that kind of work. "There's a shitload of them," he said to Delgado. "I guess if you were Otto Petrenko, an out-of-work elevator fix-it man from Cleveland, New York would be the place to go to."

"Yeah," Delgado said.

"Went to Cleveland once. The downtown's got a few tall buildings, but there's this one huge skyscraper, looks like a mini–Empire State Building. Key Tower. Fifty-seven stories. Tallest building in Ohio."

Delgado glanced at him. "Only you would know that."

Their drive took them into the Hunters Point area of Queens. Vernon Boulevard was a north-south industrial street that followed the East River, just south of the Queensboro Bridge. When they found Simpson Elevator, Delgado drove through the open chain-link gate and parked between two pickup trucks. They'd learned from Eileen that the name of Otto's boss was Gunther Willem.

They opened the door to the office. A chest-high counter topped with peeling linoleum greeted them. Bourque rested his elbows on it and called out "Excuse me" to a heavyset, gray-haired woman sitting at a desk.

When she turned, Bourque could see she was on the phone. She put her hand over the mouthpiece and said, "Help you?"

"Looking for Gunther Willem," Lois said.

"Not a good time," she said. Before she could go back to her call, Bourque waved his badge. "Oh," she said.

She rested the receiver on her desk and shouted, "Gunth!"

From an adjoining office, a gruff voice replied, "What?"

"Visitors."

There was a grumbled yet still audible, "Fuck," and seconds later, Gunther Willem appeared. He had a crew cut, a round face, stood about five-five, and was nearly as broad as he was tall. His meaty arms hung out from his body and seemed to bounce as he walked. He spotted Delgado and Bourque and squinted.

"Yeah?"

Bourque still had his badge out. "Detective Bourque, and this is Detective Delgado."

"I'm up to my eyeballs in shit," he said. "Whatever this is, can it wait?"

"No," Delgado said.

Willem took a second, accepted defeat, and waved for them to follow him back to his office. He dropped himself into an office chair that creaked under his weight, and the detectives sat in two plain wood chairs opposite his cluttered desk.

"I'm shorthanded and I got the city breathing down my neck, so make it quick," he said. "This about some of the robberies along the street here? Guys stealing tools? Because we're okay. I got two Dobermans in the yard at night, got no trouble on that score."

"No," said Delgado. "We're here about Otto Petrenko."

"Oh, him. He was a no-show yesterday and today. His wife's goin' bananas. He finally come home? Was he out on a bender or something?"

"We're investigating," Delgado said.

"Investigating what?"

"What happened to him."

"What *has* happened to him? Because, like I said, I'm shorthanded."

"What can you tell us about Mr. Petrenko?" Bourque asked.

Willem looked from one detective to the other. He quickly figured out the drill. They would ask the questions and he would answer them.

"I don't know," Gunther Willem said. "Reliable. Understands how things work, you know? Some people are born with it. They look at a machine and it's like they've got X-ray vision. They can see the parts inside it. He's pretty smart that way."

"He came to you from Cleveland?" Delgado asked.

"Yeah. The company he worked for, they were mismanaged, went bankrupt. We were hiring. So he moved here. Guy's good. Got two people out of a stuck elevator in the new Trade Center Tower one time."

"Any problems?" Bourque asked.

"Like?"

"You tell us."

"No, no problems. He does his job."

"How about when he was off the clock?" Delgado asked. "Any issues you're aware of? Drugs? Women? Trouble on the home front?"

"Like I said, nuthin'."

"He socialize with the other guys who work here?"

Willem shrugged. "Some. They go out for a drink sometimes. Give each other the gears. Maybe they get together with the wives once in a while, do some barbecue."

"You part of that?" Delgado asked.

Willem shrugged. "Not so much."

"You got along with him?"

"Yeah." His eyes narrowed when Delgado used the past tense. "What's this about, anyway?"

"You know anything about who he might have hung out with who's not with the company?"

Willem shook his head. "No. Not really." He paused, as if remembering. "Well, there was that one guy."

"What guy?" Delgado asked.

"Dropped by to see him once in a while."

Bourque felt as though he'd gotten a carpet shock. "Who was he?"

"Just some guy, is all. I'd see the car pull up on the street there and Otto would go out and talk to him."

"Did Mr. Petrenko say who he was?"

"I didn't ask. You want to go talk to somebody, it's none of my business."

"Can you describe him?" Delgado asked.

Willem sighed with exasperation. "It was a guy. Whaddya want from me?"

"White? Black?" she asked, persisting.

"White. Uh, grayish hair."

"Old guy?"

Willem looked up at the ceiling, as though the answer were written there. "No idea. He was too far away to tell."

"Car?" Bourque asked.

"Jesus," Willem said. "I don't know. Something blue. Basic sedan, I think."

"How many times did you see Petrenko meet with this man?"

"Two, maybe three times? Definitely more than once. I think I might have asked Otto once what the guy wanted."

"What'd he say?" Delgado asked.

"I don't remember exactly. I got the idea maybe Otto was helping him, like he was giving the guy some kind of advice."

"About elevators?" Delgado asked. "Wouldn't it make more sense to talk to you? Being the boss?"

Gunther shrugged. "Otto knows as much about elevators as I do. Probably more. And maybe it wasn't advice about this kind of work. Maybe it was about something else. Maybe it was his long-lost cousin. I don't know." He paused, thinking. "There was one thing, though."

They waited.

"Whenever he's come back in from talking to that guy, Otto's kind of quiet."

"What do you mean, quiet?" Delgado asked.

"Just . . . like he's got something on his mind." He shrugged. "I don't know. Worried, like. Maybe he owes this guy money or something and is having trouble meeting his payments. Although I don't know why he'd have money problems. He's pulling down seventy grand a year from me."

"You got cameras?" Bourque asked.

"What?"

"On the property. Surveillance. That would pick up someone on the street."

"Yeah, sure, of course. But the last time he was here was weeks ago. They don't go back more than forty-eight hours."

Delgado asked, "Did he ever talk about the Flyovers?"

"What's that? A singing group?"

"Did Otto have strong political views?"

"We don't talk a lot of politics here," Willem said. "Well, other than shittin' all over our useless president and useless governor and useless senators and useless mayor. But that's about it. Listen, if you're looking for Otto, I hope you find him. He's one of the best guys I got. But the way you guys are talking about him, sounds like something's happened."

The detectives exchanged looks. Delgado said, "Mr. Petrenko is dead."

Willem's face fell. "Shit. What the hell happened?"

"That's what we're looking into," she said.

He shook his head sadly. "Man oh man. There's so many ways to get killed on the job here, and he buys it on his day off? Was it a car accident? Something like that?"

"Like I said, we're looking into the circumstances."

"Son of a bitch. I should give his wife a call. Soon as I get out from under all this other shit that's going on."

"What other shit would that be?" she asked.

"Like I said, the city's on my ass. When two elevators go down in two days, and your company was one of the ones that ever did service calls in both those buildings over the past decade, that's a fucking problem. They'll be looking for someone to blame it on, you can be sure of that. But we do good work. And it might have been another company, or maybe we serviced an elevator there but not that one. No one is going to hang this on us, believe me."

"Two elevators in two days?" Bourque asked.

"I heard about one yesterday," Delgado said. "Was there one before that?"

"One *since,*" Willem said. "Few hours ago."

"Would Otto Petrenko have worked on them?" Delgado asked.

"I hope *no one* here worked on them. But if anyone did, I hope it was Otto."

"Why would you say that?"

Willem shrugged. "First rule at engineering school. Whenever something bad happens, you blame it on the dead guy."

Seventeen

Y ou almost ready?"

Eugene Clement was standing outside the bathroom of the InterMajestic Hotel room he and his wife, Estelle, had rented for their New York stay. The door was open an inch, giving her privacy, but still allowing her to carry on a conversation with her husband.

"Three minutes," she called out.

Clement knew that meant at least ten, so he stopped hovering by the door and walked over to the small desk, where his phone was recharging. He detached it from the charging cord, took a seat on the end of the bed, and opened one of his news apps.

"I'm starving," Estelle said. Her words were immediately followed by the sound of a hair dryer.

"Me too. If you'd hurry up, we could eat," he said, thumbing through the latest news stories.

"What?" she shouted over the roar.

He didn't respond. He was scanning the most recent headlines. One, in particular, caught his eye. An elevator accident. The second in two days. There were few details. The story was developing.

"My my," Clement said softly.

The hair dryer went silent. "What did you say?" Estelle asked, opening the bathroom door wide.

"Nothing," he said, turning to look at her. She was wearing one of the robes supplied by the hotel.

"You know where I'd like to go?" she said.

"Where?"

"I'd like to see Radio City Music Hall. I think they have tours."

Clement nodded. "We can look into that. We could walk it from—"

The room phone started ringing.

"Who would that be?" Estelle asked.

Clement got up, walked around the side of the bed, and snatched up the receiver. "Hello?"

"Mr. Clement?" A woman's voice.

"Yes?"

"Eugene Clement?"

"Who is this?" he asked.

"I'm Sheila Drake. I'm a booker for *New York Day*. It's a—"

"I know what it is."

"Who is it?" Estelle asked.

He covered the mouthpiece and snapped at her, "TV show."

"Mr. Clement?" Drake said.

"Here."

"We know you are in New York and would like to have you on the show today. We can send a car."

"How did you know—"

"The Flyovers group is believed to be responsible for several recent bombings in—"

"That's ridiculous. We can't control people saying we had anything to do with those events. They're horrible tragedies. We're all about awareness, raising issues."

"We'd like to talk to you about that. Give you a chance to make that point."

"We're here celebrating our anniversary. I don't have time for—"

"Let me try to lay it out for you, Mr. Clement. We can pursue you down the sidewalk, shouting questions at you, and when we broadcast that you're going to look like some kind of criminal. I think you'd be doing yourself a favor to come into the studio for a sit-down interview where you could make your case calmly, without creating some negative impressions. What do you say?"

Clement thought for a moment.

"Mr. Clement?"

He cleared his throat and asked, "What time?"

Eighteen

Chris Vallins was leaning up against the window of Block-heads, a small restaurant across from the Morning Star Café. He was tucked under the awning and, he thought, reasonably invisible, especially considering how wide Second Avenue was. The restaurant didn't open until eleven, so no one was going to come out and tell him to move on.

He had a phone in his hand, set to take photos. He would have liked a camera with a telephoto lens, but even in New York, standing on the sidewalk wielding one of those was likely to attract attention.

He'd followed Barbara Matheson from her apartment to the café. Barbara, clearly, was a walker. She lived in Murray Hill on East Thirty-Seventh, between Lexington and Third. She came striding out of her place, headed for Third and turned left, staying on it for thirteen blocks, then hanging a right on Fiftieth and east one block to Second. The Morning Star was right around the corner. Chris had stayed half a block behind all the way, usually on the same side of the street. Barbara gave no indication of knowing she was being followed. She never looked back. She had met Chris only the one time, in the back of the mayor's limo, but he figured his bald head was pretty distinctive, so he'd worn a Knicks ball cap. And unlike when he was in the limo, when he was wearing a suit, Chris had dressed this morning in old jeans, a button-down-collar blue shirt, and a brown leather jacket.

It wouldn't have much mattered if he'd looked exactly as he had the day before. Like a lot of people, Barbara had her eyes glued to her phone even while she was walking. She seemed to possess a requisite skill for the modern world. She knew what was in her path without looking up. Her gift, however, had yet to be perfected. When she failed to notice a dog walker's leash stretched out across her path, she tripped and nearly hit the sidewalk. If she was at all rattled by the near miss, she didn't show it.

When she turned into the café, he kept on walking, then crossed the street at the next light and took up his position in front of Blockheads. Barbara had taken a seat in a booth close to the window. Chris couldn't make out every detail, but at least he knew where she was. A few minutes later, another woman arrived. Younger, early to midtwenties. She slid into the booth opposite Barbara.

While they talked, Vallins mentally reviewed what he had already learned about Barbara Matheson.

The first bit of information was probably the most valuable. This thorn in the mayor's side was not using her real name, at least not when she wrote her columns. Her real name, and the one she used for all her financial transactions, was Barbara Silbert. Vallins was well aware that novelists often chose to publish their books under pseudonyms, but was that an acceptable practice when it came to journalism? Could you really take potshots at politicians and others while hiding behind a name that was not your own?

Once he had determined Barbara's true last name, he was able to find out plenty of other things about her. She was living in a sublet, paying $1,100 a month, which was a pretty good deal, considering the average was more than $3,000. Just as well her rent was a deal, considering that *Manhattan Today* was paying her a few pennies under a hundred thousand a year. That might have sounded like a lot to some, but you needed a lot to live right in Manhattan.

Barbara paid off her cards every month and was rewarded for that with a decent credit score. What was interesting about the statements he'd been able to access was not so much what was on them, but what was not. No Bloomies, no Saks, no Nordstrom. When Barbara bought clothes, she was not extravagant. The Gap, Macy's, maybe Club Monaco if she really wanted to splurge. Not a shocker. All Vallins had seen her in was jeans and a top and a light jacket. Barbara spent most of her money at bars and restaurants. It didn't look as though she ate much at home. Lots of diners, like the Morning Star. There were a few charges at liquor stores, so even if she didn't make many of her own meals, at least she drank at home.

About fifteen minutes after the younger woman joined Barbara, she got up to leave.

Chris took off his right glove so that the camera icon on his phone would work when he touched it with his finger. Barbara exited the restaurant. Chris hit the button and held it, firing off multiple shots as the unknown woman stood briefly, got her bearings, and started walking south. Chris lowered the phone as she crossed Fiftieth and hailed a cab. She got in, and the cab took off down Second.

Barbara stayed. She appeared to be ignoring her breakfast.

Chris wondered who the young woman might be. If Barbara'd had a Facebook page, Chris might have found a picture of her there, if she was a friend. But Barbara was not on Facebook. She had a substantial Twitter following, though. Just under thirty thousand. But Twitter was not typically where one posted photos of friends. It was for mouthing off, something Barbara did plenty of.

Five minutes after the young woman left, Barbara got up, paid the bill, and emerged onto the sidewalk. Would she head back toward home? Walk to the *Manhattan Today* office? These days, what with half the world working from home, there might not be much reason for Barbara to show up at an actual office.

She headed north. As she walked, she did the same thing she'd done earlier. She took out her phone. It was welded to her palm, Chris thought.

She glanced down at it as she crossed Fifty-First. Chris let out a derisive sigh. All these people, looking at their phones when they should be watching where they're going. Getting hit by cars, walking head-on into other idiots who were also staring at their phones. There was a video on the news the other day of a woman falling into some open sidewalk cellar doors, the kind you saw all over the city to accommodate deliveries.

Barbara barely took her eyes off the device the whole next block, but somehow she knew there was a red light at Fifty-Second, and she stopped instead of stepping into the path of a panel truck.

Chris was only a few feet behind her. Close enough to hear her phone when it started to ring. A curious ringtone, at that. It sounded like someone tapping away furiously on an old manual typewriter.

Barbara put the phone to her ear. As the light changed, she continued walking north.

Chris couldn't make out anything she was saying. But whatever the caller was telling her was serious enough to make Barbara stop dead in the middle of the sidewalk and listen.

Chris had to hit the brakes to avoid walking into her. He sidestepped around her and kept on walking. When he reached the next corner, he turned and looked back. Barbara was tucking her phone into her purse and stepping out into the street to hail a cab.

Shit.

He looked north and saw several available ones coming their way. Second Avenue ran only southbound, so the cabs were spread out across its width. One on the far side veered across, aiming for Barbara and cutting off several other vehicles in the process.

Chris waved and caught the attention of another cab driver. The car swerved toward him. By the time he got into the back of his taxi, Barbara was pulling away.

"Where to?" asked the driver, a heavily bearded man with one hand on the wheel and the other holding a half-eaten apple.

"That taxi right ahead? That picked up that woman? I'm going where she's going."

"Where's that?" the driver asked.

"Don't know. Just follow it."

"Ah, like in the movies," the driver said, taking one last huge bite of the apple, powering down his window, and tossing the core.

The miniscreen bolted to the back of the Plexiglas partition was playing some snippets from daytime TV. Chris made several unsuccessful attempts to mute it before giving up. He was thinking if he could get his hands on Barbara's phone long enough to fiddle with the settings, he'd be able to track her location without having to chase after her.

Barbara's cab was continuing straight on down Second. Past Forty-Second, past Thirty-Fourth, finally hanging a right on Twenty-Seventh. The cab went halfway down the block toward Third before it pulled over.

"Stop here," Chris said when his own cab was about ten car lengths back.

He tossed a ten through the partition window and was out of the car before Barbara had exited hers. He pulled out his phone and pretended to look at it while Barbara settled up with her cabbie. She got out, walked a few doors west on the north side, stopped to study the building she was in front of, and went in.

Chris crossed the street so he could check out the address without standing directly in front of it.

Barbara had gone into a funeral home. Clappison's Funeral Services, to be exact.

Nineteen

Arla grabbed a cab.

When the taxi was half a dozen blocks from her destination, it stopped dead, not going anywhere. Traffic was insane. Arla bailed and ran the rest of the way. She jogged Central Park three mornings a week, so she didn't get winded, but she sweated through her work clothes. Glover had texted her the York Avenue address, and she got there before the mayor and his entourage.

Along the way, her mind went back to the brief meeting she'd had with her mother. It had gone pretty much as she'd expected. Maybe it would have been better to break the news to her about her new job in an email. Face-to-face, things had a way of getting unpleasant in a hurry.

Arla wondered if that awkwardness was what she'd wanted all along. To see the expression on her mother's face when she told her whom she was going to be working for. To revel in her shock and disappointment. Of course, if that really *was* why Arla had told Barbara in person, it meant her mother wasn't wrong suggesting Arla took the job just to get under her mother's skin.

In the moments when Arla was honest with herself, she had to admit there was something to that. Arla had, to put it mildly, conflicted feelings about her mother. At some level, yes, she loved her. After all, she was her *mother*. And there were even times when Arla could understand what it must have been like for Barbara, to have found herself pregnant at such a young age, to not want to have to give up a career.

At least she didn't abort me, Arla told herself in moments when she was inclined to be generous.

But then there were the other times, when she just didn't give a shit about her mother's feelings. *She should have been there for me, each and every fucking day.*

So yes, maybe she was sticking it to her mother. But the flip side of all this was: Should Arla have turned down a great opportunity just because it would make her mother unhappy? Didn't she have her own life to live? Wasn't she entitled to make her own choices? Arla had actually been concerned, when she'd applied, that her potential employer would make the connection. If they found out Barbara was her mother, they'd probably deny her the job. Would that have been fair?

She stopped thinking about all that when she reached the scene.

York Avenue was blocked off. There was no sense of pandemonium, but there were half a dozen FDNY vehicles, as many marked police cars, and two or three unmarked ones. There was one lone TV van, and not an ambulance in sight. Arla was guessing the scene had been busier earlier. A couple of hours must have gone by since the accident.

Flimsy police tape served amazingly well to keep people from entering the building. Without any official City Hall ID—she was hoping she'd have one before long—Arla wasn't expecting anyone to let her pass. She'd have to wait for Glover, once he had arrived with his father and whoever else was coming, to see if she could get in.

Looking south down York she saw a black town car approaching. It stopped and Glover got out, followed by Mayor Headley. A woman Arla knew to be Valerie Langdon emerged from the other side. One of the news crews spotted their arrival and went charging in their direction. Arla expected the mayor to stop and say something for the cameras, but instead he made a path straight toward the building.

As the three of them got closer, Arla tried to catch Glover's eye. But he was walking directly alongside his father, glancing down at his phone, presumably looking for updates he could pass along to the mayor. When they reached the tape line, close to where Arla was standing, she worked her way through the crowd, reached out, and tapped Glover on the arm.

He glanced her way, reacting with mild surprise, as though it had slipped his mind that she was going to find her own way here.

"Hey," he said, blinking. Then, it all came back. He glanced at Headley, who was several steps ahead, having already ducked under the tape line.

"Right," Glover said, seizing the opportunity and lifting the tape for Arla. "Come on."

She slipped under it. The closest NYPD officer, having seen she was with the mayor's party, made no attempt to stop her. Arla stuck close to Glover. He was her hall pass. If she got separated from him, the police might boot her ass out of there.

Arla felt her pulse quickening as she headed for the entrance. Here she was, on her very first day, walking alongside one of the mayor's key advisers, strolling right past the police barricades, a dozen steps behind the mayor himself (and hoping he would not see her and ask who the hell she was), getting an up-close look at a tragedy that would be all over that evening's news.

Did it get any better than this?

They went into the building's large atrium-style lobby. The bank of four elevators was along the back wall, and the doors to one were wide open. Standing outside, peering in, were two men and one woman in firefighter garb, and what Arla guessed were a fire department captain—in dress blues, the FDNY patches on his shoulders—and a woman Arla recognized as the city's new chief of police. Bringing out the big guns, she thought. Sure, an elevator accident was a tragedy if someone got killed, but it wasn't exactly John Lennon getting shot out front of the Dakota, was it?

As if he could read her mind, Glover sidled up to her and whispered, "She was a big deal."

"Who was a big deal?" she asked, leaning her head toward his.

"The woman who got killed. Some scientist from Russia."

"What happened to her? Where's—"

Arla stopped herself. She'd spotted what everyone was looking at. On the floor of the elevator was a bloody, pulpy mass, about the size and shape of a cabbage. Next to it, what appeared to be an arm in a blue sleeve. The elevator floor was a blood-covered mess.

When Arla suddenly turned away she found herself up against Glover Headley's chest.

"Oh, God," she said.

But she quickly pulled away before he could place a comforting hand on her back. Her sense of horror and revulsion was displaced almost immediately by the feeling that she needed to be professional. She was not going to be that horror movie heroine who clung to the male lead for comfort. So she spun about and looked back in the general direction of the elevator without focusing on the head and the arm and the blood.

I will not throw up.

Mayor Headley joined the bigwigs huddled in conversation.

"What's happening?" Arla asked Glover.

"Getting up to speed," he said. "Stay here. I gotta go."

Arla did as she was told as he went to this father's side. There was more discussion; at one point, the chief of police whispered something to the mayor while she pointed to the far end of the lobby.

Arla looked that way. A man in his mid- to late thirties was sitting on a lobby couch with his arm around a young boy. A father and son, Arla guessed.

The mayor nodded and broke away from the crowd. He headed for the father and son and said a few words to them. The man's head went up and down once, at which point the mayor perched his butt on the oversized coffee table in front of the couch, which put him only inches away from the boy.

Arla desperately wanted to know what this was about.

She slipped around the outer perimeter of the lobby, coming at the couch from the other side. There was a large pillar behind it, and she took a position along one side where she was unlikely to be seen. As cover, she took out her phone and pretended to be checking something.

Although the pillar blocked her view, she could make out the conversation reasonably clearly.

"Your name's Colin?" the mayor asked.

"Yes," the boy said softly.

"You know who I am?"

"You're the mayor?"

"That's right."

"My dad told me when you walked in. You're like the mayor of all of New York?"

"I am."

"I thought you'd be bigger."

Headley chuckled at that. "It's like with movie stars. When you see them in person you wonder why they aren't twenty feet tall. The police were telling me what a brave young man you are."

"Oh?"

"You went through something pretty horrible. But here you are, with your dad here, and you're holding up okay, aren't you?"

"I guess."

"Missing school."

"Yeah," said Colin. "My dad phoned and told them I'd be late."

"Well, you ask me, I think you should get the whole day off. What do you think, Dad?"

Arla heard the father speak for the first time. "Yeah. I'm thinking we might go to the movies, or maybe the Museum of Natural History."

"I like the whale," Colin said.

"Oh, yeah, the whale is something," Headley said. "You wonder, how can it float up there, right? The police and the fire department folks say that not only were you brave, you were very helpful to them, explaining what happened."

"Her head came right off," the boy said, keeping his voice steady. "The rest of her is still upstairs in the hall. They should tell people so they don't come out of their apartments and see her there."

"I think that's been done, Colin, but that's a good idea, and nice of you to be thinking of other people's feelings. Anyway, I want to talk about you for a minute. I'm gonna give you my card here, and one for your dad, and what we're going to do is have you for dinner at Gracie Mansion."

"At what?"

"That's where the mayor—that's where I live. I get to stay there while I'm serving the people. If I get voted out in the next election, then they kick me out."

"You could live with us," Colin offered. "Could he live with us, Dad? We have the spare room."

"I would imagine the mayor has a backup plan," the father said.

"I do," Headley said. "But I'll keep your offer in mind."

"Why do they call it Gracie Mansion?" Colin asked.

"Good question," the mayor said. "It was built, way back in 1799, by a man named Archibald Gracie."

"Oh."

"I'll show you all around when you come."

"I've never been in a mansion," the boy said.

"Anyway, you, and your dad, and your mom will be most welcome."

"She lives in Omaha," the boy said. "I see her at Christmas."

"Okay then. You and your dad will be my dinner guests."

"What will we be having?" the boy asked.

"Colin," the father said, gently reproachful, "you don't—"

"It's okay," Headley said. "What would you like?"

"Hot dogs."

"I think my chef can handle that."

Arla moved toward the edge of the pillar, hoping to get a peek.
Headley extended a hand for Colin to shake, but instead the boy
slipped off the couch and threw his arms around the mayor's neck.
Headley wrapped his arms around the boy and held him for several
seconds.

When they let go, Headley said, "You call me anytime."

The mayor stood, shook the father's hand, and went back to rejoin the other emergency officials.

No cameras, Arla thought. No TV crews. No reporters hanging
about. They were all still outside, beyond the police tape. Not even
Glover or Valerie Langdon had witnessed Headley's visit with the
boy and his dad.

They'd hired her to analyze data. But that wasn't going to stop
Arla from suggesting that they find a way to highlight some other
sides of Headley's personality.

That was what her gut was telling her.

Twenty

A silver-haired man in a black suit spotted Barbara Matheson entering the lobby of Clappison's Funeral Services and approached noiselessly, as though floating on air.

"May I be of assistance?" he asked in a soft, unctuous manner.

"I'm looking for the Chatsworths," she said. "Ken and Sandy. Parents of Paula."

"Yes, of course," he said solemnly. "A terrible, terrible thing. This way."

Barbara realized she was speaking barely above a whisper, and this man's reply was equally sedate, even though there was no one else around. There was something about entering a funeral parlor that made people act like they were in a library. Someday, she thought, she'd like to throw a party in a place like this. Take her best shot at waking the dead.

Barbara followed the funeral director through a set of doors and down a hallway to a small receiving room. Broadloomed, four big comfy chairs, velvet drapes at the window. Barbara thought that if it weren't a room for grieving, it would be perfect for choosing which whore you wanted to spend the next hour with.

In one of the chairs was a woman Barbara assumed had to be Paula Chatsworth's mother, and the man pacing the room with a phone to his ear must be her husband, Ken. Sandy Chatsworth had no phone in her hand, and seemed to be staring off into space. Dazed, numb with shock, Barbara guessed.

But she did look up when Barbara came into the room. Her eyes were pink and puffy.

"Ms. Chatsworth?" she said.

"Barbara?" Sandy said, suddenly focusing, extending her hands, which Barbara took in hers. Ken was still pacing the room. "Ken, it's—"

He held up a finger. The introduction would have to wait.

"Hello?" he said into the phone. "Listen, I've been on hold for fifteen goddamn minutes. I want someone to tell me—hello? All I want is some answers about—"

He took the phone away from his ear, his mouth wide with astonishment. He looked ready to spout a series of obscenities, but then, mindful of where he was, changed his mind.

"I got cut off," he said, looking at his wife. "After waiting that long, they hung up on me! The sons of—Jesus!"

"Keep your voice down," Sandy said.

He shook his head, still not believing it. Finally, he looked blankly at Barbara, as if wondering who the hell she was.

Barbara reached out a hand. "Mr. Chatsworth. I'm Barbara."

"Oh, right, sorry," he said, hitting his forehead with the butt of his hand. "God, you got here fast."

"You caught me at a good time," she said. "How are you doing? A dumb question, I know, but—"

"They're getting Paula ready to send home," Sandy said. "We're going to have a service in Montpelier on Friday. So many people back home want to pay their respects to Paula. Everyone is devastated."

"Of course," Barbara said.

"All her friends from school, at least those who haven't moved away like Paula did, are coming. Flowers have been coming to the house. Thank goodness our neighbor's been watching, taking them in. And one of her friends set up some kind of Facebook page, but I don't know much about that." Sandy's voice trailed off, as though she realized that flowers and Facebook pages weren't very important.

"How'd you get here?" Barbara asked Ken, since he'd been so worried about the logistics of coming to New York.

"Flew," he said. "I don't think . . . I don't think I could have driven in this traffic." He turned his head, as if looking through the walls to the street outside.

Barbara nodded. "Even those of us who live here can't get used to it." She paused. "Who were you trying to get on the phone?"

"Someone with the city."

"Who? What department?"

"I've been getting bounced all around. I want to talk to whoever's in charge of making sure the goddamn elevators in this city are safe. I want to know how this happened. I want to know who screwed up and got our daughter killed."

"Sure," Barbara said. "You want answers. I understand that."

"No one's telling us anything," Sandy said.

"Sometimes," Barbara said slowly, "and I certainly don't want to be making apologies on behalf of the city, but things can get overlooked. I don't mean with the elevators, but maybe that's true. I mean the personal touch. People doing their jobs forget about how this is all actually affecting you. They forget there are folks like you who are really hurting and deserve to be updated on what's going on. And everyone thinks it's someone else's job to talk to family. But an accident like what happened with Paula, that's the sort of thing that's going to be fully investigated. At some point, someone will talk to you."

"Oh, someone already came to talk to us," Sandy said. "That's why we called you."

"Yeah," Ken said.

"Who?" Barbara asked.

"Didn't give us a name," Ken said. "Sandy asked if he had a card or anything he could leave with us but he didn't give us one. He just said he'd find a way to get in touch with us if and when he needed to."

"He was," Sandy said slowly, "kind of nice. I mean, he said all the right things, about expressing his condolences and all."

"But he didn't say who he was or who he represented?" Barbara asked. "Was he someone who works here, at the funeral home?"

Sandy shook her head. "He made it sound like he was with the city, you know, the city government. Whoever looks into these types of things."

"So what did he say? What did he want? Did he find you here?"

Ken nodded. "He said he'd called around, found out where Paula had been taken after she . . . after she left the hospital."

Sandy said, "He said he wanted us—"

"—to keep our mouths shut," Ken said, cutting her off.

"What?"

"He didn't say it like that," Sandy said. "But that was the implication."

"Tell me what he said," Barbara said, feeling a tingling at the back of her neck. "Exactly. Or as best as you can remember."

Sandy thought a moment. "He said he was very sorry for our loss. He said it was a very terrible thing that happened. He said all aspects of the incident were being looked at and—"

"Is that the word he used? 'Incident'? As opposed to 'accident'?"

She looked to her husband, who nodded. "Yes. He called it an incident. Anyway, he said they were looking into it, and asked for our patience, and said we weren't to talk to anyone about it."

Barbara blinked. "Why?"

"He didn't mean, like, friends and family," Ken said. "He meant, well, people like you."

"He didn't want you talking to the press? To the media?"

Ken nodded. "He said we needed to keep a lid on this while the cause was being determined. So, anyway, this was early this morning, and after he left, I started thinking, what the hell, this is America, last time I checked, right?"

"Pretty sure," Barbara said.

"And if we want to talk about what happened to our daughter, and we ask for answers, that should be our right. But first I wanted to call around and see what they'd found out. Maybe find out which department that guy was from. And no one wants to talk to me. I keep getting passed from department to department."

"I don't understand why they'd want to keep you from talking to the press," Barbara said. "I wonder if they've approached the families of others who were in that elevator."

Sandy said, "At one point, he said they needed time to find out who did this, and then he corrected himself right away, and said, how it happened."

Barbara blinked. "Who?"

Sandy nodded. "But he took it right back."

"What'd this guy look like?"

Sandy said, "About six feet tall. Black hair, very short and trim. Nice suit and tie. Clean shaven. And his shoes," she said slowly. "I remember his shoes."

"What about his shoes?"

"They were really nicely shined. Remember that, Ken?"

"I didn't pay any attention to his goddamn shoes," he said.

"And his car was parked right out front in a no-parking zone," she said. "I watched when he left. He got in the passenger side, but whoever was driving wasn't worried about parking it illegally."

"Can you describe the car?" Barbara asked. "Any city markings on it? Did it say NYPD on the side?"

Sandy shook her head no. "It was a big SUV. All black, with dark windows."

Ken asked, "Who drives around in a car like that?"

A couple of people came to mind for Barbara. Well, not people, exactly, but agencies. Why would those agencies be interested in an elevator mishap, tragic as it was?

Twenty-One

Richard, oh, Richard!"

The mayor turned when he heard his name and saw a woman heading his way. Early eighties, her slender frame draped in black silk. Her billowy pants were half covered by a blouse that came down nearly to her knees. Her silver hair was pulled into a tight bun at the back of her head, and she viewed the world through oversized, round glasses with thick rims. Heavy on the makeup, huge black eyebrows.

She had her arms outstretched as she closed the distance between them.

"Margaret," Headley said, placing his hands on her shoulders and delivering air kisses to both cheeks. "The Queen of the Sycamores. I knew I'd been in this building before."

When he'd first heard the address of this second elevator catastrophe, he was sure there'd been a campaign fund-raiser here. Margaret Cambridge had invited all her wealthy friends to a party so extravagant they'd all felt obliged to give the maximum contribution allowed under the law to Headley's campaign. It was a shame about the rules that prohibited massive infusions of cash from individuals. Margaret's late husband, whose name adorned half a dozen buildings in the city, had left her a billion or two, not that anyone was counting, and she'd have given Headley a million bucks if she could get away with it.

"I heard you were here," said Margaret. "I walked down the whole way."

"Good God," he said. "From the penthouse?"

"Well, I didn't have much choice," she said. "They shut all the elevators down when that one went haywire. I hope they open the others before long because there's no way my ticker's going to survive the walk back up."

He rested a comforting hand on the woman's shoulder. "I'm sure they will."

"If not, a couple of those handsome firemen can carry me back up," she said, and cackled. She then quickly put her hand over her mouth and glanced around. "I better not laugh. Considering what's happened." She lowered her voice to a whisper. "It was Dr. Petrov, wasn't it?"

He nodded solemnly. "A terrible loss to the scientific community, I'm told."

"Maybe, but she was a total b-i-t-c-h," Margaret said. "I don't move as fast as I used to, and she'd see me coming for the elevator but do you think she'd hold it? Not a chance. The Commie slut."

"Well," said Headley.

Margaret leaned in closer and whispered conspiratorially, "She was Russian, you see."

"Yes, I know. I heard from the ambassador a short while ago."

"I don't like it when we've got any of those in the building. They're all spies, you know. Rockefeller's full of them."

Headley smiled. "Always good to be on your guard."

She smiled. "Will you be at the party Thursday?"

Headley had to think a moment. "Top of the Park?" he said.

Margaret nodded. "It's going to be the event of the year. A party in the sky."

"I'll be there. Wouldn't miss it. Are you on the list?"

Margaret looked incensed at the suggestion she might not have been invited. "Please," she said. "It's Rodney Coughlin's project. He and I go way back." She winked.

Headley grinned. "He's been a close friend to me for a long time, as well. Perhaps not *as* close."

Margaret sniffed. "He only gave you a bigger party to show me up, you know."

Headley gave her bony arm a friendly squeeze. "You could always throw another one."

She laughed.

"Mr. Mayor?"

Headley turned. Annette Washington, the city's chief of police, the first black woman to ever hold the position, wanted his attention. "Chief," he said.

"Sorry to interrupt." She tipped her head to draw him away.

"See you Thursday, Margaret," Headley said. "Bring your dancing shoes."

He pulled himself away and followed Washington into the building's management office off the lobby. Already there were the fire chief and a small, balding man in his forties, and a formidable-looking man in a dark suit. Early sixties, just over six feet, strong jaw. The kind of guy who, if he wasn't already in charge, looked like he was about to assume that role.

Headley looked at him and thought: *Federal.*

The man extended a hand. "Mr. Mayor. Brian Cartland, Homeland Security."

Yup, Headley thought.

What was a guy from Homeland doing at an accident like this? It didn't make any sense to Headley, unless it had something to do with the fact that the person killed in this accident was some noted Russian scientist who was an expert in who the fuck knew what?

What a crazy world, where a malfunctioning elevator could lead to a diplomatic incident. Headley was betting the ambassador had been on the line to the White House before he'd called him at City Hall. That would explain Homeland's attendance.

"Good to meet you," Headley said warily. "What's going on?" He looked at the fire and police chiefs and then turned his attention to the small, balding man.

He said, "Mayor Headley, Martin Fleck. I work for you." He flashed a smile. "Department of Buildings, elevator inspection division."

"So again I ask, what's going on?" Headley asked.

"That's very much what we want to determine," Cartland said. "Elevator accidents don't happen every day. You've had two this week, and it's only Tuesday. As a matter of routine, after yesterday's incident, we got in touch with Mr. Fleck here. As it turns out, Homeland has a suboffice in that building, so our interest was piqued. Needless to say, how an elevator goes up and down is not Homeland's area of expertise, so Mr. Fleck was able to enlighten me."

"It's true," Fleck said. "Elevator accidents *don't* happen every day. Although about thirty people, on average, are killed in elevator mishaps every year, and some seventeen thousand Americans are injured on an annual basis, although those numbers also include escalators."

"Okay," said Headley slowly.

"And of those thirty who are killed, probably about half of them are going to be folks who work on them. An elevator technician slips and falls down the shaft, or he's at the base of the shaft and an elevator comes down and crushes him, or he gets caught between the moving parts. All totally avoidable, but someone gets careless. Horrible when it happens, but not totally shocking, given the dangerous conditions in which an elevator technician works."

Headley was getting impatient, but decided to let Fleck continue with Elevator 101.

"Stats show that one in every twelve million elevator trips results in a mishap, and often that may be as simple as a door failing to close or open properly," Fleck continued. "When passengers in an elevator are injured, it's not usually a fault of the elevator itself. For example, a woman goes into an elevator with some big flowing scarf and it gets caught in the doors, and the elevator stars to rise and that scarf is stuck at the floor below and the other end is still wrapped tightly around the woman's neck and—"

"I get the picture," the mayor said.

"Sometimes you get an idiot who wants to elevator-surf and—"

"I'm sorry, what?" asked Headley.

"Elevator-surf. Gaining access to the shaft and riding on top of the car for the thrill of it. Kids do it. The problem is, there are cables galore and parts that stick out, and the cables are greasy, and you're either going to fall and get caught between the car and the shaft, or—"

"Just tell me what happened here," the mayor said.

"Well," Fleck said, "Petrov, this Russian science lady, she's partly to blame."

Headley gave the Homeland agent a weary glance. "If it was her fault, why are we all standing here?"

"It wasn't her fault that the elevator stopped," Fleck said. "It was her mistake to climb out. Actually, if she'd stopped there, she'd have been okay, but according to the boy, she reached back into the opening for her purse and that was when the elevator suddenly continued its descent, and she got caught and, well, lost her head. But the fact that the elevator stopped in the first place is the thing we're looking at."

"We think it may have been sabotaged," Cartland said.

"Sabotaged how?"

"We're not sure," the Homeland Security agent said.

"Not sure?"

"It might have been hacked."

The mayor's eyes widened. "Hacked? Is that possible?"

"Yes," Cartland said. "It's not an easy thing to do, but it can be done. The elevator system here was recently upgraded. Loads of high-tech stuff. The more high-tech things get, the greater chance there is of messing about with them. Those old-fashioned ones, with the big metal gates you had to close, that needed a guy to run them, those didn't get hacked."

"But you don't have any actual proof that that's what happened," the mayor said.

"No," said Cartland.

This time, Fleck weighed in. "In yesterday's incident, as far as we can tell, given that there are no survivors, the car started acting like it had a mind of its own. Passing floors riders had pressed buttons for. That part sounds a bit like a hack, like someone was messing with the system. They've got an upgraded system over there, too. So up and down they went, and then, when they were around the twentieth floor, the car plummeted. That suggests a total override of the system."

"How could that happen?"

"If someone had control of it. Someone outside the elevator itself."

Headley looked at Cartland. "What the fuck are we looking at here?"

The Homeland Security agent looked grim. "We're still assessing. But we have to consider the possibility that one or both of these elevator accidents were not accidents at all."

Headley studied the man. "So if they weren't accidents, who's doing it? If you're here, does that mean terrorism? Does ISIS know how to hack elevators? They've decided to stop running cars and trucks into crowds? Do you know how ridiculous that sounds? I mean, as far as terrorism is concerned, it's about the most inefficient method I can imagine. And not only that, the level of expertise required would be off the scale. You want to kill a bunch of people, there are lots of easier ways to go about it."

"I don't disagree," Cartland said. "But it doesn't change the facts that have been presented to us."

"Let me see if I get what you're saying. Someone *might* have tampered with one or two elevators. Someone *might* have hacked in, or sabotaged the mechanism, but you really don't know yet. Has anyone claimed responsibility?"

Cartland shook his head. "Not for this, specifically."

"Is there anyone you think *might* claim responsibility?"

"We have been dealing, lately, with an uptick in domestic terrorist acts. In Seattle, in Portland. Just yesterday in Boston. The group responsible for those incidents might be looking for a higher profile. They're very much on our watch list. But there's no shortage, in this country, of crazy individuals with an ax to grind."

"But so far, no one's taking credit."

Cartland shook his head again.

"Could it be you guys are blowing something out of proportion, looking for something that's not there, to justify your existence?"

Cartland clearly did not think that deserved a response, and said nothing.

"What would you have me do?" Headley asked. "Tell New Yorkers to stop using the elevators until further notice? You have any idea what kind of chaos that would create in a vertical city like this? The entire fucking town would come to a halt."

"We should show him," Fleck said to Cartland.

"Show me what?" the mayor said.

Cartland said, "Let's take a walk upstairs. There's something you need to see."

Twenty-Two

Welcome back to *New York Day*," said the woman, looking into the camera. "I'm Anjelica Briscoe."

Briscoe adopted a stern expression. "A bombing in a Seattle coffee shop. More bombings in Portland and Boston. People dead, and wounded. Disgusting, cowardly acts. What do they have in common, and what do these cities have in common? Many things, of course, but one is that they're coastal cities, and that makes them, symbolically, targets for those who identify themselves as members of the Flyovers, a domestic extremist group whose somewhat self-deprecating name is actually a shot at the so-called coastal elites, the people who fly from New York or Boston to Los Angeles and San Francisco and back again. They feel these elites literally *look down* on the rest of the country and hold the people who live there in contempt. Our guest here today is the head of the Flyovers, Eugene Clement. Mr. Clement, thank you for coming in to speak with us here today."

The camera panned to the other end of the desk, where Clement sat, grim-faced.

"I think your characterization of what the Flyovers stand for is grossly unfair and inaccurate," Clement said.

Briscoe looked him straight in the eye and said, "The Flyovers has been branded by some as a terrorist group. Is it?"

"Absolutely not. That's a reckless assertion," he said. "The Flyovers is made up of good, decent American citizens who want nothing more than to be recognized for their contributions to this great country."

"You heard what I said off the top. Law enforcement officials say these bombings in various coastal cities are very possibly the work of Flyovers adherents."

The blood vessel in Clement's right temple could be seen pulsing as he leaned forward in his chair and said, "These bombings are despicable, horrible acts. To even suggest they have anything to do with us breaks my heart, outrages me."

"So the Flyovers eschew violence as a means to highlight their issues?"

"Without question," he said.

"And yet, you were among the armed militants involved in the occupation of a national wildlife refuge in Colorado last year. Are you going to tell me that wasn't a violent act?"

Eugene Clement appeared slighty taken aback by the question. He took a moment to respond. "A couple of things, Anjelica. First, that was not an event connected in any way to the Flyovers. Second, no one was injured in that, well, what you call an occupation. I would call it a demonstration against abusive federal authority. Washington controls millions of acres of land in the state that it has no business being involved in. That was a protest aimed directly at the federal government. Which, thank God, did not come in with guns blazing and kill a peaceful protester, as they did at a similar demonstration a few years ago."

"But there's a lot of crossover in beliefs between those groups and the Flyovers."

"Some, perhaps," he acknowledged. "But that's very true on the left, as well. We haven't held all liberals to account for the actions of the Black Panthers or the Symbionese Liberation Army or, more recently, groups like Antifa."

"Yes, but—"

"What the Flyovers is seeking to address is the current cultural divide, not government interference in our lives. Our goal is an attitude change. We want to . . . educate the Americans living along the coasts, the folks who seem to be unaware that there is *another* America. We're more than a caricature, more than a bunch of NASCAR-loving, rib-eating, beer-swilling rubes. Not that being a NASCAR-loving, rib-eating beer drinker is anything to be ashamed of." He managed a rueful smile. "That sounds like a great afternoon to me. Anyway, the coast is something of a metaphor. There are people throughout the country who hold the views we seek to challenge. You can find them right here in New York, I would imagine."

"But isn't that exactly what *you* have reduced the so-called coast-ers to? A cliché? Sushi-eating, latte-drinking, gluten-avoiding, Prius-driving elites?"

Clement shook his head. "Not at all. As I said, we're just trying to educate."

"By blowing things up."

Clement's cheeks flushed. "No. That Greatest Generation you've heard so much about? You'll find it in the heart of the country. And you'll find their sons and daughters and grandsons and grand-daughters there, too. But some of this country's most prominent pol-iticians seem to have forgotten that. Only a couple of years ago, that woman who nearly became president, who even won the popular vote, said, and I quote, 'I won the places that are optimistic, diverse, dynamic, moving forward.'" He sneered. "You know, coastal places. What an insult to the rest of the country."

"You have to admit that many of the people who swear allegiance to the Flyovers organization—"

"That's laying it on a bit heavy. We hardly have a pledge of alle-giance."

"Many of your followers, your adherents, those that speak their mind on your comments page, have advocated the kinds of terrorist acts we've seen lately."

"You know, Anjelica, many urbanites believe the only amendment we care about is the second one. Well, nothing could be further from the truth. We believe, as all good Americans do, in the First Amendment. Freedom of speech. I may not like what some of these people have to say, but I would defend their right to say it. Just as I defend your right to speak to me in condescending and belittling terms."

The host was unfazed. "Some of the things your followers say constitute hate speech."

Clement frowned. "What is hate speech, exactly? It's hate speech when you don't like something I've said. But when you attack me for what I said, can't your words also be defined as hateful?" He leaned in again. "What we need to do is find common ground. You speak your mind and I'll speak mine, and that way we'll find a way to meet in the middle. Think of all the things that we have in common. We want good jobs, we want the best for our families, we want a secure future."

"You make yourself sound like a peacemaker when the FBI and Homeland Security have suggested the exact opposite. Many of your members also belong to white supremacist, white nationalist organizations. Some are members of the KKK."

Clement shrugged. "And I can find you plenty of people of color who share their sentiments when it comes to coastal folks looking down their noses at us. That's what I mean about meeting in the middle, which is an apt metaphor when you're talking about the middle of the country. We've got people talking to each other who otherwise might never do so. We *want* to bring people together, to start a dialogue. We won't get anywhere throwing insults at each other."

The interviewer grinned slyly. "If you can take a mild criticism here, Mr. Clement, wouldn't it be more accurate to call your group the *Flown Overs*, since that's who you are. It's the coastal folks who are flying over you."

Clement gave her a withering look. "And there you have it in a single question. The contempt. The 'we're so much smarter than you' comeback."

Briscoe suddenly looked regretful, aware she had gone too far. She touched her ear, an indication she was getting a message from the control room. "Mr. Clement, we've run a bit over here, but I wanted to thank you for agreeing to come in and speak to us."

He said nothing.

"I do have one last question."

"Of course."

"Given the way your organization feels about coastal cities and the people who live there, what are you doing in New York?"

"My wife and I are celebrating our anniversary. Or we were, until you dragged me in here." He offered up a self-deprecating laugh and a smile. "The fact is," he said, "I love New York."

———————

"How dare she say those things to you," Estelle Clement said when her husband returned to the TV studio's green room, where guests waited for their turn to go on air. There was a monitor in the room, and she had watched the segment. She lowered her voice and said, "What a bitch."

Clement scowled. "The way she talked to me," he said, his voice trailing off as he grabbed her by the arm and steered her into the hallway.

"You're hurting me," she said.

He eased his grip but did not let go of her as they headed for the lobby.

"You should sue," Estelle said. "You could sue her for what she said."

The studio was on the fourth floor of a building on Columbus Circle. There were several people waiting at the bank of elevators by the reception desk. Clement said, "Let's take the stairs."

"Do we have—"

"I just want to get out of here as fast as I can," he said, already leading her toward a door with an Exit sign over it. Estelle, sensing his anger, did not object.

When they came out onto the street, Clement stopped for a moment to compose himself.

"Did you hear what I said up there?" Estelle asked. "You should sue her and the network for—"

"No," he said firmly. "It's more than just one arrogant TV host or one network. It's a bigger battle than that."

Estelle placed a hand on his arm. "What do you want to do? Do you want to go home? We can, you know. If this has ruined everything, we don't have to stay. I can see if I can get our money back on the tickets."

"Tickets?" he said.

"You remember we have tickets for that show tonight. But it's okay, we can—"

"No, we're going." He lifted his head and gave it a small shake, as though trying to rid himself of the anger he felt. Then he forced his mouth into a smile. "We're not going let them stop us from having a good time."

Estelle smiled. "You're sure?"

Clement nodded. "I'd forgotten about the show. What are we seeing?"

"It's that one with all the dancing," Estelle said. "I know that doesn't exactly narrow it down. You're probably going to hate it, anyway."

"All those nancy boys prancing about the stage? I wouldn't miss it for the world. In the meantime, I'm going to take you out for a fabulous lunch. How does the Capital Grille sound?"

"Sure," his wife said.

"I'll get us a cab," he said. "You stay here."

He stepped off the sidewalk and walked out between two parked cars. He came up around the side of one of them as he waved his hand in the air.

Behind him, he heard a window power down.

"Hey," someone said.

Eugene Clement did not turn around when he heard Bucky's voice. Looking up the street, Clement said, "Still on track?"

"Yes."

"Keep your eyes open. The world knows I'm here. There's probably a heightened alert already."

"Got it."

"We're good to go."

Clement heard the window power up as a yellow cab swerved across the street and came to a stop in front of him. Clement opened the back door and called out to his wife.

"Madam," he said, "your chariot has arrived."

Twenty-Three

Barbara had been in the funeral home for the better part of half an hour.

Chris Vallins was getting tired of waiting across the street for her to come out. It wasn't hard to figure out why she might be here, given that in her column she'd written about losing a friend in the Monday elevator accident. The dead woman's name had been Paula Chatsworth.

To confirm, he had looked up this funeral home on his phone and called to ask if the Chatsworth service would be held there. *And if so, when? Asking for a friend,* he said. The woman who answered said that while the home had been involved, the service for the Chatsworth woman was going to be held up in Montpelier.

Ah, well, thank you very much, he said.

Chris believed he was going to have to do more than just follow Barbara Matheson around and make a few online inquiries. If you really wanted to find the dirt on someone, you broke into their place. You got on their computer and read their emails. You looked into the bottom bedroom dresser drawer and checked out the sex toys.

But one thing had come out of today's efforts that had piqued his curiosity. Who was the woman Barbara had met with at the Morning Star? They hadn't talked long. The other woman hadn't even ordered breakfast. Was she a source? Was she someone passing along information to Barbara? Vallins could not recall seeing the woman in the time he had been working for the mayor's office, but the city employed a lot of people who could be privy to the kind of information Barbara would like to have. Even though Chris had seen her from across the street, he was confident he'd recognize the woman if he saw her again. And he had her picture.

Vallins started hearing music and glanced to the north. A shabbily dressed man was coming his way, pushing a rickety shopping cart with nothing in it but an '80s-style boom box that was playing at full volume.

"You can't always get what you want . . ."

Wasn't that the truth, Vallins thought, giving the man a nod as he wheeled his cart past him. The man was bobbing his head to the music and took one hand off the cart's handle long enough to give Vallins a thumbs-up.

Vallins couldn't help but smile.

Finally, Barbara emerged from the funeral home and started walking back toward Second Avenue.

Vallins was on the move again.

When the *Manhattan Today* writer got to the corner, she crossed Twenty-Seventh, looking down at the phone in her hand the entire time. A cab shot past, the driver giving her the horn. Without even looking up, Barbara sent her free hand skyward and gave the cabbie the finger.

She went into the Duane Reade on the corner.

Chris followed her in, still keeping his distance, and found that Barbara had gone down the feminine hygiene products aisle. He knew he was going to look especially conspicuous hanging around that part of the store, so he decided to go back outside and wait for her to emerge. He found a spot a few yards down the sidewalk where he could watch the door of the drug store.

While he waited, his own phone rang. He dug it out of his jacket, saw *Valerie* on the screen.

"Yeah," he said.

"Where the hell are you?" Valerie asked.

"I'm running an errand for the mayor."

"What kind of errand?"

"If he wanted you to know I'm guessing he would have told you."

A sigh at the other end. Then, "There's been another elevator plunge."

"You're shittin' me."

"No."

"Where?"

"On York, just south of Rockefeller University. Some big-deal Russian scientist got killed."

"Jesus," Chris said. "Are you there?"

"Yeah. Homeland Security's here, too."

"What?"

"Yeah. Maybe because of who it was who got killed. You ever heard of Fanya Petrov?"

"No. Should I?"

"Beats me."

Barbara, a small Duane Reade bag in hand, came out of the store. She glanced into the bag, as if checking that she remembered everything.

"I gotta go," Chris told Valerie. Without waiting for a response, he ended the call and slipped the phone back into his jacket.

Barbara was heading north, holding the bag in her left hand, her phone in her right. As she crossed Twenty-Eighth Street, she put the phone to her ear, spoke to someone. The call lasted little more than thirty seconds, which led Chris to think maybe she'd only left a voice mail.

As she continued on, she appeared to be searching for something on her phone. Maybe another number, someone else she wanted to get in touch with. Or maybe she was on some site, thumbing through headlines.

She did write a column, after all, Chris thought, making an allowance for how she never put the phone away. She probably read through several dozen news sites every day. And then she'd be calling people and interviewing them and turning the shit they said into a piece for *Manhattan Today*. But right now, in the wake of what she had written lately about the mayor, it would be nice to know exactly what she was reading and who she might be getting in touch with. And why had she gone to the funeral home, anyway? Was it simply to offer condolences, or was there more to it than that?

Chris found himself closing the distance between himself and Barbara, fooling himself into thinking that if he got near enough, he'd be able to see what was on her phone before she put it away, or to her ear. Chris had an astounding number of talents, skills that no one even knew about, but there were limits to what he could do.

Between Thirtieth and Thirty-First, Barbara nearly walked into an elderly woman coming in the other direction. Her bat-like radar had her dodging out of the way just in time.

As they neared Thirty-Second Street, Chris started to worry.

If Barbara had been looking up as she approached the intersection on the west side of Second, she might have noticed the Don't Walk warning blazing from the traffic signal on the other side. But Barbara, oblivious, kept on walking.

Coming from the left, a once-white van nearly eaten away by rust was approaching at high speed. It careened around a taxi that had pulled over to pick up a fare. The driver was flooring it, hoping to make it across Second before the light turned red. The engine roared hoarsely, as if suffering from automotive emphysema.

Barbara stepped off the sidewalk and into the intersection.

Everything happened in milliseconds. Chris expected Barbara's seemingly innate sense of where she was and what was going on around her to kick in.

As the truck bore down on her, Chris realized with startling clarity that was not going to happen.

Fuck, he thought.

Twenty-Four

When Jerry Bourque and Lois Delgado finished talking to Gunther Willem, manager of Simpson Elevator, they went into the back shop to talk to the other employees. The company, counting Willem and the woman in the office, had nine. Eight, now that Petrenko was going to be removed from the payroll. Four more were on the premises, two were out on a call together.

Bourque and Delgado split them up, each interviewing two men. All four were asked further questions about the dead man, whether they had noticed anything out of the ordinary with him in recent weeks, whether he seemed on edge, worried about anything. Did Petrenko have any vices he kept secret from his wife? Did he gamble? Did he use drugs? Was he seeing anyone on the side? Did he frequent prostitutes?

And, finally, who was the man who'd come to visit him? The one he went out onto the street to talk to?

None of the four claimed to have seen Petrenko talking to the mystery man.

The two employees not on-site were on a call at a twelve-story apartment building on Clermont Avenue in Brooklyn, just south of the Brooklyn Navy Yard.

Delgado drove. They parked on the street and buzzed the superintendent when they entered the lobby. The building's two elevators

were out of commission during the servicing, and the two technicians from Simpson Elevator were on the twelfth floor.

"Can they get one going?" Bourque asked.

The super said, "I told them, can you do one at a time? But no,
they shut them both down at once. Everyone in the building is complaining."

"No problem," Delgado said. "We'll take the stairs."

A wave of anxiety washed over Bourque.

His lungs felt absolutely fine. He hadn't taken a hit off his inhaler yet today. Climbing eleven flights of stairs shouldn't have been
a problem for him. A few months ago, he might have taken half those
flights two steps at a time.

But that was before.

Could he make it to the twelfth floor? What if his airways started
to constrict along the way? And Bourque had been dealing with this
issue long enough to know that just worrying about an attack was
enough to bring one on.

I'll be fine, he told himself. *I can do this. Just don't think—*

It was like, Bourque realized, when someone told you not to think
about an elephant, Dumbo popped into your head.

So when Bourque told himself *Don't think about the drops,* he
thought about the drops.

"You coming?" Delgado said to her partner.

"Right behind you," he said.

It hit him by the fourth floor. His windpipe started to shrink
down to the size of a straw.

When they were nearly to the fifth, Bourque called up to Delgado, who was half a dozen steps ahead, "I just got a text."

Delgado glanced back, stopped.

"Just go on, I'll catch up," he said, taking the phone from his jacket, looking at the screen and nodding as if to confirm he was right about receiving a message.

"What is it?" Delgado asked.

"I got it," Bourque said dismissively.

Delgado climbed on.

Once she'd made a turn in the stairwell and was out of sight, Bourque put the phone back into his jacket. He gripped the railing with one hand to steady himself, then dug into his pocket with the other and came out with his inhaler.

But before wrapping his mouth around it, he decided to give his doctor's advice one more try.

Focus.

What had he suggested? Focus on five things you see. Five things you hear.

I'm in a fucking concrete stairwell. There aren't five things to see or five things to hear.

That was okay. He could wing it. Like, think of five Paul Newman movies.

There was *The Sting. Cool Hand Luke. Harper.* That was three. Oh, and *The Verdict* and that one where he was the pool hustler, what the hell was that one called. Weren't there actually two? There was the original, that was—fuck, *The Hustler.* A movie about a pool hustler might just be called *The Hustler.* But then, twenty-five years later, he reprised the character in a movie with Tom Cruise. Had *Color* in the title. What the hell was that one—

He was still wheezing.

From a couple of floors above, Delgado's voice echoed, "You okay down there?"

"Yeah!" he managed to shout. "Coming!"

The hell with it.

He exhaled, put the puffer between his lips, squeezed it, and drew the medicated mist deep into his lungs. Keeping his lips sealed, he did a mental count to ten, then exhaled. He repeated the process, then slipped the inhaler back into his pocket.

Christ, it was all he could do to hold his breath for ten seconds. You watched these movies, where James Bond is rescuing someone underwater for minutes at a time without coming up for air. How the hell was that even possible?

Plenty of takes, that was how.

Bourque felt his windpipe enlarging, his lungs filling with the stale air of the stairwell. Time to move on.

He caught up with his partner at the tenth floor. Even she had stopped to catch her breath, and Bourque took pleasure in overtaking her. "Haven't got all day," he said.

"Bite me," Delgado said.

They came out onto the twelfth floor and at the hallway's end, directly in front of an open elevator door, were two men on their knees, huddled over a large toolbox. One was white, thin, probably midforties; the other was black, heavyset, late twenties. Even from the end of the hallway, the detectives could tell that there was no elevator car beyond the opening. What they could see was the cinder block back wall of the shaft and various vertical cables.

"Hey," Bourque said.

The black one turned, then said to his partner, "Cops are here."

The two men stood. Bourque and Delgado showed their badges and offered hands to shake but the repairmen begged off, displaying oily, greasy palms.

"I'm Walter," the older man said. "This is Terrence."

Terrence nodded. "They told us you were coming."

"So you know what this is about," Delgado said.

"Can't believe Otto's dead," Walter said. "Jesus. You do what we do for a living, you figure if you're gonna go, it'll probably be because you went through an open door by mistake," at which point he nodded toward the elevator shaft.

"Yeah," said Terrence, and then, gesturing toward his coworker, "or some moron knocks you in."

"What happened to him?" Walter asked.

Bourque did the usual dance of not answering and asked the two men the same questions he and Delgado had asked the others. Had they noticed anything odd about Otto in recent weeks?

They had not.

Had they seen the man who'd dropped by to see him at Simpson Elevator?

Again, they both shook their heads.

"Why?" asked Walter. "You think this guy did something to Otto?"

"We'd like to talk to him," Delgado said.

Terrence said, "Hang on."

"What?" Delgado asked.

He dug a rag out of his pocket and started to wipe off his hands. "So I've been wanting to buy a car. Like, I always liked Mustangs, so I've been going through the online ads, you know, seeing if someone has a decent used one, because no way I can afford a new one, and I'm not totally nuts about the latest design, anyway. I kind of like the ones from around 2005, 2006, you know?"

"Okay," said Bourque.

"So I find one in Queens and I call the guy. It's a 2005, and he's asking about thirty-five hundred for it, and I tell him I want to have a look at it, but I'm kinda busy, and he says, where d'ya work, I could run it by, you could check it out. Which makes the guy sound a bit desperate, so I'm thinking he might take a lowball offer, so I say okay.

So he comes over, this is like, two weeks ago. Parks it at the curb and I come out to have a look at it."

Walter said, "Terrence here takes a long time to get to the point."

"That's okay," Bourque said.

His hands cleared of the worst of the grease, he pulled a phone from his pocket and tapped on the photos icon.

"I wanted to take a few pictures of it, from all angles. Told the guy I wasn't ready to make up my mind but having some shots to refresh my memory later would be a good idea. So, like, here's the shots."

He held the camera in front of the detectives and swiped through the pictures. Many of them were close-ups of parts of the blue car, including one of the rear wheel well.

"A lot of rust there. I could probably fix it myself, but if I made a big deal about it he'd probably come down a bit more. Okay, here's the one I was thinking of."

The photo he'd landed on was a full shot of the car, parked on the street.

"So, if you look back here, that's Otto," he said. "On the sidewalk."

"May I?" Bourque asked, holding out his hand.

Terrence gave him the phone. With his index finger and thumb, Bourque enlarged the photo, zeroing in on the background. There was another car beyond the Mustang. A plain, dark sedan. One man was leaning against it, arms folded, talking to Otto, perched on the curb. The man was white, maybe six feet, gray hair. He looked to be wearing a suit. But the bigger Bourque made the picture, the less distinct it became.

"What about the car?" Delgado asked.

Bourque shifted the focus to the car. The Mustang in the foreground cut off the left half of the orangey-yellow plate, and the part that could be seen was blurry.

"New York plate," Bourque said.

"That narrows it down," Delgado said.

"Last two numbers 1 and 3."

"Maybe."

Bourque tapped the screen a couple of times. "Just want to know when. . . . this was taken." He squinted. "Here we go. This looks like middle of last month? The fifteenth?"

"That sounds right," Terrence said.

Bourque said, "I'm going to email this to myself."

"Sure, yeah, okay."

Bourque did a few more taps, then hit Send. Seconds later, there was a familiar ding from his jacket pocket.

Terrence had never gotten a closer look at Otto's friend, and had never learned anything about him. Same with Walter.

"Did you buy the Mustang?" Bourque asked.

Terrence grinned. "I did. Got it for two grand."

Delgado asked, pointing toward the open door, "What's wrong with the elevator?"

Walter shrugged. "Just routine maintenance."

Delgado took a step closer, stuck her head beyond the door's edge, and peered down the shaft. Twelve floors down to the bottom.

The car was twelve floors down, at the bottom.

"Yikes," she said.

Walter chuckled. "That's nothing. Come into Manhattan sometime. You look down, you think you can see all the way to hell."

When they returned to their car, Delgado got behind the wheel of their unmarked cruiser, waited until Bourque was settled in beside her, then got out her phone. She began tapping at the screen.

"What?" Bourque said.

"Hang on," she said. Her phone made a brief *woop* sound. She'd sent a text.

Before Bourque could quiz her again, he heard the ding of an incoming text on his own phone. He reached into his jacket, saw the one-word message from Delgado:

HI.

He looked from his phone to her.

"I heard that one," she said. "Funny I didn't hear the other two. In the stairwell, or on the High Line."

She put the car in drive and hit the gas.

Twenty-Five

*S*ave her? *Or not save her?*

It was incredible how many thoughts could go through one's head so quickly. But even in the fraction of a second that Chris Vallins had to make a decision, he realized what he had here was an opportunity. As that truck bore down on Barbara, whose eyes were still focused on her damn phone, Chris saw that a solution to the mayor's problem had presented itself. In a millisecond, this walking-talking-writing thorn in the mayor's paw could be dead.

A gift has been handed to us.

Some gifts, it turned out, were more difficult to accept than others.

He darted into the street like an Olympic runner who'd just heard the shot from the starter's pistol. His left arm went into the air, palm facing the truck, as if he were Superman and could stop its progress. Even if he could have, the truck swerved.

Barbara looked up from her phone.

Her head turned a couple of degrees in the direction of the truck, but there wasn't time for her to get a full view of it. Chris had thrown his right arm around her waist. He was moving so quickly that she was literally swept off her feet.

And then, basically thrown.

It was, pretty much, a football tackle. Barbara went down, hitting the pavement just shy of the opposite corner. Chris went down with her, the knuckles of his right hand scraping the pavement, tearing his glove. Barbara let out a scream as her right elbow hit asphalt, but it was drowned out by the brake squeal, and the subsequent gunning of the engine, from the truck. It sped through the intersection. The driver, knowing that at least he hadn't killed anyone, evidently saw no reason to hang around.

Barbara's phone slipped from her hand and skittered across the pavement, bouncing off the curb. Her Duane Reade bag was airborne. When it landed, some twenty feet away, its contents—a box of Tampax, a stick of Halls lemon cough candies, and a bottle of shampoo—scattered across the pavement.

"Shit!" she cried. Instead of trying to get up, she rolled over onto her back. She winced as she gripped her elbow. "Fuck!"

Chris had hit the ground hard, too, but at least he knew what was coming, and had thrown himself into a roll as he struck pavement. As he slowly got to his feet, half a dozen people gathered. An elderly woman who'd gone to fetch Barbara's phone glanced at Chris and said, "Well done!"

As she stood over Barbara, ready to hand her the phone, she asked Barbara, "Do you need an ambulance?"

"I think . . . I think I'm okay," Barbara said. "It just hurts like a motherfucker, is all."

Chris watched Barbara working her arm, try to determine whether her elbow was broken. She could move it without screaming, so that was a good sign. He was pretty sure, despite the close contact he'd had with Barbara, she'd not actually seen him. She didn't know who had pulled her from the van's path. The identity of her Good Samaritan could remain a mystery.

Perfect.

All he had to do was walk away, blend in with others on the sidewalk. He started heading north.

"Hey!"

Chris was pretty sure who was doing the yelling, and who was being yelled at.

"You! With the hat!"

Chris pulled the ball cap lower onto his forehead and slowly turned. Barbara had gotten to a standing position. The old woman had moved on, but a young man in a U.S. Postal Service uniform and a short, round-shouldered woman with a wheeled, wire cart full of groceries were on either side of her, offering support. Someone had gathered her Duane Reade purchases and put them back in the bag. Barbara, now standing on her own, was staring at him.

Chris slowly pointed a finger to his own chest, pretending to be puzzled.

"Yeah, you!" she said, pointing. "Jesus, you play for the Jets?"

She's going to recognize me. Get ahead of this. Don't let her be the one . . .

He took a step toward her, let his jaw drop with feigned astonishment.

"Christ, it's you," he said.

Barbara blinked a couple of times, as though trying to focus. "What?"

He took off the hat. "I was in the limo. Yesterday. I work for the mayor."

Barbara's astonishment appeared 100 percent genuine. "I don't believe it. It *is* you. Uh . . . Chris something."

"Vallins," he said, moving in closer. He looked at the man and woman flanking her. "It's okay," he said. "I got this."

They nodded with relief that they didn't have to hang around.

"What the hell were you doing, walking off? You fucking saved my life."

He shrugged. "You looked okay, so I didn't think I was needed. *Are* you okay?"

"I think so, but my elbow hurts like a son of a bitch."

"You should get it checked out. You should go to the hospital."

"I've had enough of hospitals," she said. "I just need to put some ice on it."

Chris appeared to be considering something. "Look," he said, "my place is only a couple of blocks from here, and if I don't have ice, I've probably got some frozen dinners that'd do the trick."

She eyed him warily.

"How'd you do it?" she asked.

"It was a simple tackle. Nothing to it."

"No, not that. Was the guy driving the van in on it? He waited until I got there, and you were in position?"

He met her skeptical eyes with his. "You figured it out. I come from a long line of conspirators. My dad helped fake the moon landing. You want some fucking ice for your elbow or not?"

Twenty-Six

Mayor Headley followed Brian Cartland, of Homeland Security, NYPD chief Annette Washington, and Martin Fleck, from the city department that oversaw elevator operations, to a stairwell. The fire chief, who'd evidently been up here earlier with Fleck, had stayed in the lobby.

Headley had been worried they were heading all the way up to the hallway where they'd find the rest of Fanya Petrov. But it turned out that, for now, they were going only as far as the second floor.

They came out onto a hallway and approached the four elevators. Only one had the doors in the open position. A police officer was standing guard, keeping people away, because there was no elevator car beyond the opening. At least, not one that anyone could step into.

But someone could step *onto* it.

Given that the car was one floor below, at lobby level, what the mayor and others were looking at was the roof of the elevator car. Two large steel beams ran crossways, left to right, across the top of the middle of the car. Attached to it were various cables and metal boxes with large buttons on them. More cables, electrical ones, were snaked neatly across the top of the car. In the far left corner was what appeared to be a hatch.

Headley pointed. "That's where people can get out?"

"They can be rescued from there," Fleck said. "But it's not like in the movies where you see passengers pushing it aside and getting out themselves. It's locked. It can only be opened by rescue workers."

Headley pointed tentatively into the shaft. "Can I poke my head in there?"

Fleck nodded.

The mayor stood at the edge, braced himself with one hand where the door slid into the wall, and leaned in. He craned his neck around to look up. The shaft's four corners appeared to disappear into infinity.

"Christ," he said, and pulled himself back into the hallway. "So what did you want to show me?"

Cartland pointed to something close to the hatch. "You see that?"

Headley squinted. "What?"

Cartland looked at Fleck. "Can you help us here?"

Fleck stepped from the hallway, directly onto the roof of the elevator. Headley was the only one to give a short gasp. But the elevator was as solid under Fleck's feet as if he were standing in the lobby. He lifted his leg over the beam to get closer to the far side of the car's roof.

He knelt down and indicated, without touching it, a small black box, not much bigger than a cell phone but thicker, that had a short black wand attached.

"This is an antenna," Fleck said. "And this," he said, pointing to the box, "is a remote pinhole camera."

Headley watched. "Go on."

"Someone's drilled a small hole here that provides a view of what's happening inside the car."

Fleck stood, used one of the beams to lean against. He looked as relaxed as if he were sitting on a park bench.

"Cameras in an elevator don't seem all that unusual," Headley said.

Fleck said, "People think cameras are everywhere, but that's not necessarily so with elevators. There may be cameras in the hallways and the lobbies so you see who's going in and out of the elevators. But while they're inside? Not so much. Freight elevators, that's a different story sometimes. Security likes to keep tabs on those."

"But some buildings must have cameras in the regular elevators," the mayor said.

"You're right," Fleck said. "But we've talked to building management. They don't have them here. The other elevators? No cameras in those."

Headley looked at the man from Homeland Security and the police chief. Their faces were grim.

"Only this one," Cartland said, for emphasis. "Well, and one other."

Headley waited.

"We had a look at the elevator from yesterday. There was a camera attached to the roof of that car, too. Like this one. It was the only elevator in the building outfitted that way."

"Jesus Christ," Headley said.

"We have a definite link between both events," Annette Washington said. "Same kind of camera, identical placement."

"What you're telling me," Headley said, "is that somebody could have been watching everything that happened. Somebody could have watched those people die yesterday. Somebody could have watched that scientist's head come off."

No one said anything.

"Fucking hell," Headley said. He pointed first to the camera, then to the beams and other equipment that sat atop the elevator car. "Fingerprints?"

"Working on it," Washington said.

"And what about surveillance cameras? In the halls, and the lobby?"

Cartland said, "We don't know when this camera might have been placed here. It could have been a week ago, a month ago, or a year. Fleck here is going to have to go back and see when this elevator was last inspected. It's doubtful this would have been overlooked during an inspection. That'd mean it was outfitted with the camera since then." He sighed. "We don't know how far ahead this was planned."

Fleck said, "My experience, someone walks in wearing maintenance coveralls and a hard hat, he can pretty much get into any part of a building he wants."

"This is unbelievable," Headley said. He turned on Fleck. "It's your fucking department! Aren't your people looking for this kind of thing?"

Fleck didn't flinch. "No. We're looking for mechanical and safety problems, although like Mr. Cartland said, I'd like to think that our people would have noticed this."

Headley tried to stare him down. "'Like to think'?"

Cartland cleared his throat. "If you've got the strength to walk up a few more floors, Fleck's got something else to show you."

Headley trembled at the thought of having to look at the headless corpse. Surely they didn't need him to see that.

"If you're asking me to see what's left of Dr. Petrov up there, you can spare me the trouble," Headley asked. "*Is* her body still up there?"

Cartland nodded gravely.

"Seeing her head was enough," the mayor said.

Fleck threw his leg back over the beam, got himself off the roof and back into the hallway. He dusted himself off and then looked at the mayor.

"That's not what we want you to have a look at," he said.

"What then?"

"As bad as what you've seen so far," he said, "it gets worse."

Twenty-Seven

Driving back into Manhattan, looking straight ahead as she drove over the Queensboro Bridge, Lois Delgado said, "So talk to me."

Jerry Bourque said, "Talk to you about what?"

She glanced his way. "What's with the texts that aren't texts? I've got ears, you know. If someone had sent you a text, I'd have heard it."

Bourque ignored her, watched the traffic.

"You can't breathe," she said. "You're sneaking puffs on that thing."

Now Bourque shot her a look.

"What?" she said. "What kind of detective would I be if I hadn't noticed?"

Bourque, looking away, said, "I use it, the odd time."

She sighed. "It's not allergies or bronchitis or anything like that, is it? If it was, you wouldn't be hiding it. It's in your head, right?" Before he could reply, she said, "Shit. It's not like cancer, is it? Emphysema? I've never seen you smoke."

"I don't have cancer and I don't have emphysema."

"So it's the other thing."

Bourque said nothing.

"Maybe you came back too soon."

"I took two weeks. I was fine. I could have taken two years. It wouldn't have made any difference."

Delgado said, "You don't know that. What happened to you, that kind of shit can mess you up. There's no shame in not coming back until you're ready."

She decided not to push, and drove a few more blocks without saying anything, except for one "Fuckin' asshole" when a cab cut her off.

"The doctor says there's nothing physiological," Bourque finally said.

"Okay."

"It's . . . like you say. It's a reaction to stress."

She nodded. "So . . . at those times, your windpipe starts shrinking on you?"

He nodded. "More or less. Couple hits off the inhaler usually takes care of it. Until the next time."

"And this has been going on since it happened?"

Bourque shook his head. "No. Maybe three, four months after. I'd been having a lot of trouble sleeping. And when I did finally nod off, there were nightmares. And then, through the day . . . there'd be times when I found myself struggling to catch my breath. The memory gets triggered, and it starts."

"You can't blame yourself," Delgado said. "It wasn't your fault. Is that what this is about? Guilt? Because you didn't do anything different than I would have done."

"Tell that to the kid," Bourque said.

"You know and I know the only person who gets the blame is Blair Evans. What were you supposed to do? Stand there and let him shoot you? There was a review. You did nothing wrong."

"I should have taken the bullet. He might have missed anything vital."

"Listen to you. More likely he would have put it right between your eyes."

Bourque's voice went low. "I should have been ready. I was going for my weapon but I wasn't fast enough."

"Well, the son of a bitch got what was coming to him anyway. Running into traffic right in front of a double-decker tour bus. Wham. Look, you're going by the Waldorf when you hear a shot. This Evans asshole comes running out the front, armed, before you've even got a chance to react. You yell, 'Freeze.' He's aiming right for you, he pulls the trigger, and you dive out of the way. Exactly what I would have done."

"I didn't know she was behind me," he said so quietly that she almost didn't hear him.

"How could you, Jerry? You got eyes in the back of your head? If it hadn't been her, that bullet would have kept heading up Park Avenue until it found *someone*."

"Her name was Sasha."

Delgado nodded. "I know."

"And her baby's name is Amanda."

"I know that, too."

Bourque's voice went even quieter. "There were drops of blood on Amanda's face. She's in a baby carriage, on her back, she's looking up. Imagine being fourteen months old . . . and seeing your mother . . . take a bullet through the head. Tasting her blood as the drops land on your lips."

Delgado could find no words.

"It's the drops I see," Bourque said. "Whenever I close my eyes, I see the drops."

"You should talk to someone."

Bourque looked at his partner. "I'm talking to you." And when he breathed in, they both heard a whistle.

"Oh, shit," he said.

He took his inhaler from his pocket and uncapped it. Before he could put it to his mouth, it slipped from his fingers and landed in the footwell in front of him.

"Damn thing slips out of my hand half the time," he said. The inhaler was beyond his reach. He briefly unbuckled his seat belt so he could shift forward to scoop it up.

He took a couple of hits from it before tucking it back into his jacket.

"If you didn't have that thing, what would happen?" Delgado asked.

"Asked my doctor the same question," Bourque said. "He never really gave me an answer."

Twenty-Eight

Chris Vallins said to Barbara Matheson, "Here."

He'd stopped in front of the doors to a plain, white brick apartment building on the south side of East Twenty-Ninth Street between Second and Third.

"My place," he said.

Sitting on the sidewalk, his back supported by the apartment building, was an unshaven man in his forties or fifties, a paper coffee cup on the ground in front of him with a few coins in it. His clothes were worn and dirty, but he was wearing a blue pullover sweater that looked relatively new.

"Hey," Chris said to the man, who gave every indication of being homeless.

He looked at Chris and smiled. "My man!" he said. "How's it going?"

"Not bad," Chris said. "You?"

"It's a beautiful day in this neighborhood," he sang. "A beautiful day for a neighbor. Will you be mine?"

Chris grinned. "How's the sweater working out?"

The man gripped the front of the sweater, gave it a tug, then let go. "Mighty fine. Nice to have when there's no room at the inn overnight. Got any more?"

"I'll look through my closet again. In the meantime," Chris said, taking off his gloves, "you might as well have these." The leather on the fingers of the right glove was torn in several places from when Chris had hit the pavement.

"No, I couldn't," the man said, but reached up anyway to take them.

"The right one's a bit ripped up, I'm afraid." Vallins glanced at his bruised knuckles. "Me, too, apparently."

Barbara looked at Vallins's hand. "I'm sorry. That's because of me."

Vallins shrugged, his attention still focused on the homeless man, who was already trying the gloves on for size. "They fit?"

The homeless man grinned and said, "Not bad. Got a receipt in case I need to return them?"

"Think I lost it," Vallins said.

The man finally looked at Barbara and said, "He's a keeper."

She said, "Oh no, we're not—"

"This is a friend of mine, Jack. Barbara."

"Hi, Barbara."

"Hello, Jack," Barbara said.

"Jack served his country with honor and distinction in Afghanistan," Chris said.

Barbara gave the man a solemn nod as Chris opened the door and said, "See ya later, Jack."

The homeless man gave them a thumbs-up.

As they entered the lobby, Barbara said, "I should have given him something."

Chris shook his head. "Don't worry about it. Drop a buck in his cup on the way out if you feel like it."

They took the elevator to the fifteenth floor, walked to the end of a hall, and entered his apartment. Chris went straight to the kitchen. "Take the tour while I find some ice."

He shuffled things around in the freezer compartment of his refrigerator while Barbara admired the view from his apartment window.

"If you look between those two buildings over on the left," he called out from the kitchen, "you can see a small sliver of the East River."

"I bet when they advertised this place, they touted the *river view*," she said, one arm crossing her midsection so she could hold her elbow.

"You guessed it. Allowed them to add another two hundred a month to the rent," he said.

"When a boat goes by, it's like looking at it through a keyhole."

While the view was not spectacular, it was a decent apartment. Spacious enough living room, a sliding glass door that led to a balcony big enough for two chairs. A peek down the hallway showed three doors, so a bathroom and two bedrooms. Not bad. Barbara would have killed for an extra bedroom that she could have turned into an office, instead of always using her kitchen table to do her work. The furnishings were modern, and there was the obligatory wall with the flat-screen TV, audio equipment, and shelves for speakers, CDs, DVDs, books, and a few framed snapshots.

Barbara ran her finger across the spines of the books. She never went into a house without seeing what the residents read, or at least displayed. Vallins's taste ran to mostly nonfiction. History, politics. He even had a copy of that sports star's memoir, the one Barbara had ghostwritten.

Maybe I should autograph it, she thought.

She stopped and looked at one of the photos. A young, grinning Chris, maybe seven years old, standing between what she presumed were his mother and father, the three of them leaning up against a rusted minivan. It looked like a vacation shot, and whoever'd snapped it was one of those amateur photographers who thought you must show the entire person, from shoes right up to their heads. All three were in cutoffs, short sleeves, and sneakers, and there was what looked like camping gear strapped to the roof racks. Everyone looked happy. You didn't need to vacation at the Ritz to have a good time.

Barbara glanced into the kitchen. Sleek cupboards, small granite-topped island, Wolf stove with the red knobs, Sub-Zero fridge. If Vallins had come from humble beginnings, he appeared to be doing okay now.

Vallins pointed to the small, round table tucked into the corner of the kitchen by the window. There were two open laptops with darkened screens sitting there. "Let me make some space," he said, closing them, setting one atop the other, and moving them to the kitchen counter. "Sit," he ordered.

Barbara sat.

He brought over a bag of frozen vegetables from the freezer, set it on the table, and gently lifted Barbara's arm and rested her right elbow on it.

"Oriental stir fry," she said, glancing at the bag. "So this is like Chinese medicine?" She winced. "Fuck, that's cold." She'd rolled her sleeve up, but the bag was too cold on bare skin. She rolled her sleeve down and put her elbow back on it.

"I still think you should go to the hospital."

"I'm not dying." She almost managed a grin. "I'm not that bad. You tackle like a girl. What about your hand? Doesn't it need some frozen veggies, too?"

He waggled his fingers in the air. "They work fine." He went back to the freezer. "Hey, this might be better." He held up a pliable, blue-gel ice pack.

"The veggies are doing the job," she said.

He closed the freezer. "You want a coffee? I got a one-cup maker."

"You never have company?" she asked.

Vallins ignored the question. "Yes or no on the coffee?"

"Actually, just some water, and some Tylenols, if you've got them."

He opened one cupboard to get a glass, and another to get a small bottle of pills. He filled the glass from the tap and shook out two pills onto the kitchen table. She popped the pills into her mouth and washed them down with her free hand.

"I've yet to encounter a problem that can't be solved with drugs and/or alcohol," she said.

"So you want a beer with that, then?"

She shook her head. "Water's fine." She paused. "Tell me about your friend."

"Nothing to tell, really. Served his country. Came back. PTSD. Couldn't hold a job. Lost his family. No support. End of story. There's a million of them."

"But you help him," Barbara said.

He shrugged. "Not really. Not as much as I could, or should."

Barbara narrowed her eyes as she looked at him, as if intensifying her focus would provide some greater insight.

"So," she said slowly.

"Yeah?" Chris looked at her with raised eyebrows.

"You were following me," she said.

"Nope."

"You had to be."

He shook his head very slowly. "You think you're that important?"

"Why are you dressed like this?"

"Like what?"

"Baseball cap. Leather jacket. Jeans. Give me a break. You didn't want to look like you did in the limo yesterday."

"On my day off," Chris said, "I lose the suit and tie."

"It's Tuesday."

"The mayor has weekend events. Sometimes I work Saturday or Sunday. So I get a day off midweek instead."

"Not buyin' it," Barbara said.

"Okay, so let's say I was following you, which I was not. This kind of blows my cover, doesn't it?"

Barbara considered that. "Maybe the whole thing was a setup, a way to gain my confidence. So you *rescued* me."

"Yeah. I cleverly arranged for that truck to come along at just the right moment as you were crossing the street, and you helped immeasurably by staring at your phone the whole time like a complete and total idiot."

Barbara bit her lower lip. "Okay, so, where were you going if you weren't following me?"

"There's a bar up the street where I have lunch sometimes." He cast a suspicious glance her way. "What are you doing in *my* neighborhood? How do I know you weren't nosing around up here looking for me?"

"Please," she said.

"Let me ask you this," Chris said. "Is this your routine when someone saves your life? Interrogate them? A simple thank-you would do."

Barbara was quiet for several seconds, as though working up her nerve to say something nice. "Okay," she said slowly. "Thanks. And I'm sorry you scraped your hand."

"Stop gushing," he said. "You're embarrassing me."

"You could still have been following me, but had to do the right thing when I nearly bought it. Felt you had no choice. That's why you tried to take off without my seeing you."

"The veggies working?" he asked.

She lifted up her elbow momentarily. "I think a piece of frozen cauliflower is digging into a bone."

He got up, went to the freezer, and brought back the proper ice-pack. As she set her elbow on it, he tossed the bag of frozen vegetables back in.

"You got any real food here?" she asked.

He opened the fridge compartment wide enough for her to see. It was nearly empty.

"This could be my place," Barbara said. "You don't get to the store much?"

Vallins shrugged.

"Let me ask you something," Barbara said.

"More questions about how I staged your near-death experience?"

She shook her head. "Sit down." He did. "So, Headley. What exactly do you do for him? What's your title?"

"I was recently knighted, so you might want to call me *Sir* Vallins."

"Funny, I would have pegged you for the court jester."

"I'm an assistant to the mayor. I assist."

Barbara smiled. "In what ways do you assist?"

Chris leaned in closer. "Any way I can. Security, policy implementation, research, whatever."

"Security?"

He nodded.

"You got a conceal and carry license?"

"I'm sorry?"

Barbara rolled her eyes. She knew he knew what she was talking about. "Are you packing?"

"Did you seriously say 'are you packing?' Are we in a Scorsese movie?"

"Show me your gun," Barbara said.

"First of all," Chris said, "I am not going to answer that question, and if I *were* packing, which I am not saying I am, I wouldn't be doing it on my day off."

Barbara sighed. "Fine. So you *assist* the mayor. So following me around, that would fall into the category of *assisting*."

"You're a one-trick pony."

"Okay," she said, switching gears. "Tell me about him."

"Off the record?"

"Off the record. Cross my heart and hope to die."

Vallins shrugged. "He's an asshole."

"I wouldn't call that a keen insight. A lot of us have figured that out."

"But even if he is, you don't get how things work in the real world."

"I think I've heard this speech before," Barbara said.

Chris said, "Nothing gets done in this town without cutting corners."

"Cutting corners shouldn't mean rewarding people who donated to your campaign."

"Did you ever get a job because you knew somebody? A friend who put in a word for you? Do you know anyone who hasn't, somewhere along the line, gotten a job that way? One hand washing the other?"

"It shouldn't work that way at City Hall."

"Suppose, right now, you became mayor. Or . . . I don't know, managing editor of the *Times*. Who would you bring in to help you run things? People you'd worked with in the past, people whose abilities and reputations you knew? People who'd supported you along the way that you wanted to help out in return? Or total strangers, so as not to look like you were practicing favoritism? And then those total strangers turn out to be total fuckups?"

She decided to go in another direction. "What's the deal between the mayor and Glover? Who hates who more?"

Vallins spoke slowly, as though choosing his words carefully. "The father-son dynamic can be a complicated thing."

"Diplomatic."

"Glover . . . never stops trying to impress his father. It's not easy."

"Because Headley's hard to please, or the boy's just not up to it?"

"Bit of both."

Barbara nodded. "Why are the feds involved in the elevator crashes?"

Vallins blinked. "I think I just got whiplash there. We're done with Glover?"

"Is it Homeland?"

"What are you talking about?"

"At least one set of relatives who lost someone in yesterday's crash was told not to talk about it or ask questions. By a guy in a dark suit with a dark SUV who sounded like he was right out of central casting. Everything but the Ray-Bans."

"I've got no idea," Chris said. "So ask Homeland. What do you want to talk about next? It's like you've got this list in your head, you're checking things off."

Barbara looked into his brown eyes for several seconds. "What's your story? Who are you? Where do you come from?"

"Grew up in Queens. Moved into Manhattan in my twenties."

"What'd your folks do?"

"Dad worked construction, died when a beam landed on him. My mom was a traditional wife until he passed and she went out to work for a couple of years."

Her face softened. "Sorry."

He shrugged. "I was ten when my dad died."

"College?

Chris shook his head. "No money for that. Whenever I need to know how to do something, I find someone who already knows and learn from them. Did all kinds of jobs from the age of, like, thirteen. Even before then, I had an aunt who helped me as much as she could with money, but she wasn't rich or anything. Worked in a butcher shop, computer repair store, did some security work in my twenties. Sometimes I'd be doing them all at once, finishing up one shift at one gig and heading off to the other." He smiled. "I'm a quick study. Show me how to do something once, I'll know it forever."

"So, you never played college football, then. Where'd you learn to tackle?" She smiled.

"Tackling girls just comes natural."

"How'd you connect with Headley?"

"Worked low-level on a campaign, got discovered. Like a movie star." He shrugged. "What about you?"

"What about me?"

Chris moved in closer. "Why are you so angry?"

She scowled. "I'm not angry."

"Please. I've been reading you for years," he said. "You are one pissed-off bitch, and I mean that as a compliment. The best writing comes from outrage, right? You use words like a weapon."

Barbara shifted her elbow on the icepack. "It's not anger," she said defensively. "I just don't like injustice and hypocrisy."

"Nah," he said, shaking his head. "It goes deeper. Something happened to you. Something changed you. What was it?"

"Don't psychoanalyze me," she said.

He studied her for several seconds. "You think who you are doesn't come through in everything you write? I may not know your shoe size, but I know who you are."

"And who's that?"

"Someone looking to settle a score," he said. "Let's have a look at that arm."

He gently took hold of her wrist with one hand, as though she might try to escape, while he lightly touched her elbow with the other. Barbara made no effort to stop him.

"So this bald thing you got goin' on," she said, looking at his scalp. "You after the Dwayne Johnson look? You shave it, or did you lose your hair before your first prom?"

"I don't have money for combs and conditioner," he said, still holding her arm.

They didn't say anything for several seconds.

"I don't sleep with the enemy," Barbara said.

"Did I ask?"

"No," Barbara conceded. "Not yet."

"I'm heading into kind of a busy week and don't think I could handle anything more than heavy petting."

She appeared to be considering it, then glanced at her elbow. "And I do my best work with this arm, and until it mends . . ."

She pushed back her chair and stood. She handed Chris the ice-pack. "Gotta go."

"Let me walk you out."

"I can find my way."

He followed her as far as the door. She turned, went up slightly on her toes, and kissed him on the cheek. "Thanks for the Oriental veggies."

"My pleasure."

"I know you were following me," she said.

He smiled. "Then you won't be surprised the next time it happens."

On her way out, she gave Jack a ten.

Twenty-Nine

They had to walk up twenty-seven floors.

They couldn't be sure that the other elevators in the York Avenue building had been sabotaged in any way, even though there was no evidence that they'd been fitted with pinhole cameras.

Martin Fleck offered to save the mayor the hike, saying he could take video and email it to him. But Fleck had also set the hook, promising to show something significant to the mayor, and Headley wanted to see it for himself.

"I still hit the StairMaster four times a week," the mayor said. "So lead the way."

Brian Cartland, of Homeland, was okay with making the climb, as well, but police chief Annette Washington begged off, but not because she wasn't up to it. She had a meeting at One Police Plaza.

In the lobby, Arla had found Glover and was going to tell him about the exchange she had just witnessed between the mayor and the boy, but she didn't have a chance. The sound of a text notification came from inside Glover's jacket. He looked at the phone to find a message from his father.

On second floor but on the move. Get up here.

"Gotta go," he said. "You might as well head back to the office. The others should be back by now and you can get started."

Arla was dismissed.

Glover found the entrance to the stairwell and was just about to exit onto the second floor hallway when the fire door opened and his father, Fleck, and Cartland entered.

"We're going up," Headley said.

"How far?" Glover asked.

"You'll see," his father said.

Fleck led the way, followed by the mayor, then Cartland, and finally, Glover. Everyone except Glover was careful to pace himself, taking the stairs at a steady rate. Glover, however, in struggling to keep up, occasionally took the steps two at a time, which only tired him out even more, causing him to stop several times to catch his breath.

Once they'd reached the twenty-ninth floor, Cartland said of the yet-to-be seen Glover, "Shall we wait for your son, Mr. Mayor?"

Headley had a hand on his chest, feeling the pounding inside. "That . . . really was a workout," he said. "You think you're in shape, but . . . No, let's get started. Glover will get here when he gets here."

Fleck led them down a corridor around the corner from the elevators until they reached a locked, green door marked Equipment Room Keep Out. Fleck produced a key to open the door, and once he had, they heard the soft humming of machinery and cooling fans.

Cartland and Headley followed him in. As the door was about to shut, a hand shot in to keep it open. A breathless Glover stepped into the room behind the others.

"Good of you to join us, Glover," Headley said.

The room, about thirty feet square, was filled with several tall, locker-like units in the center that were constructed of green metal. Along one wall were the tops of the machines—massive pulleys that housed the belts and cables responsible for raising and lowering the elevators through the shafts. They were, at this time, idle, given that all the elevators were shut down.

Attached to one of the locker units, at eye level, was a black box about the size of a thick, paperback novel, or an oversized TV remote.

"Whoa," said Glover, scanning the machinery like a wide-eyed kid. "Never been in a room like this."

Fleck walked over to one of the green metal units and, with another key, opened one. Inside, from top to bottom, were countless wires and circuit panels. Lights flickered on and off while small digital readouts provided information.

Headley glanced at it all, clearly flummoxed by what any of it meant.

"This is the brains and the guts of the elevator system," Fleck told the other men. He reached for the black box attached to the next unit and dislodged it. It had evidently been attached magnetically. It had a small screen at the top and several rows of small buttons below. A cable with a jack at the end dangled from the bottom. Fleck plugged it into one of the circuit boards, and the screen came to life with a series of numbers and symbols.

"Okay," Fleck said. "I'm now, with this box, in control of the elevator system to this building. I can move them from floor to floor, open the doors and close them, send them straight to the bottom or the top. I can do any damn thing I want."

He continued. "Before I can do any of this, of course, I have to punch in a slew of codes to establish an interface between this device and the elevator system. But if you know the codes, you're in business. And here's the thing." At this point, he unplugged the unit, and started tapping the various buttons with his index finger.

"If I'm outside the building, at home, or at my office, and if I want to do all these same functions, I can, as long as I have this box or one just like it with me. Admittedly, that's a little trickier, because first I have to get through the entire building's security system to access the elevator system. But if I know those codes—and it would be easier to get them if I've already been in here to set things up—I'm in business. I can make this elevator do whatever I want, and I don't even have to be here. So if you're thinking of reviewing the surveillance tapes from the time of the event, well, that's not necessarily going to be of any help."

"Jesus," said Headley. "But the codes and everything, those can't be easy to crack."

"They aren't," Fleck agreed. "But it can be done."

"So," Cartland said, "you'd either have to work in the elevator business and understand all this shit, or—"

"—know someone who did," said Glover, who had been watching intently.

Headley gave his son a dismissive look. "Thanks, Glover. I think we'd all pretty much figured that part out." To Fleck, he said, "Or anyone who works for the city's elevator inspections division."

"Yes," said Fleck.

Headley looked at Cartland. "What do you suggest?"

"Off the top," he said, "we need to get people checking every single elevator in the city, looking to see if a camera's been surreptitiously installed. So far, the two elevators where people have been killed have had that camera."

"Christ. How long could that take?" Headley asked Fleck.

"Seventy thousand elevators, and roughly a hundred and forty inspectors," Fleck said. "Do the math. That's about eighteen hundred elevators per person, you figure maybe they can do half a dozen a day, and—"

"That's insane," Headley said.

"But," Fleck said, "if we make this public, get every building maintenance team involved and they do the inspections themselves, at least a simple visual, well, that would speed up the process."

Headley looked back to Cartland. "Go public?"

Cartland's face was granite.

"We go public with this," Headley said, "and let everyone in New York know that somebody may be fucking with the elevators, and they know that every time they get into one of these things they're gambling with their lives . . ."

"Pandemonium," said Glover.

"Yeah," said Cartland. "This is a vertical city. You got eight and a half million people afraid to go to work. Terrified to ride the elevators in their own building."

"The city'll come to a fucking standstill," Headley said. "Unless we can find the son of a bitch who's got one of those boxes there."

"Yeah," said Cartland. "And if this is, as we suspect, sabotage, we have to start asking why anyone would *want* to do this."

"Do terrorists need a reason?" Headley asked.

"This is a very sophisticated way to go about killing people. It would take a lot of thought and planning and expertise. To go to all this trouble, you can bet your ass there's a reason. Even if it's one that might not make sense to us."

Headley had turned his attention back to the box Fleck was holding. "How many of those can there be? Not that many, right? You go to every elevator maintenance company, find out if one of these has been stolen."

Fleck looked grim.

"Mr. Mayor, you remember, before we came up here, I said what I had to tell you was worse than what you already knew?"

Headley made a face that suggested he'd had a bad burrito. "I think we know what that is now. A paralyzed city."

"Well, yeah, that's pretty bad. But what I wanted to tell you was about this box."

Fleck held it up in his hand, next to his face, like a *Price Is Right* girl, but without the fake smile.

"Anybody can get one of these off eBay for five hundred bucks."

Thirty

Jerry Bourque was slipping on his jacket and getting ready to leave the station at the end of his shift when his desk phone rang.

Lois Delgado had left early to look after her sick kid, so he couldn't hand it off to her. Before departing, she'd gotten back to Gunther Willem to find out if he'd learned whether Otto Petrenko might have worked on one, or both, of the elevators that had killed people in the last two days. Bourque, checking his phone on the way back into Manhattan, got up to speed about the York Avenue elevator mishap that had claimed the life of some Russian scientist.

"I hate coincidences," he'd said. "Two elevators drop and we've got an elevator technician beaten to death."

Once they were back at the station, she'd called Willem. He promised to get back to her as soon as he could. Shortly before Delgado left, he phoned in and reported that according to company records, Petrenko had never done work in those two buildings, but the company had in years past.

Even so, Delgado had made a point of telling their captain that while there might be no connection whatsoever, she and Bourque were investigating the death of an elevator technician. The captain said that if those two elevator incidents were anything more than straightforward accidents, the information hadn't been made its way to their precinct yet.

Now, on his own, Bourque was standing by his desk, thinking

about what he would pick up from the hot table on his way home, when the phone rang. He snatched up the receiver and put it to his ear.

"Detective Bourque," he said.

"Is this Detective Bourque?" a woman asked.

It never mattered that you gave your name when you answered. People had to make sure.

"That's right."

"This is Misha Jackson? You were trying to reach me?"

"Yes," he said, slipping back into his chair, reaching for a notepad and taking a pen in hand. "Thanks for returning my call."

"I work in the casino and don't get off work till about four in the morning, and I turn off all the phones so I can get a decent sleep. When I woke up"—and at this point she started to cry—"I had calls from my brother and Eileen. I can't believe this. Who would do something like this to Otto?"

"I'm sorry for your loss," Bourque said.

"I can't get my head around it! Otto was . . . he was an okay guy. I don't know why anyone would do this."

"That's what we're trying to find out."

"Anatoly—my brother—said you'd already talked to him."

"Yes. I'm wondering if your story is similar to his."

Misha Jackson made sniffing noises at the other end of the line. "Yeah, I guess. It was weird. I mean, we didn't hear much from Otto. He was always the odd one out of the three of us, you know?"

"Explain."

"Well, he was always more of a loner, more to himself. Me and Anatoly had lots of friends, but Otto was the one who kept to himself. He was kind of a mechanical geek from the get-go. He'd have never gone outside the house if our mother hadn't forced him."

"Mechanical geek?"

"Even as a kid, he always took apart everything to see how it worked. Toaster, TV, you name it. Computers, too. He could just see the inside of a machine in his head, you know what I mean?"

"Sure. His boss said as much."

"I'd get a Christmas card from him and Eileen every year. But even that, she wrote it and put the stamp on it and walked it down to the corner mailbox. Otto didn't give us much mind. But we were still family, you know? Just because he didn't pay much attention to us didn't mean he didn't give a shit. If something happened to either one of us, he'd be there. Four years ago, my husband had a heart attack, and it was looking bad there for a while, and when Otto heard about it, he was on the first plane out to see how I was doing."

"Sounds like, on balance, a good brother."

Another sniff. "Yeah."

"Tell me about his recent calls."

Bourque heard the woman take a breath. "It was strange, him calling for no obvious reason. Wasn't my birthday or Christmas. He just calls and asks how we're doing. But here's the part that's strange. He wanted to know what hours I work, and I told him, and next thing you know he's calling me at the casino, and not from his home phone. A different phone."

"Hmm," said Bourque.

"And on this call, he's all, hey Misha, you need to watch yourself. Make sure you lock your doors, make sure you put on the alarm at night. He even wanted to know if I carried a gun. Why the hell would I want to do that? He tells me it's legal to carry a concealed gun in Nevada, that I should think about doing that, and I'm thinking, where is this coming from? And I ask him, and he says it's nothing, but the world's changing, you can't be too careful."

"That sounds like what he told your brother. He wanted him to carry a gun, too."

"I asked him if he was in trouble and he said no. But I could tell he was lying. It was in his voice. He was definitely on edge about something."

"Did he say whether he was being threatened in any way?"

"No."

"Did he talk about the Flyovers?"

"The who?"

"An activist group."

"I don't remember any talk about that."

"It sounds as though your brother was trying to put you on guard, that he believed there was some threat to you that he wasn't willing to share."

"Well, no one's threatened me, except for a guy who lost a hundred grand the other night on blackjack. He wasn't too happy, and security had to remove him. But that's work stuff. Happens now and again. But outside the casino, going about my business, I haven't noticed anything out of the ordinary. No one waiting by my car when I finish work. No one watching the house, at least that I've been able to see."

"Is that what Otto was suggesting? That there could be someone watching you?"

Misha Jackson paused. "That reminds me of something he said. I only just thought of it now."

"What did he say?"

"I kind of forgot about it, because it seemed so crazy, I thought he had to be joking. He said, just because you don't see them doesn't mean they aren't there. Kind of a variation of the line about being paranoid. It doesn't mean they're not out to get you. That's why I thought it was a joke, that he was referring to that. But now that I think about it, maybe he meant it. Why would anyone be watching me and my brother? That makes no sense."

"And yet, someone did kill Otto. Can you think of anyone who might have a grudge against your entire family?"

"Christ, you think we're next?"

"I don't know anything like that, Ms. Jackson. But Otto was murdered, and clearly he was trying to warn you."

There was a long silence at the other end of the line.

"Ms. Jackson?"

"I'm gonna get it."

"Get what?"

"That gun."

Thirty-One

So how'd your first day go?"

Glover Headley raised an eyebrow as he asked Arla the question. He was nursing a Stella while Arla was waiting to take her first sip of a Kir Royale. They were seated at a table at Gran Morsi, an Italian place a short walk from City Hall.

"Yeah, right, wow," she said. "It's not every job where the first thing you see is some dead scientist in an elevator."

"That's why I wanted to check in on you. I hope this wasn't too forward, asking you here for a drink. I wanted to get away from the building, see how you are. That was a pretty traumatic thing to have to deal with."

"Yeah, sure, I get that. Look, aside from the decapitation, it was a pretty good start. You know, like, 'Other than that, Mrs. Lincoln, did you enjoy the play?'"

Glover couldn't help but chuckle. "God, that's awful. But the way you put it, that made me laugh. When you got back, the rest of the department was there?"

Arla nodded. "Everyone was great. I think, tomorrow morning, I can really hit the ground running."

"That's terrific."

"But listen, I'm glad we've got a second to talk, because I saw something kind of interesting today."

Glover took a swig of his beer. "Oh, yeah? In the office?"

"No, at the building where it happened." She described how his father had dealt with the boy who'd been in the elevator when the woman was killed. "He was great with that kid. That's a side of the mayor we don't see often enough."

"Yeah, that's for sure," Glover said, an edge to his voice.

Arla caught the tone. "What?"

Glover put his elbows on the table and leaned in. "My dad is a guy with . . . many sides. There was a time, from all accounts, when he was a complete jerk. Back when he worked for his own father, looking after the buildings he owned. There are stories, and they're not pretty. But once he got out from under his dad's thumb and started out on his own, I think he started to change, become more empathetic. To actually care about people, you know? At least to some degree, and with some people. But there's always been this part of him, a side he tries to keep buried, where he's still that young man who's stuck doing Daddy's dirty work. A cold son of a bitch. It comes out every once in a while."

Arla smiled. "Like with you, sometimes."

"Like with me *most* of the time," he said. "It's kind of an open secret." He sighed. "There's even a 'poor Glover' hashtag on Twitter where people post times when my father humiliates me."

"That's awful."

"Yeah, well, I guess it balances out, considering there's like half a dozen other Twitter accounts devoted to making fun of *him*."

Arla gave him a sly look. "Which one of them is yours?"

That made him laugh again. "I'll never tell. The thing is, I get what he's trying to do. His dad was tough with him, and that turned him into someone with drive and ambition. He figures, if he's tough with me, he'll get the same result. He'll turn me into the kind of man he is." He paused. "I don't know that I want to become the kind of man he is."

"Sure," Arla said. "I get that. We all have to be, you know, our authentic selves." She rolled her eyes self-deprecatingly. "Or some new age bullshit like that."

Glover nodded. "God, I can't believe I'm telling you all this." He ran his hand over his head. "Well, look, I don't want to keep you from anything. I wanted to buy you a drink and make sure that you survived."

Arla paused a moment before asking, "You wanna get something to eat? I mean, we're just sitting here and it's dinnertime and all. But you totally don't have to. You probably have to go help the mayor do something."

"I don't."

"Great," Arla said, smiling. "And listen, I'll get this because you've been so—"

"No, that's nuts." He grinned. "I can bill the city for this one. I'll write if off as employee training."

"Well, you strike me as a very good trainer," Arla said.

As soon as she said it, she thought, what the hell was that? *You strike me as a very good trainer.* Why did she say something like that? As soon as the words left her lips she realized it sounded like some *Fifty Shades* come-on, which it was not.

Unless it was.

No, it was *not.* She had to come back with something else.

"The whole department," she said, "seems very equipped to bring new people up to speed, to train them in the latest data analysis."

Okay, she thought. Not a bad recovery. She couldn't tell, from Glover's expression, whether he'd interpreted her previous comment as sexual. That was probably a good sign.

But then Glover leaned in even closer.

"You know, we have to be very careful these days. I don't want my sitting here with you, having a drink, having dinner, to be seen in any way as inappropriate. You're not under any pressure to stay. We're living in a post-Weinstein world now."

"Dinner was my idea, remember?" she said.

Glover smiled. "It's nice talking to you."

"Yeah," Arla said slowly.

Glover sat back in his chair and raised his palms. "You know, about work. It's good, talking about all the things that need to get done."

"Of course, right," she said.

He turned his head, scanned the room. "If you see a waiter, let me know and I can score us some menus."

"So," Arla said, signaling a change in the conversation's direction, "what did your dad want?"

"Hmm?"

"When we were at the accident, and he texted you to come upstairs?"

"Oh, yeah, we had to walk all the way to the top." He stopped looking for someone to bring him a menu and leaned in conspiratorially. "I don't even know if I should tell you about it."

"Why? What?"

Glover rubbed his chin, trying to decide how much to share with Arla. "You have to promise not to tell anyone."

Arla felt her pulse quicken. "Yeah, sure, of course."

"There was this guy from the building department, and this other guy from Homeland Security or something."

"You're kidding. Why would someone from Homeland be there?"

His voice went even quieter. "They think the elevator was sabotaged."

Her mouth dropped open and her voice rose. "Seriously?"

Heads turned at a nearby table.

Through gritted teeth, he said, "Shh. I can't tell you this if you're going to look like I just told you I'm gay or something." A pause. "Which I'm not."

"Okay," she whispered.

"Anyway, it looks like the 'accident' was deliberate. Yesterday's, too." His face grew grim, yet he also looked excited to be able to share privileged information. "Looks like, by the same person."

"Oh my God. So, it's terrorism?"

"Could be," he said. "It would have to be someone very smart to be able to pull it off. Lots of technical know-how required." Glover smiled, as if in admiration of whoever had done it. "And this is kind of curious, although I haven't mentioned it to my dad because he's been such a prick lately—pardon my French—but people who supported my father lived in both of those buildings."

"You think that means anything?"

Glover shrugged. "Probably not. I mean, there's probably people in every skyscraper in Manhattan who supported him." A pause. "Hard as that is to believe at times."

"So what are they doing about it?" she asked.

"Last I heard, they're quietly putting out the word to every landlord in the city to check the elevators. Not giving the real reason why. They're making up some excuse. Maybe to do with the cameras that were installed."

"Cameras?"

He filled her in about what had been found on top of the elevator cars. "If that's all that it was, it might just be a Peeping Tom thing. But it's way worse than that."

"But if it's happened twice, it could happen again. Don't people need to be warned?"

Glover shook his head. "They don't want to start a panic. Listen, I'm gonna go find us some menus."

He got up from the table in search of a waiter.

Arla watched him walk away, thinking, *Oh my God, my mom so needs to know this.*

Thirty-Two

My feet are dead," Estelle Clement said to her husband, Eugene, as she sat on the edge of the bed in their hotel room. She had kicked off her shoes and was massaging her right foot with both hands. "What an idiot I was, wearing heels to the show tonight."

"I told you," Eugene said.

"I thought we'd be able to get a cab after. I never dreamed we'd have to walk all the way back. We should have gotten one of those Ubers."

"I never take those," he said. "There's a record. Where you were, where you went, when you took the trip."

"You don't want the world to know we went to a show and came back to the hotel?" she asked.

"I just . . . don't like being tracked," he said.

"You've been on edge ever since that TV thing," she said.

The mention of TV prompted Clement to pick up the remote. He pointed it at the television and turned it on. He flipped through channels until he found news.

"Did we come all the way from Denver so you could watch TV?" she asked.

He ignored her.

Estelle said, "Fine." Having massaged her feet enough that she felt she could walk, she strolled over to the window. "There's not much of a view. You should have booked us on a higher floor."

"This was all they had," Clement snapped. On the screen was a reporter, standing out front of a high-rise building. The chyron across the bottom read: *Second Elevator Disaster in Two Days.* He had the volume set too low to make out what she was saying.

His wife reached across the bed for her purse and dug out her cell phone. "I'm gonna text the kids."

"Do that."

"We've got two more days," she said, with what sounded like a hint of resignation in her voice. "What about tomorrow?"

"Why don't we talk about it at breakfast?" he said. "I'm trying to watch this."

She hadn't started texting yet. She was glaring at her husband.

"Eugene," she said.

"Hmm?"

"Look at me."

He sighed, turned and said, "What?"

She asked, "Who was that man?"

"What man?"

"The man sitting in the car, after the interview, when you were getting the cab. The one you talked to with your back to him."

Clement's face grew concerned. "I'm not sure I'm following you."

"He put down his window and he said something to you. You had a conversation."

"He was probably telling me to stop leaning on his car," Clement said.

"Do you know him?" she asked.

"Of course not," he said.

"Because I think I've seen him before."

"What are you talking about?"

"I only had a quick look at him. But at home, I thought I saw you talking to him once. On the street. And I even thought I saw him in the lobby."

"I'd never seen him before in my life."

"So you *did* see him? Today you had your back to him when you talked to him."

Clement was briefly flustered. "I didn't see him. I didn't see any-body. I don't know what the hell you're talking about."

Estelle was quiet for a moment before she asked, "Why did we do this trip?"

"What? It's our anniversary, for Christ's sake."

"I was surprised when you proposed it."

He tossed the remote onto the bed and rolled his eyes. "Why wouldn't I?"

"Because it's the first really nice thing you've done in a long time."

"This is what I get. I plan a trip, I fly us to New York, and now I've done something wrong. What do you want from me, Estelle?"

She considered the question. "Well, for starters, to love me again, if that's not asking too much."

He looked at her, said nothing.

She sat back down on the bed. "You don't even . . . I know I'm not twenty-one anymore, that the years take their toll, but . . . I'd like to think you still found me even a little . . . attractive."

"Of course I do," he said without conviction, glancing for half a second back at the television.

"The prescription . . . worked, but you still don't seem to want—"

"I really don't want to have this conversation again, Estelle."

"You never want to have this conversation."

"Maybe because we don't *need* to have this conversation."

"If you would just talk to—"

"I don't need to talk to anyone."

Estelle said nothing for several seconds. Then, "It's a myth that it's always women who lose interest."

Clement briefly closed his eyes and sighed. "This has been a very stressful year for me. Getting the organization up and running. Getting the word out. Dealing with all these baseless accusations. It's taking a toll. Surely to God you can see that. Maybe you need to stop thinking about yourself all the time and try to imagine what I'm going through."

That cut deep. She eyed him scornfully. Her voice was cold and even when she said, "Everything I do is for you."

He waved his hands in the air, let them fall to his sides. "Fine, okay, you do."

"I think the reason we came here has nothing to do with our anniversary."

"That's ridiculous," he said.

She got up from the bed, went to the bathroom, and closed the door. When Clement heard her turn the lock, he grabbed the remote.

Maybe, he thought, he could catch the rest of that elevator report on a different newscast.

Thirty-Three

Barbara, as was her routine at night before turning off the lights, was sitting cross-legged on her bed, MacBook in her lap. She was jumping from website to website, reading the latest from the *New York Times*, *Politico*, the *Hill*, The Huffington Post, CNN, BuzzFeed.

She'd taken some more painkillers for her elbow, which still hurt like hell. Despite Chris Vallins's plea, she had not sought medical attention. She fell. No big deal. People fell all the time. And her elbow still worked. She knew this for a fact because she had used her right arm to empty a bottle of chardonnay into a wineglass when she'd come home.

She'd had a hard time getting Chris Vallins out of her head the rest of the day. She was feeling things for him she did not want to feel. *Get over it,* she told herself.

Barbara had made some calls when she returned home. She wanted to reach family members of the others who had died in Monday's elevator crash and ask if any spooky officials in black SUVs had come to see them, too, to tell them to keep their questions to themselves, to not speak to the media. She figured that was a better place to start, since she was going to run into more problems—especially considering she did not speak Russian—trying to find relatives of the woman who'd died in today's elevator incident.

She had no luck getting any of Sherry D'Agostino's relatives to call back. Ditto for the family of Barton Fieldgate.

But she did get through to Stuart Bland's mother.

Stuart, as it turned out, had still lived at home.

"I told him to leave that lady alone," she said tearfully once Barbara had identified herself. "He went to her house and nearly got in trouble. He wouldn't have been in that elevator if he'd listened to me."

It took several more questions for Barbara to get the full picture, that Stuart was trying to get a producer to look at a script he had written. That was what had taken him to the Lansing Tower.

"At first, they thought he had something to do with it," Bland's mother said. "Because he was using a phony ID. For FedEx. So that made them suspicious. But he couldn't have had anything to do with it. That's just crazy. He could barely get his bicycle chain back on. I think I convinced them. But I shouldn't even be telling you this."

"Why?"

"The man said."

"What man?"

"The man who came to see me. From the government."

"Did he say which department?"

"He didn't say. But I could tell."

"What was his name?"

"I'm not sure he told me. He didn't leave a card. I have to go."

And she hung up.

Barbara wrote a piece for *Manhattan Today*, but it didn't take long and she wasn't very happy with it. Recounting her conversations with Bland's mother and Paula's parents, she asked her readers, "Who is this mystery man?" Why would someone want the families of the victims to keep a low profile while the elevator accident was being investigated? Why would they be pressured not to ask questions? Barbara did not speculate in her piece. She did not mention the FBI or CIA or Homeland Security. She didn't have anything solid enough to do that.

And Vallins hadn't been any help when she'd asked him about it. If he knew anything, he wasn't saying.

And he never did answer the bald question, the bastard. Okay, so maybe that was too personal. Just as well she'd resisted the urge to run her hand over his head.

Looking again at the story she posted, she fretted at how light it was on facts. But maybe someone who did know something would read it and get in touch. That was often how it worked. A story that was incomplete could produce more leads than a story that didn't run at all.

It had produced a few responses already, not that they were in any way useful. Just comments from, as Barbara's father once referred to those who call in to radio talk shows, a "cavalcade of nincompoops." There was **spicydragon**, who said, "Anybody that old who still lives with his mommy deserves to die." And there were these words of wisdom from **DeepStateHarry**: "We r all being watched. There r black vans everyware."

Barbara was about to move on from the *Manhattan Today* website when one other comment caught her eye.

"Hope you are feeling better."

It was from **GoingDown**.

Barbara felt, along with the persistent, dull pain in her elbow, a chill run down her spine.

"Hope you are feeling better."

Barbara thought back to when Chris Vallins had tackled her in the middle of the street. All this time, she'd thought *he* was the only one keeping an eye on her. Was it possible someone else was, too? Whoever this **GoingDown** person was, had he—or she—seen that van nearly hit her? When she screamed in pain about her elbow, had this person heard her?

Barbara tried to think back to the scene. There was the old lady who got her phone. That postal worker. The woman with the shopping cart. Was it one of them?

GoingDown had been the one, in a response to her last article, to express condolences about Paula Chatsworth.

Okay, that's what GoingDown is referring to. Not my fall today.

Barbara touched her hand to her chest. Her heart had, briefly, raced at the thought that she was being watched. She was getting paranoid. Thinking about mysterious men in black SUVs had prompted her mind to go places it shouldn't.

"Chill out, girl," she said under her breath.

That was when she moved off the *Manhattan Today* site and started surfing all the other news outlets.

The so-called experts said screens should be avoided an hour before bedtime. Artificial light from phones and tablets and laptops messed up sleeping patterns, they argued. Bullshit, Barbara thought. This was what she did every night. Even if she had someone over. If some man wanted to roll over and go to sleep after a fuck, that was fine with her. But don't expect her to ignore what was going on in the world. Frankly, this was one of the reasons why she didn't like having men spend the night. Not only did they want you to put the laptop away, they expected you to make them breakfast.

Fuck that.

Barbara closed the laptop, killed the lights, and put her head on the pillow. She was about to close her eyes when she noticed her phone, sitting screen-side up on the covers next to her, light up with a text. Barbara glanced over.

It was Arla.

There really hadn't been a moment all day when Arla wasn't in her thoughts. Even when Barbara had been with the Chatsworths, or talking to Stuart Bland's mother, Arla was on her mind. Barbara had been unable to stop thinking about Arla's new job and what had motivated her to go after it. Had she done it to drive her mother nuts, or was it really a position she wanted, that she believed would challenge her?

Barbara, in one moment, would think her reaction to Arla's news at breakfast had been perfectly justified. And in the next, she would feel she'd totally blown it. She replayed the conversation in her head countless times.

I should have said . . . and I shouldn't have said . . .

Barbara picked up the phone and read the message.

You up?

Barbara typed **YES** in return.

Is it too late to call?

Barbara quickly tapped **NO**.

She only had to wait ten seconds for the phone to ring with its distinctive typing chime.

"Hey," Barbara said.

"Hey," Arla said. "I know it's late and all but—"

"No, it's okay. I'm still up. Everything all right?"

"Yeah, sure, things are good."

Barbara hesitated before asking, "How was the first day?"

"It was . . . interesting."

"That doesn't sound good."

"No, I mean, it really *was* interesting. I hadn't even started and I ended up going to that second elevator accident."

Arla filled her in.

"God," Barbara said. "You saw what happened?"

"Yeah."

"You okay?"

"I guess. Although I'm sure I'll have nightmares or something. When I saw it, I thought, don't be a wuss. Don't freak out. Believe me, it wasn't easy."

Barbara hesitated before asking, "Did you meet him?"

"You mean the mayor?"

"Yes."

"No. And Glover didn't introduce me, either. I'm too low level."

"Glover? You met his son?"

"Yeah. He oversees the department that hired me. So he showed me around because everyone else was off at a seminar."

"Glover's your boss?"

"I'll have several. There's my immediate supervisor, then Glover, and then, I guess, well, ultimately we're all working for the mayor, right?" Arla paused. "Look, Mom, about this morning—"

"Yeah, it's okay. I—"

"No, I said some things and I'm sorry. I've been working through a lot of stuff. I'm trying to sort them out. I didn't take this job to be all in your face. I mean, maybe a little, but this is something I could—"

"It's okay," Barbara said again, her voice soft, reflective. "It's your life."

"The mayor's hard to get a handle on. I saw him do something really nice today, when no one was watching, with this kid who'd been in the elevator where this woman got killed. But with Glover, for example, he's a shit."

"Well."

"He was telling me tonight—we grabbed a bite—about how complicated his relationship with his father is. But listen, that's not why I called. It's kind of tricky to talk about and I probably shouldn't say anything, but Glover said—"

"Getting this close to the mayor's son, you need to be careful about that."

"What?"

Barbara thought a moment before offering a reason. "If they find out who your mother is, they'll question your motives."

"I told you. This job has nothing to do with you."

"I'm just saying, watch your step with him."

"I don't need your advice," Arla said, an edge in her voice.

"I don't—I'm just trying to—"

"You know what?" Arla said. "You're right. I was going to tell you something, but now I realize that's not a good idea."

"Tell me what?"

Arla didn't answer.

"Arla?"

It took Barbara a moment to realize her daughter had ended the call.

"Shit," she said and tossed the phone onto the floor.

She flopped back on the bed, her head crushing the pillow. A minute later, she turned out her light, and stared at the ceiling until dawn.

Thirty-Four

I'm going to say something to him," the boy says. "I am. I don't care if he gets mad."

His mother shakes her head angrily. "No, you're not. I've known him longer than you have. There's no talking to him."

"He's so mean. You should—"

But the boy stops himself. What he wants to tell his mother is that she should stand up for herself. That she shouldn't take any more shit from this man. But he can't bring himself to do that because he knows that everything she does, she does for him. She does not deserve his scorn or criticism.

And yet.

"If something isn't done," he says, and it is at this point that his voice starts to break, "you could, you know . . ."

"Don't be silly," she says. "Nothing is going to happen to me." She smiles. "I'm made of tough stuff. Don't you worry about me."

"But last night," the boy says, "you said your heart felt like—"

"Enough," she says sternly. "Go do your homework."

Wednesday

Thirty-Five

I *will never come to this hotel again.*

Elliot Cantor pressed the Down button for what had to be the tenth time. No, not pressed. He *stabbed* the button. He was *angry* at the button. Elliot wanted to kick this button's ass. He wanted to put this button in a blender and slice and dice it to death.

Elliot *loathed* this elevator. This one, and the one next to it. A thirty-story hotel with a dozen or more rooms per floor needed more than two elevators. Both of them were always busy.

"I don't believe this," Elliot said.

His partner, Leonard Faulks, said, "It's okay. It'll get here eventually."

"I've got my doubts," Elliot said.

Elliot and Leonard, both thirty-one years old and both from Toronto, were on a weeklong trip to New York. They'd both been here before on business in their respective jobs—Elliot was a financial adviser and Leonard a freelance book editor—but they had never visited together. A friend had recommended to Elliot that they stay at the Klaxton 49, one of four Manhattan hotels owned and managed by the small Klaxton chain. Elliot did the booking online after reading good things on TripAdvisor. Well, his review was not going to be like the others. He'd already been writing it in his head. It was going to read something like this:

"This 30-story hotel may be clean and centrally located and the staff are nice enough but DO NOT GO HERE UNLESS YOU LOVE TO WAIT FOR FIVE FUCKING HOURS FOR THE ELEVATOR TO ARRIVE."

This had been their experience since day one. They were on the fifteenth floor, the building's midpoint. Had they been given a room on a lower floor, they would have used the stairs. And even now, Elliot was considering them. Descending was a lot easier than ascending. Not that the two of them weren't in good shape, but sometimes, after seven or eight hours of walking all over Manhattan, the last thing you wanted to face when you got back to the hotel was a grueling climb.

Elliot was watching the numbered lights to see where the two elevators were. One was at the fifth floor and moving up. The other was on the twentieth floor and moving down. And the time the elevators were spending on each number was evidence that many guests were boarding and exiting.

The ascending elevator stopped at seven, then nine, then twelve. Elliot was hopeful that last person to disembark would be at fifteen, meaning they could step right on and go down. But the descending elevator was now on the move, heading toward them. Only two floors away now.

"Why don't you press it again?" Leonard said.

Elliot gave him a look, knowing he was being needled, but that didn't stop him from doing exactly what Leonard asked. He hit the button.

He *attacked* the button.

The descending elevator stopped one floor above them.

"This has to be it," Leonard said, striking an optimistic note, hoping his partner would calm down.

The elevator moved. They heard it whiz past in the shaft.

It did not stop for them.

The light flashed at fourteen, twelve, nine. It was heading straight to the lobby.

Elliot, in a sign of defeat, slowly leaned his head forward and rested it on the wall above the buttons.

The elevator coming up went right past fifteen and stopped at twenty-two. Leonard watched, wondering if it would keep on going up, or start coming back down.

Now it was coming down.

"Elliot," he said cautiously.

Elliot raised his head slowly, then looked up at the numbers. The second elevator was three . . . two . . . one floor way.

They did not hear the sound of something whooshing past. The elevator sounded as though it was coming to a stop.

And then the doors opened.

"Sweet Jesus, it's a miracle," said Elliot.

That was the good news. The bad news was that the car was nearly full. Jammed into the back were an elderly couple who were clearly at the end of their stay, each one clutching the handle of a wheeled carry-on bag. Also on board were a fortyish woman in a pink tracksuit and two teenage girls, also in matching tracksuits and running shoes. Elliot didn't have to be Sherlock Holmes to figure out these were the woman's daughters.

At least there was still just enough room for him and Leonard to get on without having to scrunch shoulders.

No one said anything as they boarded, but there seemed a collective sense of despair in the car; the others had been waiting an eternity as well for this ride to street level.

Leonard went to press the L, for Lobby, but it was already lit.

The car began to descend.

And then stopped.

They had gone one entire floor.

One of the teenage girls said, "Of course."

The doors parted to reveal a young couple and—Elliot wanted to scream—a stroller with a small child in it.

"Uh," said Elliot, "I don't think so. We're pretty full here."

"No, we can do it," the father said, pushing in the stroller first, bumping the tiny rubber wheels over the metal edge.

Everyone else in the elevator had to back up. Once the father had the stroller in, he positioned it sideways so as to make space for the mother. She stepped in and waited for the doors to close.

"I always wanted to feel like a sardine," Leonard whispered into his partner's ear.

Someone had to say it, Elliot thought.

The elevator descended one more floor, and then stopped *again.*

A groan slipped through the lips of everyone in the elevator, with the exception of the couple who had just entered, and their child, of course, who was oblivious to everyone else's aggravation.

"Seriously, this is too much," said the elderly man to his wife.

"The way this is going we'll miss our flight," she said softly. "If there's traffic, we'll never get to LaGuardia in time."

The doors parted.

Everyone thought, *Jesus Christ no.*

Before them stood a man in his early twenties, about five-ten and easily three hundred pounds. He was decked out in a pair of shorts, and a pair of oversized, unlaced sneakers, and an "I Love New York" sleeveless shirt where "Love" was a heart symbol. The thick laces trailed behind him like bright orange worms.

"I *really* think you're gonna have to wait for the next one," Elliot said.

"Fuck that," he said. "I've been standing here ten minutes."

He started to board, forcing his body into the mass of human flesh. The small boy in the stroller looked up, wide-eyed, at this towering mass of person hovering over him.

The large man continued to force everyone to squeeze back even farther. The older woman said, "I don't think I can breathe," although that might have had less to do with being compressed and more to do with the newest passenger's sleeveless shirt.

He was, not to put too fine a point on it, aromatic.

Everyone was jammed in so tightly that the man did not even try to turn around. He faced the back wall of the elevator and said to one of the teenage girls who was closest to the panel of buttons, "Can you hit Lobby?"

"It already is," she said.

Her sister said, "Hit the Close button."

"The what?"

She pointed to the button with the two triangular symbols pointing at each other. Her sister hit the button.

The doors started to close, then bounced back. The newest passenger's butt was in the way.

It was the girls' mother's turn to speak up. "Honestly, I think you're going to have to take the next—"

But rather than get off, the man pushed in even farther, his belly hovering over the head of the child in the stroller. The girl pushed the button again.

The doors once again attempted to close, and this time they made it.

"Shit!" said one of the girls, looking down.

The door had closed on a trailing orange shoelace from one of the big man's unlaced sneakers. As the car started to move downward, the slack went out of the lace. In less than a second, the shoe it was attached to was dragged suddenly to the door, which pitched the large man forward.

As his meaty leg was yanked upward, the top half of his body toppled. Like a great oak falling in the forest, he went straight to the floor, narrowly missing the child, but hitting the arms of the stroller, pitching the boy upward, like he was on a teeter totter and someone had dropped a boulder at the other end.

Everyone screamed. The teenage girls' screams came out more like shrieks.

No sooner had the big man hit the floor than he started to lift up as his one leg headed toward the top of the door.

But then the shoe was ripped from his foot. He came crashing down again. The shoe sailed up to the center of the door until the lace snapped, and it dropped back down.

"Benjy!" the mother screamed, reaching over the man to see that her child was okay.

"Fuckin' hell!" Elliot shouted.

Somehow, impossibly, everyone had pushed back to allow room for the fallen man. The girls were literally perched on Leonard's feet. The child's father's arms were spread wide against the wall of the car.

The toddler was crying. The stroller was a write-off.

And then the doors opened.

They had reached the lobby.

Half a dozen people waiting to board recoiled in horror at the sight of the collapsed man. The girls managed to step around him, quickly followed by their mother. Once out, they stopped and turned to offer help.

The big man slowly got up off the floor. Elliot actually extended a hand to help him.

"You okay?" he asked.

The man nodded, then spotted his shoe, minus half a lace, on the floor of the car. Leonard grabbed it and handed it over.

"Please!" said the older woman, still at the back of the car. "Let us out! We have to catch a plane!"

She and her husband navigated their way around the others, but as soon as they exited the elevator they were faced with a throng of people who'd been waiting for it.

"Look what you did!" said the small child's mother, who now had the toddler in her arms and was pointing to the mangled stroller.

"Uh, sorry," he said.

"You should never have gotten on," the father said. "And Christ, maybe this'll teach you to tie up your shoes."

"I said I was sorry. Anyway, it's the hotel's fault. The door grabbed my lace."

The parents shook their heads as they hauled the busted stroller off the elevator.

"You sure you're okay?" Leonard asked.

The big man nodded slowly. "I might have twisted my ankle," he said, looking down at his socked foot. "But I guess I'm all right."

"Okay," he said, then looked at Elliot and gave him a shrug that said, *I guess we're done here.*

As the two headed through the lobby, Elliot said, "I thought that guy was going to lose his leg or something."

"I want my granola parfait from Le Pain Quotidien," Leonard said, "and then we're going to see if we can move to another hotel."

Elliot smiled. "So now *you're* the one who's fed up."

As they came out of the hotel, Leonard said, "That guy could have crushed us to death."

"So, what, you're looking for a hotel that bans fatties? That sounds very un-PC."

They took a moment to get their bearings as they stood on the sidewalk. A yellow Prius cab was working its way down the street.

Leonard pointed east. "It's that way."

"No," Elliot said, grabbing his arm. "I'm pretty sure Le Pain's that way."

The cab was sixty feet away.

"Wait," Leonard said, looking one way and then the other. "I hate to admit this, but I think you're right."

The cab passed by the hotel doors.

"Okay, then let's—"

And that was when the bomb in the Prius exploded.

Thirty-Six

Three minutes after the taxi explosion on East Forty-Ninth Street, eight people were huddled out in front of the three elevators in the lobby of the twenty-story Gormley Building on Seventh Avenue between Sixteenth and Seventeenth Streets. A man and a woman who were closest to the closed doors were both gazing at their phones. The woman was reading the *New York Times* and the man was scanning information from an app that tracked the stock market. He shook his head slowly, not liking what he was seeing.

Of the six people behind them, most were on phones, others sipped expensive lattes from Starbucks cups. Every few seconds, someone would glance upward to see what floor the car was currently on.

It had been up on the eighteenth floor, but was heading their way.

About ten seconds later, the doors parted.

The man and woman who'd been standing closest each took a step forward without looking up from their phones.

And went down.

There was no car.

Odds were, they might have survived. It was not as though they stepped into the shaft twenty floors up.

They plunged, but only as far as the basement. There was only one floor below the lobby level. There was no parking garage beneath the Gormley Building, so the elevator did not go any great distance below the street.

The shaft, however, did extend slightly farther than the basement level, into a pit that accommodated elevator servicing.

It was into this pit that the two people fell.

As they pitched forward through the open doorway, screams erupted from those directly behind them. No one else blindly followed them into the shaft.

Once the cries of "Oh my God!" and "Holy shit!" and "Fuck!" subsided, a casually dressed man with buds in his ears leaned into the opening and looked down. The two people were rag dolls, their arms and legs a twisted mess. The floor of the shaft was dirty, and the grimy cement walls were lined with cables and tracks.

The fallen man was struggling to move one of his arms. The woman could be heard moaning.

"They're alive!" said the earbuds guy, glancing back at the others as he yanked on the wires that led up to his head. "Call 911!"

Someone with a phone in hand was already punching in the three numbers.

The man with the earbuds leaned back into the shaft and shouted down to the two injured people. "Help's coming! Hang in there!"

A breathless uniformed security guard arrived, pushing his way through the onlookers until he got to the opening. "What's going on? What's happened?"

The earbud guy said, "Door opened, no car, they went straight in."

The security guard's eyes went wide. "Basement," he said. "We can get closer to them if we open the elevator doors in the—"

And that was when they heard a mechanical noise. They both looked up.

What they saw was the bottom of the elevator car, which had been, all this time, sitting at the second floor.

It was now slowly moving in a downward direction.

"Fuck me," said the security guard, backing out of the shaft and pulling the other man with him.

The car's descent was bafflingly and maddeningly slow.

The base of the car had now moved below the top of the opening to the shaft. The inner doors of the elevator car were closed. While there was still a chance to see to the bottom, the earbud guy noticed that the fallen man had actually managed to get to his knees. He was leaning over the woman, checking on her.

As the car descended halfway past the opening, the security guard said, "Shit." He reached over and hit the Up button, hoping that would halt the elevator's progress, or at least make it come to a stop at the lobby level.

That way, rescue crews would still be able to reach the injured by way of the basement elevator door. All the security guard had to do was grab the special elevator key. All elevators had a small, peephole-sized opening in the door into which the key could be inserted. Once turned, it would open the doors.

It seemed like a plan.

Briefly.

The elevator car maintained its slow descent.

It did not stop at the lobby level.

It continued, slowly, on its inexorable downward path.

The injured man, no longer visible, could be heard shouting, "Make it stop! Stop the fucking thing!"

Frantically, the security guard, unable to think of anything else to do, kept jabbing at the button. "Come on! Stop, you son of a bitch!"

The top of the elevator car now dropped below the level of the lobby floor.

The screams from the man in the pit grew more intense, and were joined by the woman. A bone-chilling, two-person chorus of death.

The elevator car, like some cunning animal moving in on its injured prey, maintained its slow descent until it finally came to a stop.

The screaming ceased.

Thirty-Seven

Eugene Clement was reading a print edition of the *New York Times* while, across the table from him in the hotel restaurant, his wife was looking at stories on a tablet. On the plate before her was her unfinished breakfast. Some scraps of scrambled eggs, one and a half slices of toast, a rasher of bacon.

They'd exchanged only a few words since the night before, when Estelle had started asking him about that man he'd been talking to, then tried to move on to the subject of their sex life, which he had no interest in discussing. He'd been partly honest with her when he'd used stress as an excuse. He had been under a considerable mental strain lately. But the real truth was, he *had* lost interest. Not in sex. Just in sex with Estelle.

He'd found ways, back in their hometown, and when he traveled the country, without her, on business, to meet his needs.

Discreetly.

What worried him as he sat here at breakfast had nothing to do with coming up with excuses for why Estelle didn't get his motor running the way she once did. What had him worried was her suspicion that their trip to New York had nothing to do with their anniversary.

Which was, of course, correct.

He'd been having to enjoy the Flyovers' activities from afar. It just wasn't very satisfying, watching a bombing in Seattle when you were several hundred miles away. But he wanted to have a front row seat to see how the New York coastal elites reacted when the rubes struck back. Clement believed he had been successful, up to now, in keeping his wife from thinking that the Flyovers would ever resort to violence. She appeared persuaded that the criticisms of the Flyovers were unfounded.

But then she started asking about the man he'd spoken to briefly. Said she had seen him on more than one occasion.

Clearly, Clement and Bucky had to be more careful moving forward.

Eugene looked over his newspaper to find his coffee, noticed the food still on his wife's plate, and asked, "You didn't like your breakfast?"

"It was fine," Estelle said, not looking away from the tablet.

"I liked mine," he said. "Not that you asked."

She looked up from the tablet. "What?"

"Nothing," he said.

Estelle said, "Maybe you need to let someone else lead the charge."

Clement blinked. "I'm sorry, what?"

"You say you're stressed out," she said. "So let someone else do it. Let someone else speak for the Flyovers."

"The work's not done," he said. "I have much to do."

"And when will it be done?" she asked. "Tell me. What is it, exactly, that you're hoping to achieve? What is it you want?"

This was not like her. Challenging him on his mission.

"Awareness, Estelle," he said. "I want to raise awareness."

She sighed. "Like with that godforsaken occupation?" she asked, loudly enough to be heard beyond their table.

Clement glanced around quickly to see whether any of their fellow diners had noticed, then leaned over the table and glared at her. "For God's sake, keep your voice down," he whispered. "And we achieved a lot with that."

Estelle shook her head sadly. "A bunch of grown men having a sit-in in a national park, looking like fools. Ten days you were there. It was ridiculous. God knows how long it would have gone on if one of your brilliant partners in crime hadn't tried to sneak out to get Kentucky Fried Chicken and got himself nabbed by the FBI."

Clement leaned back in his chair. "What's gotten into you lately?"

"Certainly not you," she said icily.

He felt his cheeks go hot. "You don't win a war with a single battle," he told her. "What we achieved with the occupation may not be evident for some time. These things are cumulative."

She kept her voice to a whisper this time, but her anger was evident. "Who are you at war with, Eugene? Tell me? The other people in this restaurant? Our waiter? The people at the front desk? Are you at war with them?"

Eugene breathed in slowly. Estelle had never been able to see the big picture.

"A revolution takes time," he said.

"A revolution," she said dismissively. "You're Paul Revere, is that it?"

"Don't mock me."

"And all these people who follow you, your acolytes. Half of them are out of their minds, you know. They're lunatics. Blowing up coffee shops. The things you write, the things you say, they get people riled up." She paused. "I know you'd never want them to do those things, but you have to know you have an influence."

Clement took a moment to compose himself. Slowly, he said, "I am here, right now, in this city, to celebrate our anniversary. I do not want to talk about my work. I do not want to talk about . . . *us*. So get out your goddamn guidebook and pick some goddamn thing for us to do today while I go take a goddamn piss."

Estelle's jaw dropped.

He threw his napkin onto the table and pushed back his chair. As he walked away, he took out his phone, opened an app, and scanned the latest headlines. There were two breaking stories. Details were sketchy, but there had been another elevator accident. Two people were believed dead. And on West Forty-Ninth Street, a taxi had exploded, killing two on the street, and the driver.

Clement slipped the phone back into his jacket and continued to the men's washroom, which was down a short hallway off the lobby. He pushed open the door and walked in slowly.

The room appeared, at first, to be empty. He stood, briefly, in front of the mirror, ostensibly checking his appearance, running his hand over his thinning gray hair. He turned and took a step toward a row of urinals, glancing over his shoulder at the three stalls. Two of the doors hung open, but the third was closed. In the gap at the bottom could be seen two shoes.

Eugene chose the middle urinal and unzipped. While he stood there, he cleared his throat. Not once, but three distinctive times.

From behind the closed stall, a voice Clement recognized as Bucky's said, "You up to speed?"

"Yes," Clement said. "It's been quite a morning for the good folks of New York."

"Yeah," Bucky said from inside the stall.

"Any problems?"

"No." Bucky paused, then said, "The cab was a Prius."

"Nice touch," Clement said, giving his dick a shake.

"I set it to go off sixty seconds after I got out. Any longer than that and another passenger might have noticed it in the back."

"Where exactly did it go off?"

"Out front of the Klaxton Hotel."

"Nice that it wasn't this one," Clement said. Sarcastically, he added, "I would hate for anything to put a damper on our anniversary weekend." He paused, then said, "Speaking of which, you need to be more careful. My wife's noticed you."

"Shit. What'd you say?"

"I said I didn't know what she was talking about." Clement zipped up. "At least Estelle isn't going to find us talking in here."

He went back over to the row of sinks, where he washed his hands slowly and methodically. The door opened and another man walked in.

Clement said, "Morning."

Just loud enough to send a signal to Bucky that their conversation was over.

He held his hands under the dryer, but they were still damp when he returned to the hotel dining room. When he went back to the table, Estelle was not there. He scanned the room for her before sitting down.

She'd gone back to their room, he figured. She was still angry with him. *Fuck it,* he thought. *I'm going to have another cup of coffee.*

He spotted the waiter and waved a hand in the air. But then Estelle appeared and sat back down in her seat. She had several flyers in her hand advertising various city attractions.

"Where were you?" he asked.

"Just sorting out what I'm going to do today," she said. "I got tired of hunting through the guidebook. I got these by the front desk."

She fanned them out on the table like playing cards, saw one she liked, and picked it up.

"The Guggenheim," she said.

Clement nodded. "Sure, we can do that."

Estelle shook her head. "That's what *I'm* doing." She gathered up the other flyers and tossed them to his side of the table. "I'm sure you'll find something just as interesting."

Thirty-Eight

Barbara saw a tweet about the exploding taxi on East Forty-Ninth Street. She went to the link but there wasn't much more detail there than there had been on the Twitter feed.

She was in her kitchen nook, the laptop on her table, sipping on cold coffee, and had been thinking maybe she should get dressed, wishing she had an apartment as nice as Chris Vallins's, when she saw the news.

"God," she said, reading about the taxi.

Another ISIS-inspired nutcase, she figured. Once or twice a year, it seemed, New York had to endure some numbnut, would-be terrorist, acting alone, who had put together some half-assed bomb and then tried to detonate it in Penn Station or the Port Authority or Times Square. Sometimes these assholes did real damage, and other times the things went off before they could even get them out of their apartment. The ones that often created the most mayhem didn't have to build a bomb at all. They just got behind the wheel of a truck and ran people down.

These days, any time anything bad happened, the first thought was: Is it terrorism? But what happened on Forty-Ninth Street might turn out not to be a bombing. Maybe a gas main under the street blew up as the taxi was driving over it. It was possible the cab blew up for reasons unrelated to a bomb. The incident had only happened in the last half hour, and not much was known.

Barbara briefly considered turning on the TV, then decided she'd check later.

She reread the column she had posted late the previous day. There were a few more comments, none remotely helpful. She was going to try again today to get some kind of statement from any governmental body that would talk to her. Homeland, FBI, the NYPD, somebody. She'd call Animal Control if she thought anyone there had a clue. Why, she wanted to ask them, had at least two families connected to these elevator deaths been asked to keep their mouths shut?

Barbara looked through her own contacts in her phone, making a note of those who might be helpful, then went online looking for other possible leads. She made a list of the people she wanted to reach.

She had a source inside the NYPD. Not an actual cop or a detective, but a woman in the city's public information office. Barbara had her private cell phone number. She brought up the contact on her own phone and tapped it.

Several seconds later, a woman said, "Hey."

"Yeah, hi. It's me. Long time no chat."

"I was starting to feel neglected. And relieved at the same time," the woman said.

"Look, I'm trying to nail something down and I'm not getting anywhere yet."

"On what?"

"The elevator accidents on Monday and Tuesday. I'm getting the sense interest in those has gone way up the food chain but I don't know why. Like maybe Homeland or the FBI is sniffing around. Why the hell would that be happening?"

"If that's true, I haven't heard anything. But—"

"They're like industrial accidents. But some of the families of the victims have been told to keep a low profile on this. Not raise a fuss. So—"

"Shut up and listen."

Barbara paused. "Okay."

"It's not two. It's three."

"What?"

"Are you near a TV?"

"No, I live on Neptune. Of course I'm near—"

"Turn it on."

Barbara got up out of the kitchen chair and strolled into the living area of her apartment, the cell phone still glued to her ear. She picked up the remote with her free hand, fired up the flat screen, and went to one of the twenty-four-hour news channels.

"—in three days," said a woman with a mike in hand. While Barbara recognized the reporter, Liza Bentley, she did not recognize the building she was standing out front of. But she watched the crawl at the bottom of the screen, which read: *Two Dead in 7th Avenue Elevator Disaster.*

"This is not happening," Barbara said under her breath.

"You talking to me?" said her source.

"What's going on?" Barbara asked. "This can't be coincidence."

"Well," the woman said slowly, as if debating if she should continue, "I did hear *something.*"

Barbara muted the TV. "What did you hear?"

"There was nothing on paper, no emails. But a lot of calls have been made to landlords."

"Landlords?"

"Building owners, property managers, that bunch. The word was to keep it on the down-low."

"'Down-low'?"

"I've always wanted to say that," the woman said. "Anyway, the city doesn't have enough elevator inspectors to do this on their own, so everyone's been asked to check their buildings."

"For what?" Barbara asked.

"I don't know," she said. "But whatever's happening—a defect or whatever—they're afraid it's going viral."

"Can elevators get a virus?"

"I don't mean it like that." The woman paused. "Unless, you know, maybe I do. Thing is, there's more than sixty thousand elevators in the city. It's going to take a while to get to all of them."

"Then why *not* go public?" Barbara asked. "Get the word out? Why haven't you put out a statement?"

"Hey, I just work here. They want to tell the world something, I'm on it."

"Panic," Barbara said.

"What?"

"They don't want to start a panic."

"If there's anything to actually panic about."

Barbara laughed. "People don't always need a sound reason to go into panic mode."

"Look, I gotta go. Let me leave you with one bit of advice."

"Okay."

"Take the stairs."

Thirty-Nine

I don't think you can wait any longer," Valerie told the mayor. "You have to say something. A press conference."

Richard Headley was circling his desk, pacing, running his hand slowly over his head. "Christ," he muttered. "What the hell am I supposed to tell people? Don't use the fucking elevators? In this city? Might as well them not to honk their horns."

Valerie nodded sympathetically. "I know. If we put our heads together, maybe we can come up with something that—"

"And where the hell is Glover?" he asked, stopping and looking at the door, as if expecting his son to walk through it at any second.

"I don't know," Valerie said. "I'll text him."

Headley waved a dismissive hand. "Never mind. I don't know what help he'd be anyway."

Valerie, who had been standing in the middle of the room, took a step closer. "Mr. Mayor." A pause. "Richard."

He stopped pacing at the sound of his name, looked at her, and waited.

"It may not be my place to speak to this," she said.

"I'm sure it isn't," the mayor said.

"I say this with the best of intentions."

"Go ahead, Valerie. Just say it."

"About Glover."

"What about Glover?"

"I think . . . I'm worried about his self-esteem."

The mayor cocked his head slightly to one side. His look bordered on amused. "Self-esteem?"

"I know we talked about this the other day, that his real talents lie in other areas, but you're awfully hard on him. He's trying so hard to please you, but he can't seem to get anything right in your eyes. And I'm not just worried about him. It's you I'm worried about."

"Why?"

"Things get out. People talk. People observe. Moving forward, we're working very hard to craft an image of you that voters will like." She cleared her throat. "Like *more*. They see the way you treat Glover, they form an opinion. That you're, well, something of a bully where your own son is concerned. It doesn't play well."

Headley grunted.

Valerie stood a little straighter, steeling herself for the onslaught she thought was probably coming. "Look, you're a complex individual. You can be tough, even cruel. But there *is* another side to you, and I've seen it. You can be compassionate. I know there are things you care about. The environment, for one. But it's not enough to care about the planet. You have to care about the people on it."

Headley looked bemused.

Valerie continued. "There are going to be more stories about you moving forward. Profiles. We're looking for someone else to ghost-write your bio, now that Barbara Matheson has taken a pass."

Headley snorted derisively. "One of Glover's bright ideas."

"Maybe it was a better one than we think. She could have done a good job if we'd agreed to give her a bit of leeway."

He shook his head.

"As I was saying, there will be more profiles, many of which we'll have no control over, and that means people who work for and with you will be approached. There's a good chance a lot of them will speak off the record, especially if they feel they've been insulted or slighted by you. They'll talk about what they've seen. How you've treated Glover might be one of the things that comes out. And it will reflect badly on you. The fact is, there's already talk about it. There's even a Twitter account that—"

Headley raised a hand, silencing her. He slowly wandered behind his desk and sat in his plush, oversized chair. He lowered his head briefly, placing his palms on his forehead before looking up again.

"Okay, so I'll never win Father of the Year," he said. "But the fact that I have him here, working in this administration, is to try to make up for the missteps I've made over the years. If he were anyone else . . . I'd have fired him by now, most likely."

"He's a bright kid, Richard. He's the most tech-savvy guy I know. Policy, okay, that's not his strong suit. He's too young, doesn't have the experience. Put him somewhere where he shines, twenty-four/ seven. Like polling and data analysis. He just did a new hire down there. Liberate him from being part of the inner circle. Let him do his thing without having to make you happy every day."

The mayor appeared to be considering Valerie's words. He looked away and said, quietly, "He . . . humiliated me. It took me years to live that down."

Valerie sighed. "You're better than this."

"You can bet, when and if I announce for anything, they'll dig up that clip of him crying for the cameras."

"He was a kid," Valerie said. "He was a kid who watched his mother die while you were out—"

She stopped herself.

Headley gave her a cold stare. "—fucking her nurse?"

Valerie nodded slowly. "I might have put it another way. But yes."

The mayor's face softened. "My own father was a son of a bitch."

"I know."

"Treated me like shit." He shook his head. "I hated him. I *still* hate him, and he's been dead for sixteen years. The shit he made me do. But at the same time, I'm grateful, you know?"

"I . . . think so," Valerie said.

"He gave me the strength to make hard decisions. I had to execute his orders or face his wrath. It made me tough." He paused, struck by a memory. "One time, he made me evict this couple. The husband had lost his job and his wife had just had a baby. Had some sort of health complications. But they were four months behind in the rent. We were a business, not a charity. They had to go."

Valerie looked as though she'd caught wind of a sewage leak. "Jesus, you tell that story like you're proud of it. God help us if that finds its way into your bio."

Headley blinked, as if not realizing how the tale made him look. "Yeah, okay, I take your point. But it was *not* the point I was trying to make. I learned to do what had to be done. I grew a spine working for my dad."

"Except when it came to standing up to him. You could have said no when he told you to put that family onto the street."

Headley gave his assistant a withering gaze. She just wasn't getting it.

"All I'm trying to do with Glover is make him tough, too."

"I see," Valerie said.

"God, you're looking at me just the way his mother used to," the mayor said.

Now it was Valerie's turn to gaze witheringly. "You don't have to make the same mistakes with your own son that your father made with you."

The look he gave her was a mix of contempt and admiration. "You got some balls talking to me this way."

"If you don't want to hear the truth, Richard, hire someone else."

His mouth slowly morphed into a crooked smile before his face once again turned grim. "Set it up. A presser, with the chief and that smug asshole from Homeland."

"Maybe not Homeland," Valerie advised. "We don't want to scare everyone to death. You put Homeland on stage and we're talking terrorism, no doubt about it."

Headley gave that a thought. "Okay. And we better bring in what's-his-name, our elevator guy, in case there are any technical questions."

"On it," she said. As she went for the door, it opened. Glover strode into the room.

"There's been another one," he said breathlessly. "Another elevator tragedy."

Headley looked at his son pityingly, then at Valerie. "Breaking news."

She gave her boss a sharp, disapproving look that said, *You just can't help yourself, can you?*

Forty

Alexander Vesolov, the Russian ambassador to the United States, was walking through Grand Central Terminal when he turned into Hudson News.

He perused the front pages of the various newspapers and settled on a copy of the *Wall Street Journal*. He picked it up, his eye immediately going to a story, above the fold, about the death of Dr. Fanya Petrov in an elevator mishap. Shouldered into the piece was a one-column sidebar story with the headline: "Is it Safe to Ride a City Elevator?"

He took a ten-dollar bill from his pocket and handed it to the woman behind the counter. Once he'd pocketed his change, he folded the paper once and tucked it under his arm. He did not head back out into the terminal, instead deciding to peruse the periodicals. Hudson News had hundreds of magazines to choose from, as well as a selection of books.

Vesolov first wandered over to the newsmagazines. He glanced at the covers of *Time* and *The Economist*, leafed through the pages of *The New Yorker* and read the captions on the cartoons and didn't laugh at a single one. He'd never understood them.

He put *The New Yorker* back and moved to the car section. Articles about cars needed no cultural translation. Vesolov reached for a copy of *Automobile*, lightly bumping shoulders with another man who was glancing through the pages of *Motor Trend*.

The other man was several inches taller than Vesolov, and in much better physical shape. Vesolov's shoulders were permanently hunched; he was round in the middle and thick in the neck, his skin sickly pale. The other man was lean and trim, tanned, and his black business suit fit him perfectly.

"So," Vesolov said quietly, his eyes focused on the magazine.

"Yes," said the other man, his voice low.

"It's done. There's nothing else for you at this time." Vesolov flipped the page, saw an article about an upcoming, all-electric Porsche. "If we need you, we'll be in touch. A deposit has been made in the usual account."

"You didn't need to do that."

"We had a deal. Petrov is no longer a threat."

"Yes, but—"

"Don't protest. We had an arrangement. Things turned out a little differently than expected, but we have the result we wanted. Maybe the next one, you'll give us a discount."

"Seems fair," the other man said.

"You have a bit of extra time. See the sights."

The man chuckled. "Maybe not the Empire State Building."

"No, it does not seem like a good week for those kinds of attractions."

"You know where I would like to go? Iowa."

"Iowa?" said Vesolov. "Nobody comes to America and goes to Iowa."

"You see *Field of Dreams*? It is my favorite movie."

Vesolov shrugged. "Fine. Go to Iowa. See corn."

The ambassador put the car magazine back, turned, and walked away without saying another word. The second man waited the better part of a minute before heading back out into the terminal.

A third man, who'd had his back to the other two as he leafed through the pages of a *Sports Illustrated*, took out his cell phone.

He entered a number, placed the phone up to his ear. Someone answered before the first ring had finished.

"Get me Cartland," he said.

Forty-One

Jerry Bourque had staked out a spot on Grove Street, leaning up against a tree growing out of the sidewalk between Bedford and Bleecker. Beautiful old brownstones, tall, leafy trees. Plenty of interesting shops and cafés and restaurants. Bourque had always loved Greenwich Village and wished he lived here. You could almost imagine that you were in a world separate from the rest of New York City. Maybe it was the trees that worked to muffle the horns and sirens and growling engines that were only a block away.

Some mornings, like this one, he'd come here before the start of his shift to see how she was doing.

Amanda.

She would have had her second birthday by now. She was only a year and a half old when her mother, Sasha Woodrow, was shot to death by Blair Evans.

Bourque had been here enough times to know the routine. The nanny—a young woman in her twenties—would arrive at half past seven, on the dot, every morning, Monday to Friday. Sasha's husband, Leslie, would leave roughly fifteen minutes later. The front door would open, and Leslie, dressed nattily in suit and tie, would carefully bring out a bike and gingerly roll it down the steps to the sidewalk. He would then mount it and pedal off to his Wall Street job.

Bourque thought it was foolish of him not to wear a helmet.

Amanda had already lost one parent. Why was he willing to take the risk that she might lose two? It was all he could do, every morning he was here and saw this, not to say something to him.

But he held his tongue, because if he were Leslie Woodrow, his comeback would be, "Well, maybe if you hadn't dived out of the way, Amanda wouldn't already be down one parent."

Bourque surmised that Leslie got Amanda up and dressed, and that he also gave her breakfast, because most mornings that he was there, he witnessed the nanny emerging from the brownstone within twenty minutes of the father's departure. Clearly, there was not enough time for the nanny to accomplish all those things. Bourque often imagined Leslie sitting at breakfast with his daughter, sharing a piece of toast with her, giving her some Cheerios to play with, hopeful that more of them would end up in her mouth than on the floor.

The nanny—Bourque wished he knew her name, and even though he had the skills to find out, he had resisted doing so—liked to take Amanda out for a stroll first thing every morning, unless it was raining.

Today was no exception.

The door to the brownstone opened and out came the nanny with Amanda in one arm, and a small, folded-up stroller in the other. Once she had locked the door and made her way down to the sidewalk, the nanny set Amanda down briefly and quickly unfolded the stroller before the child could wander off. Once Amanda settled into it, the nanny buckled her in.

Very smart, Bourque thought.

Bourque believed the nanny was from France. Here on a visa, perhaps, maybe a student taking courses at night while she worked for Leslie Woodrow through the day. Bourque often heard her

264 | Linwood Barclay

speaking French to the child as they went past. How nice for Amanda, to acquire some proficiency in a second language at such an early age. Too bad about the way it had to happen, of course.

Bourque was discreet. He kept his distance. He turned away, or crossed the street, when the nanny approached with the stroller. He knew he shouldn't be spying this way, but Bourque needed constant assurance. He needed to know Amanda was okay.

He needed to know she was happy. That she was not traumatized. Like him.

If Amanda happened to be kicking her feet, or babbling cheerfully, or looking at the world with wonder and curiosity, Bourque felt hopeful. Those were all good signs, weren't they? If you were consumed with the memory of your mother being shot, of her blood spilling directly onto you like warm, red rain, those things would not be possible, right? Bourque wanted to believe Amanda had a chance of being a normal, healthy, happy child. Sure, not having a mother put her behind the eight ball from the get-go, but Bourque had to believe that eventually she would get past that. And who knew? Perhaps, one day, Leslie would find someone else. A new wife, a mother for Amanda.

Hell, maybe he'd marry the nanny. It had happened before.

Bourque watched Leslie for signs every morning, too.

Those first couple of months, Leslie did not ride his bike. After the arrival of the nanny—and Bourque believed the woman had been hired only after the mother's death—he would come down the steps to the street like a dead man walking. He shuffled more than walked. The man was visibly consumed with grief.

The next time Bourque staked out a spot in the morning, Leslie had the bike. To Bourque, the bicycle represented some level of recovery. A desire to face the day with more energy, to embrace it with *speed*.

In fact, as the weeks and months went on, he took off from his Grove Street residence with what struck Bourque as enthusiasm.

Good, Bourque had thought. *That's good.*

Guilt-ridden as he was over the woman's death, he was desperate for evidence that Leslie and Amanda were moving forward. Not that Sasha's death wouldn't haunt them forever. It certainly would Bourque. Maybe he was kidding himself. Seeing signs that were not there in a bid to ease his conscience. He wasn't looking for forgiveness. He had no reason to expect that. But if Leslie and Amanda could build a future together, maybe Bourque could breathe a little easier.

Literally.

As the stroller approached, Bourque saw Amanda was playing with something. It was a small rubber airplane, and Amanda was zooming it around, holding it up against the sky, imagining it up there.

Her lips vibrated as she mimicked the sounds of the jet engine.

The lips that tasted her mother's blood.

Bourque felt his windpipe tighten. He stood up straight, no longer using the tree to support himself. He reached into his pocket for his inhaler. Just one quick shot. That was all he needed. He uncapped it and brought it up to his mouth.

"Hey," someone said.

Bourque brought the inhaler down and shoved it into his pocket as he turned to find the nanny looking at him.

"Yes?" he said.

"Who are you?" she asked. She enunciated perfectly, but her French accent was impossible to miss.

"I'm sorry?"

"I've seen you before. Are you watching us?"

"No, I'm just waiting here to meet a friend. I—"

"I know I've seen you. Next time, I'll call the police."

Bourque, feeling his air passages constricting further, said, "I am the police." He quickly flashed his ID. "I'm keeping an eye on someone farther down the street. I'd appreciate it if you didn't say anything."

The nanny's mouth went round in an *Oh!* gesture. "Sorry," she whispered, and moved along, red-faced.

Bourque put the inhaler into his mouth and squeezed. He'd initially thought he only needed one shot, but now he took two. He fumbled as he tried to put it back into his pocket and dropped it instead. He bent over, snatched it up off the sidewalk, and dusted it off before tucking it away.

He could never do this again. If the nanny spotted him a second time, he'd have too much explaining to do.

The cell phone in his pocket rang. He brought it out, saw who it was, and put the phone to his ear.

"Yeah," he said.

"Where are you?" Lois Delgado asked.

"On my way in."

"Yeah, well, get a move on. We've been reassigned."

"To what?"

"They're pulling together some kind of task force on the elevator accidents. There's three now."

"Three?"

"Yeah. Two might be coincidence. But three's a clusterfuck. When the captain told them about our Otto guy, they pulled us in."

"We don't know that there's a connection." He paused. "But we don't know that there isn't."

"I'm hearing Homeland is involved."

Bourque said nothing. He looked up the street, saw the nanny and Amanda turn the corner.

"You there?"

"Yeah."

"I think they must be expecting mass panic. The mayor's about to make some kind of statement."

"I feel calmer already," Bourque said.

Forty-Two

"Thanks for coming," Mayor Richard Headley said to the gathered media in the press room at City Hall.

Valerie had emailed all the usual suspects a release saying the mayor would be making an important statement at noon. She offered no further details. At least a dozen reporters and news editors emailed back, asking what he'd be talking about. Valerie did not respond.

That pretty much guaranteed everyone would show up.

The room was jammed with reporters. Print, network, radio. Many of them were chatting, asking each other if they had any idea what was going on. Valerie provided a short introduction that amounted to little more than "Mayor Richard Headley," before turning over the podium to her boss.

Standing well off to the side were Glover and Vallins. Onstage with the mayor were Police Chief Annette Washington and Martin Fleck, the elevator expert.

The mayor cleared his throat after his thank-you and welcome, and took a drink of water from a glass left for him on the podium. He was about to speak when someone shouted out a question.

"Was the taxi explosion terrorism related?"

The question appeared to throw off the mayor before he'd had a chance to begin reading from his prepared text. That one reporter's question was a dam burster. Others began shouting questions.

"How many were killed in the explosion?"

"Was the driver a terrorist? Is this a suicide bombing?"

"Was the bomb left in the car by a passenger?"

The mayor held up a hand and waited until everyone had quieted down.

"Any questions about the taxi incident I will leave for Chief Washington here. Right now, I'm going to address another potential concern for the citizens of New York. As you know, there have been three tragic incidents involving elevators in the last three days. The first, on Monday, claimed four lives, including well-known entertainment producer Sherry D'Agostino and lawyer Barton Fieldgate. A terrible loss to the city, and to their families. At the time, it was believed some sort of random malfunction was the cause. But then, on Tuesday, another elevator incident took the life of a renowned Russian scientist, Fanya Petrov, who was here doing work at Rockefeller University. I have been in contact with the Russian ambassador and assured him we are doing everything we can to find out what happened. But even before I could make much headway there, we had another incident this morning in which two people were killed."

A stirring went through the crowd.

Headley said, "We have reason to suspect that these three incidents are not coincidental and are in fact related."

"How?" shouted one reporter.

"I'm getting to that," the mayor said, giving the reporter a harsh *shut the fuck up and let me finish* look. "Without getting into the details, there is a commonality to all these events that has raised our concern level. So I have directed the city's inspection force to begin a comprehensive check of all elevators in all five boroughs. Needless to say, this is a time-consuming task, so we are asking for the assistance of property management departments to initiate their own inspections."

The assembled media was getting increasingly restless. Another reporter shouted out, "So are we talking a mechanical issue here?

Some failed part that's in lots of different elevators across the city? And if so, why are the failures happening at the same time?"

"This is the sort of thing we're looking into," Headley said, irritated. The constant interruptions were throwing him off his game. "I can say that—"

"My information is that the FBI or Homeland Security are involved, which would be kind of weird if it's just a mechanical issue."

A different voice. Female. Headley squinted, trying to see past the lights to spot who had asked the question.

"Would that be Ms. Matheson?"

"Yes," said Barbara. "Am I wrong about that? That the feds have taken an interest?"

The mayor paused a moment. "DHS is involved, yes," he said slowly.

"Was it Homeland Security, then, that was going to the families of the deceased and asking them to keep a low profile? To not ask too many questions, at least at this stage?"

"I'm not in a position to answer that," Headley said. "We'd need someone from Homeland to field that."

"Is it because they didn't want to cause a panic before they had more details?"

"I'd encourage you to give them a call."

"Oh, I've been trying," Barbara said. "Wouldn't Homeland's involvement suggest what you're dealing with here is, in fact, terrorism? That these elevator malfunctions are actually sabotage? That they're deliberate acts?"

The buzz that was moving through the room began to grow louder.

A reporter from the *Daily News* shouted out, "If this is deliberate, who's doing it? Has anyone claimed responsibility?"

The mayor looked to Chief Washington. She nodded and stepped forward to the microphone.

"No one has claimed responsibility," she said. "And just to clarify what the mayor was saying, we do not know with one hundred percent certainty that there was deliberate tampering. But we are seriously looking at that possibility."

"Is this related to the Flyovers?" asked a woman from Fox News.

"We have no reason to—"

"Because," she continued, "someone claiming to be inspired by them just claimed responsibility for the taxi bombing. It's on Twitter."

Washington blinked. Everyone in the room turned to look at the woman from Fox.

"I'm not familiar with that tweet," Washington said, grimacing. "Twitter is not my number one news source."

"Is it possible the explosion and the elevator incident at the Gormley Building on Seventh Avenue are linked? They happened at exactly the same time."

"Again, that will be part of our investigation. We're in the very early stages. I'd like to turn it back over to the mayor."

The mayor resumed his spot at the podium and said, "Thank you, Chief. Moving on, I'd like to point out that—"

"Is it safe to take an elevator in this city?"

It was Barbara's question. The room went silent as everyone waited for the mayor's answer. But instead of doing that, the mayor turned to Fleck and waved him forward.

"Um, I'd like to introduce Martin Fleck, from the Department of Buildings. He can speak to the issue of elevator safety and deal with the more technical questions."

As Fleck approached the mike, the mayor whispered, "Try to keep it upbeat."

Fleck gave him a sharp look, as if to say, *Seriously?* But as he stood before the podium he did his best to project calm.

"To address that last question," he said, "the facts bear out that elevators are very, very safe. Accidents are extremely rare. In fact, most fatalities related to elevators involve servicemen, not the general public. There are many safety features built into any elevator system that—"

A woman from the *Post* cut him off: "Yeah, but we're not talking about that kind of thing. We're talking about terrorists cutting the cables."

Fleck held up a palm to the crowd. "No one said anything about cutting cables, and no one up here used the word 'terrorist.' The cables were not, as you say, cut on these elevators."

"Then what did happen?"

Fleck said, "It's more like they were hacked."

There was a sudden eruption of questions. With everyone shouting queries at once, Fleck looked like a bunny cornered by a wolf pack.

"How," Barbara managed to shout over the others, "do you hack an elevator? Is that actually possible?"

"Well, it would be very difficult," Fleck said. "It would demand a very high level of expertise. And even if you had that kind of knowledge, you would need a device that—"

"What kind of device?" It was the woman from the *Post* again.

"In simplest terms, it's like a TV remote that allows one to control all of an elevator's functions."

The guy from NY1 said, "That sounds like something out of a *Mission: Impossible* movie. You can't do that in the real world, can you?"

"If you knew all the various security codes, yes, in fact, you can. It can be plugged right into a building's elevator system. Now, if someone were outside the building, and knew how to access the overall security system, one could then tap into the elevator system."

Fleck, now that he was really getting into his area of expertise, was starting to look more comfortable, but Headley appeared increasingly uneasy.

"Holy shit," one of the reporters exclaimed.

A tall, handsome man from the local NBC affiliate finally got a question in. "But a device like that would be very hard to get hold of, wouldn't it?"

"In fact," said Fleck, "no. You can buy one for about five hundred dollars on—"

The mayor came up alongside Fleck and edged him away from the microphone. "Thanks very much, Martin. I'll take it from here. The reason I called this news conference was to inform the public that we are investigating all of these incidents very carefully and asking that if anyone sees something that is remotely suspicious, to please alert—"

Barbara called out, "Excuse me!"

The mayor ignored her. "What we are imploring people to do is—"

"I had a question that never got answered," Barbara said, making herself heard above the mayor.

Headley, looking visibly pained, looked at Barbara and asked, "What question was that?"

Barbara took half a second to compose herself, then said, sounding out each word clearly and succinctly, "Is it, or is it not, safe to take an elevator in the city of New York?"

The mayor looked grim. Everyone in the room seemed to be holding their breath.

"I don't know," he said finally.

Forty-Three

Within minutes of the mayor's "I don't know," the story was the lead item on all city, state, and national newscasts. CNN interrupted regular programming with its *BREAKING NEWS* logo, and a grim-faced Wolf Blitzer told the world how the mayor of one of the biggest, and most vertical cities in the world could not say, with any assurance whatsoever, that the city's thousands of elevators were safe.

"After three elevator tragedies in as many days," Blitzer said, "New York is now facing the possibility of a serial saboteur. There is evidence to suggest that all three incidents, in random buildings across the city, are connected. Stunningly, it was revealed moments ago that these elevators may have been hacked, raising the horrifying specter that these conveyances that carry millions of people every-day could be remotely manipulated. This startling news comes at the same time as the Flyovers, a militant domestic group believed to be responsible for terrorist acts in several coastal cities, has claimed responsibility for a taxi bombing in New York that claimed not only the life of the driver but two visitors from Canada who had just stepped out of a hotel on East Forty-Ninth Street. The head of the New York Police Department could not say, one way or another, whether the Flyovers group is actually behind the taxi bombing, or if it has a hand in the elevator crisis."

The *New York Times* website updated within minutes of Mayor

Richard Headley's news conference. Its banner headline read: "Elevator Plunges Linked, Sabotage Suspected." Below that ran a secondary headline: "Mayor Headley Fails to Calm a Nervous City."

The *New York Daily News*, predictably, was less subtle about the mayor's inability to reassure his constituents that it was safe to get into a city elevator. Paired with a picture of the mayor looking glumly down at his notes was the headline "Nice Going, Dick," followed by a secondary headline reading: "Head Case Doesn't Know If Hacked Elevators Safe."

Immediately after the news conference, with two thumbs working at lightning speed, Barbara wrote a column on her phone and emailed it to her editor at *Manhattan Today*. It was posted to the website less than a minute later, under the headline "Mayor Gives City the Shaft When it Comes to Elevator Safety."

By Barbara Matheson

In what has to go down in the books as one of the most disastrous press conferences in New York City history, an inept Mayor Richard Headley told the city two startling things. The first was that someone, or some group, is deliberately killing New Yorkers by taking over the operation of elevators with malicious intent. But as troubling as that news is, the second tidbit is worse: our mayor hasn't got a clue what to do about it.

Appearing with the chief of police and a flunky from the city department that oversees elevator safety, the mayor offered a blunt "I don't know" when asked whether you can get into one of these devices and expect to get out of it alive. Consider what has happened since Monday. Four dead when an elevator in the Lansing Tower plunged. A visiting Russian scientist beheaded as she attempted to escape her car when it was stuck, with the doors open, between floors. And early this morning, two people crushed to death in the Gormley Building after they fell into the bottom of the shaft, and the car came down on top of them. What may happen tomorrow, and what plan, if any, does the city have to deal with this?

As if that weren't enough to worry about, a New York cab blew up this morning killing at least three people, but don't ask the mayor if that has anything to do with the elevator mishaps, because he doesn't know. What we do know is that someone claiming to be part of the Flyovers activist group posted on Twitter to claim responsibility for the bombing. Maybe they'd have copped to the elevator sabotage, too, but ran out of characters. So, bottom line is, we don't know whether it's safe to ride in an elevator, or a taxi. Have a nice day.

The hashtag #goingdown started trending on Twitter within ten minutes of Headley's remarks.

And then *big* news broke.

Media outlets were alerted to a second City Hall press conference less than an hour after the first one.

Mayor Headley, instantly feeling the heat about not knowing how to respond to the crisis, issued a statement that he was, after consultation with the city's police and fire chiefs, ordering that every elevator in the city be taken out of service until it could be determined that they were safe.

Every. Single. One.

But rather than face the press again after his disastrous earlier appearance, Headley sent someone to speak on his behalf.

His son.

A nervous Glover Headley took to the podium to say that the city was calling on landlords and property managers everywhere to make their elevators inoperable until they could be inspected and deemed safe, and by "safe," he meant "not tampered with." Instructions on how to determine whether they had been would be posted on the city's website so as to expedite the process. Among other things, inspectors would be told to look for unauthorized modifications to the cars, and to change any passwords into building and elevator security systems.

Glover said the mayor appreciated the magnitude of the inconvenience this would pose to the people of New York, but he was hopeful the measure would be short-lived. Inspections were to start immediately, and it was possible many elevators would be back in operation by the end of the week, many much sooner. The non-news networks canceled regular programming to give the story blanket coverage.

"This is an outrageous overreaction," said one male political commentator on CNN, part of a *Hollywood Squares*–like cluster of pundits. "You simply cannot shut down every elevator in the biggest city in the country. We have no idea how real this threat is, and chances are more people will get hurt *not* being able to use elevators than might be hurt in them. This is like shutting down every road in America because there might be a couple of weak bridges out there somewhere."

A woman in the box next to him shot back, "Are you kidding me? Would you get on an elevator in New York today?"

The man shot back, angrily, "Yes I would, and you know why? Because this is all a load of fake news designed to frighten people and make them submit to the will of—"

Another man in the box above him cut in and said, "For the love of God, that's just about the stupidest thing I've ever heard from you, and that's saying something. Every time you're warned about a possible threat, you think it's some conspiracy to make you submit? Come on, what are you—"

"Oh," the first man shot back, "and I suppose you think 9/11 wasn't an inside job. Well, I have it on good authority—"

On Fox, the conspiracy theories went even further, where one guest speculated that the mayor, with his left-leaning, Democratic background, had manufactured the crisis as a way to make New Yorkers more fit by forcing them to take the stairs. After all, this was the same mayor who wanted all the city vehicles to be emissions free. Could you really trust someone like that? "This is the most ridiculous thing since former mayor Michael Bloomberg tried to legislate the size of soft drinks," the guest said.

Over on NBC, a so-called expert had been brought into the studio to tell viewers how to survive an elevator plunge.

She said, "A lot of people think if you're in an elevator that's hurtling downward, and you jump off the floor just before it hits the bottom of the shaft, that somehow that's going to save you. Well," and at this point she chuckled, "there's a whole lot wrong with that supposition. The first is, you're not really going to be able to time it right. You can be looking at the numbers next to the door and figure, okay, we're just about to hit the basement, jump now! But even if you could do that, which is pretty much impossible, it wouldn't save you. Your body is still traveling downward at the same rate of speed as the elevator, so one way or another, you're going to hit bottom and you're going to hit it hard. The only real hope you have of surviving is to lie down on the floor of the elevator, on your back, spreading out your arms and legs like you're a starfish. What this does is more evenly distribute your weight across the surface of the elevator floor."

The host asked, "Okay, but what if you're in an elevator with ten other people and can't do that?"

The expert shrugged. "Well, in that case, you're going to become elevator pizza."

On MSNBC, the elevator crisis was a financial story.

"The New York Stock Exchange has closed three hours before the ringing of the bell," one analyst said. "The business of the city has effectively ground to a halt. Millions of dollars are being lost every second that this goes on. Mayor Richard Headley has created a panic. He needs to get back out there in front of the cameras and come up with something better than 'I don't know' and 'We're shutting down the elevators.' This has to be the most astonishing example of incompetence I have ever seen."

The only group alleged to have taken responsibility for anything that had happened in New York in the previous three days was the U.S.-based Flyovers, and even its connection to the taxi bombing had not been independently confirmed. But that did not stop many individuals, including more than a few politicians at very senior levels, from arguing that this was more evidence that America needed to curb immigration and tighten its borders.

"We cannot," said one bombastic talk radio host, "allow these illegals into our country to wage war on us. But yet, that's what we do! Just how stupid are we, ladies and gentlemen?"

Nearly every TV channel—with the possible exceptions of those devoted to weather updates, cartoons, and repeats of *The Big Bang Theory*—was featuring nonstop talking heads offering plenty of opinions based on almost no information whatsoever.

In that sense, it was pretty much like any other day.

Forty-Four

Barbara had not left the City Hall media room after the mayor's statement. She'd taken a chair in a back corner, sat down, and written her piece with her two amazing thumbs. The room had pretty much cleared out, but reporters started filing back in when word got out that the mayor's son was going to make a follow-up statement. So Barbara was already sitting there when Glover went to the podium to announce the mayor's decision to shut down all city elevators.

"Holy shit," Barbara said under her breath. The magnitude of this story was growing exponentially by the hour.

She wasn't surprised Headley had sent the boy to deliver this latest bulletin. The mayor had done enough damage to himself in his earlier appearance when, in response to Barbara's question, he could not say whether it was safe to ride a New York elevator. Glover's statement had pretty much made it clear that the answer was no.

Glover declined to take questions after making the announcement, but as he tried to escape the room he was cornered by several news crews and reporters shouting out more questions. He kept raising his hand in front of his face, as much to keep the blinding lights out of his eyes as to keep the media hounds at bay.

Barbara saw nothing to be gained by joining the scrum. No reporter ever got an exclusive by following the pack. She glanced out the media room door and spotted Chris Vallins's bald head. He was walking speedily, as though he wanted to distance himself from the chaos as quickly as possible.

Barbara chased after him. When she was within a couple of feet she reached out and grabbed his arm, spinning him around. His startled expression lasted only until he realized who it was that had a hold on him.

"Hey," she said. "Tell me. Just how bad is this?"

He glanced about nervously. "You're the last person I should be seen talking to."

Barbara turned her head to the closest door, a sign screwed to it that read Ladies. She hooked her arm deeper into his and dragged him toward it.

"You gotta be kidding," he said. By the time he got his arm free, they were already inside, in an area with some cushioned chairs ahead of where the room opened up and the stalls could be found.

Barbara pushed Chris into a chair and dropped into one next to it.

"Spill," she said.

"I've got nothing to say," he told her as he turned his head to the door, clearly worried that another woman might walk in at any moment.

"How big is this? Who's behind it?" she asked.

"They don't have any idea," he said.

"What about these Flyover nuts?"

Vallins shrugged. "They're looking at them. But no one really knows anything."

"What's connecting the elevator events? Is there some commonality?"

Vallins pressed his lips tightly together, as though conducting an inner debate. "Okay, I shouldn't be telling you this, but . . ."

"Come on," she said anxiously.

"Cameras," he said.

"Cameras?"

"Someone installed tiny cameras to monitor what was happening in the elevators that killed people."

Barbara's eyes went wide. "Jesus. Why would someone do that?"

Another shrug. "Maybe to see that someone was inside before making them go haywire. No sense dropping an elevator if there's no one inside to fuck with." He sighed. "You really made Headley look like a fool in there."

"He doesn't make it that hard. What else can you tell me?"

"Nothing. I shouldn't even have told you that much. But it's going to come out. Landlords are being told what to look for. They see one of those cameras mounted on top of an elevator, they know it's an elevator that might be targeted."

"This is insane," Barbara said. "Why would anyone do this?"

"You can be sure there's a reason," Vallins said. "And I'm betting that eventually it'll come out."

Barbara said, "You have my number?"

"Oh, I think everyone's got your number."

"Fuck off. My phone number."

"I've got it. And your email."

"How'd you get that?"

Vallins gave her a *duh* look. "It's at the end of your column."

"Oh, right." She rolled her eyes at her stupidity. "If there's anything else you can tell me, off the record, get in touch."

"Don't hold your breath." His face softened as he asked, "How's the elbow?"

"Aches like a motherfucker," Barbara said with a hint of smile. "But it's fine."

The door started to swing open. A woman took one step in and stopped when she saw Chris. Before he could say anything, Barbara pointed to the hall and said, "Find another one."

The woman disappeared.

Chris said, "You really are a piece of work."

"You're not so bad yourself. And I still say you were following me."

Chris shook his head and sighed. "Lucky for you. Or you wouldn't be here, now, being a pain in the ass."

She eyed him slyly. "He's got you checking up on me. Looking for some way to discredit me."

"I'm not saying that's true," Chris said, "but even if it was, I think he's got bigger things to worry about now."

"So I better stop looking at my phone when I cross the street, then. My guardian angel is otherwise engaged."

"Something like that," he said.

"Too bad," Barbara said.

The sound of a text came from inside his jacket. He dug out the phone, looked at the message, grimaced.

"What?"

"They need me," he said, then rolled his eyes. "The mayhem has begun."

Forty-Five

Amad Connor, fourteen years old, and his friend, Jeremy Blakelock, who had turned fifteen the week before, were pulling the same stunt they'd pulled several times before.

They had both left their Hell's Kitchen apartment building after breakfast, supposedly on their way to a full day of school, where they were both in the ninth grade. Their parents—Amad lived with both of his, but Jeremy lived with his mother during the week and then went to live with his father, in Brooklyn, most weekends—always left for work later. Amad's dad was employed in the massive shoe department at Macy's, while his mother was a secretary for a condo development firm in the Upper West Side. Jeremy's mother was the head, dayside chef for a restaurant just off Union Square.

Amad and Jeremy actually showed up for homeroom, when attendance would be taken, but they vanished on their way to first period. That way, it would take longer for school officials to figure out they were absent, at which point there was a chance they would call their parents and ask where they were.

But they also knew, from past experience, that often the school didn't make that call. After all, they were teenagers. They weren't some kindergarten toddlers who'd failed to show up. So what if they didn't get to class? Odds were they hadn't been kidnapped.

With an entire city at their disposal, one might have thought they'd explore it. Ride the subways, go to Midtown Comics and steal some graphic novels, then hit the multiplex and take in the latest adventure featuring the stars of the Marvel Cinematic Universe.

But they did none of these things. They headed home.

They were going to surf.

From watching various YouTube videos, the two had learned that once you were inside an elevator, if you kept the doors open, looped a wire over a small bracket tucked in the upper corner where the doors retracted, and pulled down on it, the outer doors would remain open even after the elevator had moved on. So, they'd send the elevator one floor down, jump out, and once the elevator had stopped one floor below, step through the opening and stand atop the car.

To cover their tracks, they would make sure the door closed behind them. (Later, when the elevator stopped for long enough, they would pry open the doors one floor above the car and leap out.)

Up and down the shaft they'd go. They had no control over the elevator at this point. That would be determined by whoever got on it, and it was the unpredictability that made it so much fun. The elevator would be summoned to a floor, but which one? Someone would board, but where would they want to go? Whispering back and forth so as not to alert anyone they were there, they would take bets on where they might end up.

They'd recorded some of their earlier adventures on their phones and posted them anonymously to YouTube. The site was filled with this kind of stuff. They only wished they lived in an even taller building, so they could go on longer, wilder rides.

It sure beat school.

Except that afternoon, something odd happened.

It seemed that no one needed the elevator. They had been sitting on the roof of the car, at the top of the shaft, crouched below the ceiling and above the exit to the twenty-fifth floor without a door beside them to crack open. Ten minutes had gone by and they had not moved. And they could hear neither of the other elevators moving, either.

That had never happened before.

"What the fuck?" Jeremy said to Amad.

Amad said, "Maybe there was a fire drill and everyone's outside."

"There was no fire alarm, dipshit," Jeremy said.

After twenty minutes, they started to get worried.

Jeremy suggested they open the escape hatch on the top of the car. If they could get into it, and hit the elevator buttons, they could probably get out. But the hatch did not lift off. It was bolted on, and they had not exactly brought along a tool kit.

They did not want to get caught on top of the car. They'd be in trouble not just with the building management, but their parents. All the other times they'd elevator-surfed, they'd gotten away with it.

But at the half-hour mark, they started shouting.

"Help!" they cried together. "Help us! We're in here! Somebody get us out!"

No one heard them.

———

Connie Boyle's phone buzzed.

It was screen side down on her desk at an investment firm in one of the uppermost floors of One World Trade Center, the tallest building in the Western Hemisphere, sixth tallest in the world. Although technically 104 stories tall, there were only ninety-four actual stories, and when Connie chose to look out the window, which was not often, she felt overwhelmed by the view.

And not in a good way.

It had taken Connie, forty-three, a long time to get used to the idea of working up here in the clouds. First of all, she was uncomfortable with heights. It wasn't a totally crippling fear, but it was bad enough that she had insisted, when her firm moved here, on a work station well inside the building, away from the windows. She could go entire weeks without ever looking outside. Her friends would say to her, "Wow, how cool to work up there! Do you ever get tired of that view?"

"What view?" she often replied.

Connie's anxiety about working here was not due solely to her uneasiness with heights. One World Trade Center had been erected on the site of the old World Trade Center. Connie could never get over the fear that the new building was a target. Whenever she heard a passing jet she felt a wave of anxiety. She felt relief at the end of every day, when she put her feet back down on Fulton Street.

Her phone buzzed, and she saw that it was her husband. When he asked her in a panicked tone—before she'd even had a chance to say hello—whether she was okay, her heart began to race and she almost instantly began to feel faint and dizzy.

"Why?" she asked.

"The elevators," he said. "Have they shut down your elevators?"

She had no idea what he was talking about, but before she could ask him what he knew that she did not, a woman's voice came over the building's public address system.

"May I have your attention, please," she said.

Connie's dizziness intensified. Her heart was a jackhammer.

"Oh my God," she said. "Oh my God."

"It's going to be okay," her husband said. "I just wanted to be sure you were—"

Connie was half listening to her husband, half listening to the voice emanating from the speakers.

"They're shutting down the elevators," she whispered. "We . . . we can't use the elevators. We're. . . . Oh God, we're stuck up here. We're sitting ducks."

She dropped the phone onto her desk as she stood up out of her chair. She looked over the partitions to the north window.

"We're trapped," she said. Her voice grew louder, and shakier. "We have to get out of here! We have to get out!"

Several coworkers leapt from their chairs and gathered around Connie, attempting to console her. But the woman was in the throes of a full-scale panic attack.

"Connie, Connie, it's okay," said one woman. "It's just a precaution. Yeah, we've got a long walk down the stairs to get home but—"

But Connie didn't hear her. She had passed out and collapsed on the floor.

———

Retired librarian Zachary Carrick went to Zabar's Monday, Wednesday, and Friday.

Zachary bought only as much as he could carry. Like many New Yorkers, he did not drive. Unlike most New Yorkers, he did not like to take taxis, and hated the subway. If Zachary was going to go someplace, it had to be within walking distance. Which meant that Zachary pretty much never left the Upper West Side. His world these days had become limited to roughly a nine-square block area. Zabar's was only around the corner, at Broadway and Eightieth. He liked to walk, but he didn't like to walk far.

So Zachary would buy what he needed for two days. On Fridays, he would buy a little extra, to get him through to Monday. It wasn't just that Zachary Carrick only purchased what he could carry. He figured, at the age of eighty-seven, he didn't want to buy too much food if there was a chance he might not get the opportunity to consume it. This worried him most on Fridays. Suppose, he often thought to himself, I pop my clog Friday night, and I've gone and bought enough provisions to get me through the entire weekend? What a waste of money that would be.

Zachary had been on his own since his wife, Glenda, passed away nearly twenty years ago, but he had never left their eighteenth-floor apartment on West Eighty-First. Why move? The place wasn't huge to begin with. Why mess with a perfectly good routine?

Although he'd spent a career surrounded by newspapers and periodicals filled with current events, Zachary didn't give a rat's ass about what went on anymore. He didn't get any papers and almost never turned on his TV, unless it was to watch what he called the Lobby Channel, where he could see who was coming in and out of the building. Out of the hundreds of channels available to him, this was, without question, the best reality show on TV.

Zachary was not prepared for what awaited him upon his return to the building today.

There were Out of Order signs taped to all three elevators.

A dozen other residents were milling about in the lobby, grousing about the inconvenience. Most of them were, as Zachary himself might say, getting on. A few of them were even as old as he was. One of them was Mrs. Attick, who was in a wheelchair. She looked the most distressed of any of them.

"What the hell is going on?" he asked, setting down his two Zabar's bags. Even though they weren't that heavy, his arms felt like they were going to pop out of their sockets. The other residents quickly brought him up to speed.

"It was Headley gave the order!" one man said. "Shut 'em all down! All over the city!"

"That son of a bitch," Zachary said. "How the hell am I supposed to get upstairs? I can't walk up to eighteen. I'll be dead before I get to ten."

Mrs. Attick said, "What about Griffin?"

"Who?"

"My cat. The super said there's no way to know how long this is going to go on. Could be hours or it could be days! Who's going to feed Griffin?"

Zachary hated cats and didn't much care what happened to Mrs. Attick's. He just wanted to get back up to his apartment, where he could watch what was happening here on his TV while he made himself some coffee.

"My daughter came and took me to lunch," Mrs. Attick said in her high-pitched voice. "But she dropped me off without knowing what had happened! She would have gone up and fed Griffin. She works out four days a week. She could have run up those stairs like it was nothing. Griffin's going to be worried sick."

Zachary was more worried about his yogurt. He needed to get it into the refrigerator.

He was about to go hunting for the super when the main doors flew open and in came two male paramedics—one short, one tall—with a wheeled gurney. They looked frustrated, but not shocked, when they saw the Out of Order signs.

"Did you reach the super?" the short one said into the small radio attached to a strap just below his chin. "We need a working elevator."

His radio crackled. "On his way," a voice said through static.

"Yes!" said Zachary under his breath. They'd have to get the elevators operational if there was a medical emergency somewhere in the upper reaches of the building.

Seconds later, the superintendent, a heavyset, olive-skinned man, came into the lobby from a nearby stairwell door.

"You got to get one of these going," the paramedic said.

"Yeah, yeah," the super said. "I just got the middle one back on. It's Mr. Gilbert, in 15C."

A stir of excitement from the residents. What a break, that Mr. Gilbert was having another one of his heart attacks.

The super hit the Up button and the center elevator doors opened. But Mrs. Attick had already positioned herself close to them, and when they parted, she wheeled herself in like someone trying out for the Paralympic Games.

"Lady!" the tall paramedic shouted. "Get out of the way!"

"My cat!" she cried.

She hadn't yet turned around, so the shorter paramedic was able to grab the handles on the back of her chair. But as he attempted to pull the wheelchair back out, Mrs. Attick grabbed the railing on the elevator wall. That only slowed the paramedic for half a second, who yanked harder.

Everyone heard a snap.

Mrs. Attick screamed.

"My wrist! Oh God, my wrist!"

At which point, Zachary wondered if they would treat her first, right here in the lobby, which would allow him to use the elevator to get to his apartment and put his yogurt into the fridge.

It did not work out that way.

They got Mrs. Attick out of the elevator, tipped the gurney up on one end, hit "15" on the pad, and up they went.

They were too late.

Mr. Gilbert was dead, and had been for the better part of half an hour.

As was Zachary Carrick, who had decided, what the hell, he would make the climb. He was rounding the stairwell by the door to the fifth floor when his heart exploded.

The good news was, a sixth-floor tenant, Grant Rydell, twenty-three, an unemployed Broadway actor who was heading down to the lobby to check the mail—he was hoping his mother, back home in Saginaw, had sent him a check to cover that month's rent—discovered Zachary in the stairwell and, before calling 911 on his cell phone, helped himself to his Zabar's purchases.

Turned out that he and Zachary both loved strawberry yogurt.

———————

"Terrorist!"

Ettan Khatri turned around when he heard someone shout the word. Not because he thought anyone was shouting at him, but because when anyone shouts "Terrorist!" you want to look around and see what's happening.

Was somebody waving around a machine gun? Had some nut wandered into the lobby of this office tower on East Fifty-Seventh Street with dynamite strapped to his waist?

But when Ettan turned around, he saw a man pointing straight at him.

Of course, this kind of thing had happened before over the years. His parents were from India, and he was born and raised in the United States. Nevertheless, if your skin happened to be a little bit darker, and your hair was jet-black, there was always some asshole who thought you were an Islamic extremist. You could tell them you were Hindu, but they'd just look at you and say something like, "Same difference!"

Ettan, twenty-eight, was in the building for a job interview at a gallery that specialized in rare posters. Ettan had an art degree from Boston College, but he'd spent the last three years working behind the counter at the McDonald's on Third just north of Fiftieth. When he saw the online posting for an assistant sales position at the gallery, he applied immediately.

So here he was, and given that the gallery was on the fifth floor, getting there by stairs was not going to be a hardship. He'd already checked in with security and was told he would find the stairwell door just beyond the bank of elevators.

It was as he was walking past the elevators, each decorated with a strip of yellow tape reminiscent of the kind used at crime scenes, that he heard the man yell.

He was a big man. Three hundred pounds, easy. Wearing khakis and a checked shirt and a ball cap with no logo on the front.

"Did you sabotage *these*?" the man asked, pointing a thumb at the elevators as he closed the distance between them.

"What?" Ettan said, at which he raised his palms in a defensive gesture, but not quite quickly enough.

The man drove a fist into Ettan's mouth.

The world went black.

It started in the Spring Lounge when, sitting across from him at their table, Faith Berkley slipped off one shoe and ran her foot up the inside of Andre Banville's leg.

Supposedly, this meeting had been to discuss purchasing one of Andre's French landscapes. The bar was just around the corner from his gallery, but also just happened to be very close to Faith's new, twentieth-floor luxury condo on Broome Street.

"Maybe," Faith said, "if you saw our place, and our color palette, and how the light filters through the blinds, you'd have a better idea of our needs." She put a little spin on the last word.

"Excellent idea," Andre said. "Will Anthony be there to offer some suggestions?"

"As it turns out," Faith said, "my husband won't be home until later. We'll have to manage."

"Why don't you finish that drink and we'll do just that."

They were on each other the second after the elevator door closed and Faith had tapped the button for her floor. Andre pushed her up against the back wall, put his mouth hungrily on hers, slipped his tongue between her teeth. He untucked her blouse and ran his hands over the lacy bra she'd bought the day before from Agent Provocateur, while she reached down to stroke him through his jeans.

"Jesus," she gasped, "you could cut glass with this thing."

A button popped off her blouse as Andre explored beneath it with his hands. "When we get to your room," he whispered, "I'm going to pull down your panties and I'm—"

The elevator stopped. They were at the twelfth floor.

"Shit!" Faith whispered, pushing Andre away and frantically tucking in her blouse. "It's not supposed to stop! It's supposed to go directly to our floor."

But the doors did not open. And the elevator did not move.

"What's going on?" Faith asked.

She pushed the button for her floor again. Nothing. Then, a static crackle. A male voice emanated from a speaker next to the buttons.

"Is there someone in there?"

Faith said, "Elmont?"

Andre looked at her, eyebrows raised. She whispered, "Doorman."

"Ms. Berkley? Yes, Elmont. We're bringing all the elevators back down to the first floor and taking them out of service."

"Why on earth are—"

"Some kind of emergency, ma'am. Happening all over the city. They say—"

"Faith?"

Another man's voice.

Her husband.

"Anthony?" she said.

"I'm here with Elmont, honey. Raced home from the office soon as I heard what was going on. Wanted to be sure you were—"

"I'm fine!" she said, glancing at Andre. "It's okay! Go back to—"

"Not a chance," Anthony said. "I'll be right here when the doors open."

At the Empire State Building, hundreds of people who had bought their tickets and lined up to be taken to the 102nd-floor observation deck were told that they wouldn't be heading to the top of the city's most famous building after all. There was grumbling and confusion as tourists formed new lines to get their ticket money refunded.

It was a different story on the observation deck, where dozens of visitors were informed their trip back to street level was going to be somewhat more arduous than their ride to the top. Soon, the stairwells were filled with people, and not only those who'd been to the top, but also the thousands of people who worked in the building and were heading home.

A similar scene was playing out over at the Top of the Rock, the viewing area atop Rockefeller Center. Managers of almost all city tourist sites, even those that did not soar into the sky, decided to close their doors. Museums shut down. The guards on the various floors displaying art at the Guggenheim, which could have been accessed by walking up the gradually sloped floor that circled the atrium, announced that everyone was to leave the building. The consensus was that if the city's elevators were a possible terrorist target, so might be notable landmarks.

The fear was that whoever was messing with New York was just getting started.

The millions who traveled countless stories upward every day were cutting out early. Anxiety around being trapped at work had prompted many to get out while they knew they could. But what awaited them when they got home, if they happened to live in a towering apartment building, was the same situation in reverse. Thousands decided to delay their return and went out to dinner, hoping that within a few hours the city would announce that the crisis was over and the elevators were once again safe to use.

Tourists arriving at JFK and LaGuardia, unaware of the mayor's decree, were stunned when they got to their hotels and learned they could not get to their rooms if they weren't prepared to take the stairs. Not good news if you'd brought half a dozen suitcases with you. Hotels reported scores of cancellations from those who had not yet left for New York but had seen the news.

In short, it was one big shitshow.

Forty-Six

The mayor, in his City Hall office, jumped from channel to channel, seeing reports from all corners of the city. In the room with him were Valerie, Vallins, and Glover.

"What a goddamn clusterfuck," Headley said, shaking his head with despair.

"It is that," Valerie said.

"You heard anything?" he asked her.

"I just got off the phone with Homeland, and the chief. There's nothing new."

"We have to get a fucking handle on this," he said. "They've got to find whoever did this and they have to do it right fucking now! I'm being crucified out there. We need to come up with a new statement, something that offers some reassurance."

Valerie said, "Inspections are being made. I'm hearing that a few elevators are already back in service. But I think we're looking at a couple of days before things are back to normal."

"Jesus Christ."

The cell phone on the mayor's desk started buzzing. Vallins was closest, and grabbed it.

"Mayor Headley's office," he said.

"Put the son of a bitch on," a man said.

"Who's calling?"

"Rodney Coughlin."

Vallins said, "Hang on." Headley looked at him. "You're probably going to want to take this. It's Coughlin."

Headley took a moment to prepare himself, then took the phone. "Rodney," he said.

"What the fuck are you thinking?" Coughlin said.

"Listen, I know—"

"Maybe you've forgotten what's happening on Thursday. Does Thursday ring a bell, Dick? Huh?"

"I know. I know."

"How do you think my guests will like walking up ninety-seven flights of stairs for the official opening of Top of the Park? Better have some pretty fucking amazing appetizers to make that kind of trek."

"It's a temporary measure," Headley said.

"Who found a way around the rules to give half a mill to your campaign?" Coughlin asked. "It's slipped my mind."

"Rodney, I know. Look, have your people do a complete sweep of the elevators. I'm guessing they've already been told what to look for. I'm sure—"

"You know who's going to be here, for the opening of the tallest residential building in the entire fucking country?"

"Rodney, I—"

"I'll tell you who. *Everybody.*"

Vallins waved a hand, trying to get the mayor's attention. Headley put his hand over the phone and whispered, "What?"

"Send me," he whispered.

"What?"

"Tell him you're dispatching one of your aides to personally make sure everything will be okay."

Headley squinted. "What do you know about elevators?"

Vallins shook his head, signaling that wasn't his point. He whispered, "I'll get someone. I'll oversee it."

Headley nodded, then went back to the phone. "Rodney, listen to me."

The mayor made his pitch. The second he ended the call, his face went red and his body shook.

"That fucking son of a bitch," he said, and then pitched the phone in his hand directly at the TV screen, which had been showing a YouTube video of several people stumbling all over each other in a high-rise stairwell.

The screen shattered.

Valerie stifled a scream.

"Goddam fucking hell," Headley said. "Who does Coughlin think he is, talking to me like that?"

Glover, who had said nothing through any of this, walked over to the mayor's office window and gazed out at the city.

And smiled.

Forty-Seven

More than two dozen NYPD detectives crowded into the small, rectangular conference room. Some had taken chairs, others were leaning against the wall along the perimeter of the room. Nearly everyone had a takeout coffee in hand.

Jerry Bourque and Lois Delgado stood off to one side, arms crossed. At one end of the room, with an oversized computer monitor on the wall behind, were Chief Washington, a woman from the Federal Bureau of Investigation, and Homeland's Brian Cartland.

The detectives summoned to this meeting had originally been told they'd be focusing on the three elevator tragedies, but the scope of the investigation had been broadened.

They were now also looking at the taxi bombing on East Forty-Ninth Street. While there was not yet anything specific to indicate a connection between the elevator events and the bombing, the fact that the two incidents happened within minutes of each other could not be ignored. It was possible, the chief speculated, that the goal of the person or persons responsible had been to sow chaos by triggering simultaneous crises.

Attempts were being made to acquire whatever surveillance video existed from the three buildings where the elevators had been sabotaged. Two detectives across the room from Bourque and Delgado said these efforts were being undercut because none of the buildings had cameras set up in the elevator control rooms, where they believed the perpetrator would have had to make some initial connections between the main system and the portable controller. And as for saved video or images from other cameras, they had no idea when the elevators might have been tampered with. Should they start looking at video from last week, or six months ago?

But for sure, someone had to have gotten into those shafts at some point to mount cameras that would provide a view to what was happening inside the cars. Computer experts, the detectives said, had been brought in to determine whether it was possible to tell where the images being transmitted by the cameras had gone. They hoped to have more on that within twenty-four hours.

Street surveillance video was being gathered to help with the taxi explosion investigation. The car's route that morning, up to the moment of the blast, was being traced, and once that was nailed down, cameras along that path would be found and video examined. A preliminary examination of the destroyed vehicle suggested the explosion had originated in its center, suggesting further that the bomb had been left on the floor of the backseat by a passenger.

"They seem like very different crimes," observed a detective at the back of the room.

"True," said Washington. "And they may very well have been executed by different individuals or groups with no connection to each other. But I want those following the taxi bombing and those on the elevator incidents comparing notes, in case there are links."

"Yeah," said Delgado. "A bomb left in a car is pretty low-tech compared to the elevator stuff. One requires a tremendous amount of planning, the other, not so much. Who we looking at?"

Washington went to a laptop set up at the front of the room. The screen on the wall lit up with photos of a bombed coffee shop.

Cartland said, "The list of groups that might want to set off a bomb in New York is long. We've had a few ISIS and ISIS-inspired events in recent years. But also on our radar are people identifying with the Flyovers movement. They're believed to be behind this bombing in Portland, Oregon. These Flyover types are taking credit for similar events in coastal cities in recent weeks and have, indeed, claimed responsibility on Twitter for the taxi explosion, although we've not been able to confirm the claim's legitimacy. Agent Darrell, from the FBI, can speak to this."

A short black woman with closely cropped black hair moved forward. "Hi. Diane Darrell. This taxi bombing does have some of the earmarks of other acts that adherents of the Flyovers have said they perpetrated. What's interesting is that the man who leads the activist group—who has, at least publicly, disavowed all acts of violence—is currently in New York, supposedly on a pleasure trip with his wife. Do we have that shot of Clement?"

A new picture came up on the screen of Eugene Clement and a woman crossing a New York street.

"This was just after he did a TV interview. We've been keeping an eye on him."

Delgado leaned in close to her partner and whispered, "Could that be our guy?" When Bourque gave her a puzzled look, she added, "Standing by the car. Talking to Otto? In the picture?"

Bourque gave a noncommittal shrug.

Darrell was still talking. "Is it just a coincidence that he's here in New York when that taxi thing goes down, and the Flyovers say it was their doing? I don't know about the rest of you, but I've never been a big believer in coincidences."

Diane Darrell cracked open a bottled water and took a sip.

"A straightforward bombing is easy enough to understand. You're a group with a message, and the easiest way to get it across is blow something up. Or get behind the wheel of a truck and mow some people down. All in the name of Allah. Or, perhaps in this case, to express contempt for left-wing ideology. It may not make sense in our minds to make a statement by murdering innocents, but we've come to understand the profile."

She paused.

"The elevator thing is trickier. What's the message? What's the statement someone's trying to make? So far, no one's claimed responsibility. We're looking for a motive here, and so far it's elusive." She looked at Cartland. "Unless you'd like to share your theory."

Cartland made a tiny shake of the head.

"Okay, then," Darrell said. She looked to the chief. "What about this homicide your people have been working?"

Washington nodded and scanned the room. "Where are Bourque and Delgado?"

Delgado raised a hand as Bourque said, "Here."

Washington said, "Fill us in."

Delgado told them about finding the body of Otto Petrenko on the High Line more than forty-eight hours earlier. "An elevator technician."

A murmuring went through the room.

"Fingertips cut off, face beaten beyond recognition. To slow us down on an ID, in case he was in the system. Which he was, for a minor event a few years ago."

"Where are you on this?" the chief asked.

Bourque weighed in this time. "Workin' it. His boss says he didn't service any of the buildings where elevators were sabotaged. But he might have been doing something on the side. But a couple of curious things. Petrenko had been in touch with relatives—those living outside the city—to warn them to be on guard. Told his sister, living in Vegas, that she should think about getting a gun."

"Why the paranoia?" Cartland asked.

"Don't know," Bourque said. "Couple of other things. He'd

expressed views that sounded sympathetic to the Flyovers, accord-ing to his wife. But I don't have anything to suggest it went beyond that. We've done a check of his computer. No communications that stuck out."

"But there was someone he'd met with a couple of times," Delgado said. "Came to his place of employment. Nobody Petrenko works with has any idea who this guy was. We're trying to get a lead on him."

Cartland, who looked as though he'd been scowling ever since Delgado started talking, said, "Petrenko?"

The homicide detectives nodded.

"Is that a Russian name?" Cartland asked.

Bourque said, "His wife said he was born there, and his parents escaped to Finland shortly after he was born, then moved to America when he was four. Been in the U.S. ever since."

"So far as we know," Cartland said.

Bourque nodded. "Yeah."

"So if he ever made any trips back to Russia in his later years, you don't know that."

Delgado said, "No, we don't. We can look into that. Can you tell us why that might be relevant?"

Cartland hesitated. "Agent Darrell, a moment ago, alluded to a theory I have, which I was not particularly eager to share because it's a bit out there." A pause. "But I think we're in a situation where every possibility needs to be explored, no matter how far-fetched it might seem."

The room waited.

"The sole fatality in yesterday's incident was Dr. Fanya Petrov, a renowned Russian scientist temporarily attached to Rockefeller University. Her area of expertise had something to do with nonge-netic hereditary characteristics, and not for a second do I understand any part of it. But Dr. Petrov also had considerable background in another area of study, one that made her very valuable, potentially, to the United States. That was pathogens. Bacterial pathogens. She knew a lot about the Russian government's research into bioterrorism. She did not want to go back to Russia. She wanted to stay here." He paused. "And we believe the Russians knew that."

"Jesus," said Bourque. "Are you saying—"

Cartland held up a hand. He wasn't finished. "Not long after Dr. Petrov literally lost her head, the Russian ambassador was on the phone to the mayor very quickly. He wanted answers. What I'd like to know is how the ambassador found out about this accident so quickly. I think they knew she didn't want to go back to Russia. They'd been watching her."

At this point, Cartland scratched his forehead, then crossed his arms in front of his chest.

"I think the ambassador's call of outrage to the mayor was a performance. He had to have been pleased by this turn of events. Things couldn't have worked out better for him than if he'd planned it that way." He paused. "Then again, maybe he did."

He glanced down at the laptop, searched briefly for something, then clicked.

On the screen there appeared a photo of a man walking along a New York sidewalk. It was a side shot taken across the street without the subject's knowledge. He was tall and trim with dark hair, dressed in a black suit.

"This," Cartland said, "is Dmitri Litvin. A freelancer for SVR, the Russian foreign intelligence service."

"Just what sort of freelance work does he do?" asked someone in the room.

"Pretty much what anyone needs. Want someone to disappear? Litvin can make it happen. But his skills go beyond assassination. He's also believed to be a brilliant computer expert."

"By 'expert,' do you mean 'hacker'?" Delgado asked.

"Possibly," Cartland said. "Litvin met this morning with the ambassador, in Grand Central. Dr. Petrov was described, essentially, as a neutralized threat. And Litvin made a joke about not going up the Empire State Building."

"He's not the only one," quipped someone.

Cartland acknowledged the comment with a nod. "True. Their conversation was interesting but not conclusive. But we have to consider the possibility that the scientist's death was a hit."

Bourque said, "So you create a series of accidents, a kind of smokescreen. The only one you want to kill is the doctor, but if you only kill her, you raise too many red—no pun intended—flags. It looks like a Putin hit, plain and simple. But you let a few others perish in the process, we don't know where to focus our attention."

Cartland nodded. "Like I said, it's kind of out there. But *someone* has gone to a lot of trouble to sabotage these elevators, and the Russians have people with the expertise to get it done. Now you tell me you've got a Russian-born elevator technician who was murdered two days ago. That lengths were taken to make it difficult to ID the body. That members of his extended family had the fear of God put into them."

He uncrossed his arms. "My theory's starting to sound slightly less fanciful."

Forty-Eight

Following the mayor's disastrous media event, Barbara could have wandered the city—and she would not have had to wander far—compiling stories about the chaos that had been launched by shutting down all the elevators in New York.

But that was the story every other media outlet in the city was chasing, and the truth was, they could do a much better job of it. Hundreds of people working their way down concrete stairwells, person-in-the-street interviews, frustrated tourists who'd come all the way from Flin Flon, Manitoba, wanting to go to the top of the Empire State Building and being turned away—these were tales made for TV. Lots of visuals. Angry people. *Collapsing* people. Network news crews were fanning out across the city.

Barbara figured, let 'em have it. Let them do what they're good at. After her brief meeting with Chris Vallins, she hurried back to her apartment, hoping she could get there before her landlord shut down the elevators. If they were working, she was going to take one of them, figuring the odds it would take her to her death were slim. But she was too late. The elevators were plastered with two signs written in Sharpie that read: Closed by Order of Mayor Richard Shithead.

Barbara had always harbored a fondness for her landlord.

Once she'd reached her apartment and had taken a moment to catch her breath, Barbara put on a pot of coffee, sat down at the kitchen table, and fired up her laptop.

Barbara didn't need to know how many elevators New York had. Barbara didn't need to know how many millions of people were inconvenienced. Barbara didn't need to know how many people would drop dead of heart attacks by the end of the day from taking the stairs up to their thirty-fifth-floor apartments, although that would be an interesting statistic. Barbara thought it was entirely possible more people would die *not* using elevators than would die in them.

No, what Barbara needed to know was *why,* and *who.*

Why would someone who wanted to kill people decide to do it by sabotaging elevators? Why not just pick up a gun and shoot them? Why not run them down with a car? Why not start a fire in an apartment hallway in the middle of the night? If you wanted to kill a few people, any of these methods would be easier.

Why not, well, blow up a taxi?

A bomb in a cab was very effective at taking out a few innocent people. It was pretty random, but if you were looking to make some kind of demented statement, it would do the trick.

Was the elevator saboteur trying to make a statement with the elevator deaths?

Were the victims random? Were the buildings random?

Barbara thought about that.

Even if you could take over an elevator's controls, could tell who was in it at any given time by looking at them with a camera—*thank you very much for that tip, Chris Vallins*—it didn't strike Barbara as a very efficient way to kill a specific person.

How long would you have to wait for your potential victim to board the elevator? What if the person took the stairs? What if the person went out of town? And if there were several elevators in this particular building, how long might you have to wait for the person to take the one you had rigged to fail?

Let's say this person you wanted to kill finally got on the right elevator at the right time. Was there any guarantee that when the elevator went haywire, the person you wanted dead would actually die? Paula Chatsworth had survived, at least for a while. And from what Barbara knew of the second incident, that Russian scientist would still be around if she hadn't decided to crawl out of that stalled elevator when it was stuck between floors. No one could have predicted she'd do that.

And the event this morning, where two people fell into the bottom of the shaft?

Barbara pictured people crowded around an elevator first thing in the morning, waiting for the elevator to arrive. The people who might be standing closest to the doors, waiting for them to open, would be totally left to chance. Completely random. And if someone had pushed them into the shaft, they would have been seen.

All of which led Barbara to conclude that the victims really *were* random.

But what about the locations? Why was the Lansing Tower on Third Avenue targeted on Monday? What was it about the Sycamores Residences, just south of Rockefeller University, that made it the saboteur's choice for Tuesday? And today it had been the Gormley Building on Seventh.

Was there a common thread tying these locations together?

The coffee machine beeped. Her fresh pot was ready.

"What was I thinking?" Barbara said, getting up and walking right past the coffee machine to the refrigerator. She took out a bottle of chardonnay, unscrewed the top, and found a glass to fill.

She sat back down and began an internet search on the buildings, starting with the Lansing Tower, site of the first incident. There were, not surprisingly, hundreds of stories that mentioned the building. It housed a company devoted to movie and TV production— Cromwell Entertainment, the one Sherry D'Agostino had worked for—as well as top legal firms, even an office for the Department of Homeland Security.

That last tidbit of information was interesting, Barbara thought. She filed it away for possible future reference.

There was also a profile of New York real estate developer Morris Lansing, who had named the building after himself. Hey, if Trump could do it . . .

Lansing, sixty-nine, had been one of the city's more illustrious characters for the better part of thirty years. And in those thirty years, he had probably made himself a few hundred friends and a few thousand enemies. You didn't get that far up the city food chain without pissing off a lot of people. Had Lansing angered someone to the point that they'd fuck up his building?

Finally, there were real estate type ads. While the Lansing Tower was mostly commercial, there were some residences on the upper floors. Barbara had to fend off pop-up inquiries.

Next, she did a search on the Sycamores Residences. What came up first, of course, was the tragedy from the previous day. She ignored the recent news items, refining her search so it excluded this week.

Once she had done that, up came more real estate ads. There were several available units in the Sycamores. Some of them offered a view of the East River, and all touted the building's amenities, including a playground for kids, a gym, and large party rooms that could be rented for special occasions. Did Barbara want to buy or rent? Boxes kept popping up on her screen, inviting her in to chat with an agent. She kept clicking on X's to get rid of the boxes, which couldn't have been more annoying if they were a swarm of mosquitoes buzzing around her head.

Once she got through the real estate ads, she found a couple of other news stories. A kitchen fire on the sixth floor that was quickly extinguished, an entertainment feature about a visiting stage director who happened to be staying there.

Half an hour and two-thirds of a bottle of chardonnay later, nothing in particular had jumped out at Barbara. Maybe the answer to her question was there in what she had read, but if it was, she had failed to spot it.

Barbara sighed.

She rubbed her weary eyes and flopped herself onto the couch for several minutes, staring at the ceiling, trying to think of her next step. The only thing she could come up with was to finish off that bottle.

She got back up, emptied the rest of the chardonnay into her glass, and sat back down in front of her laptop. The screen had gone dark. She ran her finger over the mouse pad and brought the computer back to life.

One more building. The Gormley.

Here was another developer who believed you couldn't go wrong naming a building after yourself. The structure had been started in 1967 and finished in 1969 under the able direction of Wilfred Gormley, who had passed away in 1984. Again, there were real estate listings advertising residences and office space.

Barbara scanned through the names of businesses that occupied the building. An insurance company, a talent agency, accounting services. On the first floor, a barber and a florist.

I am wasting my time.

Barbara put the glass to her lips, tipped it back and emptied it. She folded the screen down and slowly leaned forward until her forehead was touching it. She had to find another angle, another strategy, think of someone new to talk to, check in with her various contacts, make a call to—

I'm an idiot.

She raised her head and reopened the laptop.

If you wanted to find out what was common about the three buildings, she thought, you did a search on all of them at once.

So she typed in the names of the three buildings and hit Enter.

The results loaded in a millisecond. Barbara blinked when she saw what popped up first. She wasn't quite sure whether to believe it.

It was an itinerary for mayoral candidate Richard Headley.

It covered one week during his election campaign a couple of years earlier. Barbara scrolled through the listing of events, looking for the highlighting of the words she had entered into the search engine.

The Sycamores reference came up first. Headley attended a fund-raising party hosted by Margaret Cambridge, who lived in the York Avenue building's penthouse. Margaret was one of the city's major, and aging, philanthropists. She'd never be able to go through all her husband's money, so she liked to give it away, and Headley was someone she wanted to give it to. Of course, there were rules governing large donations, but Margaret had strong-armed enough of her friends to come and give the max.

Barbara went back to the itinerary, looking for the word "Lansing." The reference turned out not to be about the Lansing Tower, but about Morris Lansing, another major financial backer of Headley's who'd hosted a campaign rally for Headley. Searching his name and the mayor's together, Barbara learned that they were longtime friends.

On to "Gormley."

The day after the Lansing rally, Headley had paid a visit to the Gormley Building because the person who lived in the penthouse was holding yet another fund-raiser for him. That person turned out to be Arnett Steel, president and CEO of Steelways, which was the firm the mayor had been pressing the city to hire for major, multi-million-dollar improvements to the city's subway switching system.

"Fuck me," said Barbara.

She looked to see what other stories came up that linked Lansing, the Sycamores, and Gormley.

Nothing else of consequence came up in her search results.

Okay, okay, she told herself. *Take a breath.*

Just because Richard Headley had something in common with these three buildings—or, at least, with people who had a connection to them—did not mean *this* was what linked the three elevator incidents.

But damn, it was pretty fucking hard to ignore. Barbara's pulse was racing.

Suppose this is it, she thought. Suppose Headley is what connects these events.

That would suggest that if someone was sending a message through these horrific acts, the message was for him.

Barbara closed her laptop, stood, grabbed her jacket, and headed out of her apartment.

She wanted to talk to Richard Headley. She wanted to talk to Richard Headley, face-to-face, and she wanted to talk to him right now. She'd make some calls along the way to find out where he was. City Hall? Gracie Mansion? One Police Plaza? Wherever the son of a bitch was, she would find him.

Barbara went to the elevator, pressed the down button, and stood there. Glanced impatiently at her phone.

When the elevator did not immediately show up, she hit the button again.

And then it hit her.

"Jesus Christ, I'm losing my mind," she said to herself, and headed for the stairs.

Forty-Nine

It was only Day Two at the new job for Arla Silbert, but wow, the shit that had happened.

Her first day—her first *morning*—she was off to a grisly disaster scene and ended up having dinner with the mayor's son. On top of that, he disclosed to her something Arla just knew her mom would be dying to know. Which, if she hadn't turned into such a bitch on the phone, Arla might have told her.

Anyway, it didn't much matter that Arla didn't pass on Glover's tip that there was something fishy about those elevator accidents. The whole world knew that now. Just as well Arla hadn't said anything. If she had, and Barbara had posted something on the *Manhattan Today* site twelve or more hours before Richard Headley held his disastrous news conference, the leak might have been traced back to her.

You don't exactly want to be found out giving away your employer's secrets your first day on the job. That's definitely not going to help you get a good reference at your *next* place of employment.

So here she was, buried down in the data analysis department on her second day, and what with that Headley presser, and the shutdown of the city's elevators, there hadn't been a dull moment. Sure, she wasn't ducking under police tape today, attending accident scenes with the mayor's son. But there was plenty to do.

There was a hastily called meeting in one of the conference rooms midafternoon. Arla and her coworkers were tasked with monitoring media coverage of the crisis. Was the city's messaging getting out there? Were property managers going to the city website to learn everything they could about how an elevator might be tampered with, how to recognize it, and how to stop it from happening?

At one point, Arla raised her hand.

"I saw something yesterday that really made an impression," she said.

The others looked at her blankly, a kind of collective "Who are you again?"

Arla told them about being at the Sycamores Residences observing as the mayor comforted the boy who'd been in the elevator when the Russian scientist had been killed. Even with no cameras present, Headley took his time with the child, praised him, even invited him to Gracie Mansion for a hot dog.

"That was a side of him I hadn't seen, that most New Yorkers haven't seen," Arla said. "A really *human* Richard Headley. For anyone who thinks that news conference today didn't go well, maybe a way to offset that is to get him out on the street, and into those stairwells that everyone's having to go up and down. Have him deliver some groceries to some elderly person on the fifteenth floor. Only, you know, have someone cover it."

"Yes, well, thank you for that," Arla's new boss said, and then moved on to the next item.

In her head, Arla could hear the whine of a bullet-riddled fighter plane plunging earthward, the explosion as it hit the side of the mountain. There'd been no time for the pilot to eject to safety.

Humiliated, she went back to her computer after the meeting. Okay, maybe, for a newbie, she had overstepped. No one liked a smartass know-it-all, and maybe that was how she had come across. But that didn't mean her idea wasn't a good one. Maybe the problem was that she'd delivered it in the wrong venue. This department was not a campaign office. Yes, they gathered and analyzed data, but they were not strategists. These people, technically, worked for the city, not the mayor. It wasn't their job to advise Headley on his image. He had political advisers for that. People like Valerie Langdon.

And Glover.

As the afternoon dragged on, Arla kept thinking about him. He was the one who needed to hear her idea. She should text him. Or . . . maybe not. He might react the way her supervisor had. Who did she think she was? Did she think those closest to the mayor had no clue how to present him during a crisis?

Or might Glover think she had an ulterior motive? Was she just looking for an excuse to talk to him again?

Yeah, well, maybe.

Just as she'd come to question her motives for taking this job in the first place—had she done it, at least in part, to piss off her mother?—she was now asking herself why, exactly, her thumb was poised over her phone, ready to send a text to Glover.

Wasn't it possible she wanted to share her idea, *and* see him again?

She wrote: HEY, DONT WANT TO MAKE SUGGESTIONS ABOVE MY PAY GRADE BUT THINK RH COULD WIN NYERS OVER BY DOING A COUPLE OF THINGS DIFFERENTLY.

Arla reread the words several times. To send, or not to send?

She made her decision. She tapped the tiny, blue, upward-pointing arrow, heard the soft *whoosh* of the departing message. Arla left her phone, screen up, next to her keyboard and tried not to look at it any more often than every four seconds.

After a full minute had gone by, she believed she'd made a grave miscalculation. Glover had not responded. She'd made a fool of her-self. She was some lowly new hire thinking she knew how to run the place. As the minutes ticked by, Arla realized the only thing worse than Glover not replying would be if he *did* reply. How would *that* play once the rest of her department found out? Arla Silbert, doing an end run around her boss on her second day.

Stupid stupid stupid—

The phone rang. Arla jumped. Not enough for anyone else in the room to notice, but she'd felt her entire body jolt.

It was not her cell phone that had rung. It was her desk phone.

She picked up. "Hello. Arla Silbert."

"Hey," said a voice that she recognized instantly. "So what's this great idea of yours?"

Arla felt a hammering in her chest. "Listen, I'm sorry," she said, keeping her voice low so none of her coworkers would hear her. "I never should have—"

"No, no," said Glover. "Look, we're in the middle of a crisis. We need to consider everything. Even," and at this point Arla thought she heard a light chuckle, "from the new kid on the block."

"If you really think—"

"I do. Why are you whispering?"

"I don't think the others here appreciate my suggestions. Like you say, I'm the newbie."

"Okay, look, your day's just about over, right?"

"Yeah, the whistle blows in twenty minutes. But the way things are going, I wouldn't be surprised if we're asked to hang in."

"If you aren't, come by my office when you're done."

"Yeah, okay, sure."

Arla hung up, looked around to assess whether anyone had been listening in. Everyone else appeared transfixed by whatever was on their screens.

I don't know what the hell I'm doing, Arla thought.

Some of the more experienced staff were, in fact, asked to stay late. A few who lived on the upper floors of tall residential towers volunteered to work overtime, hoping that if they hung in long enough, the elevators would be working again by the time they did go home.

Arla was not asked to stay, nor did she volunteer to.

She found a place in the hallway a couple of doors down from Glover's office. Thank God for cell phones. In the olden days, when dinosaurs ruled the earth, if you were just hanging around, someone might approach and ask if they could help you, or demand to know what you were doing there, even if you did have a City Hall ID hanging around your neck.

But today, all you had to do was lean up against the wall and look at your phone. Your phone gave you cover in almost any circumstance, especially if it appeared you were dealing with an email or a text. That said you were *working*. You were *dealing* with something. You might not even have any business with anyone on this floor, let alone in this hallway. You were en route to someplace else, but had only stopped here because you'd received, or had to send, an urgent message.

So that was what Arla was doing. Leaning up against the wall, engrossed in her phone. For real. She was reading the latest updates about the elevator crisis when she sensed someone approaching. She looked up.

Glover smiled. "Hey," he said. "You made it."

"Hi," she said, tucking the phone into her purse. "Okay, so you remember last night, I was telling you about when your dad— sorry—when the mayor was talking to that kid and—"

He put a hand on her arm. "We don't have to do this in the hall."

His hand felt warm through the sleeve of her blouse. "Yeah, sure, okay, that sounds great."

"I need to get out of here for a few minutes, anyway," he said. He tapped his chest by the handkerchief pocket of his jacket. "They can get me if they need me."

Glover had been looking Arla in the eye, but something, or someone, farther down the hall had distracted him.

"Hang on," he said.

Arla turned, following his gaze. A tall, broad-shouldered, and entirely bald man was walking toward them.

"Chris," Glover said.

The man stopped, nodded. "Glover," he said, his tone flat.

"You coming back from Top of the Park? Coughlin cooled down some?" There was an air of authority in Glover's voice, but it sounded somehow hollow to Arla. Puffed up.

Chris looked at Glover through narrowed eyes. It reminded Arla of someone doing a Robert DeNiro impression, the way you'd stare someone down as you said, "You talkin' to *me*?"

Finally, Chris said, "It's handled."

Glover nodded. "Great, just what I was hoping to hear."

Arla sensed what was happening, and it made her sad for Glover. He was hoping to impress her, suggest that this Chris guy, whoever he was, reported to him. But it was clear this man felt no such obligation.

In a bid to break the tension, she extended a hand and said, "Hi. I'm Arla."

Chris's eyes widened and he smiled graciously as he took her hand. "Chris Vallins. Arla, you said?"

"Yes. Arla Silbert."

Vallins's eyes seemed to flicker. "Pleasure," he said.

"Ms. Silbert has just joined us," Glover said. "She's a whiz at data analysis."

Vallins smiled. "Well."

"Listen, we're just on our way," Glover said.

"Of course," Chris said. "Nice to meet you, Ms. Silbert."

Glover lightly touched Arla's arm to propel her down the hall. Once they were walking, she asked, "What's he do?"

"Whatever my father asks," Glover said.

"That all seemed, I don't know, a little awkward."

Glover shot her a look that seemed to confirm her assessment. "I feel like he doesn't trust me, or respect me. It's like he's watching me half the time."

Arla gave him a sympathetic look. "It's not like you've got anything to hide," she said. "I mean, you're the mayor's son."

———

Chris Vallins watched as Glover Headley and Arla Silbert walked away. Once they'd turned the corner at the end of the hall, he got out his phone and pulled up the pictures he'd taken when Barbara Matheson visited the Morning Star Café.

Using two fingers, he zoomed in on the photos of the young woman who had joined her. He'd taken a few shots as she was leaving the restaurant.

Without question, this was the woman he had just met.

Hanging out with the mayor's son.

His preliminary research had determined that while Barbara wrote under the name of Matheson, her legal last name was Silbert.

There was, Vallins believed, more than a passing resemblance between the two. He was willing to lay odds that the woman he had just met was Barbara's daughter.

Vallins shook his head with no small measure of admiration. You had to hand it to Barbara, he thought. She'd installed a mole in City Hall. A mole who was cozying up to the mayor's son.

The only thing to do now was figure out what to do about it.

Tell the mayor? Or warn Barbara that she was pushing her luck? Vallins had to admit, he was warming to her.

But for now, telling the boss was the way he was going to play it.

Fifty

Bucky heard a knock at his second-floor hotel room door.

"Hello?" he said.

"Housekeeping?" a woman called out.

"Look at the sign!" he shouted. He'd left the Do Not Disturb card hanging off the door handle since checking in days earlier.

"I know, but—"

Bucky got up from the bed where he had spread out everything he needed, went to the door, and opened it a foot. Any further, and someone would be able to see what he had spread out all over the bedspread. A woman was standing in the hallway with a large cart stocked with sheets and cleaning supplies and tiny bottles of soap and shampoo.

"I haven't serviced your room since you got here," the woman said. "Are you sure you don't need—"

"I don't need anything," Bucky said.

"Fresh sheets?"

"No."

She held up a tiny bottle of shampoo. "This?"

"I'm good. The room is fine. I don't need a thing."

Bucky started to worry when the maid eyed him suspiciously. Maybe she thought he had a dead body in there. Or that he'd kidnapped a girl or something. Or was on some kind of porn-watching binge. He needed to give her a story.

"I've got the flu," he said, and placed a palm over his stomach. "I come to New York to see my girlfriend and soon as I get here I come down with something. Musta caught it on the plane. Right after I check in I start throwing up and then I got the runs." Then he made a waving motion in front of his nose, clearing the air.

"Oh my," the maid said, taking a step back from the door.

"I'm taking it easy till it blows over," he said.

"What about food? I don't see any tray from room service outside your door."

"Been too sick to eat," Bucky said. "Maybe tomorrow."

"Okay, okay, you get better," the woman said, pushing her cart on to the next room.

Bucky closed the door and sighed with relief. He wouldn't have wanted to be asked to explain the items strewn across the bed and desk. Certainly not the empty pizza boxes, which would have put a lie to the story he'd just told. But especially not the various containers of chemicals. The wires. The timers. The two open laptops. The two burner phones and other electronic devices.

The gun.

Bucky had driven all the way across the country to New York. It wasn't like he could get on a plane with all this stuff, especially the silencer-equipped Glock 17.

He'd brought everything up to the room in two trips, which wasn't all that difficult given that he had booked himself into a two-story motor court. No high-rise hotel for him. Wouldn't want to be trekking up all those flights of stairs these days. Once he had everything in the room, he set it all up the way he liked. It was here that he'd put the finishing touches to the bomb he'd left in the Prius. It was here that he was preparing two more. And it was from the laptops he did any necessary research, and watched reports about what he'd accomplished.

Bucky was going to have another talk with Mr. Clement tomorrow. He had some ideas about what to do next, maybe up their game, but he wanted to clear them with the boss. It was a conversation they would have in person. Mr. Clement didn't like communicating through landlines or cell phones. The old man avoided texting. He didn't like when things were written down. The guy wouldn't even take an Uber. Only cabs he could pay for in cash. So they'd set up meetings at the zoo, or on the street, or in the hotel men's room.

They'd have another meeting there in the morning. He'd just have to be careful not to be seen by Mrs. Clement. She'd spotted him, Mr. Clement said. She was getting a little suspicious.

Bucky didn't like that. He knew Mr. Clement kept her in the dark about the worst of his activities. But women often had ways of figuring things out. They were sneaky. They couldn't be trusted.

Bucky wondered what Mrs. Clement would do if she knew the things her husband had set in motion.

Maybe nothing.

Maybe something.

Anyway, he couldn't worry about that now. He had work to do.

Fifty-One

Jerry Bourque and Lois Delgado had already put in a twelve-hour day and were both starting to get a bit punchy. Delgado had phoned her mother-in-law to babysit, again, because her husband had pulled a late shift at the firehouse. She'd talked to him a couple of times, the two of them wondering what the night might bring in a city without elevators.

On Delgado's computer screen was the picture Jerry had emailed to himself from Otto Petrenko's coworker's phone. It showed, in the distance, Otto talking to the tall man leaning up against the dark sedan.

Delgado had placed on the same screen, off to the side, a photo of Eugene Clement. She and Bourque did not necessarily have a reason to believe it was Clement who'd come to see Otto at his place of work, but it was a starting point.

"I just don't know," said Bourque, who had wheeled his office chair around to the other side so he could sit shoulder to shoulder with his partner and stare at the screen. "It could be him, but then again, it could be just about anybody."

"Clement and this guy are about six feet, but so are half the men in the world, so that's no help. And they both have gray hair. But . . ."

"What do you see?"

"I'm just looking at our mystery man's hair. It seems . . . off."

Bourque leaned in closer. "Off, as in . . . ?"

"Kilter. It doesn't look natural. I think it's a rug."

Bourque nodded. "Maybe. So . . . it's part of a disguise? He doesn't want people to recognize him?"

"Or he's just vain," Delgado said. "Let's go back to the tag." She zoomed in on the back of the sedan. That part of the car was in shadow, and the color of the license plate was difficult to determine. Plus, it was nearly 50 percent obscured by the used Mustang, in the foreground of the picture, that the elevator technician had been thinking about buying. Immediately to the right of the plate was a scratch in the paint where the bumper had been dented.

All they could make out were the last two numbers of the plate: 13. Even those numbers were somewhat blurry. The plate could be a New York State one. Below the numbers were what appeared to be the letters TATE. Most New York plates had the words "Empire State" across the bottom. But then again, most New Jersey plates said "Garden State" in the same place. And Connecticut plates featured the words "Constitution State" along the bottom edge. Rhode Island had "Ocean State."

Most New York plates were an orangey yellow, but some were white with blue numbers, and others were blue with orange numbers. New Jersey plates came in yellow, or blue, or white.

What proved more helpful were the words across the top of the plate. Jerry pointed to the screen. "Looks like an *R* and *K* there." The last two letters in New York.

"Yeah. So it's a New York plate. That narrows it down to only a few million," Delgado said.

Bourque pointed. "What is that?"

"What is what?"

He put his finger directly on the screen.

"Do you mind?" Delgado said, brushing his hand away. "You're gonna leave a smudge. You're as bad as my kid."

"Just look," he said, pulling his finger back half an inch.

Delgado leaned in, her nose only four inches from the screen. Bourque was pointing to a small sticker of some kind on the bumper, just below the plate.

"I can't tell what it is," she said.

It was not the size of a traditional, rectangular bumper sticker people put on their cars to advertise where they'd gone on vacation, or who they were supporting politically. This sticker was round, and about the size of a paper coaster, if not slightly smaller.

"It looks like it's got letters on it," he said.

"Yeah. Maybe three. Reminds me a little of a New York Yankees logo. You know? With the *N* and the *Y* on top of each other, except here they look separated."

"So it's an *N*, and a *Y*, and what's the third letter?" Bourque asked.

"Maybe a *C*?" She shook her head. "It's just going to get fuzzier if I blow it up any more."

"Hang on," Bourque said slowly. "I think I've seen this before but I'm not sure where. I just have to think . . ."

He got up out of his chair and rounded the desks until he was back in front of his own computer.

"Want your chair?" Delgado asked, watching as her partner leaned over to tap away on the keys.

"No, it's okay," he said. He squinted at his screen and muttered to himself, "Okay, yes, yes, okay."

"What is it?" Delgado asked.

"Give me a sec. I'm printing it out."

"Printing what out?"

A few steps away, a printer started to hum, and seconds later a piece of paper dropped into the tray. Bourque walked over, retrieved it, then sat back down in the chair next to Delgado.

He held the sheet of paper in front of her. "What do you think?"

He had printed out a picture of a logo with the letters *NYG* grouped artistically together.

"Pretty," she said. "What is it?"

"Remember how Headley's been going on about making this a more livable city?"

"Yeah, well, that's really going well," she said. "So long as you like stairs."

"It was all part of his campaign. Reducing greenhouse gases, that kind of shit. He's been doing a big push about making all city cars environmentally friendly. Either making them all electric, or at least hybrid. Part gas engine, part electric."

"Okay," Delgado said.

"He kicked it off with his so-called New York Green initiative. They made up these stickers."

"So . . . this is a city car," Delgado said slowly.

Bourque nodded. "Yeah."

"Well, then maybe this is a dead end," she said. "I mean, it makes sense that someone from the city, like the building department, the one that looks after elevators, might come by and see the folks at the good ol' elevator repair shop."

"Yeah, but then why wouldn't they talk to the boss? To what's-his-name, Gunther Willem. And supposedly Otto never mentioned this guy he went out to talk to. According to Willem, Otto didn't say a word about what his visitor wanted. Why wouldn't he want to reveal a conversation he had with someone from the City?"

Delgado took her face away from the screen and leaned back into her chair.

"That's a good question," she said.

"So all we have to do," Bourque said, "is find an environmentally friendly sedan that belongs to the City, with a plate ending in 13, and a scratch in the bumper right there, and find out who signed it out on this day."

"Well," Delgado said, "how hard could that be?"

Fifty-Two

Once she'd managed to hail a cab and was safely ensconced in the backseat, Barbara started making calls on her cell. Her first was to the mayor's office, but she couldn't get through. When the line wasn't busy, it rang endlessly.

Not surprising. Given the kind of day it had been, Headley and his team might well have adopted a bunker mentality. Hole up, wait for things to blow over. So far, the fallout from the mass elevator shutdown was not good. At least eight dead. Six of those were possible heart attacks, two were stairway falls.

There were probably a hundred media inquiries per minute coming in to City Hall. The city's ability to deal with incoming requests for information and interviews had probably already collapsed.

But heading south in a cab, Barbara was struck by how calm—almost convivial—things were. Manhattan sidewalks were always thronged with people moving hurriedly from place to place, and, not surprisingly, given that going upstairs was suddenly a pain in the ass, they were more packed than usual. But people were hardly running about, panicked. Not many of them were even putting one foot ahead of the other. They were standing around, leaning up against buildings and lampposts, chatting with each other, laughing. Every café, bar, and restaurant with outdoor seating was overflowing with people making the best of an emergency.

Can't get up to your apartment? Might as well have a drink till they give the all clear.

Fuckin' New Yorkers, Barbara thought. *It doesn't matter what you throw at us. We just carry on.*

She threw a twenty at the driver and leapt out of the cab two blocks from City Hall. She ran the rest of the way.

She had always loved this part of Manhattan. The park and fountain south of the city's seat of government. People playing chess, kids on school tours, the nearby stands selling New York souvenirs and trinkets and hot dogs and pretzels. Tourists heading off to cross the Brooklyn Bridge on foot.

But Barbara didn't really see any of this now. She had her mind on one thing and one thing only: telling Richard Headley that he, and his supporters, were what linked the elevator incidents.

As she reached the gate to get onto the City Hall grounds, her way was blocked by a uniformed officer. She'd been through this security checkpoint so many times that often she was waved through without flashing her media credentials.

This time, the cop on duty wouldn't let her through. He said, "Hold it right there."

"I need to talk to the mayor," Barbara said.

The cop smirked. "Oh, well, sure. Head right up. I'm sure he's free." But he did not let her pass.

"No, seriously," she said. She dug into her purse and handed him her credentials. "I go in there all the time. Come on, you know me. Right? You haven't seen me go through here a hundred times?"

"I still have to check your ID and confirm that you're legit. Threat level's been raised, in case you hadn't noticed."

Barbara sighed, turned around in a gesture of frustration.

Something caught her eye.

Two people heading down the sidewalk. A man and a woman. The woman, at least from where Barbara stood, looked a lot like Arla, and the man had more than a passing resemblance to the mayor's son.

"Shit," she said.

"Huh?" the cop said.

Barbara spun back around. "Nothing."

He handed back her credentials. "Go on in."

Barbara ran into the building, cleared further checkpoints, and headed to the mayor's office, where she encountered even more security.

"Please," she said to the female guard. "I need to see him."

"You're gonna have to deal with the media liaison department if you—"

The door to the mayor's office opened. Valerie Langdon emerged.

"Valerie!" Barbara shouted. She quickly followed that with, "Ms. Langdon!" She and the mayor's assistant had never been on a first-name basis.

Valerie turned, saw who it was, and hesitated.

"It's important," Barbara said.

Valerie approached. "What do you want?"

"I need to talk to him."

"You and every other reporter between here and California," she said.

Barbara took two seconds to compose herself. "I think I know why," she said.

Valerie's head tilted to one side. "Why what?"

"Why it's happening."

"Tell me."

"I think it's about him," she said.

"Say again?"

"I think the elevator incidents are about the mayor."

"That's insane."

"Maybe," Barbara said. "But I want to bounce something off him."

Valerie took ten seconds to make up her mind. "Come with me," she said.

Valerie made Barbara wait outside the door to the mayor's office. She reappeared less than a minute later.

"He'll see you," she said, a hint of surprise in her voice.

Valerie did not follow Barbara into the office. The mayor was leaning up against his desk, watching the TV on mute.

"Close the door," he said.

Barbara closed the door.

"Have a seat," he said.

Barbara took a spot on the couch and Headley sat in a chair opposite her. He slapped his palms on top of his thighs and leaned forward. "So, what's this important thing you want to tell me?"

"There's a common thread to the elevator events," Barbara said.

"I know," the mayor said, shrugging. "Similarities in . . . technique."

"I'm not talking about the cameras."

Headley's eyebrows went up. "So you know about that."

She nodded. "I'm not talking about *how* it was done. I think I know *why* it might have been done."

Headley leaned back in his chair, crossed his arms, as if daring her to impress him. "Shoot."

"I think it's about you."

A long pause. Then, "Go on."

"All three buildings are either owned, or occupied, by major supporters of your campaign. Especially the one this morning. The Gormley Building."

"I don't know anyone named Gormley."

"Maybe not, but you do know Arnett Steel. He lives in the pent-house."

Headley said nothing.

"And the Sycamores, that was where—"

"I know," he said. "Margaret Cambridge."

"I think someone is sending a message to you, and those who've enabled you," Barbara said. "I think this . . . I think this is about revenge."

Headley slowly shook his head. "Your theory seems . . . thin."

"Do you have a better one?" Barbara asked.

"Several leads are being followed. An alt-right domestic terror group could be behind this. That theory is already out there. It strikes me as the most credible one. My guess is you'd just *love* for these events to have something to do with me. It'd fit the narrative you've set forth."

"That's not true," Barbara said. "I'm not here as a reporter. I'm— okay, that's bullshit. I *am* here as a reporter. But I want to see whoever's doing this caught just as much as you do. I want this to end." She paused. "I watched Paula Chatsworth die. This isn't just another story for me."

"It's personal," the mayor said.

Barbara nodded.

"Personal in more ways than one," Headley said with a sly smile.

"I don't know what you mean."

"I think you do." He smiled. "Were you surprised when I so read-ily agreed to see you?"

"Um, maybe a little."

"I had Valerie show you in because I wanted to congratulate you."

"For?"

"Your audacity. The genius of it. Planting someone right here at City Hall. Getting someone on the inside. I have to hand it to you."

He suddenly got up, went back to his desk, shuffled some papers, trying to find something. "It's here somewhere," he said. "I asked for the file. On new hires."

Arla.

"Doesn't matter," Headley said, abandoning the search and heading for the door, getting ready to show her out. "I'll find it later. But I've been informed that you have a member of your family working for us. Am I right about that?"

Barbara nodded slowly. "Yes."

"Your daughter?"

"Yes. But it's not what you think. She did it entirely on her own. If you want to know the truth—"

"That'd be a twist."

"If you want to know the truth, I think she took the job, in part, just to get under my skin. She knew that working for your administration would not go over well with me. Our relationship is . . . complicated. But she got the job because she's good at what she does. She deserves it."

"So you say," Headley said. "Forgive me for being skeptical. Anyway, whatever game you and your daughter may or may not be playing here, it's over. As is her employment with the City of New York."

He opened the door, inviting her to leave. But instead of walking out, Barbara went to his desk and grabbed the sheaf of papers he'd been going through.

"Hey!" the mayor said. "Don't touch my—"

She quickly found what she was looking for. She waved one sheet in the air and scattered the rest onto his desk. "You were hunting for this. My daughter's job application."

"I hadn't had a chance to read it yet. But I know what I need to know."

"Do you? Do you know her name?"

The mayor shrugged. A no.

"Arla," Barbara said, heading for the door. She slapped the sheet of paper against Headley's chest as she passed him. "Arla Silbert."

She met Headley's eyes for a fraction of a second as she walked out.

Fifty-Three

Barbara had her head down as she walked briskly away from the mayor's office, but not, as was most often the case, because she was looking at her phone. Her head was down because she did not want anyone to see her cry.

If it had not been for the tears blurring her vision, she might have seen Chris Vallins instead of running right into him.

"Sorry," she blurted, and looked up. "Oh, shit."

"Jesus," he said, seeing the tears. "What's happened?"

"Nothing," she said, trying to steer around him. But this time, it was his turn to hold her by the arm and steer her toward the closest door.

It wasn't a ladies' room this time, or a men's. He ushered her into a conference room that was outfitted with one rectangular table and about a dozen wheeled office chairs.

"Talk to me," he said, putting her into one of them. He took another one and wheeled it around so he was facing her, knees touching.

"I don't want to talk about it," Barbara said. "I'm fine."

She dug into her purse for a tissue and dabbed her eyes.

"You were in talking to Headley?"

She nodded.

"About?"

Barbara swallowed, sniffed. "He's the link. Wherever an elevator's gone down, it's been a building with a major political donor. To his campaign. I think that's what this is about."

Vallins said, "Whoa."

Another sniff. She went into her bag for another tissue and blew her noise.

"What did the mayor say?"

"He dismissed it," she said.

Vallins leaned in close, his head nearly touching hers. He saw a tear running down her cheek and caught it with his finger.

"That's why you're crying?"

She shook her head. "No. It's . . . I think everything's about to unravel."

"What do you mean?"

Barbara raised her chin, looked into Vallins's eyes. "I don't know what to make of you. You work for that asshole, but there are times when you seem like maybe you've got an actual conscience."

He smiled. "I don't know about that." He paused. "I . . . sometimes I have to play both sides."

"That sounds like the shortest definition ever of 'politics,'" Barbara said.

"Maybe."

"My daughter got a job with the city. She did it totally on her own. Headley found out, somehow. He thinks I engineered it. That I got her in here as a spy, for fuck's sake." She shook her head. "It's not true."

Vallins inched back slightly. "I can see why he might have thought that, though."

"He's going to have her fired, Chris," Barbara said. "It's not fair."

"I'm sorry," he said.

Barbara shrugged. "It's not like it's your fault."

Vallins said nothing.

"I have to go," Barbara said. "I have to find her. I have to talk to her."

As she started to rise from her chair Vallins gently gripped her shoulders and held her in place. "Wait," he said. "Just . . ."

"What?"

Vallins swallowed, took a breath. "I like you. I mean, I've always liked what you've stood her. I've been reading you for a long time. And, well, yeah, I like you."

Barbara sniffed again. "Okay. I'm guessing the mayor doesn't know you're a fan."

He managed a smile as he struggled with what to say next. "Maybe sometime I'll be able to explain. But for now, I'm sorry."

And then he did something she was not expecting. He leaned forward, kissed her lightly on the forehead, then released his grip on her shoulders and wheeled back in his chair.

Barbara stood and studied him for a moment.

"Thank you," she said, and left the room.

Fifty-Four

I'm an idiot," Arla said. "It should have occurred to me that you'd already thought of this."

She and Glover had settled into a booth at Maxwell's on Reade Street. He smiled and took a sip from the copper mug that held his Moscow Mule. Tito's vodka, ginger beer, and lime. Arla had gone for a glass of Sancerre. Glover had offered a taste of what he was drinking, and the face she'd made when she got a little of it on her tongue had made him laugh.

Arla had told Glover she thought the mayor had to get out there, be seen by and with all those New Yorkers struggling through the elevator crisis. Climb a few flights to take dinner to a shut-in, she'd said. Deliver a prescription from Duane Reade to an apartment dweller too ill to make the trip down and back up again.

"Yeah, those are good ideas," he said to her, sitting across the table from her.

"You're already doing this, aren't you?" she said.

"I'm setting up something," he said. "But great minds do think alike."

"I brought this up at our department meeting," Arla said, "and everyone looked at me like, 'Who do you think you are?' Sorry if I've wasted your time."

"Not at all," Glover said, leaning forward so he wouldn't have to speak loudly. "The truth is, I was happy to get out of the building. It's pretty tense in there."

Arla had her fingers over the base of her glass, holding it securely between sips. Inches away, Glover lay his hands flat on the table, his fingers splayed as if reaching out to Arla, waiting to make a move.

"I'll just bet it is," Arla said.

"Yeah. Dad's kinda freaking out. The news conference didn't go well. All the TV pundits are ripping him to shreds."

"When can people start using the elevators again?"

"Once landlords and property managers have done inspections, they should be able to start up the elevators in their buildings. So, maybe tomorrow? And you can be sure that nothing, absolutely nothing, will stop the Top of the Park grand opening tomorrow night."

"That skyscraper at the north end of Central Park?"

"Right. Rodney Coughlin's massive steel and glass erection."

Arla smirked.

"After the Freedom Tower, it's the tallest building in the city. He's one of my dad's biggest backers. We're going to the opening tomorrow night."

"Yikes. I'm not sure I'd want to be in on one of *those* elevators."

"No kidding," he said. "But I'm sure everything will be safe. Who knows. They might even catch whoever's doing it by then."

"I wonder who it is," she said.

"Whoever it is, you gotta admit, he's pretty brilliant. I mean, yeah, you have to condemn the act, but it's hard not to be impressed by the ingenuity of it all. Being able to take over control of a building's elevators. It's amazing."

Arla shook her head. "I don't know. I don't see much to admire." She turned over her phone, which had been resting facedown on the table, to check the time. "Look, if you have to go, I'll understand."

"I'm in no rush," Glover said.

He inched his fingers forward until the tips of several were touching Arla's. She did not pull back.

"I wondered how you'd feel about, you know, getting together outside of work."

"You mean, like right there?" Arla asked.

Glover laughed nervously. "This sort of started out as a drink about work. But maybe sometime we could—"

"Sure," Arla said. "I'd like that."

He smiled. "Great. Do you have a favorite resta—"

"Hey," said a voice.

They both turned to see Barbara standing at the end of the table. While Arla struggled to hold her jaw in place, Glover appeared unfazed to see her there.

"Barbara," he said, taking his hand away from Arla's. "Nice to see you."

Barbara attempted to offer Glover a smile, but her face was glass on the verge of shattering as she focused on Arla.

"Uh," Glover said, still not sure why Barbara was standing there, since she had not yet said why, "let me introduce you. Arla, this is Barbara Matheson, who you may know from her *Manhattan Today* column." He managed a smirk. "Maybe not my father's favorite writer, but believe me, he always reads her. And Barbara, this is Arla Silbert. She's—"

"We've met," Arla said.

"Oh," Glover said, surprised. "Where do you know each other from?"

To her daughter, Barbara said, "I need to talk to you."

"How did you find me?" Arla asked.

"I saw you coming out of City Hall. This is about the hundredth place I've gone into, looking."

Arla said, "I *have* a phone."

Barbara shook her head. "I had to talk to you face-to-face."

Glover, watching this conversation, had the look of a bewildered puppy. "I feel a bit out of the loop here," he said.

Barbara said to him, "I went to see your father." She paused. "It's all about him."

Glover shrugged. "It's always all about him."

"That's not what I mean. All this shit with the elevators. It's a message, meant specifically to get his attention."

Glover was instantly alarmed. "What are you talking about?"

"Ask him. I'm done. I gave it my best shot. Anyway, you're not why I'm here. I'm here to talk to my daughter."

It was Glover's turn to keep his jaw from dropping. Speechless, he looked at Arla, who had briefly closed her eyes, as if trying to make her mother disappear.

"Arla," Barbara said.

She opened her eyes. "Please go."

Barbara's face began to crumble. "I'm so sorry. Somehow . . . he figured out who you were . . . are . . . to me." A long pause, then, "Maybe even to him."

Glover found his voice. "That's your mother? And you just happened to land a job helping the mayor? Are you some sort of spy?"

"No," Arla said. "She didn't even *know* I was applying for the job." She looked at Barbara. "I'm fired, right? Did Headley tell you that?"

Barbara nodded. "Pretty much."

"Terrific," Arla said, tearing up herself now. "Fan-fucking-tastic."

Glover was still struggling to put it all together. "I don't—I had no idea. You don't . . . have the same name." He reached back across the table for Arla's hand before she could pull it away. "I'll talk to my father. He can't fire you like that. I oversee your department. I'll handle this."

Barbara couldn't stop looking at Glover's hand on Arla's.

"Don't," Barbara said quietly. Glover, startled, slowly withdrew his hand as Arla's cheeks flushed.

Glover took a moment to compose himself and said, "I should go." He tossed some bills onto the table to cover their drinks and slid out of the booth. Before walking away, he looked at Arla and said, "I'm going to sort this out."

But Arla couldn't look at him. Her head was bowed, she had one hand over her eyes. Barbara sat where Glover had been.

Without looking at her mother, Arla said, "I hate you."

Barbara said, "I don't blame you. And I think maybe you're about to hate me even more."

Arla took her hand away from her eyes and looked at her mother through tears. "That seems unlikely. You've lost me my job." She tilted her head toward the door, in the direction Glover Headley had gone, and said, "Maybe more than that."

"It wouldn't have worked out with Glover," Barbara said.

"Oh, and why's that?" Arla asked. "Because you hate his father? If you'd been there for me more, you'd know I've got a mind of my own and don't care whether you approve of people I see, or who their parents might happen to be."

"It's not . . . like that," Barbara said.

"What, then?" Arla said. "Tell me. I'd really like to know."

"It could never have worked out with Glover," Barbara said slowly, "because he's your brother."

Fifty-Five

When she comes through the doorway, she is panting, desperate for air. "I think I need a drink of water," she gasps. And then she begins to stagger.

The boy is sitting cross-legged on the floor, watching an episode of Star Trek. He jumps to his feet.

"Mom?" he says.

She puts a hand to her chest. "It hurts so—"

And then she goes down. First to her knees, then the rest of her pitches forward. She doesn't even manage to get an arm in front of her to help break her fall. Her face has turned slightly, so she lands on her right check.

"Mom!" the boy screams, running to her.

She moves her lips, whispers something to her son. "I need . . . call your father." Her eyelids close.

"Mom? Mom? Say something. Mom. Please don't die. Mom? Mom. Open your eyes. Look at me. Mom. Mom! I love you, Mom. I love you. Oh, Mom. No no no no no."

Thursday

Fifty-Six

No elevators plummeted Thursday morning. No bombs exploded.
But the day was young.

Fifty-Seven

Eugene Clement, seated one table over from where they were in the hotel dining room the day before, asked, "Are you all packed?"

Estelle didn't look up from her menu. "Yes. I'm good to go."

"I'll get us a car to the airport around ten," he said. "I'll have someone bring our bags down."

"That sounds fine," she said.

Things were less frosty than they'd been twenty-four hours earlier. They were speaking. Current events had brought about a thaw in relations.

After Estelle had toured the Guggenheim the day before, she'd crossed Fifth Avenue and strolled through Central Park for a couple of hours. It was while wandering the park's paths that she heard people talking about something to do with elevators. She went onto her phone and read about the crisis engulfing the city. It was then that she suppressed the animosity she was feeling toward her husband and called to ask if he knew what was happening, to warn him not to use the hotel's elevators. Or any other elevators in the city, for that matter.

"Good thing we're on one of the lower floors," he said.

So that evening they walked over to Pera, both ordering the lamb chops—their last New York dinner before heading home—and that evening, Clement even made love to her.

The things you had to do sometimes.

Clement still had another matter to take care of before they departed. One more meeting.

"I think I'll have the eggs benny," Estelle said.

"Sounds good. If the waiter comes while I'm away, make it two. And would you ask him to bring more cream for the coffee?"

As he started to push back his chair, she asked, "Where are you going?"

"Where do you *think* I'm going?"

"You haven't even had a second cup yet," she said. "You already have to go?"

"I'd love to discuss my urinary tract with you, dear, but could it wait till I get back?"

He strode off.

Clement exited the dining room, crossed the lobby, then entered a hallway around the corner from the elevators. He pushed open the door to the men's room. Standing at the last in a row of sinks was Bucky, leaning in close to the mirror, trying to pluck a hair from his nostril.

Bucky turned and offered the hand he'd just been working with to his boss, who declined to take it.

Bucky grinned as he withdrew his hand. "Sorry."

"We leave at eleven," Clement said.

"Sure, that's fine," Bucky said. "So you won't be here for the next ones."

"No, but I've been thinking, maybe the timing's not right. We've been overshadowed. I think we should hold off for a while, or try a new location. There's too much else going on here. Everyone's on high alert."

Bucky frowned. "I'm ready to go. I wanted to talk locations. What do you think about a subway station in rush hour? Or maybe a department store?"

Clement motioned Bucky over to the far wall. They each leaned a shoulder into it as they continued to confer.

"Listen," Clement said, "you've done good work. And there's more to be done. But it's time to take this show someplace else, cities we haven't hit before."

Bucky couldn't hide his disappointment. Clement offered a regretful smile. While he didn't want to shake the man's hand, a pat on the shoulder seemed appropriate. As he lay his hand there, he said, "We'll find a way to talk when I get home."

"Okay, that's a good—"

"I knew it," someone said.

They both turned. Estelle Clement was standing just inside the door of the men's room.

"Jesus Christ," Eugene said, taking his hand off Bucky's shoulder. "You can't be in here."

She took five slow steps into the room. She glanced, briefly, at her reflection in the massive mirror that ran along the wall.

"It all makes sense now," she said. "I think I've known all along. At least, for a while. The . . . lack of interest. How distant you've been. I . . . didn't want to see the signs."

"Shit," said Bucky.

"How long?" Estelle asked, looking at her husband. "How long has it been going on? Is he the first, or just the latest?"

Clement was on the verge of a smile. "Wait, what is it you think—"

"I hid down the hall," she said. "Yesterday. This man came out seconds after you did. The same man I'd seen before. Too many times for it to be a coincidence." She shook her head sadly, then eyed her husband pityingly. "It's all so pathetic. An entire hotel at your disposal, and still you meet in here. Is there some thrill attached to that? Tell me. I really want to know. God, it's such a stereotype. Such a cliché."

"Dear, you've misunderstood," Clement said. "Bucky here—"

At the mention of his name, Bucky cleared his throat and gave Clement a disapproving look. Clement, realizing his mistake, paused to start again. But he didn't get a chance.

"I kept wondering, why New York?" Estelle said, her voice shaking. "At first I thought, maybe you were trying to make a point. That it was some bizarre Flyovers statement, walking into the enemy camp, looking—I don't know—for some kind of dialogue or confrontation or whatever. Then," and she suddenly laughed, a short, almost hysterical hoot, "I even wondered, was it you? Did you make those elevators crash? Hire some genius to do it?"

"That's absurd, Estelle," Clement said.

"Well, I know that now!" she said. "I almost wish that was what you'd been up to." She touched the corner of her eye to catch a tear. "It would certainly be less humiliating than this." Her lip quivered. "God, I feel like such a fool. How long, Eugene. How many other men?"

Behind her, a man came striding into the room, already tugging at the top of his zipper. But he hit the brakes when he saw Estelle, then spun around and left.

Clement began to laugh.

"Oh, this is too much," he said, and the laughs turned into guffaws. "Really, really, this is beyond outrageous."

He looked at Bucky, clapped his hand on the man's shoulder again and continued laughing. Bucky, however, did not see the humor in the situation. He pushed Eugene's hand away and started heading for the door.

Estelle sidestepped to block his path. When he attempted to dodge around her, she moved again.

"Bucky, is it?" she asked. "Are you married, too? Does your wife know she's married to a queer?"

"For fuck's sake," he said, glancing back at Clement. "Mr. Clement, with all respect, you need to straighten out your lady here."

Clement nodded. "Estelle, I can tell you, in all honesty, that I am *not* having an affair with Bucky." A short laugh. "If I was thinking of switching teams, it'd be with someone a little better looking." He grinned at Bucky. "No offense intended."

Bucky looked increasingly distressed.

"Then what the hell *is* going on?" Estelle demanded.

"Bucky here is . . . a business associate."

"Oh, please, Eugene. Don't treat me like a moron. What the hell business would anyone conduct in *here*?"

Bucky said, "Mr. Clement, I don't think you should get into—"

"Bucky here is my number one . . . man in the field. An operative, you might say. He—"

"Is he one of your followers?" Estelle asked. "Goes around blowing things up?"

Clement blinked. Bucky said, "Shit."

"You think I don't know?" Estelle said, looking at her husband. Her voice rose. "The thing is, I don't know which is worse. If he's your boyfriend, or one of your bombers?"

"Lady—Mrs. Clement—you need to shut the fuck up," Bucky said.

Clement shot him a look. "Don't speak to my wife that way, Bucky."

Bucky looked at Clement as though he'd never set eyes on him before. He was seeing him in a new light. No longer the mentor. Now a threat.

"Or maybe he's both," Estelle said, not shutting up, and definitely not getting any quieter. She glared at her husband and shrieked, "Maybe makes your bombs, and then he gets down on his knees and—"

That was when Bucky shot her.

He'd quickly taken the silencer-equipped Glock from where he'd tucked it into the back of his jeans, hidden under his jacket, pointed it at Estelle and pulled the trigger.

The bullet caught her in the throat, passed through her neck and struck the closest urinal, shattering porcelain and spilling the deodorizing urinal puck to the floor.

Estelle went down.

Clement screamed *"NOOOOO!"* and, momentarily paralyzed by what he'd seen, looked at Bucky, eyes wide, mouth open.

"What in God's—"

Bucky shot Clement in the chest. He staggered back a step, looked down disbelievingly at the blossom of red on his shirt. He dropped to one knee.

Bucky put another bullet into him, this one into the forehead. Clement went down.

"I'm real sorry, Mr. Clement," Bucky said. "Especially this being your anniversary and all." He tucked the gun back into his pants, straightened his jacket, and walked out of the men's room.

Fifty-Eight

Barbara threw back the covers and padded quietly on her bare feet to the kitchen.

There was a pounding in her head demanding coffee, but it was calling out for painkillers even more insistently. Barbara opened the cupboard, tapped out two pills from a container, popped them into her mouth, and washed them down with a handful of tap water.

She put a paper cone into the coffee maker and spooned in twice as much ground dark roast as she usually put in each morning. Once the water had been added, she pushed the button and waited for the first drops of coffee to appear. The pot could not fill quickly enough. She glanced at the four empty wine bottles on the counter. She was, to put it mildly, very hung over.

When the coffee was ready, she filled a mug and stirred in some sweetener. Then she stepped quietly back into the bedroom and sat down gingerly on one side of the bed.

"Hey," Barbara whispered. "I made some coffee."

Arla, sleeping on her stomach, had her face buried in the pillow. She made a low, barely audible grunting noise, then slowly rolled over, her hair dragging across her face.

Blinking several times as she adjusted to the light coming in through the window, Arla said, "I feel like a piece of shit that's been stuffed inside another piece of shit."

"Join the club," Barbara said. "You want some Tylenol or aspirin or anything? You want it, I've got it."

Arla started to pull herself up, her back resting against the headboard. As she reached for the mug, she said, "Let me see if this does the trick first."

She glanced at the cell phone on the bedside table, picked it up. "It's dead. What time is it?"

"Nearly ten," Barbara said.

Arla snorted. "Looks like I'm gonna be late for work."

Barbara said nothing. With her free hand, Arla patted her mother's knee. "Joke."

"I'm sorry."

"You've said that enough." Arla took a sip of coffee, closed her eyes briefly. "Bliss. You did it just right. What time did we finally fall asleep?"

"Around five, I think," Barbara said.

"God."

"Let me get a cup. I'll be right back."

Barbara slipped out to the kitchen, filled a mug for herself, and returned. Arla hadn't moved. Barbara went around to the opposite side of the bed and got in it, back to the headboard, next to her daughter.

"I haven't got much in the way of breakfast," she said apologetically. "Does Uber Eats deliver this early?"

"I need a hangover breakfast bad," Arla said. She glanced down at herself, took in the blue T-shirt and white pajama bottoms she was wearing. "Thanks for the PJs," she said.

"No problem," Barbara said, her shoulder touching Arla's. It was, she thought, the greatest feeling in the world.

"It's all really fucked up, isn't it?" Arla said.

"That's an understatement."

"The mayor of New York is my father."

"Yeah."

"And he's never known anything about me."

"That's right."

"And Glover is my *half* brother."

"Yup."

"And he's never known about me, either."

"That's right." Barbara paused. "And that's all on me."

Arla ran her finger around the rim of her coffee cup. "I wonder if that's why I was feeling this, I don't know, kind of attraction. To Glover. Maybe I saw something of myself in him. We were connecting on some genetic, sibling-like level."

"I guess that's possible."

Arla put her coffee on the table and half turned to face her mother. "These days, like, right now, does Headley have any idea?"

"About what?"

"That this Barbara Matheson who's writing about him, that you're that person? The one he slept with years ago?"

Barbara slowly shook her head. "No. I'm sure of it. I don't look much like I did at that age. My hair's a different color and, well, I'm a little chunkier. I wrote under a different name. It was a long time ago. And we only met a couple of times. The night it happened, and then when I told him."

"And he denied it. Said he had no memory of you, or the party, or anything."

Barbara nodded.

This was not the first time Arla had asked the question. Barbara had told her story—the unexpurgated truth—several times since they'd arrived at her apartment the night before. After Barbara had dropped the bombshell in Maxwell's about Glover, she'd persuaded

Arla to leave with her, promising to tell her all the things she had wanted to know since she was born.

They had gone back to Barbara's apartment—after climbing several flights of stairs, they were pretty weary by the time they got there—and opened the first of four bottles of wine. Barbara told Arla her story, stopping and answering, as honestly as she could, every question that Arla had along the way.

Arla had thought the reason there was no father listed on her birth certificate was because her mother really wasn't sure.

"You kind of, you know, as I got older, let me think you were— God, this is going to sound so judgy—a bit of a slut," she had said at one point. "You said my father had gone to the other side of the country, found a life there."

"Yeah," Barbara said. "I guess I thought that would discourage you from trying to find him, to make a connection. Telling you, when you were little, that he was out west, it was like saying he was on another planet. It was the same lie I told my parents, so they wouldn't go looking for him, trying to get him to do the right thing. Thing is, he might as well have been a thousand miles away instead of right here in the city. I've always felt you can't force someone to care. I wasn't going to go after Richard, make him submit to a blood test, to prove what I already knew. If he didn't want to be a father, I wasn't going to coerce him into being one."

"But you could have at least gotten support. Made him help financially."

"I probably should have. I guess I was too proud. Too headstrong. Independent to a fault. I thought, 'Fuck you, I don't need your help.'"

"But you took your parents' help," Arla said. "You made me a burden to them, when you could have lightened the load for them by making Richard assume some responsibility."

"You were *never* a burden to them," Barbara said. "They loved you more than you can ever know."

"Just a burden to *you,* then," Arla said.

Barbara looked away.

"I'm sorry," Arla said.

"That's okay. I deserve that. I can't change what I did. All I can do is try to make better decisions moving forward."

Arla was quiet for several seconds before she said, "Do you think he'd want to know now?"

Barbara said, "I don't know." She thought for a moment. "I think he might have recognized the name."

"What do you mean?"

"When I was in his office, all he knew was that a child of mine was working in his administration. He didn't know your name. When I walked out, I told him. I said 'Silbert.'"

"Which was the name he'd have known you by. If he remembered."

"Yeah." Barbara shrugged. "I just don't know."

Arla sipped some coffee. "I'd like . . . to talk to him."

"I get that," Barbara said. "But I'm not sure it's a good idea."

"It's not really your decision."

Barbara looked at Arla. "I know." She looked into her cup. "I need more coffee. You?"

Arla handed over her mug. As Barbara was heading into the kitchen, Arla called out a question: "Is it revenge?"

"Is what revenge?"

"Writing about the mayor. Going after him. Is it all about getting even?"

There was silence while Barbara filled the cups. When she came back into the bedroom, she said, "No. I mean, for years I never wrote about him at all. I was already covering the New York political scene. And then he came onto it, and attracted a following, and ran for mayor, and won. I'd have written about anyone who did that."

She handed Arla her coffee.

"Yeah, but didn't you see that as a chance to finally go after him?"

"No," Barbara said defensively. "I don't believe so."

"Have you told your editors? You sure haven't told your readers."

Barbara took a moment to answer. "No."

"What do you think they'd say if they found out, if they knew?"

Another pause. "They would probably say I have a conflict. That I can't be objective."

"Would they be right?"

"They'd have a point," Barbara said. "But they'd be wrong."

"So if I confronted the mayor, and this all got out, you could lose *your* job," Arla said. "Payback."

Barbara got back onto the bed, careful not to spill her coffee.

"You know," Arla said, "if you did lose your job, you should write a book."

"I have written books."

"*Ghost*-written. You should write your *own* story. You become a reporter when you're a kid. You get knocked up, but that doesn't stop you. Your parents raise the baby. Okay, some people may judge. But you get a rep as a tough journalist in the craziest city in the world, and then you have to confess to your daughter that the mayor is her fucking father. It writes itself."

"Stop," Barbara said.

"I would read that. Like, if I were somebody else." Her eyes lit up as she remembered something. "You know, there's a woman in my building who's some hotshot editor at one of the big publishing houses. You should talk to her. I bet you could get a book deal, easy." Arla's stomach growled. "I have *got* to find something to eat."

She swung her legs down to the floor and went into the kitchen. Barbara could hear the fridge door opening.

"You weren't kidding," Arla said. "How do you feel about frozen pizza for breakfast? Or—hello, what's this?"

Barbara came into the kitchen and saw Arla holding up two tickets the size of postcards, words in fancy script printed on the high-stock paper.

"These were by the toaster," Arla said.

"They're media invites to tonight's Top of the Park opening. The ribbon-cutting for that zillion-story condo tower that overlooks Central Park. Probably won't even happen if the elevators are down." She thought about that. "Although, knowing Rodney Coughlin, he'll find a way."

"Will the mayor be there?" Arla asked.

"*Everybody* will be there," her mother said.

"I see two passes here," Arla said. "Have you got a plus-one yet?"

Fifty-Nine

Given that the FBI were keeping tabs on Eugene Clement, there was an agency presence in the hotel.

An agent by the name of Renata Geller had observed Clement leave the dining area, where he and his wife were having breakfast, and head down the hallway where the men's room was located. She could not exactly follow him in there, and at the moment, she was on her own. Had she been partnered with a male agent at the time, they might have discussed whether he should wander in there, too.

Only moments after Clement got up, his wife, Estelle, did the same. Within seconds, Agent Geller realized she was also heading down the hall to the washrooms. She thought that was odd. Dining couples tended to go in shifts, unless they were done with their meal. The Clements hadn't even ordered yet.

When Agent Geller and her husband went out to dinner, that was how they did it. One at a time. You didn't want the waiter to think you'd walked out. You didn't want to lose your table.

Oh, well, Agent Geller thought. *When you have to go, you have to go.*

Two minutes went by. Then three. Neither Clement nor his wife returned.

Shit, Agent Geller thought. The Clements knew they were being watched, and had given them the slip. They weren't coming back to their table. They'd found a back way out of the hotel. How was she going to explain this to her—

And then she heard the scream.

A man's scream.

"NOOOOO!"

She started running down the hallway toward the washrooms.

A man came charging out of the men's. Midthirties, scraggly hair. He was tucking something into the back of his jeans. Agent Geller was pretty sure what it was.

She looked at him, raised her weapon, and barked: "Stop! FBI!"

The man looked at her, wide-eyed, then reached for the gun he'd slipped under his belt. Before he could raise it, Agent Geller fired.

The man's body spun so quickly that the gun flew out of his hand. He hit the hallway floor. Writhing, he looked for the gun, which was some ten feet away. He started crawling toward it, leaving a red, bloody streak on the hotel floor.

But within a second Agent Geller was standing between him and the weapon.

"Do. Not. Move."

"Oh, shit," he said. "Shit, shit."

Blood continued to drain out of him. The bullet had gone into his right shoulder.

"The Clements," she said. It was a question.

"She shouldn't . . . have come into the men's," the man said, struggling to get the words out. "You're . . . not supposed to do that."

Sixty

Mayor Richard Headley was about to come out of the stairwell on the twelfth floor of an East Ninetieth Street apartment building, clutching a takeout bag from Brew Who, a coffee shop on Lexington. Inside the bag were a granola parfait, a butter brioche, and an Americano.

Waiting in the hallway for him was a camera crew from NY1. They were posted outside the apartment door of Dorothy Stinson, eighty-two. Dorothy was standing in the open doorway, waiting for the mayor's arrival. She looked as excited as a young girl waiting for Santa to come down the chimney.

Valerie Langdon and Chris Vallins were huddled behind the news crews. At the sound of an incoming text, Valerie glanced down at her phone. It was Glover, who was coming up the stairs with the mayor.

One floor away.

"They're almost here," Valerie whispered to the cameraman.

The news reporter holding the mike had already done her setup. She'd interviewed Dorothy, who told the story of how every *normal* morning she took the elevator down to the lobby, then walked to Brew Who for her treat. She'd been doing this daily for five years, ever since her husband had died. He used to make her breakfast every morning, and after his passing, she'd decided she wasn't going to start doing it for herself.

She might have dared to walk down the twelve flights to the

lobby, although this gave her pause, given that she'd had a couple of tripping incidents in the past year. But even if she could get to street level without incident, there was no way she could the climb twelve flights back up to her place. One of Dorothy's neighbors had written about her situation on the City Hall website, and it was Glover who'd spotted it.

Despite Headley's renewed reluctance to embrace Glover's suggestions, he thought this one was worth a shot.

"Let's do it."

As Valerie and Chris huddled, waiting for the mayor to appear, Valerie whispered, "Has he seemed a bit . . . off lately?"

Chris leaned in close to her so as not to be heard by the camera crew. "A little, maybe."

"I noticed it after Matheson left yesterday," she said. "He seemed, I don't know, preoccupied."

"There is kind of a lot going on," Vallins said. "Could be—"

He stopped talking when he saw the stairway door open at the end of the hall. Headley emerged, all smiles. He walked briskly to Dorothy, giving her a hug, and then handing her the bag with a Brew Who logo on the side. A few seconds later, Glover entered the hall.

Dorothy giggled. "It's not every day the mayor pays a visit. Won't you come in?"

"Love to," Headley said, following her into the small apartment. The TV crew slipped in after him.

Dorothy didn't have so much a kitchen as a nook. The apartment, except for a bathroom off to one side, was a studio. A bed on the far wall, a couple of chairs and a television, and just inside the main door, a short counter, hot plate, and cupboards. Dorothy directed the mayor to a small, badly chipped, Formica-topped table and two padded chairs with aluminum framing. They both sat.

"This is so kind of you," she said.

Valerie and Chris and Glover huddled in the doorway, behind the cameras, watching.

"I wish I could do this for everyone in the city like yourself, Dorothy," he said. "And I want you to know that we're going to have everything back to normal very, very soon."

She reached into the bag and took out the granola parfait, then two cups. A slender string and a tiny label was hanging from under the lid on one.

"Mine's the tea," the mayor said.

"This looks delightful," she said. "How much do I owe you?"

Headley chuckled. "It's on me."

She peered down into the bag at the one remaining item. It was the butter brioche, wrapped in wax paper. "My favorite," she said. "But I usually start with the parfait, while the yogurt is still cold."

"Makes sense to me," Headley said. A plastic spoon had been tossed into the bag. He handed it to her.

"So, Dorothy, how have you been managing through the crisis?" he asked. He already knew the answer. Dorothy had been interviewed ahead of time by the staff, and her answers passed along to the mayor.

"My landlord, Janos, is checking out the elevators right now. If he gets them up and running soon, I think I'm going to go out for lunch."

"Sounds like a good man," Headley said as Dorothy dug into her parfait. She slid a spoonful of yogurt, strawberry, and granola into her mouth.

The mayor took the lid off his tea, lifted out the bag, and let it drain against the top edge of the cup before setting it on the lid. "We think just about every elevator in the city will be back in service by the afternoon. Everyone's really pulled together to—"

"Oh my God!" Dorothy said.

She had her spoon back in the yogurt and had unearthed something small and dark that appeared to have tiny legs and a tail attached to it.

It was a dead mouse.

Dorothy started to make gagging sounds, turned away from the table, and vomited onto the floor.

"You can be sure we're going to be taking this up with Brew Who," Glover said, trailing after his father as they came out of the apartment building, headed for his limo. "This is outrageous. I'll call the health department, get the inspectors in there, shut them down."

Valerie was already in the back of the car, phone in hand. The two TV stations covering the event had posted the video within minutes. By the time the mayor had raced down twelve flights of stairs, it was already trending.

"How bad is it?" Headley asked as he got in the car.

"It'll blow over," Valerie said. "You can make a joke about it later. I don't see that you have any choice."

"It'll be on every late-night show," Headley said.

Glover came around the other side of the car and opened the door.

"No," his father said, raising a hand.

"What?" Glover said.

"Find your own way back," he said. "This stunt was all your idea. I never learn."

"Dad!" he said. "It should have worked. How could I know there was a mouse in her yogurt? You think I put it there?"

"Close the door!"

"Richard," Valerie said softly. "You can't—"

"Now!" Headley shouted.

Glover closed the door. Through the window, Valerie gave him a sympathetic tip of the head as the car pulled away. Then she shifted in her seat to look at her boss.

"Don't start with me," he said.

"He's your son," she said.

"He walked me right into that. God damn it, if he excels at anything, it's making me look like a fool."

"Look, if you—"

Valerie's phone shouted out news of an incoming text. She quickly dug it out of her purse and looked.

"Something's happened," she said.

"What?"

"It's Chris. Details just coming in."

"Of what? Christ, not another elevator thing."

"No, it's a shooting. In a hotel." She waited as more words appeared on her phone's screen. "Two dead. The FBI took down the shooter. He's . . . still alive."

"Who's dead?"

"Hang on . . . there's a link." She tapped on the screen. "That Flyovers guy. And a woman. It's not clear. Wait, Chris is writing something else. The man the FBI shot, he could be the one who shot the Flyovers person."

"This isn't clear at all," Headley said.

"Let me make some calls. But from what Chris is saying, this guy the FBI got, they like him for the taxi bombing, and maybe the elevator stuff, too. You're gonna want to make a statement. That mouse in the parfait just got kicked off the six o'clock news."

Sixty-One

Jerry Bourque and Lois Delgado had spent the morning working the phones, tracking where city-owned cars were garaged, and working up a list of vehicles that were not only part of the "green" pool but had plates ending in 13. Once they'd tracked down the car, they wanted to know who'd taken it to Simpson Elevator for a chat with Otto Petrenko.

But then the captain showed up and told them to get their asses over to the Westerly Hotel in Fort Lee, on the other side of the George Washington Bridge, in New Jersey. There was a chance, the captain said, that what was going on there might have something to do with what he and Delgado were working on.

Bourque made the case that just one of them should go. The other should stay back and try to make headway on finding that car.

"Flip for it," the captain said.

They didn't have to. Delgado said she was happy staying on the car, so Jerry headed off to New Jersey.

On the way, he found out what made the Westerly a place of interest, beyond its usual charm.

A week ago, a forty-four-year old man from Tulsa, Oklahoma, by the name of Garnet Wooler had rented a room on the second floor. This same Garnet Wooler, had, two hours earlier, been shot in the shoulder by an FBI agent in the lobby of the InterMajestic Hotel in midtown Manhattan as he was drawing a weapon. It was believed this same gun had been used to kill Eugene Clement and his wife, Estelle, just moments earlier in the men's bathroom just off the hotel lobby.

Wooler had been rushed to the hospital, where he was listed in serious but stable condition. And while he was able to talk, he had so far chosen not to. But police had found, in his pocket, a key card for the Westerly in Fort Lee.

A quick check found that Mr. Wooler was not unknown to police, at least out in Tulsa, who knew him better as Bucky. There were two minor assault charges. One, on an ex-wife, was five years ago, and the second, eight years back, stemmed from a disagreement in a bar with someone who had opened his door into the side of Wooler's pickup truck.

Four years ago, Wooler had also been treated and released for burns to his upper body after goofing around with explosives on a buddy's farm. He had, off and on, worked for a company that removed tree stumps by using dynamite. Given his history, it wasn't a stretch to think he had the wherewithal to blow up a New York cab.

Bourque's captain had dispatched him to the scene because Clement had been, up until the moment he was fatally shot, the head of the Flyovers activist group, which might or might not have had something to do with taxi explosions and elevator plunges, and maybe even the murder of Otto Petrenko.

While police had arrived on the scene nearly ninety minutes earlier, it was only moments before Bourque's arrival that they gained access to Wooler's room. Given that this man might be their bomber, they were proceeding with great caution. First, they didn't know whether Garnet Wooler had been acting alone, or if he might have associates holed up at the hotel. Second, they needed to determine that the room had in no way been booby-trapped. No one wanted to trigger an explosion when they entered it.

So a crane was used to lift police up to the second floor hotel room's window so that they could scope the place out. In addition, a high-tech camera on the end of a wire was inserted under the door to give a full view of the room's interior.

Confident, at last, that the room was safe to enter, police did so.

Similar precautions were taken with the 2004 Dodge minivan registered to Wooler that was sitting in the hotel parking lot. As Bourque arrived, the van was being loaded onto the back of a flatbed truck and being taken to a forensics lab for examination.

Judging by the number of official vehicles in the hotel lot and the surrounding streets, one could be forgiven for thinking a Newark-bound jet must have come down here. There were countless New York and New Jersey state police cruisers, cars bearing the NYPD logo, fire emergency vehicles, and enough black Tahoe and Suburban SUVs—most likely Homeland and FBI—to start a GM dealership.

Bourque found a spot for his unmarked car and killed the engine.

Flashing his badge, he got into the hotel and up to the second floor. The hallway outside Wooler's room had been turned into a law enforcement convention. He made his way to the door, flashing his badge again. A rosy-cheeked FBI agent named Ben Baskin invited him in once Bourque had explained his interest.

"Oh, yeah," said Baskin. "I saw you at the meeting."

"What have you found?"

"Shitload of stuff. The guy did not travel light. We've found rifles, couple more handguns, in addition to the one found on him. Ammunition. We think we're going to find more weapons in the van. Also, some ammonium nitrate, Tannerite, some wire and—"

"Bomb-making materials," Bourque said.

"Yeah."

"Same materials used in the taxi?"

Baskin shrugged. "To be determined."

"How about any kind of electronics?"

"Plenty. Couple of laptops. Burner phones. Other stuff."

"Anything that might be used, say, to hack into an elevator's control system?"

"Still searching. And like I say, we've still got the van to get through. We're also trying to find out if our friend here was working with anyone else."

"What happened at the InterMajestic?"

Baskin shook his head. "Our guy shot and killed Clement and his wife but we don't know why, because it looks like Wooler was on the same team as Clement. Maybe Clement was telling him what to do, or came to New York to be closer to the action when it went down."

"But if they were somehow working together, why'd he shoot Clement and the wife?" Bourque asked.

"Good question. Wooler's said next to nothing, but he made one comment, something along the line that Clement's wife thought they were gay. Wanted us to know that was not the case, at least where he was concerned."

"Guy's facing terrorism charges, but that's what he'd worried about." Bourque shook his head. "You come across anything yet that connects Wooler to a guy named Otto Petrenko?"

"No. If we do, you'll be the first to hear about it. Anything else?" Baskin asked.

Bourque thought a moment. "I don't think so."

"You don't want to know if I have a partner named Robbins?"

Bourque grinned. "No."

"You're the first."

———

Before crossing back over the George Washington, Bourque pulled into a McDonald's lot on Lemoine Avenue. He was starving, and didn't have the time or inclination to find anything of higher nutritional value.

He was wolfing a Big Mac and slurping down a Diet Coke when his cell phone, which he had placed on the table, rang.

"Bourque," he said, although with his mouth full it came out more like *Burfk.*

"Get the marbles out of your mouth," Lois Delgado said.

"I'm grabbing a bite," he said.

"Where?"

"McDonald's."

"Yeah, thought I could smell it," she said. "What'd you find?"

He filled her in. When he was done, she said, "So, guess where I am."

Bourque took a sip of Coke. "In a room at the Plaza with Ryan Gosling."

"I mean right now, not where I was last night," she said.

"Tell me."

"I'm in the City Hall garage looking at a boring sedan with a license plate that ends in 13, and it's got a dent in the bumper identical to the one in our picture."

"Whoa," Bourque said, feeling his pulse quicken. "Now we just have to find out who signed it out that day."

"Already have," she said.

"Are you going to make me beg?" Bourque asked.

"That's exactly what Ryan said."

"Tell me."

"Here's a question. Why do you think the mayor's son would be wanting to meet with Otto Petrenko?"

Bourque set down his drink. "The mayor's son?"

"Glover. Glover Headley. He's one of his dad's aides or advisers or whatever."

"Huh," Bourque said. "I guess we should ask him."

Sixty-Two

T hanks for coming."

Richard Headley gazed out over the assembled media. He couldn't recall the press room ever being this crowded. There were even more representatives from TV and radio and print here today than there had been the day before. He hadn't had very good news for them then. Today was looking a little better.

"I just want to say a few words before Chief Washington arrives. She'll be able to answer a lot of your questions in more detail. But there has been an arrest. Most of you already know about the shooting at the InterMajestic."

He quickly told them that the man who'd been arrested was a suspect in the taxi bombing.

"At this time," he said, "we can't say this person is connected to the elevator tragedies, but I can confirm he is a person of interest. There is a strong link with the Flyovers group, which has, in recent months, established a pattern of fomenting chaos in coastal cities, of which we are definitely one. So with that possibly hopeful news, and reports coming in from across the city about the progress that is being made in restoring elevator service, I think it's fair to say that things are looking up."

Several questions were shouted out, and Headley did his best to answer them, but in most cases said they would have to wait for the chief. To his relief, there was not one question about the granola parfait rodent.

On the pretext of having to leave for another meeting, Headley offered his apologies and excused himself from the press room. When he returned to his office, Glover was there. Sitting on the couch, a remote in hand, watching CNN on the new TV that had been installed after the mayor had shattered the other one the day before.

Glover stood.

"I see you got back okay," Headley said.

Glover nodded. "I walked."

Headley's eyes went wide. "From Ninetieth Street?"

"Took me about two and a half hours. But it gave me lots of time to think." He reached into his pocket and withdrew a white envelope, which he handed to his father. "About this."

"What's this?" he asked. Written, in hand, on the front of the envelope was the word *Dad*.

"I wasn't sure who to make it out to," Glover said. "I didn't know whether to write 'Dad,' or 'Father,' or 'Mayor Headley.'"

The envelope was not sealed. Headley withdrew the single sheet of paper tucked inside, unfolded it, tossed the envelope onto the coffee table. He scanned the words. It didn't take him more than ten seconds to read it.

"What the hell is this?" Headley asked.

"You'll notice, on the actual letter, I made it out to the position, to Mayor Richard Headley. I guess, between that and the envelope, I covered all bases."

"You're resigning?"

Glover nodded. "Yes. As it says, in the letter, effective tomorrow. Or, I guess, midnight tonight."

"Why? You don't give a reason in your letter."

"Because I'm tired of disappointing you. And I simply can't take it anymore."

"Can't take what?"

"The constant belittling. The put-downs. The eye rolls. Anyone else with an ounce of self-respect would have quit long ago, wouldn't have put up with it for so long. Maybe that's what took me so long. I'm all out of self-respect."

Headley was shaking his head. "This is ridiculous."

"More likely a relief, for you. Now you don't have to actually fire me." He took a breath. "Mom's been dead a long time, Dad. If you've kept me on out of guilt, thinking maybe you owed it to her, you don't have to feel that way any longer. I *want* to leave. Maybe my quitting will be my one chance to make you happy."

"Christ, Glover."

"The resignation, as it says in the letter, is effective at midnight. I'd still like to attend the Top of the Park event tonight, however. If it's still on."

"It is," Headley said. "Coughlin messaged me a while ago. He's got the elevators working. Of course you can come." He paused, then said, "That woman you hired. Arla Silbert."

"The one you fired," Glover said. "Because she's Barbara Matheson's daughter."

Headley nodded quickly, as though wanting to brush over that part. "What else do you know about her?"

"Nothing. Why?"

"No reason. I just . . . wondered."

Glover turned and started heading for the door. He was almost out of the office when his father called out his name.

"Yes?" Glover said, stopping and looking at the mayor.

"I'm sorry about kicking you out of the limo." He swallowed, hard. "That was wrong. It wasn't your fault there was a goddamn mouse in that old lady's breakfast."

"Actually, it was," Glover said. "I put it there."

The mayor was standing by his desk, numb, when Valerie came into the room three minutes later.

"What did Glover want?" she asked. "I saw him leaving and he looked kind of shook up."

He handed her the resignation letter. She scanned it quickly, then said, "Oh. Did you accept it?"

Headley nodded. "He told me something that he did . . . I should be angry. I should be livid. But I'm not. I feel like I had it coming."

"What did he tell you?"

The mayor shook his head. "Maybe you're right. What you've been telling me, that I've been too hard on him. I'm seeing now how that can end up biting you in the ass."

"Richard, I wish you'd tell me what you're talking about."

"Glover may think I'll have changed my mind about letting him come to Coughlin's thing tonight, but I haven't." He smiled grimly. "I want him there."

Valerie was about to press harder about what had gone on between him and his son, but she was interrupted by a text. "What's this?" she said, reading it.

The mayor raised his head, waiting.

"It's reception," Valerie said. "The police are here."

"Probably Chief Washington," Headley said. "Maybe she knows more about this Wooler guy they've arrested."

Valerie slowly shook her head. "No. It's two detectives." She looked up. "They're looking for Glover."

The mayor went ashen-faced. "They have detectives in the health department?"

"What?" Valerie said. "What are you talking about?"

"Never mind," Headley said.

Valerie entered a number, then put the phone to her ear.

"Hey, it's Valerie. Are those detectives still there? Okay, yeah, put one of them on." She waited a few seconds, then said, "Yes, hello? Who's this? Delgado? What can I do for you, Detective Delgado?" She listened, then said, "Well, I'm sorry but Glover is not here right now. Perhaps this is something I can help you with?"

She listened some more. "I see."

"What is it?" Headley asked.

Valerie put her hand over the phone and said, "They specifically want to talk to Glover."

"You better call him," Headley said, his voice weak, tipping his head at the landline on his desk.

Valerie told Delgado to hold on, picked up the receiver for the mayor's phone, and entered the number for Glover's cell.

She waited several seconds before finally saying, "Glover, it's Valerie. Can you call me the minute you get this?"

She went back onto her cell and said, "I tried his cell but he's not answering. I'm sorry. His home address? I don't—"

Headley reached across the desk and snatched the phone out of Valerie's hand.

"This is Mayor Headley," he said, with more courtesy than usual. "Who's this I'm talking to?" He listened for a second. "Can you tell me what this is about?"

He held the phone to his ear for another five seconds, said, "Okay," then, without saying anything further, handed it back to Valerie. She put it to her own ear, said, "Hello?"

"She hung up," the mayor said.

Valerie lowered the phone. "What did she say?"

"They're coming here. To talk to me."

Sixty-Three

Bourque and Delgado had never before been in the office of the mayor of New York City. If they were impressed, they were trying very hard not to show it. Valerie had met them just outside the door, and when she took them in, Headley was pacing the room. He had taken off his jacket and loosened his tie.

"Detectives Bourque and Delgado," Valerie announced.

The two detectives each introduced themselves so the mayor would know who was Bourque and who was Delgado.

"What's this about?" the mayor asked.

"It's really your son we want to talk to," Delgado said.

"About?"

Bourque said, "It's tied to an investigation we're working on."

"So this has nothing to do with the mouse."

Bourque glanced at his partner, as if to ask *Did I hear that right?* But instead, he said, "We're investigating a homicide, sir."

Headley almost looked relieved. "By my count, there's what, ten of them? Seven deaths by elevator, three in the explosion."

"We're looking into the death of Otto Petrenko," Delgado said. "His body was found on the High Line Monday morning."

"Petrenko?"

"An elevator technician," Bourque said.

Now they had Headley's attention. "Elevator technician? Is there a connection between his death and what's been going on?"

"Possibly," Delgado said. "Before he died, Petrenko became very worried about the safety of his relatives in other parts of the country. It's possible he was being coerced to provide details on how elevators function, that he feared these relatives would be harmed if he didn't go along. At the moment, it's just a theory. Not long before he was killed, Petrenko met with a man who visited him at his place of work. No one else knew who this man was, and Petrenko didn't talk about him to anyone. We've been trying to find out who that man might be."

"Why do you think Glover might be able to help you with that?" the mayor asked.

Bourque said, "We managed to track down the car this man was driving. It came from the City Hall car pool."

Valerie, who'd been standing off to one side through the discussion, said, "It did?"

"It had one of those stickers on the back," Delgado said. "Part of your green campaign, sir. We had a partial plate and a distinguishing mark on the bumper. With all that, we were able to find the exact car."

"Hang on," the mayor said. "When did you say this was? Because it's very possible, given the events of this week, that someone from the city *would* be talking to an expert in how elevators work."

Delgado said, "As I mentioned a moment ago, Mr. Petrenko died sometime between Sunday night and Monday morning, before that first elevator event in the Lansing Tower. This meeting predates that."

"Well, I guess the simplest thing to do," Headley said, "is find out who signed the car out that day. You don't need Glover to do that for you. We should be able to get that information. Can we do that for the detectives, Valerie?"

"Absolutely."

"We've already done that," Bourque said.

The room went quiet.

When the mayor didn't say anything, it was Valerie who decided to ask the question. "Who signed it out?"

"Glover Headley," Delgado said.

The mayor and Valerie exchanged glances.

"That's why," Bourque said, "we would like to talk to Glover. We just want to clear this up. That's the way it is in an investigation. Tying up one loose end, then moving on to the next thing."

"That's right," Delgado said. "So if you could just tell us where we might find him, so we could cross this angle of inquiry off our list."

Headley turned, walked toward his desk. He ran his right hand up to the back of his neck, kneaded it like it was bread dough.

"He just . . . resigned," Headley said.

"Why?" Bourque asked.

"Because I'm a son of a bitch," he said. "Look, I'm sure there's a very simple explanation for this. I'll be talking to Glover tonight— he's coming to the Top of the Park opening—and I'll ask him what this is about and get back to you tomorrow."

"We would prefer to talk to him ourselves, sir," Delgado said. "And we need to talk to him sooner than that."

"Look, we just tried to raise him and he's not answering, so I don't know what to tell you."

Bourque said, "We need his cell number and home address."

Valerie looked at her boss, as though waiting for permission. He gave a weary nod, and she said, "I'll write those down for you."

She slipped out of the office.

Delgado and Bourque both took out their business cards and placed them on the mayor's desk. "Give us a call," she said, "if he should happen to show up sooner."

Headley looked down at the cards but did not touch them.

Valerie returned with a slip of paper and handed it to Delgado. "I gave you his email address, too," she said.

"If he's not in the building, or at home, you know any favorite places he might hang out?" Bourque asked. "Coffee shop? Bar? Park?"

The mayor looked at him blankly. "I can't think of any. Valerie?"

"No," she said.

"What did Glover do, before handing in his resignation?" Delgado asked.

"Um, data analysis, polling, techie stuff," Valerie said.

"You'd call him a techie?" Bourque asked.

"Oh, yes," Valerie said. "There's not a program or gadget in the world Glover can't figure out."

Sixty-Four

Anyone would have been forgiven for thinking the Academy Awards had been moved from Hollywood to New York.

The official opening of the Top of the Park had all the earmarks of Oscar night. Huge spotlights set up across the street in Central Park cast dancing, crisscrossing beams of light into the night sky.

Central Park North was closed off between Fifth Avenue and Central Park West. Being allowed through were dozens of limousines bearing celebrities and politicians and the city's major power brokers. Judging by the presence of TV crews from CNN, as well as *Access Hollywood* and *Extra*, this was an entertainment event as much as it was a news story.

As each vehicle rolled to a stop at the end of the red carpet that led into the cavernous atrium of Top of the Park, tuxedoed attendants rushed forward to open doors. Photographers and TV crews waited to see who might emerge. If it turned out to be a prominent actor or actress, glammed-up TV hosts would stop them as they passed for a few words of architectural insight.

"It sure is tall!" one actress said.

"I'd have gotten pretty dizzy working on that!" quipped an Oscar-nominated actor.

When New Yorkers far more powerful or influential, but whose faces did not appear on a twenty-foot-high screen at one of the city's multiplexes, stepped out of a limo—the head of the New York Stock

Exchange, the presidents of the Whitney Museum of American Art and Columbia University, to name just three—the TV types lowered their cameras and microphones until the next *beautiful* person came along.

Regular New Yorkers not important enough to get an invitation still came out in droves to catch a glimpse of those who'd made the cut. Smartphones flashed incessantly. Fans begged for selfies. The occasional celeb even obliged.

Barbara and Arla were not among those who arrived by limo. The closest they could get, by car, was Fifth and Central Park North.

"Shit," Barbara said upon seeing the barricades that kept them from getting dropped off out front of Top of the Park. "If I'd known we've got to walk this far I'd have worn flats."

If the 110th Street station, which was only a few steps from the brand-new skyscraper, hadn't been closed for security reasons, they could have taken the train and saved themselves a few steps. But Barbara had had to agree with Arla: When you're all dressed up, did you really want to trek down into the subway?

That morning, they'd opted not to order in, and instead went out for a proper hangover breakfast. Scrambled eggs, extra crispy bacon, home fries, and more coffee. Then they'd gone back to Barbara's place to go through her closet and see if she had anything glitzy enough for the Top of the Park affair.

Going through her mother's closet, Arla asked, "Just how many pairs of jeans do you have?" She found one black, off-the-shoulder dress tucked in the far corner and pulled it out. Holding out the dress at arm's length, she said, "What do you think?"

Barbara said, "How many other dresses did you find in there?"

"None."

"It's got sleeves, so no one will see my black and blue elbow. I like it."

"With the right accessories, it'll work."

"Accessories?" Barbara said.

Arla returned to her own apartment at that point, but invited her mother to come by two hours before the event, by which time she would have picked out a few necklaces and bracelets and sets of earrings for her mother to choose from.

"Maybe this is a mistake," Arla said as they made their way from the cab to the entrance to Top of the Park. "I mean, an event like this is not exactly the best place to tell someone you're his daughter."

Barbara nodded. "Let's hold back, see if he makes the first move. If he recognized your name when I said it, he might do something. If he does nothing, then we know he doesn't remember anything about that night, including my surname. And who knows? The moment Richard sees me walking into that party, he may have my ass kicked to the curb."

"It'd be a long way down," Arla said. "And besides, it's not his party."

Barbara smiled as they reached the red carpet. "No, it isn't."

The two of them stopped before approaching the front doors and looked up. They had to crane their necks back as far as they could, and even then weren't sure they could see the top of the building.

At the entrance, Barbara reached into her evening clutch and produced her invitation, which was closely scrutinized by a blond woman in a dazzling red, floor-length gown, accessorized rather incongruously by an earpiece and wires. "Have a wonderful time," she said.

And then they were inside.

"Fuck me," said Arla.

The lobby was a breathtaking amalgam of swooping steel and glittering glass and lights that seemed to float, untethered, in the air above them. There were a couple of hundred people milling about, taking glasses of champagne from the trays of wandering servers.

"Oh my God," Arla whispered, nudging her mother and getting her to look to one side. "Isn't that what's-his-name? From that movie?"

Barbara nodded. "Yeah. But don't get excited. He's gay."

"No," Arla said.

"That's the word."

"Oh, and at eleven o'clock. That's—"

"Yeah. They say she's going to run for president. She keeps saying she isn't, which tells me she probably is. Oh, look."

Coming through the crowd was the mayor, dressed in black tie. He had a broad smile pasted on his face that looked, at least to Barbara, more artificial than usual. Politicians were masters at appearing delighted to see you when they really didn't give a shit, and Headley was one of the best, but Barbara thought his bonhomie seemed particularly strained. Something about the creases coming out of the front corners of his mouth. Fault lines ready to give way.

Trailing him were Chris Vallins, also in a tux, and running shoes, a backpack hanging discreetly from his hand at his side; Valerie Langdon, in a powder blue, floor-length dress; and Glover, also in a tux, the bow tie awkwardly askew. He was engaged in what seemed to be an agitated conversation with Valerie.

"They're going to walk right past us," Arla said.

"Don't worry," Barbara said.

Arla moved so that her body was mostly shielded by her mother. "I don't want Glover to see me. I'm not ready to talk to him about . . . anything."

As Valerie and Glover walked past, the procession slowed, and Barbara heard snippets of their discussion.

"I *told* him," Glover said. "I didn't sign out that car . . . don't care what the cops say. I don't . . . anything about it."

"I don't know what . . . believe," Valerie said. "He told me about . . . mouse. What . . . you thinking?"

Mouse?

". . . amazed he let you . . . tonight," Valerie said.

". . . feels guilty, I guess. A first . . . gone soon."

The crowed opened up, allowing them to move on and out of range for Barbara to hear anything else. As Vallins passed by, Barbara reached out and touched his arm. He glanced her way, startled.

"Love the shoes," she said, looking down at his runners.

He gave the backpack a slight swing. "Got the Florsheims in here," he said, grinning. "Hey, I sent you an email."

"Okay," Barbara said as Vallins moved on.

"You know that guy?" Arla asked.

"A little," Barbara said.

"He's kinda hot."

"A little."

She took out her phone and checked her email inbox. There was nothing there from Vallins. She looked in Junk, but there was no message there, either.

Everyone was being herded toward two banks of elevators, which were just off the main atrium. There were five elevators on one side, five on the other. The numbers above the doors, etched in granite, indicated where they went. The five on the left were for the floors below the fiftieth, the ones on the right for floors fifty-one to ninety-eight, also known as the Observation Level.

It was before the doors on the right where everyone lined up. All five doors opened simultaneously. Barbara and Arla were close enough to be among the first wave of riders.

Headley and his team stepped into the first one, accompanied by,

Barbara noticed, Rodney Coughlin himself. The doors closed and the elevator departed.

Barbara and Arla boarded their car, and were followed by another eight people in tuxes and gowns.

As the doors closed, there was a palpable sense of unease inside the car. Someone chuckled nervously.

"They did get the guy, right?" a woman said.

"That's what I saw on the news," a man said. "I think they're pretty sure."

The elevator began its ascent.

Sixty-Five

Bourque and Delgado had spent the rest of the afternoon try-ing to track down Glover Headley. They'd had no luck raising him with repeated calls to his cell phone. They did not find him at his apartment. And a search of bars and restaurants in the blocks near City Hall also proved fruitless.

Bourque had given his card to the doorman of the building where Glover lived and asked him to get in touch should Glover return.

Just before seven, Bourque's cell rang.

"He just returned," the doorman said.

He and Delgado had been checking restaurants at the time. They ran back to the car and started the drive back uptown to Glover's Upper West Side residence. But as was more often the case than not, the drive north was a traffic nightmare. By the time Delgado brought the car to a screeching halt out front of the building, and Bourque ran in, Glover had already left.

"He wasn't here long," the doorman said. "He was in and out in about fifteen minutes. Looked like he just came back to get changed. Left in a tux."

When Bourque got back in the car, he turned and looked at Del-gado and said, "How do we look?"

"What are you talking about?"

"Looks like we're going to have to crash the party."

"He wasn't there?"

"He's on his way to the Top of the Park opening. Left in his penguin suit."

Delgado glanced down at herself. Black jeans, plain white blouse, jacket. "Oh, yeah, I'm good to go."

Along the way, she glanced over a couple of times at her partner, who had a big smile on his face.

"You look like a kid on Christmas morning," she said.

He grinned. "Okay, I'm excited. I've been following the progress of this building since before they broke ground, but have never had an excuse to get inside. I bought a book about it on Monday. Studied every page. Can't wait to see it. Ask me anything about it. Go ahead, ask me. You want to know the architects?"

"Not particularly."

"Svengali and Associates. I know. Svengali? But it's the guy's real name."

Delgado said, "Uh, wasn't Svengali a kind of evil dude? A real manipulative fucker?"

"Yeah. But it's a great-sounding name. The building was first conceived fifteen years ago, and it was going to be ninety stories, but then 432 Park Avenue came in at ninety-seven, so Coughlin—"

"Coughlin?"

"Rodney Coughlin, the developer?" Bourque said. "And then this other project got announced last year, at the bottom of Central Park, isn't finished yet, and it's going to surpass 432, so Coughlin said, add eight more floors, bringing it in at ninety-eight, and a height of one thousand five hundred and sixty feet, which tops anything out there, built or not-yet built. All of which makes it the tallest residential tower in the Western Hemisphere, and the second tallest building in New York, after One World Trade."

"They're just architectural penises," Delgado said. "Whose concrete-and-glass dick is bigger?"

Delgado took Central Park West all the way up to Central Park North. At that point, they encountered the police barricade that was keeping everything but VIP limos from proceeding. Delgado flashed her badge and was waved through.

She pulled the car up onto the south sidewalk about a hundred yards west of the building. Bourque was out first, and he stood there for several seconds, admiring the structure.

"I'm going to make it," he said.

Delgado, out of the car, slammed the door and said, "What?"

"Out of art board," he said. "For my collection."

Delgado had seen pictures on her partner's phone of his creations. "You're gonna need a bigger apartment."

Bourque shrugged. "A *taller* apartment."

"Ready to party?"

Bourque nodded. They headed toward the building.

Sixty-Six

T he elevator softly chimed as its destination—the ninety-eighth floor—was reached, and the doors parted.

A collective gasp erupted from inside the car. The doors opened onto a vast expanse of openness, across which could be seen a wall of floor-to-ceiling windows, and beyond that lay an even more vast expanse of sky. Looking westward, there was a distant orange sliver on the horizon as the last glimmer of the setting sun bled away.

Barbara and Arla and their fellow passengers stepped from the car and into what amounted to a ballroom in the sky. They moved hesitantly, almost fearfully, testing the solidity of the marble floor beneath them as if to be sure they weren't walking on a cloud. A reverent hush had fallen over the guests, who, only moments before, had been chatting amiably in the confines of their elevator car. It was as if each had been struck dumb, overwhelmed by the magnificent view from atop this tower in the sky.

"There are no words," someone whispered.

It was true. There were not enough superlatives in the English language to convey how dramatic, how wondrous, how absolutely miraculous, the experience was.

Arla circumnavigated the room, weaving her way around buffet tables laden with elegant displays of food and drink, and another table with a stunning, ten-foot tall architectural model of Top of the Park, until she was at the southern exposure that overlooked Central

Park and, beyond that, the skyscrapers of midtown, including the building's closest rival, 432 Park. Beyond that could be seen Rockefeller Center, the Chrysler Building, the Empire State Building, and, even farther in the distance, One World Trade Center.

"It's like we're in a plane that's holding its position in the air," Arla said, touching her fingertips to the glass as her mother came up behind her.

"Don't stand so close," Barbara said nervously. She'd never considered herself to be afraid of heights, but up here, at this moment, she felt a touch of vertigo. "Come back," she said, pulling gently on her daughter's arm.

"It's okay," Arla said, resisting. She looked down. "There's nothing around here that even comes close. We're up here all alone." She giggled and turned her head so her mother could better hear her. "You wouldn't have to worry about walking around naked with the curtains open."

"Except for maybe a jet full of passengers heading into LaGuardia."

That prompted Arla to look east. "You can see them," she said. "The planes, coming in and taking off." She shook her head in wonder. "What do you think it costs to get an apartment in this building?"

"We might not be the target demographic," Barbara said.

"But if you could, if you had millions of dollars, would you want to live here?"

Barbara thought a moment before saying, "No. It feels . . . it almost feels wrong. The building feels like it's thumbing its nose at the laws of nature. It's too incredible, too death defying. I wouldn't mind a huge loft in SoHo, though."

"Yeah, well, I think I could get used to—"

"*Good evening!*"

The voice was emanating from speakers built into the walls and ceiling.

"Welcome to the Top of the Park!"

Arla was looking, too. "Over there," she said, pointing.

Standing on an elevated platform, with a night sky for a backdrop, was Rodney Coughlin. Six feet tall, broad-shouldered, chiseled jaw, eyebrows like mutant caterpillars, he was a commanding presence. He held a champagne glass at shoulder height as he smiled broadly at his guests, his teeth big and bright enough that light was bouncing off them. The mayor stood to his right, looking somewhat distracted.

Barbara and Arla threaded their way through the crowd so they could get a ringside view. Once in position, Barbara glanced around. She spotted Glover over by one of the elevators. Valerie was standing not far off. Barbara had lost sight of Vallins.

"Oh, what a glorious night this is!" Coughlin exclaimed, and the room erupted with applause. He grinned. "How do you folks like the view?"

Scattered laughter, more applause.

"Now, I know you've all just got here and you can't stop yourselves from looking out the window and," he chuckled, "looking *down* on the rest of New York. I need to warn you, there are going to be a few speeches, and I have a number of people to thank including—Mario! Where are you?"

Standing next to Barbara, a short, bushy-headed man with dark sunglasses the size of two coasters and wearing a bright, orange sport jacket waved his hand in the air.

"Mario Svengali!" Coughlin shouted, raising his glass even higher. "The most brilliant architect in the whole fucking universe. I'm going to be having a few words to say about him, and others, and my good friend the mayor, right here!"

He gestured to Headley beside him. "Thank you very much, Richard, for letting me use the elevators tonight."

Headley blushed as nervous chuckles swept the room.

"Don't worry!" Coughlin continued. "Tonight, the people who deserve our gratitude most of all are the good men and women of law enforcement—the NYPD, the FBI, you name it—who made an arrest today in connection with the horrible events of this week."

Headley tried to interject, saying, "Actually, so far he's only—"

Coughlin quickly cut him off. "I've got plenty to say tonight, and a lot of other people to thank. But we've also got some other people who want to say a few words." He rolled his eyes. "Politicians, right? Well, so long as they're saying wonderful things about me, I say give them all the time they want."

A few more laughs.

"Most of those speeches are coming later. First, we want to have some fun. But before I command you all to eat, drink, and be merry, the mayor would like to say a few words. But you're going to be brief, right, Richard?"

Coughlin quickly whispered something in the mayor's ear. Barbara, who had always been pretty good at reading lips, was pretty sure he'd said, *Don't fuck this up*.

The mayor, a strained grin on his face, stepped forward.

"I also just wanted to extend a welcome to everyone here on what is truly a historic night in the history of New York City as this astonishing building becomes part of the Manhattan skyline. My congratulations to everyone who played a role in making Top of the Park a reality."

Arla leaned in close to her mother and said, "I think maybe I look a little bit like him. Around the eyes?"

As the mayor kept talking, Barbara replied quietly, "I don't know. Possibly."

The truth was, Barbara had always seen something of Headley in her daughter. Not just the eyes. The way her nose turned up slightly at the end, how she cocked her head when she was puzzling something out, the sharp turn in her jawbone just below the ear.

"As you all know," Headley continued, "this has been a slightly stressful week for New Yorkers, so I would urge you to take full advantage of the open bar." A forced chuckle. "I'll be first in line."

A few laughs and at least one "Hear, hear!"

"Okay!" the mayor said. "More speeches later! Let's party! Let's make this a night we'll remember for the rest of our lives!"

Headley stepped off the platform, where he was met by Valerie, who was chatting to him about something. As they spoke, they both glanced, at different moments, at Glover, standing over by the elevators.

"What do you think?" Arla whispered. "Should I go up and talk to him? Just, like, introduce myself, and see what kind of reaction I get?"

Barbara was hesitant. "I'm not sure this is the right moment. This entire *evening* might not be the right moment."

"I thought this was the plan. I talk to him *tonight*. I might not ever get this close to him again. I lost my job, remember?"

"I know, I know."

Barbara was second-guessing her decision to give Arla that extra media pass. The last twenty-four hours had been so overwhelming, she thought. Perhaps her judgment was clouded by what had amounted to an emotional breakthrough with Arla. A breakthrough of *honesty*. Hours earlier, so grateful for this watershed moment in their relationship, Barbara would have been inclined to give Arla anything she asked for. A media pass to the biggest party in town? Sure, why not?

Now she wondered if it had been such a good idea.

Did Arla have a right to know who her father was? Of course. Was Arla perfectly justified in wanting to make a connection with him? No doubt about it.

But here? Now?

The mayor had broken away from Valerie and was heading their way.

"I'm going to do it," Arla said.

But before Headley had gotten very far, an elderly woman wearing a floor-length gown and enough jewelry to open a Cartier store interceded.

"Richard!" she cried.

"Margaret!" he said, embracing her.

Barbara recognized her. Margaret Cambridge. Her name had come up when Barbara was doing her internet research.

"How do you like that view?" he asked her.

"It's worth a million bucks," she said. "Actually, more like a billion!"

They both laughed. The mayor gave her another hug, then moved on. Barbara could sense that Arla was ready to make a move. She placed a hand on her arm. "Wait, just wait a second. Maybe we should—"

"Mayor Headley?" Arla said.

Too late.

The mayor stopped, turned.

"Yes?" he said, looking at her.

Arla moved forward until there was barely a foot of space between the two of them. Seeing them that close together made Barbara light-headed.

No. Not here. Not now. Later. Somewhere private.

Arla extended a hand. The mayor took it, smiled, and said, "Nice to meet you."

Then he noticed Barbara standing right behind her. She caught his eye and he said, "Ms. Matheson."

Barbara smiled nervously. "Mayor."

Arla said, "I wonder, would there be somewhere we could talk privately, for a couple of minutes?"

"Maybe if you talked to Valerie Langdon. She's just over there? In the blue dress? You could tell her what this is about and she could see about setting something up."

Arla's face fell. "It's not a political thing. It's more a personal thing. You see, my name is Arla—"

She did not have a chance to finish her sentence. And even if she had, Headley would not have been able to hear it.

The explosion was far too deafening.

And not just the first one.

The one that came after.

And the one after that.

And the one after that.

Sixty-Seven

Bourque and Delgado flashed their IDs to get past security and into Top of the Park. Once inside, Bourque stopped, mouth agape, and took in the view.

"Unbelievable," he said.

"Yeah, pretty," Delgado said. "Let's find our boy."

Bourque approached a security guard, showed his badge again, and told him they were looking for Glover Headley, the mayor's son. The guard said that pretty much everyone was now on the top floor for the festivities. The guard had seen the mayor come through the lobby, but had no idea what the son looked like.

"Let's head up," Bourque said to his partner.

He and Delgado found themselves standing alone in front of the bank of elevators. There were three touch screens positioned atop small, granite pillars between the elevator doors with a notice that read: Enter Your Floor.

"How's it work?" Bourque asked.

Delgado studied it. "For the fifty-third floor, you tap in five, three . . ."

"But for the top?"

"Looks like . . . *O, B*. For observation deck." She tapped the OB symbol. A message appeared on the screen: *ELEVATOR 2*.

There were numbers atop the elevators, and the second from the left was marked 2.

"That one," Delgado said, pointing. They positioned themselves in front of those doors.

"What's your take on all this?" Bourque asked his partner while they waited for their car to arrive.

"I don't know. Glover's made himself very hard to find today. He signed out the car used by the man who met with Petrenko. Petrenko ends up dead. What do you think?"

"If you wanted to know everything there was to know about fucking around with a building's elevator system, someone like Petrenko would be the guy to talk to."

"Yeah," Delgado said.

"And if you led him to believe you could hurt his extended family, he'd probably help."

A soft chiming noise indicated the arrival of their car. The doors opened and, with half a second's hesitation, they stepped in.

Bourque looked for the panel of buttons to enter their floor and was momentarily alarmed when he didn't see one.

"I already did it, remember?" Delgado said. "No buttons."

"It's like getting into a car without a steering wheel."

"At least there's no chance of some smartass kid jumping on, running his hand down all the buttons, and jumping out again."

"Yeah," Bourque said. "*That's* what I'm worried about."

The car began to move, slowly accelerating. Its increasing speed seemed barely perceptible. Then Bourque put his finger to his ear.

"I can feel the pressure changing," he said, trying to gather some spit in his mouth to swallow.

"I feel it," Delgado said, touching her own ear. "Should have brought some gum." She eyed him with concern. "You okay?"

"Yeah, I'm fine."

"'Cause . . . you know. Your breathing is okay?"

"I'm fine," he said again, this time with an edge to his voice.

A few seconds went by before Bourque said, "You actually think it could be him?"

"Glover?"

"Yeah. The mayor's assistant said he was a techie."

"Why would the mayor's own kid decide to kill people by sabotaging elevators?" Delgado asked.

"Maybe we'll get a chance to ask him," he said.

They could feel the elevator decelerating.

"Wow, that was fast," Delgado said. "We're here already?"

Bourque looked at the digital readout that told them what floors they were passing. "Uh, no. We're just passing the fiftieth. Fifty-two, fifty-three."

"But we're slowing down. I can feel it. We've still got more than forty floors to go."

They both went quiet for a moment, focusing their collective attention on the sense of movement.

Bourque looked at the readout. "Sixty-five," he said. "We're holding at sixty-five."

Delgado looked at the narrow strips of brushed aluminum wall on either side of the doors. "Now I want some fucking buttons. How do I reenter the observation deck?"

"No idea," Bourque said.

"Maybe it's voice activated." She looked up toward the ceiling, as if there were a God of Elevators waiting to hear from her, and said loudly, "Observation deck!"

Nothing happened.

"Maybe you were supposed to say 'please,'" Bourque said.

"Come on!" she shouted. "Let's go!"

The elevator did not move.

"I want out," Delgado said.

"Same here."

He pressed the button bearing two triangles with their bases touching. The "open door" button.

The doors did not open.

"Try it again," Delgado said.

Bourque jabbed repeatedly at the button before giving his partner a *What now?* look.

She pointed to the emergency button. "Give that one a try."

Delgado stuck out a finger and was about to touch it when, suddenly, the elevator doors parted, giving them a view of a deserted hallway.

"Well," Bourque said, looking at Delgado. "The elevator seems to be inviting us to leave."

She hesitated. "We might have to walk up the rest of the way."

"Or walk *down* the rest of the way," he said. "If the elevators are down for the count, I'd rather head down before I start going further up."

"I vote we get off," Delgado said, stepping through the opening and into the hallway.

Bourque followed.

The second he'd cleared the doors, he heard the elevator move. He and Delgado spun around in time to see the car—with the doors still open—slowly descend.

"Jesus Christ," Delgado said.

Once the car had disappeared from view, they found themselves looking directly into the shaft. They both took half a step back.

"What the hell is happening?" Bourque said.

Within seconds, the elevator doors on the far left opened, exposing the shaft. Then the one third from the left, then the fourth, and finally, the fifth.

All five doors were in the open position, but there wasn't a car at any of them.

They were looking into five open shafts.

For several seconds, they were speechless.

Delgado crept forward to one of the open doorways and peeked over the edge. "That is one fucking long drop down," she said.

Drop.

"So what now?" she asked. Bourque said nothing. "Jerry?"

Drops.

"I'm fine," he said. "Let's think for a second."

And for several seconds, neither of them spoke.

"Wait," Delgado said. "What's that sound?"

"What?" Bourque said.

"Shut up and listen."

They both listened. Slowly, Delgado turned and looked at Bourque. "It's you," she said.

Bourque had started wheezing. He rested a palm on his chest. "Oh shit," he said. "Shit, shit."

"Talk to me."

"It's . . . been triggered."

"Can you breathe?"

"For now," he said.

"Have you got your thing?"

Bourque's chin went up and down. He patted the pocket of his suit jacket. He reached in and brought out the inhaler, uncapped it.

"One shot should do it," he said. "Two at the most."

Delgado nodded sympathetically. "Sure. Go ahead."

He was just about to insert the device into his mouth when the first explosion went off.

That first blast, which sounded well above them, was quickly followed by three others, all strong enough that they could feel the building shake ever so slightly.

Bourque was startled enough by the first explosion that he didn't need the other three to lose his grip on the inhaler.

It slipped from his fingers, bounced off the toe of his shoe, skittered across the marble hallway floor, and through the middle set of open elevator doors.

Instinctively, he darted forward to try and catch it.

"Jerry!" Delgado screamed.

She went to grab for him but he was already moving. Just not quickly enough. By the time he reached the opening, had braced himself with one hand on the wall, and was peering down into the shaft, his inhaler was already plunging past the thirtieth floor.

Sixty-Eight

Barbara grabbed Arla instinctively, sheltering her in an enveloping embrace. She wanted to run, but had no idea where to run to as people around her screamed.

The four blasts—*BOOM! BOOM! BOOM! BOOM!*—seemed to have come from all directions. Many of the elegantly dressed guests were crying, others were staring around wildly, panicked expressions on their faces.

Once the screams died down, Headley moved toward the temporary stage, leaping onto it and grabbing the microphone.

"Everyone remain calm!" he shouted. "Please stay calm!"

That was a tall order, given that there was now a strong smell of smoke and sulfur clogging the air.

Several guests were crowding around the five elevator doors, tapping away at the digital screen, entering *L* for the lobby.

"We have to get out of here!" a man cried out frantically.

"The stairs!" a woman yelled.

That prompted a ministampede. Guests were following Exit signs that directed people to four sets of stairs that would, ultimately, deliver them to street level.

"What's going on?" Arla asked her mother.

"I don't know," Barbara said, a protective arm still around her daughter's shoulders.

She scanned the room. There were plenty of others holding on to one another for comfort. Many had phones out and could be heard talking in frantic tones to multiple 911 operators about what had just happened.

"I'm thinking," Barbara said softly, "that we should get out of here."

Arla nodded. "Okay. They're already waiting for the elevators."

"Yeah," she said cautiously. "I'm not so sure I want to be first in that line."

"Jesus!"

The high-pitched cry had come from one of the stairwell doors.

"Stay here," Barbara said, releasing Arla and darting between other guests as she headed for the stairs. Arla did not do as she was told, and followed her mother as she squeezed past a group huddled around the door, which had been pulled wide open.

A section of the first set of stairs was missing.

Between every floor were about forty steel and concrete steps, each with a landing at the halfway point where the stairs reversed direction. What everyone had been looking at, through the smoke and dust that was still wafting throughout the stairwell, was the gap that began seven steps down from the stairwell door. Four steps were missing, their crumbled remains having fallen to the steps another flight down.

Four separate stairwells, Barbara thought. *Four explosions.*

When she turned around, Arla was there.

"How bad is it?" Arla whispered.

"Bad," Barbara said, coming back into the main room. "We better hope the elevators are working."

Not for a moment did she believe they would be.

But Barbara and Arla headed for them, anyway. They heard other guests confirming, in loud, panicked shrieks, that the other stairwells had been similarly sabotaged. Headley was still calling for calm but could barely be heard above the mayhem.

The sound of the chiming elevators brought an almost instant chill throughout the room.

The lights flashed over all five elevator doors.

"Thank God!" a woman shouted.

Another woman could be heard consoling her husband, whose entire body was shaking. "It's going to be okay, Edmund," she said within earshot of Barbara. "It's going to be okay. The elevators are here."

The five elevator doors opened simultaneously, but there wasn't a car in a single one of them.

The guests were greeted with five ninety-eight-story elevator shafts. All the hopefuls who'd been waiting for a ride down backed suddenly away. One brave woman in a glittery silver gown crept forward and peered over the edge and down.

"My God," she whispered. "You can't even see the bottom."

A man shouted. "Who's doing this? What do they want? How are we going to get out of here?"

"Everyone!"

It was Coughlin at the mike again, his face a mask of anguish. "Everyone, please!"

The crowd slowly went quiet and turned to look at the developer.

"Okay, I understand everyone is very upset, but I've already been in touch with building maintenance and I'm assured this is just a glitch that can be—"

He couldn't finish the sentence as various terrified guests drowned him out.

"Those were explosions!"

"How do we get down?"

"Who's doing this?"

"Why didn't you call this off? What were you thinking?"

That question prompted Coughlin to raise his hand in the air—a bid to get everyone to quiet down again—and turn and look at Headley.

"Perhaps the mayor would like to field that one."

An anxious looking Headley approached the mike. "People, people, please, listen."

A few people, anxious to hear the mayor over all the nervous chatter, went *"Shhh!"*

"Thank you," Headley said. "What I want you to know is, I personally assigned one of my own people to oversee a thorough inspection by qualified technicians of all the elevators in this building. All five were deemed to be in excellent working order. Based on the results of that inspection, I authorized resumption of services. I was told we were good to go. Where's Chris? Chris Vallins?"

Barbara's eyes darted around the room, searching him out. Finally, she spotted him, standing a few steps ahead of the middle elevator's open doors. Next to him stood Glover Headley.

Vallins raised a hand. "Here," he said.

Glover, as well as everyone else in the room, turned and looked at him venomously. *So,* they all appeared to be thinking, *this is your fault.*

"What did you find?" Headley asked.

"Find?" Vallins said. "Nothing."

"You were here, yesterday?"

Vallins nodded. "That's correct, Mr. Mayor. Today, too."

Glover was shaking his head. He looked from Chris to his father and said, "Dad always uses the best people."

The room fell silent.

"Uh, thank you, Glover," Headley said. "But as I was saying, the building had been checked as recently—"

"And yet here we are, trapped at the top of this fucking monstrosity," Glover said. "Look at all that's happened on your watch."

Valerie was moving through the room toward the mayor's son. She said softly, so as only to be heard by a few, "This is not the place."

Glover was not dissuaded, even when Vallins also started moving closer to him. To the crowd, he said, "By the way, is anyone here hiring? In case you haven't heard, I'm no longer working for the mayor of New York City."

There were murmurs throughout the room. Barbara felt a growing unease, that Glover's performance was not unrelated to what was happening to all of them.

Headley spoke. "Son, just tell me. Why did you meet with that man?"

"What man?" Glover said.

"That elevator expert. Weeks ago."

A collective gasp swept the room.

"How many times do I have to tell you?" the mayor's son said. "I don't know anything about that."

Headley searched the room, spotted Barbara, and said, "You tried to tell me. That it was personal. I had no idea *how* personal."

Barbara didn't know what to say. This hardly seemed the time for an *I told you so.*

Even if she could have thought of some response, someone else had something to say first.

"It *is* personal."

Chris Vallins was speaking.

He was standing only a step away from Glover and looked at him as he spoke.

"Someone in this room blames the mayor for how he treated his mother. How he neglected her. How he didn't give a shit about her."

Vallins turned his head to stare squarely at the mayor.

"I'm that person," Vallins said. "Mr. Mayor, you killed my mother."

More gasps. More whispers. Everyone was wondering what the hell was happening.

Including Glover. He looked at Vallins and said, "You signed out that car. You used my name."

Vallins nodded. "Sins of the father and all that," he said. "Sorry."

At which point he swiftly placed his palm flat on Glover Headley's chest, knocking him off his feet and through the open elevator doors.

Sixty-Nine

M om? Mom? Say something. Mom. Please don't die. Mom? Mom. Open your eyes. Look at me. Mom. Mom! I love you, Mom. I love you. Oh, Mom. No no no no no."

Chris thinks she is dead, but then she opens her eyes again as she lies there on the floor of their tiny apartment.

"I need . . . I need your father."

This hardly seems like the time to remind her that his father—her husband—is dead, and has been for a long time.

"I'm calling for help," he says, on his knees beside her, rubbing his hand across her forehead.

He jumps up and goes for the phone, dialing 911. He quickly tells the operator their Bronx address, that he thinks his mother has had a heart attack, that she's been complaining about pains in her chest for weeks, that she's just come up six flights of stairs carrying bags of groceries, that they need to get here quickly.

"They're coming," he tells his mother, tears streaming down his cheeks. "You're going to be okay. Just hold on until the ambulance gets here. Okay? Mom? Mom? Say something. Mom. Please say something."

She makes a low, moaning noise.

"I'm gonna be gone for just a minute. I'm gonna run down and wait for the ambulance, show them how to get up here."

Chris bolts from the room, runs down the hallway past the elevator with the Not in Service sign held to it with tape that has gone yellow *with age. He nearly flies down the six flights of steps and is running out the front of the building as the ambulance comes screaming up the street.*

Chris runs out between two parked cars and waves his arms in the air. The ambulance screeches to a halt out front and two paramedics—a man and a woman—leap out.

"This way!" Chris says.

They want to take half a second to confirm. "Maude Vallins?"

"Yes! Room seven-oh-three! Hurry! She's still breathing!"

They grab their equipment and run in after the boy. As he heads for the stairwell door, the woman says, "Where are you going?"

She points to the two elevators in the lobby. She hasn't yet noticed the Not in Service signs taped to them.

"They don't work!" he shouts.

"Ah, Christ," says the male paramedic.

Chris takes the steps two at a time, reaching the seventh floor more than a minute ahead of the other two. The paramedics enter the hall winded, sweat dripping down their temples. Chris is at the door to his apartment, waving them in.

While the two emergency workers kneel over his mother, Chris cannot stop babbling.

"The doctor's always saying she has a bad heart and it's really hard for her going up and down the stairs and I told her I'd do the shopping, you don't have to do it, or even if she goes out I can carry all the bags up, you know, because it's way too hard for her but she's always saying she can do it, that it's not my job, that my job is to go to school, but I could do it after school but she says no and I talked to the man, who comes for the rent, and I've asked him and asked him to please fix the elevators, that my mom can't handle the stairs, that one day she's going to have a really really really bad heart attack but he's this total asshole and I told my mom not to pay the rent until he fixed them but she said she couldn't do that because—"

The woman stands, turns, and asks, "What's your name, kid?"

"Christopher."

She tips her head toward the hallway.

"I can't leave my mom," he says.

"We need to talk, Christopher."

Once in the hall, she walks him a few steps away from the open apartment door. "What family you got? Brothers, sisters? Where's your father?"

"It's just me and my mom. My dad's dead. I don't have any brothers or sisters."

The woman's eyes sadden. "Uncles? An aunt?"

He nods. "Fran. She's my mom's sister. She lives in Albany."

"You got a number for her?"

"Does my mom have to go to the hospital?"

The woman swallows. "How old are you, Chris?"

"Twelve."

"We're not taking your mom to the hospital, Christopher. Maybe if we'd gotten here a little sooner . . ."

Chris says, "Like, if the elevator had been working."

The woman says, "I guess we'll never know. We need to get in touch with your aunt, tell her—"

She glances down the hallway at the sound of the stairwell door opening and closing. A young man, early twenties, dressed in a suit and tie, strides toward the paramedic.

"What's going on?" he asks in a voice that suggests he's entitled to know.

"That's him," Chris whispers.

"Him?" the woman says.

"The asshole," he whispered.

The man is now face-to-face with the paramedic. "What's happening here?"

"Emergency call. Heart attack. Who are you?"

"Richard Headley," he says. "My father owns this building, among others. I'm the property manager."

"Do you live here?" the woman asks.

Headley looks as though he's been slapped in the face. "Hardly. I come by twice a month. Check on things, collect rent."

"My mom's dead," Chris says.

Headley looks down at the boy, noticing him for the first time. "Sorry to hear that, sport."

"If they'd got up here sooner," Chris says, holding back his tears, "they could have saved her. If you'd fixed the elevators. Going up and down the stairs killed her. It's your fault."

Headley bends down so he can look the kid in the eye. "One thing you'll learn, when you get older, is you can't go blaming others for your troubles. If your mom didn't like the way things were here, she could have moved."

He pats the boy's shoulder as he stands back up. But he isn't done doling out advice for the grief-stricken young man.

"We all have setbacks in life, but we move on. If there's something you want in life, you go after it, no matter how hard it is, or how long it takes."

These are the words Chris will always remember.

Seventy

The mayor screamed, a ragged cry of pain and grief and disbe-
lief.

"Glover!"

The name resounded through the glass-enclosed space. The
crowd, transfixed in horror, suffered a brief, collective bout of heart
failure, not quite accepting what they had just seen. It was all too
impossible to believe. One moment, Glover was there, and a moment
later, he wasn't.

The mayor's son had barely had a chance to utter a scream of his
own, and his plunge down the shaft took so long that no one heard
a thing when he hit bottom.

Headley started pushing his way through the crowd toward Chris
Vallins, a wild, murderous look in his eyes. But from somewhere,
Vallins had produced a gun, and he was pointing it straight at the
mayor.

"Stop, Richard," he said. Utterly calm, utterly cold.

Headley halted, a few feet away from Barbara. A second earlier,
he'd looked ready to kill Vallins, but now the enormity, the sheer
horror, of what had just happened was overtaking him. The mayor
was on the verge of weeping, but was too stunned, too overwhelmed,
to actually cry.

"Go ahead, let it out," Vallins said, keeping his gun trained on
Headley while he crouched down and reached back with his free

hand for an open backpack that was propped against the short stretch of wall between two open elevator doors. He stood slowly, hefting the backpack over one shoulder while holding the gun in his opposite hand.

A tear escaped Headley's right eye and ran down his cheek as he stared incredulously at Vallins.

"It hurts, doesn't it?" Chris said. "It hurts a lot."

"Why . . . why did you . . ."

"You really don't remember, do you? You have no idea."

"I . . . I don't . . . I don't know what . . ."

"Let me give you a hint. A twelve-year-old boy. Mother dead of a heart attack. Couldn't handle going up all those flights of stairs anymore. You wouldn't spend a dime on that building. We had no heat half the time, rusty water coming out of the taps, mice and rats and cockroaches, holes in the ceiling where water dripped down from shitty plumbing on the upper floors. But most of all, we had no fucking elevators. The only things you ever replaced were the Not in Service signs. You killed her, Richard."

There was a dawning realization in Headley's eyes.

"Vallins . . ." he whispered. "Your mother was . . . Maude."

"I wondered if you'd recognize the name when you hired me." Chris smiled. "But it had been so long, and you never asked."

"I . . . I'm sorry," the mayor said. "But . . . Glover . . . you didn't have to . . ."

"I didn't *have* to do anything," Chris said, shifting the backpack around to the front so he could see into it. "I didn't *have* to mess with the elevators at your good friend Morris Lansing's building. I didn't *have* to have some fun with the elevators at the Sycamores, where one of your biggest fund-raisers was held. Pretty sure I saw Margaret earlier. And I didn't *have* to fuck with the elevator at the Gormley Building, where your good friend Mr. Steel lives. But I wanted to. I wanted to send a message to all those who gave you a helping hand. The kind you never gave anyone. I wanted to send a message to the people who helped put you where you are when you so don't deserve to be there."

But not the taxi bombing, Barbara thought. It didn't fit. It never had.

Vallins looked down again into the backpack and smiled. "Ah, here we go."

What he pulled out looked like an oversized TV remote. Barbara thought back to that news conference, when that city official said there were devices out there, that same size, that could allow someone to commandeer a building's elevators. He let the backpack drop to the floor.

"So," Chris said, holding the remote at eye level so everyone could see it, "this is my little friend that's your ticket out of here. With this, I can return the elevators back to their normal functions. You'll all be able to go home. Just don't anyone think of rushing me, or trying to jump me, or I'm going to toss it down the shaft. Are we clear on that?"

There were a few nods among the guests.

"Awesome," he said. "But there is an *if*. One big *if*."

"Please," Headley said. "Don't hurt anyone here. You want to toss me down there, let me be with my son? Fine. I'll jump right in if you'll let these people go."

"Here's what we're going to do," Vallins said. "I'm going to let *you* go."

"What?" Headley said, his voice cracking.

"That's right. I'm going to bring one elevator up, and you can get on it. And I'm going to send it—very safely—back to the lobby."

"I don't understand. Why would you let me—"

Vallins raised a finger on the hand holding the gun. "Let me finish."

The mayor went silent.

"You'll get off in the lobby and I'll bring the elevator back up, without you. Then you'll take the stairs and rejoin us."

"I'm . . . what?"

Vallins smiled and nodded. "You're going to walk your way back up here. Well, almost." He paused. "See how you like it. Now, you're in pretty good shape for a man your age, although I don't know how often you run to the tops of skyscrapers. We're going to make it interesting. We're going to put a time limit on it. I'm going to give you twenty minutes."

"Twenty—"

"That seems more than enough time. When they had a race to get to the top of the Freedom Tower, there were people who did it in under fifteen. So I think I'm being generous. The only thing is, the clock starts ticking as soon as you get on the elevator to go down."

"This is . . . and what if I'm late?"

"You heard the four explosions that took out the stairwells. There's a fifth bomb just waiting to go off that will pretty much take off the top of this building. Everyone here, including myself, will die. So, if you decide to run away, to not come back, that's what's going to happen."

The mayor stood there, speechless.

Barbara leaned forward, close enough to the mayor to whisper to him and be heard.

She said, "You should get going."

Richard Headley's eyes met hers.

"I'm sorry," he said. "For everything."

Barbara felt as though the room was spinning.

Then the mayor looked at Arla, took both her hands in his, and squeezed. "What a wonderful young woman you've turned out to be. I've only had an instant to be proud of you."

Arla appeared to be on the verge of fainting. "Thank you," she whispered.

"Time's a-wastin'," Vallins said.

Headley let go of Arla's hands.

Vallins looked at Barbara and said, "Do me a solid and set the timer on your phone to twenty minutes."

"Okay," Barbara said with feigned calm. She reached into her clutch and brought out her phone. At that moment, it dinged. An incoming email.

"That'll be from me," Vallins told her. "Sent on a delay. You can read it later, if you get the chance. Got the timer ready?"

She fiddled with some settings, then said, "Ready."

"Hold it up and show me," Vallins asked, and she did. Vallins looked at the mayor. "How about you? Set to go?"

Headley swallowed and said, "I'm ready."

"We're on ninety-eight, but call me when you get to the ninety-seventh floor." Vallins smiled. "You have my number. I'll send an elevator to bring you up the last story."

Headley nodded that he understood. He reached into his jacket to make sure he had his phone. He looked at it, brought up Vallins's number, then returned it to his pocket.

Vallins, keeping the gun trained on him, entered some instructions into the remote control elevator device with his other hand. Seconds later, an elevator car arrived. Vallins swept his arm gracefully toward it, inviting the mayor to board.

Headley walked forward, got into the car, turned and looked at the crowd, his chin quivering.

Vallins pressed another button and the door closed. He then looked at Barbara and said, "Go."

She tapped Start on the timer app and held the phone up to show him.

Vallins smiled. "Don't you go pausing it on me now, or I'm gonna be mad."

"Okay."

"We've got some time to kill while we wait for Richard to return," he said to everyone. "Go ahead and enjoy yourselves, have a good time, enjoy the food." He pursed this lips. "I'll tell you this. If anyone's offering, I wouldn't say no to a shrimp."

Seventy-One

Jerry Bourque was hunched over, hands on his knees, looking down into the shaft where he'd lost his inhaler.

"Oh, fuck," he said. But then he craned his neck around to get a peek up the shaft instead of down. "What the hell was that?"

"I heard four blasts," Delgado said, standing beside him and briefly placing a comforting hand on his back. She felt it rise and fall in rhythm with the wheezes emanating from his throat.

She glanced back down the hallway, at the four apartment doors.

"I can't believe no one came out to see what's going on," she said.

Bourque, slowly standing back up, said, "I read that people weren't moving in until after the opening bash. And anyone who's moved in already is probably at the party. Except for the top floor, the building's probably deserted."

Delgado slowly shook her head. "Some folks are gonna want their deposit back." She took a phone from the purse slung over her shoulder, tapped it. "This is Detective Lois Delgado. I'm with Detective Jerry Bourque and we are on the sixty-fifth floor of the Top of the Park. The elevators have been disabled and we heard explosions that sound like they're coming from the top. *Send everything.*" She listened to the person on the other end, said, "Got it," and then ended the call.

"What?" Bourque asked.

"They know. Tons of 911 calls coming in. Look, how are you doing? You sound like a tea kettle."

Bourque took several breaths, listened to the air struggling to get through his windpipe.

"I'll be okay. Come on, we have to get up there."

Delgado shook her head adamantly. "No. No way. It's like forty more stories. You take the stairs down, I'll head up."

"You're not going up there alone. God knows what's happened."

"You'll fucking kill yourself if you go up there."

"No," he said, and wheezed. "I can do it."

"There's backup coming. You don't—"

"Yeah, well, we're about sixty flights of stairs ahead of whoever's coming next to help out." He reached out and put a hand on his partner's shoulder. "It's in my head. There's—" and he stopped for another breath "—nothing actually wrong with me. I just . . . I just have to focus, and maybe I can get my wind back."

"No, you have—"

"Quiz me," he said.

"What?"

"Give me a category."

"I don't know what the hell you're talking about."

"It's a trick my doctor gave me. I think about something else, other than my breathing. Concentrate on a subject. Like the city's tallest buildings—although, right now, that's probably a bad choice. You know, five Spielberg movies. Name all the different *Star Trek* series, or what years the Yankees have won the World Series, or—"

"I've got one," Delgado said.

Bourque blinked. "Okay. Good. Hit me."

"Name five Ryan Gosling movies."

The corner of his mouth curled up. "Good one."

Wheeze.

"Okay. Um, the *Blade Runner* sequel, whatever they called that."

"That's one." Delgado held up one finger.

"And *La La Land*," he said.

Wheeze.

"That's two. Three to go."

"Uh . . . the one where he was driving the car."

"I need a title," Delgado said. "I'm cutting you some slack, missing the title of the *Blade Runner* sequel. But for this I want the title."

Bourque closed his eyes for a second. "Oh, fuck, of course. *Drive.*"

"That's three."

"Okay," he said.

Wheeze.

"There was that funny detective one he did, with Russell Crowe. Good Guys. No, *The Nice Guys.*"

"Well done," Delgado said. "Just one more."

"God, this is tough. Maybe if I dreamt about him every night like you do I'd—"

"No excuses," Delgado said.

"Oh!" he said, snapping his fingers. "That funny superhero. *Deadpool.*"

Wheeze.

"Oh, I'm sorry," she said. "That was Ryan Reynolds."

"They're not the same actor?"

Delgado's eyes softened. "You're still short of breath. I can hear it. It sounds like you're getting worse. Jerry, how bad can this get? Without your puffer?"

"Bad," he said. He had moved to a sitting position, his back to a short stretch of wall behind open elevator doors.

"We need to get you help. We need to get paramedics up here."

"Too long," he wheezed. "Too far up."

"Well, shit, what do we do? Christ, you need mouth-to-mouth?"

He had just enough air to chuckle. "That sounds lovely, but I don't think it'll do anything."

"There's got to be something. Look, I don't want to leave you here, but I've got to head up. If you don't move, if you don't exert yourself, can you get enough air into your lungs that you're not going to fucking die on—"

They heard a scream.

It had come from one of the elevator shafts.

Bourque managed to shift his position in time to see, a heartbeat later, a tuxedoed man past the open door immediately to their right.

Going down. In a hurry.

Bourque and Delgado gasped, staring for several seconds into the space where the man had appeared for only a millisecond. If they had blinked, they would have missed him.

Together, they moved tentatively to the opening and peered over the edge, Delgado standing and Bourque on his knees. Then Delgado looked up, as if checking to see whether more were headed their way.

They both moved back from the opening and looked at each other, each taking several breaths as they waited for their pulses to stop racing.

"Hey," said Delgado.

"What?" Bourque said.

"Listen."

Bourque thought, *Didn't we just do this a minute ago?*

He tilted his head, raised his chin, as if putting his ear to the wind.

"I don't hear anything," he said.

"Me neither," Delgado said.

He looked at her, confused. Then it hit him.

"The wheezing," he said. He took several deep breaths without making a sound. "Son of a bitch."

What had the doctor told him? About how a sudden shock might reverse the psychosomatic condition?

Just to be sure, he breathed in and out half a dozen more times, and felt no restrictions in his air passages.

"I know where the stairs are," he said. "I've got the book."

Seventy-Two

When the elevator doors opened onto the lobby of Top of the Park, Richard Headley was met with a crowd. Police officers, firefighters, and paramedics blocked his path.

"Out of my way!" he said. "Out of my way!"

As a few emergency workers stepped back to allow him to get off the elevator, others were getting on.

"No!" he said. "He's controlling it! If you get on it, you'll die!"

Once he was out of the car, and the others had exited, it began to go up.

Headley wasn't waiting around to watch. He was already looking for the closest stairwell door.

"Mr. Mayor." A woman's voice. Headley ignored it as he spotted a sign pointing to the stairs.

"Mr. Mayor!" Sharper this time, but he still did not respond as he looked for a way back to the top.

"Richard."

He stopped, turned, and standing there was Chief Annette Washington.

She reached out, touched his arm, and asked softly, "Do you know?"

It took him a beat to understand what she was asking him. Everyone in the lobby, he realized, would have seen his son plummet past one of the open elevator doors. Glover would have had only a few below-ground-level floors left to fall after they'd seen him. Headley nodded solemnly and said, "Glover."

She nodded back.

"Can I . . . can you see him?"

"There's four levels below street level," she said. "He's down there. We're going to get him out, Richard." She paused. "I don't think you should look."

"I will," he said. "But not now. I have to go back up. There's not much time."

"What's going on? What were those explosions?"

He spotted a door to the stairs. "I'll have to run and talk," he said, breaking away from her.

She ran after him. In the stairwell, taking the steps two at a time, he told her, in bullet form, what had transpired. That his aide Chris Vallins was behind the elevator events. That he'd given the mayor only a few minutes to climb his way back to the ninety-eighth floor. That if he didn't make it, another bomb would go off, killing everyone at the party.

"Why?" asked Washington, one step behind him. "Why is he doing all this?"

Headley stopped, briefly, on the landing of the third floor and looked at her. "I've done terrible things," he said.

"You can't do this," she said. "We'll send up a team. We'll find a way—"

He gripped both her arms above the wrists and forced her to look into his eyes. "Annette, *there is no time.* Good-bye."

He turned and kept running up the stairs.

Washington called after him, "Look for Detectives Bourque and Delgado! They're up there somewhere!"

If Headley heard, he gave no indication.

He just kept running. And climbing.

As he passed a door marked Floor 5, he started doing the math in his head. First, he needed to know how long it would take him to get from the fifth floor to the sixth. He counted.

Fifteen seconds.

Okay, he thought. Roughly ninety floors to go. Ninety times fifteen was 1,350.

So what was that in minutes?

Headley had always been good at doing math without a calculator. He could look at city budget projections and do calculations in his head as quickly as any of the bean counters from the financial department.

So, take 1,350 seconds and divide by the number of seconds per minute, which was, of course, sixty, and—

Twenty-two and a half minutes.

"God, no," he said aloud, rounding the landing between the eighth and ninth floors.

Vallins had given him twenty minutes, but the clock had started ticking the moment he got onto the elevator. He couldn't have more than fourteen or fifteen minutes left.

There was no way he was going to make it.

He increased his speed. Ten floors up now, his calves and thighs were already screaming in pain. He was still taking the steps two at a time, grabbing the railing each time and using it to pull himself upward. Like so much of the rest of his body, his shoulder was hurting like a son of a bitch.

His chest felt as though it would explode.

This is what he wants. He wants me to have a heart attack. I'm going to die the same way his mother did.

What was that last thing the chief had shouted at him? Bourque and Delgado? Weren't those the two detectives who'd come to City Hall looking for Glover? They were already in the building, somewhere?

Glover.

Headley thought his heartache was more likely than a heart attack to do him in. He thought about those last, accusatory words he'd said to his son before Vallins had pushed him into the shaft. Believing that his son could have had anything to do with this.

How he would have to live with that forever.

However long forever was.

As he passed the door marked Floor 14, he thought about what a curse he'd been to so many around him.

All those tenants in his father's buildings.

His wife.

His son.

All the bad luck he'd brought them.

Maybe it was fitting he'd think of that at this moment, passing the fourteenth floor. Given people's superstitious nature, it was actually the thirteenth.

Seventy-Three

Vallins nibbled on one of the shrimps Barbara had taken from the buffet table, put on a plate, and slid across the floor to him.

"These are excellent," he said, biting on one, then tossing the tail into the elevator shaft. He raised his voice. "Everyone, please! Eat up! Enjoy!"

While we can, Barbara thought.

While none of the guests had much of an appetite, she'd seen more than a few head over to the bar. But most were huddled in pairs, standing quietly, eyes trained on Vallins, wondering what he might do next, *terrified* by what he might do next.

Vallins shrugged when he didn't see anyone taking his advice, then looked over at Barbara and Arla, who were standing closer to him than anyone else.

"Sorry," Vallins said to Barbara. She could not take her eyes off the device in his left hand, and the gun in the other. "You were right, of course. I was following you when you stepped out in front of that van. I saw you two at breakfast earlier. Then when I saw Arla at City Hall, I put it together, and ratted her out to the boss." He gave Arla a regretful look.

"I don't understand, either," said Barbara. "You want to bring the mayor down, but you still were doing his dirty work."

Vallins nodded. "I've been doing his dirty work for some time. That's how I got close. Anyway, it's all in the email."

Barbara said, "Why didn't you just let the van run me down?"

He shrugged. "I told you. I like you."

"Enough to let me—my daughter—go?"

"How would that look, playing favorites?" he said. "If anyone survives, I hope it's you. Otherwise the email's pointless. I've always thought you were a good writer. You're the best one to tell the story."

"Chris, please. Let everyone go."

He shook his head. "Sometimes innocents are lost in the pursuit of a greater goal. If anyone here is really, truly innocent."

Barbara's head twitched. "That was you. The comments on my article. You're the one calling himself Going Down."

Vallins smiled. "That was a bit cute, I know."

"Help me out here, Chris. Haven't you sacrificed enough innocents already? Like my friend Paula? Wasn't your mom an innocent? What's happening to these people, is it any more unfair than what happened to her? Does anything you've done make sense? Does hurting all these people, here tonight, serve any purpose? You've taken his son from him, Chris. What more do you want?"

He was stonefaced. "How's our time?"

Barbara looked at the phone in her hand. "Seven minutes, twenty seconds."

Vallins nodded. "Do you think he'll make it?"

"I don't know."

"Do you think he's even trying? Maybe he got off in the lobby and buggered off home."

"I doubt that," Barbara said, although she was not 100 percent sure. It hadn't even occurred to her, until Chris had posed the question, that Headley might not even try to make the climb.

He'll try, she thought. *He's a bastard, but no one could be that big a bastard.*

"Is this how it ends for you?" Barbara asked. "I mean, you can't be thinking you're going to walk away from this."

Vallins looked thoughtful. "You know, I always used to think those suicide bombers, those Islamic terrorist crazies screaming 'Allahu akbar' as they fire their machine guns into a crowded theater, with no chance of getting out alive, what the hell is wrong with them? But I also sort of get it, you know? Because when you've been angry for so long, when the only thing you care about is justice, your own life stops having much meaning. What are we down to?"

Barbara looked. "Six minutes, twenty-five seconds."

"My mother was a wonderful woman. Strong and proud and good. Not . . . confrontational. She didn't like to make waves."

"Would your mother be proud of you now?" Barbara asked. "Would she want you to get even this way?"

He just smiled. "Save your breath."

Barbara sighed. "I'm guessing you were something of a techie," she said.

"Yup. Always messed about with computers. Taught myself, mostly. Same was true with elevators. Studied every manual I could find, memorized them. But I still needed some help with that. Found someone to fine-tune my skills. Help me figure out all the security stuff. But he and I, we had a bit of a falling out Sunday night. I had a feeling he was going to talk to the police. He'd stopped believing I had people watching members of his family. He was right about that. It was only ever just me."

He paused, surveyed the room full of his hostages. Someone, over by the window, was softly crying.

"Where are we on the clock?" he asked Barbara.

She looked at the phone in her hand, the tenths of seconds flying past on the counter.

"Four minutes, fifty-five seconds," she said.

Vallins nodded. "Doesn't look good." He glanced toward the bar. "Last call, folks."

Seventy-Four

They were making good time.

They were winded, their hearts were pounding, and their legs were killing them, but Bourque and Delgado were nearing the top.

Delgado had slowed, briefly, as she took a call from someone on the ground who wanted her to know that at some point, they might run into the mayor, who was also in one of the four stairwells, heading back up. She was quickly briefed. When she got off the phone, she called out to Bourque, three steps ahead of her, "There's some bad shit up ahead."

She told him the body they'd seen flying by in the shaft was the man they'd come to talk to, and that he had been pushed by one of the mayor's aides, who evidently was the guy behind all the elevator mayhem.

And that aide, Chris Vallins, was holding court on the ninety-eighth floor, ready to blow the whole thing up if Headley didn't make it back up in time.

"Why?" Bourque asked between pants.

"Beats me," said Delgado. "From what I gather, if we can't get to this guy in the next ten minutes or so, it's not going to matter."

As they reached the landing between the ninety-fifth and ninety-sixth floors, Bourque stopped. Some painting equipment had been left there, tucked into the corner, a not-unfamiliar sight on their trip skyward. Paint touch-ups being done throughout the building, but for the opening, workers' supplies had been tucked out of sight. To steady himself, Bourque placed a hand on one of the steps of a five-foot ladder and took a few breaths.

Delgado stopped. "Are you okay?"

"I just need one second," he said.

"Wheezing?" she asked.

He shook his head. "No. Just exhausted."

"You're a fucking medical miracle, you are," Delgado said. "Or a psychological one. Not sure which."

"Okay," Bourque said, "I'm good."

They continued on with the climb.

Bourque still couldn't believe he was okay. His doctor, Bert, had been right on the money about how he might come out of the shortness of breath that had been plaguing him for so long. Or maybe there was another explanation. Maybe it had something to do with duty. Duty to the job. Duty to his partner.

Duty to Lois.

He was not going to abandon her. He was not going to let her continue to the top of this building and face whatever was up there without him. And maybe that determination, that sense of conviction, was stronger than the mental dysfunction that had been converting his stress into a constriction of his windpipe.

And what the fuck did it matter, anyway? He could breathe, and he was doing this.

One thing he knew with absolute certainty. If he got out of this alive, he was *not* going to make a cardboard replica of this goddamn building.

Delgado, behind him at this point, said, "What's this?"

The steps were starting to be littered with tiny pebbles of concrete.

"Must have something to do with the explosions we heard," Bourque said. "We're almost there." A pause, then, "Hello."

They had just passed the door marked Floor 97. Just one floor to go. But there was a small problem.

There was a four-step gap in front of them.

"Holy shit," Delgado said.

"There are three other stairwells," Bourque said, reaching for the handle of the door to the ninety-sixth floor.

"How do you know that?" she asked.

"I told you. The plans are in the book I got."

Delgado nodded, briefly impressed. But she was still visibly worried. "If the other stairways were passable, wouldn't people already be scrambling down them?"

"Stay here," he said. "I'll check. And if they're blown up, too, I saw something that might be able to help us."

"No, we shouldn't split—"

"Two minutes," he said, and started running back down the stairs.

Not much more than a minute later, he reappeared with the painter's aluminum ladder, the one they had passed moments earlier, slung over his shoulder.

"Oh, God," Delgado said. "You gotta be kidding me."

"The other stairwells are no good. This is our best shot."

He rounded the top of the stairs, nearly clocking Delgado with the ladder as he went by.

"Is it long enough?" she asked.

"It'll have to be."

He went to the last step before the gap and placed the ladder across it. It was long enough, but there was nothing to brace it against. Once anyone actually got on the ladder, it would slide and drop into the opening.

"I'll hold it," Delgado said.

"What?"

"I hold the bottom of it in place while you climb across. Then you hold it and I'll follow."

Bourque was skeptical. "Are you sure? I'm not the svelte athlete I once was."

"Yeah, like you were ever an athlete. Get a move on."

Delgado planted her feet firmly on a lower step, knelt down, and placed both hands on the bottom rung of the ladder, which lay on a forty-five-degree angle across the opening. Bourque, delicately, grabbed hold of a higher rung, then, careful not to hit his partner in the head, put his feet on a lower one that was just above her head.

Now, all his weight was on the ladder.

"You okay?" he asked.

She grunted. "Move it, fatso."

Carefully, he made the crossing, looking ahead and not at the stairs a flight below, or the sliver of space between sets of steps that appeared to go down to the depths of hell. Gingerly, he got himself onto the step on the other side of the divide, taking his weight off the ladder.

Delgado let out a long breath as Bourque planted his butt on the second step after the gap, leaned over, and gripped the top of the ladder.

"Okay," he said.

Delgado got onto the ladder as tentatively as her partner had. She made the crossing slowly. As she reached the other side, Bourque leaned over slightly to give her room to get a grip on the closest concrete step.

As her legs were coming off the last step of the ladder, her foot slipped, and pushed hard on the upper rung. Bourque lost his grip, and the ladder fell, hitting the lower stairwell with a loud, metallic crash.

Delgado clung to the step, her legs dangling in space.

Bourque got his hands under her arms and pulled. She scrambled to get hold of the next step, and once she had it, and her waist was over the threshold of the step below, she pulled herself up the rest of the way.

"I guess we better hope there's another ladder at the top so we can get back down," she said.

They both got to their feet and, after taking a second to pull themselves together, walked up the rest of the way to the door marked Floor 98.

They each took a moment to take out their weapons. Once they both had a gun in hand, Bourque grasped the handle of the fire door.

"Kinda wish I'd worn a vest," Delgado said.

Bourque slowly opened the door.

Seventy-Five

Richard Headley knew there was no way he'd make it.

He wasn't using anything as accurate as a stopwatch app on his phone, but he'd been glancing regularly at the Rolex strapped to his wrist, and his twenty minutes were nearly up. And he had some thirty floors to go.

Not. Gonna. Happen.

Those people are all going to die. Because of me.

But even though he knew it was hopeless, he kept going. He'd taken off his bow tie around the twentieth floor so he could open up the collar of his shirt. He was soaked with perspiration. Once he'd hit the thirtieth floor, he slipped off the jacket of his tux and dropped it on the steps, making sure before he did it that he had his phone.

His white dress shirt was translucent with sweat. It was running down his neck and forehead, getting into his eyes and stinging.

Keep going. Keep going.

He glanced again at his watch. The twenty minutes had to be up.

What the hell am I going to—

And then it hit him.

Stall.

He had the messaging app open, the name *Vallins* at the top of the screen. He stopped long enough to text one word.

Here.

He kept going, looking every few seconds to see if there would be a reply. It came within ten seconds.

Wow. And with 3 seconds to spare.

Headley kept climbing.

Very impressive. Sending your ride to 97.

So the elevator was on the way. But it would be there, waiting for him, long before Headley could get to it.

How long would it take for the elevator to come from the lobby—or wherever else Vallins might have sent it in the interim—to the ninety-seventh floor? A minute?

Headley kept going, one foot ahead of the other.

His phone chimed.

Are you aboard?

Headley stopped, typed his reply with a sweaty thumb.

No.

Several seconds passed. Headley managed to ascend another story.

Get on.

Headley stopped.

Elvtr not here.

Headley knew it was a lie that would not buy him much time. All Vallins had to do was look down the shaft to know the elevator was where it was supposed to be. The elevator car would be one floor below. He'd be able to see its roof.

And then, just as he feared:

Its there.

Think, think, think.
What *couldn't* Vallins see?
Headley put his thumb to the screen.

Doors closed. Open the door.

Let him think on that for a moment.
Headley ran past Floor 72.
Still so far to go.
Three dancing dots appeared on the mayor's phone.

It should be open.

The mayor wrote back:

Its not.

And then the phone in the mayor's hand rang.
Vallins.
Headley stopped, took the call.

"What do you mean the doors aren't open?" Vallins shouted.

"I'm right here," Headley said. "The other four doors are wide open, but the doors in front of the elevator aren't."

"That's not fucking possible!" the man said angrily.

"Look, you're the guy hogging the remote, not me," Headley said. "Send me one of the other elevators. And this time, if you're such a fucking genius, make sure the doors open." He paused. "Remember, we had a deal. I get back in time, you let everyone go. Well, I made it. Only reason I'm not up there now is you fucked up. That's on you. Not me."

Vallins was silent for a moment. "I don't believe you."

"Then why don't you bring up another elevator for yourself and come down one floor and see it with your own eyes?"

Headley, waiting for Vallins to reply, passed Floor 76.

"Okay," Vallins said finally. "I'll send another elevator. Because I really, *really* want you to get back here."

Seventy-Six

As quietly as possible, Detective Jerry Bourque opened the door to the ninety-eighth floor and slipped in.

He was expecting to hear screams and other sounds of panic, but instead what he heard were soft whimpers and crying, and just one man talking very loudly.

Bourque already had a finger to his lips in case any of the hostages spotted him, which a few did almost instantly. While there were some barely audible gasps, no one did anything stupid like shout: *Police are here!*

Everyone instinctively understood that the arrival of Bourque and Delgado might be their only hope of getting out of the Top of the Park alive.

The stairwell door was tucked around the corner from the elevators, but they could hear the man continuing to shout.

"That's not fucking possible!" he said.

Bourque poked his head around the corner, far enough for one eye to take in the scene.

Vallins was by the elevator, gun in one hand, the phone in the other.

Amazingly, the first thing Bourque thought was: *This guy is bald.* The man who'd been talking to Otto Petrenko by the car had hair. But then again, it had looked like a rug.

On the floor, right by Vallins's foot, was a black box. Some kind of device.

Bourque wondered whether it could be a bomb. It did not look like one, but then again, how many bombs had Bourque seen in his career? But it looked more like a piece of electronic equipment. The good news, if there was any, was that it was not in Vallins's hands at this moment.

Bourque, like his partner, had his gun pointing toward the floor, but once they rounded that corner, they would have to be in a firing position. Could he take the shot? Was anyone standing close to Vallins? Anyone directly behind him?

There were some people to his right, a few steps farther away from the open elevator door he was standing beside. But there appeared to be no one behind him.

At one point, as Vallins continued to argue with someone on his phone, he glanced down into the shaft.

No one else is coming, Bourque thought. *Lois and I are on our own. Backup is ninety-eight floors away. We might as well be on the moon.*

He tightened his grip on his weapon.

Now or never.

It all happened in under ten seconds.

Bourque stepped out from behind the corner, gun raised. "Drop your weapon!" he shouted.

He knew Delgado had moved out, too, and was at his back.

Vallins snapped his head in Bourque's direction. Dropped the phone. Brought up the arm holding the gun.

And Jerry Bourque thought: *Lois is right behind me. Do not duck. Do not dive out of the way. Do not make the same mistake again.*

Holding his ground, Bourque fired at the exact same moment as Vallins.

Vallins stumbled backward, the bullet ripping into his right shoulder. As he stumbled, his foot knocked the device closer to the open shaft.

Bourque, hit in the stomach, went down.

Screams.

Her partner having dropped to the floor, Delgado had a clear shot at Vallins, who was still standing despite being hit.

She fired.

Four times.

Bang. Bang. Bang. Bang.

Vallins jerked spasmodically as the bullets slammed into his thigh, chest, and neck.

One missed and spiderwebbed one of the observation deck windows.

He dropped to the floor, once again knocking the black box.

It skittered several inches closer to the open elevator doors.

A woman holding a cell phone, who'd been standing closest to Vallins, dived forward, actually sailing through the air and landing across his bloodied body, her elbows hitting the marble floor as she scrambled to grab hold of the device before it had a chance to tumble out of sight.

The device was halfway over the sill of the open doorway when she snatched it with her right hand. She brought it close to her chest, smothering it with both hands as if it were a football.

"Touchdown," she whispered to herself.

Friday

Seventy-Seven

Horror at the Top of the Park
By Barbara Matheson

It's a cliché, but sometimes clichés are on the money. Our nightmare is over.

The city's, anyway. The nightmares are unlikely to ever end for those directly touched by the horrors of this week. The ripples from these events will be felt for years to come.

Tell me about it.

Anyone who was on the ninety-eighth floor of Top of the Park will never forget what happened last night, and you can count this writer among them. We all had little expectation that we would survive. Had it not been for the heroic actions of NYPD detectives Jerry Bourque and Lois Delgado, who knows what might have happened. We all wish Detective Bourque, in the hospital and listed in serious, but improving, condition, a speedy recovery.

And while it's becoming increasingly clear that the origins of this tragic week can be traced back to decisions made by a young Richard Headley, his own actions last night were probably what bought those two detectives enough time to bring down the terrorist behind the elevator disasters. Even though Headley had had no time to grieve the death, minutes earlier, of his son, Glover, he played the game that terrorist wanted him to play in a bid to save the hostages.

As everyone knows by now, Mayor Headley was found dead of an apparent heart attack in the stairwell, just shy of the ninety-fifth floor. I had, as regular readers of this column know, been a harsh critic of the mayor, but must admit I am reassessing some of my feelings about him. There are things that I, and at least one other person I know, would have liked to have told him if we'd had the chance.

Another big thank-you is owed to one of the city's elevator inspectors who managed to reach the top floor, and, using the device the terrorist had used to commandeer the elevators, bring the cars back online and safely get everyone out of the building.

There was, obviously, a sense of urgency, given that there was believed to be a fifth bomb in the Top of the Park. But as I write this, no further explosive devices have been found, although the search is ongoing and the streets around Top of the Park remain closed as a precaution.

Now, about that terrorist. I hesitate to use his name here, because people who perpetrate these kinds of acts revel in a kind of perverse notoriety. But I need to tell you about Chris Vallins.

I got to know him a little this week, before I knew he was—as the tabloids are now calling him—the Elevator Executioner. I liked him. He seemed like a decent guy. I watched him give his gloves to a homeless man.

But we know now that he blackmailed an elevator technician into teaching him everything he knew, making him believe members of his extended family would be killed if he failed to go along. We know he killed that man—beat his face to a pulp and cut off his fingertips to hinder identification—when he feared the man was going to expose him. We know he plotted, for years, to gain the confidence of the mayor to exact his revenge, and had spent months getting into a number of buildings to prepare the elevators for failure.

We know he killed many innocent people when he took over the control of three of them.

The question is why.

He explained it all to me in an email I was able to read only today. He did it out of love. Love for his mother, who had been deeply wronged, years ago, by a young Richard Headley. You've probably already read or heard all about that by now, so no sense repeating it all here.

Are there any lessons in all this? I wouldn't presume to be wise enough to know, but I can say this much.

Actions have consequences.

Maybe not overnight. Maybe not in a week, or a month, or even a decade.

But the things we do, the decisions we make, the way we treat other people, it all becomes part of the equation. Eventually, things have a way of balancing out.

Or maybe this is all just a load of bullshit. Honestly, I don't know anymore. That's why this is my last column, at least for the foreseeable future, for *Manhattan Today*.

Barbara took one last look at the piece on her screen and hit Send. The entire time she'd been typing, she'd been resting her right elbow on an ice pack. Hitting the floor, when she'd dived to grab the elevator control device, had made that earlier injury worse. Now that she was done writing her piece, the pack was warming. She flexed her arms, then leaned back in her kitchen chair, reached for her coffee, and took a sip.

She hadn't yet slept. There'd been police to talk to, statements to make. It was four in the morning before she and Arla got back to her apartment. Arla was too shaken up to head back to her own place. The good news was, she'd managed to fall asleep in Barbara's bed shortly after they'd come through the door.

Barbara had stripped off her blood-soaked gown and put on

some sweats. It wasn't long before she opened up the laptop and started to write.

Around eleven in the morning, Barbara heard rustling in the bedroom. She looked toward the door and saw Arla emerge, her hair a tousled mess.

"Hey," Barbara said.

"Have you even been to bed?" Arla asked.

Barbara shook her head. "There's always time to sleep. How are you doing?"

"Okay, I guess. A bit numb. I can't . . . I can't believe all those things happened." She brushed some hair from her eyes. "I can't believe we're alive."

"Yeah, there's that."

"Is there more coffee?"

Barbara pointed. Arla found a mug, poured herself some, and as she sat down at the table, said, "I just find out I have a brother, and find out who my father is, and then lose them both."

Barbara reached out a hand. Arla gripped it. "You're gonna want to talk to someone, maybe," her mother said. "I know you've seen someone before."

Arla looked into her mother's face. "I can talk to you."

Barbara gave the hand another squeeze.

Arla said, "I should get back to my place."

"You sure? You can stay here as long as you like."

"No. I should get back." She smiled sadly. "Need to update my résumé."

"Sure." Barbara paused. "I'll see you home."

"Can you stay awake that long?"

Barbara knew, eventually, she would crash, and crash hard. But not just yet. While Arla showered, Barbara got into something slightly more presentable than her sweats—jeans and a pullover sweater. When Arla was done in the bathroom, Barbara handed her some of her own clothes she believed would fit her.

They took a cab to Arla's. On the way, Arla leaned over and rested her head on her mother's shoulder. They didn't speak.

Barbara paid the driver and the two of them went into Arla's building.

When they got to the elevator, another woman was standing there. Nicely dressed, silvery hair, pearl earrings. She was carrying a Whole Foods bag.

Arla nodded at her. "Hey."

The woman smiled politely.

Arla turned to her mother. "This is the woman I was telling you about."

Barbara blinked, not understanding. The woman looked at Arla, who said, "You're the book editor, right?"

She nodded. "That's right."

The elevator doors parted and the three of them stepped on. The woman pressed the button for the tenth floor, while Arla hit twelve.

"My mom's got an idea for a book," Arla said, smiling. "Maybe a couple."

"Oh," said the woman, doing a very good job of concealing her excitement.

Arla prodded her mother. "Tell her."

"You'll have to be quick," the editor said. "I'm getting off at ten."

Barbara smiled tiredly. "I don't think we'll need that much time."

Acknowledgments

There are a lot of people, scattered across both sides of the Atlantic, who helped immeasurably with getting this book to you.

At HarperCollins UK, thanks go out to Charlie Redmayne, Lisa Milton, Kate Mills, Alvar Jover, Joe Thomas, Sophie Calder, Anna Derkacz, Georgina Green, Fliss Porter, and Jo Rose.

At William Morrow/HarperCollins US, I am indebted to Liate Stehlik, Jennifer Brehl, Gena Lanzi, Nate Lanman, Ryan Shepherd, Andrea Molitor, Mumtaz Mustafa, Andy LeCount, and Brian Grogan.

And at Doubleday Canada, I am grateful for the support of Kristin Cochrane, Amy Black, Ashley Dunn, and the rest of the team.

As always, I want to thank my agent Helen Heller and everyone at The Helen Heller Agency, as well as Enrique Galo, Phil Gillin, Marcie Sherwood, and Steve Fisher.

And to booksellers everywhere, thank you.